POISONED BEAUTY

C.S. HALE

Poisoned Beauty
By C.S. Hale
Copyright 2024 @ C.S. Hale
All rights reserved

ISBN: 978-1-948670-06-7
First Edition

This book is a work of fiction and does not represent any individual, living or dead. Names, characters, places, and incidents are either products of the author's imagination or are used fictionally.

Edited by Alicia Dean
www.aliciadean.com
Cover and interior design by The Illustrated Author Designs
www.theillustratedauthor.com

Published in the United States of America

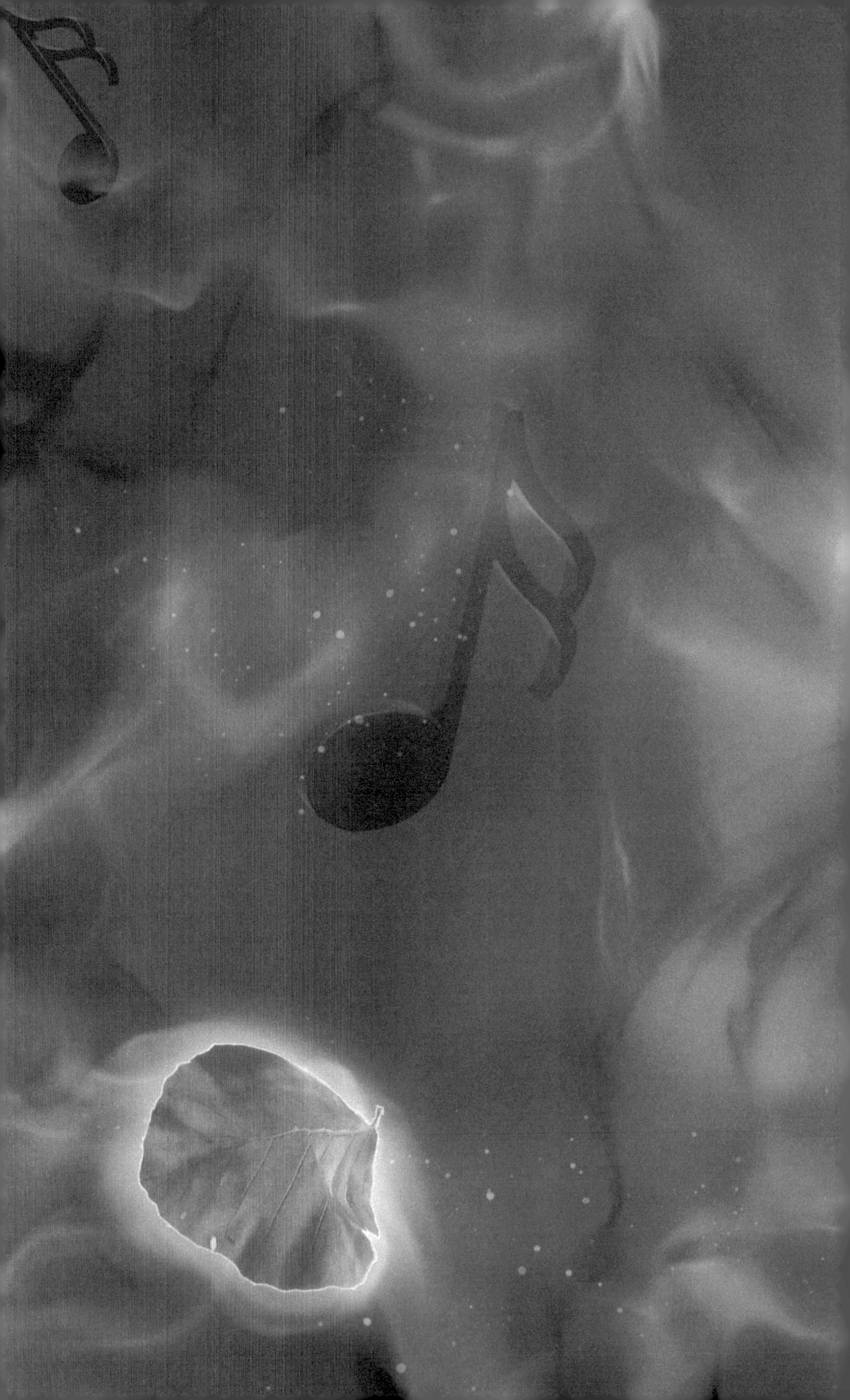

Banalfar Series
Fall From the Moon
Rise From the Ashes

All Bags Go to Cleveland

acknowledgements

This book was born where all fairytales are – rooted in someone else's "Once upon a time ..." In this case, where the worlds of Rosamund Hodge's stunning debut mashed up against Stanwood High School's staging of *Shrek the Musical*. Which got my wheels turning and wondering, *What if all fairytales do happen in the same place?* Having devoured all the fairy stories I could get my hands on since being given free rein in my elementary school library in second grade, it was wonderful to begin wandering the halls where the seed of all those stories took place. I can't wait for you to begin to wander them with Nadia.

Thank you to Lacie and Maddison for cheering me on this year as I made *Poisoned* real after many long years, and thank you Bethany for your love of this story. This one is for you. Literally. Turn the page.

Thank you Melissa for bringing Poisoned to life. I am always in awe of your work.

And thank you readers for going on this journey with Nadia. May your own hardships make you kind.

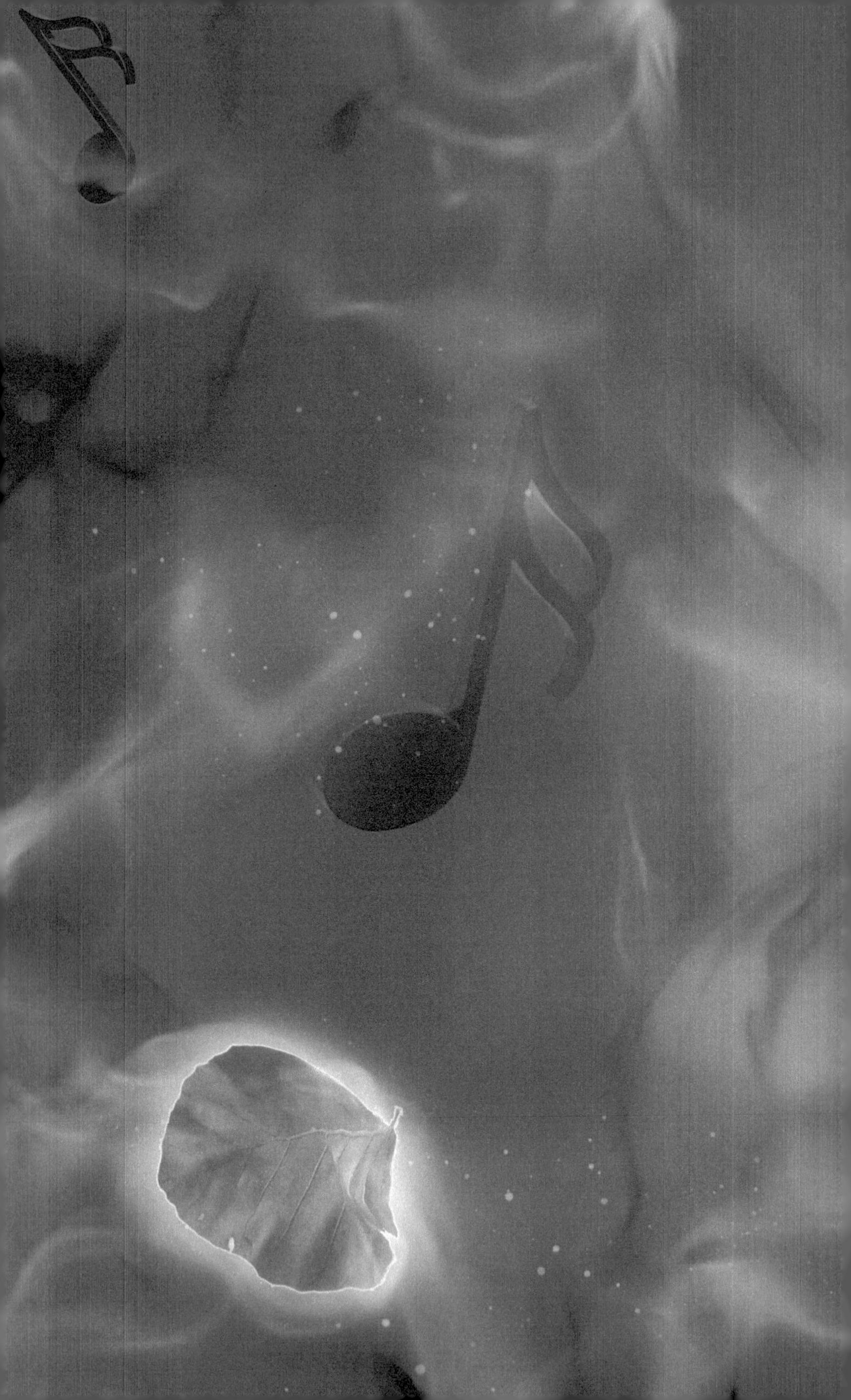

For Bethany

This one has always been yours.
I'm so glad you have always been its champion.

one

Nobody wants you. Nobody truly wants you. You are nothing but a free pair of hands. Not even a beauty. Something so broken, not even a beast would want you.

"Get up!" Cook's toe connected with Nadia's knee. "The fires aren't stoked and the water's not drawn. Why we ever took you in…" Cook's voice faded into an unintelligible mumbling of Nadia's faults as she shuffled back to the stove.

Nadia rubbed her aching knee and rolled off her pallet by the fish tank. She struggled to her feet with a groan. The fat trout in the tank stared at her with their bulgy eyes, the opening and closing of their mouths echoing Cook's command, *"Up! Up!"*

Putting a hand to her aching back, Nadia tried to stretch out the ever-present knot between her shoulder blades and limped her way to the stove. Embers glowed in its open maw, jumping and dancing as Cook shoved in piece after piece from the stack of wood at her feet.

"I've got this!" she shouted at Nadia. "Go fetch the water."

Nadia stifled a sigh as she gathered a pair of buckets and made her way out the back door. Shades of blue ate at the darkness in the east, not enough to dim the light of the morning star. Not enough to light the path, but Nadia's feet knew their way. She'd had years to count the steps to the well—ninety-eight paces. Years to make a game out of it, beginning as an eight-year-old, small and frail, barely able to haul even one full bucket down the path.

The crank complained as Nadia lowered the large fixed bucket into the dark depths. *How long ago was that?* Fifteen. Yes, it must be fifteen years for Elsbeth, Lord Braemoor's daughter had been but three when Nadia arrived and was now eighteen.

Nadia carefully poured water into her two buckets and hoisted them up. She was still small and thin but wiry. Years of strenuous work had hardened her muscles. Years of malnutrition had done little to fill her out. She was last in the pecking order at Westpark. Even Daisy and Hazel who'd come to work in the kitchen after she had, were of greater value. They had beds in the servants' wing on the second floor and were allowed to sit at the long harvest table and eat. Nadia had her pallet by the great soapstone tank that held the fish pulled from the pond and river until it was time to cook them. She was handed bread, and sometimes a hunk of cheese, to eat while she continued with her chores. Her never-ending chores.

She had stayed up well past moonrise. Bats had brushed against the windows, feasting on the bugs attracted by the light burning by the sink as Nadia washed up the mountain of pots and pans and dishes, fine plates and crystal glasses, endless silver cutlery all used at the feast in honor of Elsbeth's birthday. The rest of the servants had eaten the leftovers and gone to their beds, leaving Nadia to finish the final chores alone.

And so she'd been tired and overslept and Cook had needed to wake her.

"Lazy layabout!" Cook snapped when Nadia set her buckets on the enormous table. "I don't know why we keep you."

You keep me because you don't want to do the work. And I stay because the only way to kill myself would be to throw myself down the well. And with my luck, it would be shallow, come up only to my knees, and then I'd be worse off than I was. But Nadia only responded with a tight smile and set about preparing the oatmeal for the servants' breakfast.

The festivities for Elsbeth's birthday continued the rest of the week. Now that his beautiful daughter was of age, Lord Braemoor was eager to show her off and reel in the young men that could add to both his coffers and his prestige. Lord Braemoor held one of the fattest holdings in the kingdom and Elsbeth was his only child. While it would be beneath the crown prince to take anyone lower than a princess for a wife, Lord Braemoor's estate would be a welcome prize for one of the spare princes or any other sons, firstborn or not, of the rest of the peerage.

And so Lord Braemoor planned the celebration of Elsbeth's birthday with a weeklong tournament. It provided the men with an opportunity for some sport and Elsbeth with an opportunity to view her potential husband at his best.

Tents of all kinds had been set up in the fields surrounding the manor house. Tents for viewing. Tents for eating. Tents for resting. Each potential suitor, his intentions voiced or not, had raised one in which to house his armor and to change, each resplendent with his family's colors. The entire kitchen had been moved outside, the better to serve and feed the multitude of those in attendance. In an offer of largesse, Lord

Braemoor had even roped off an area for the town to come and view and sell their wares, which caused the common side to take on the air of a country fair.

Nadia would have much preferred to have been hidden back inside the manor for, to her, monsters prowled the world outside the kitchen and corner of the manor grounds attached to it. When she was young, Nadia had tried to be like Elsbeth, spirited and full of life, and had stood up to the monsters who sneered and belittled her. But she quickly learned. Monsters don't respect the challenge or finish you off quickly. They stand there and laugh until the laughter is a death in itself. But you don't die. There is no peace.

She learned to get up and soldier on, to hide when she could, for death was not easy to find in this green and pleasant valley full of lush fields, low hills, and shallow, slow-moving rivers. Without death, there was no end to the laughter.

Nobody wants you. Nobody truly wants you. Seven little words that had been seared into her soul.

Nadia was filling beer as fast as she could. Huge kegs had been rolled up from the cellars, braced, and then tapped on site. Daisy stood ten feet away filling glasses with hard cider. Nadia had twisted her hair up and secured it with some pins that Hazel had cast off, but tendrils of her mousy brown hair escaped and flapped in her eyes every time she bent over. She brushed them away with the back of her hand.

"Nadia! Are you really nada? I need that beer now!" Gregson, one of Lord Braemoor's squires stood, hands on his hips, toe tapping with impatience.

"I'm moving as fast as the keg is," Nadia said, and placed four more steins on the huge tray.

"You're moving as fast as the keg is..." Gregson trailed off, fixing Nadia with an expectant glare.

Nadia shrunk back. Surely he didn't expect her to call him—

"You're moving as fast as the keg is—sir!" The tray Gregson had been clamoring for only moments before sat untouched before him. His eyebrows rose expectantly.

Nadia swallowed. "I'm moving as fast as I can, sir."

"Not fast enough." Gregson hoisted up the tray and marched back into the throng.

Her hands shook as she held the next stein under the brown, yeasty stream. She shouldn't have to call him "sir." Gregson held no title. Yet. He was hardly out of pagehood. It was this tournament, the jousting and the steeplechase, that had inflated him. He had been invited into the inner circle, his service important, and now he felt himself even more superior.

Nadia gave herself over to the task, filling the steins, trying to be nothing more than a clockwork servant, like those on the glockenspiel that decorated Westfold's city hall. A roar of laughter rang out from the field, and suddenly Daisy was there, pulling on her arm, shoving her forward, closer and closer to the dais where Elsbeth stood in triumph. Person after person joined Daisy in pushing Nadia to the forefront, all of them laughing. Over on the town side, even Nadia's brother George shook with it, tears of mirth running down his bearded face.

The crowd shoved her until she stood below Elsbeth. Lord Braemoor's daughter raised her arms and quieted the crowd. Nadia could see they had come to the end of the day's sport for a score of men were mounted on horseback.

Elsbeth's voice rang out clear and strong. "Here she is gentlemen." Elsbeth gestured toward Nadia. "Your consolation prize. A kiss to the winner from me. A kiss to the loser from her."

Elsbeth raised a scarf into the air. Caught by the breeze, it snapped in purple ripples before Elsbeth dropped her arm and the men thundered off.

Dust rose as the horses raced down the road to the river. Nadia knew the route they'd take. Down the main road, across the bridge until they neared the town itself, then they'd swing across the sheep fields until they reached the fairy fort. From there, they'd turn south and race back for the manor, skirting the wheat fields, full and golden, just weeks away from the fall harvest, then cut through the coppices and back around the manor proper until they reached the sheep mown fields from which they'd started.

Elsbeth and her father had raced it often enough. A trip of no more than fifteen minutes, maybe less with the fine horse-flesh mounted today.

Minutes enough to return to conversation and eating and speculation. Minutes enough to stay pinned where she was. No one had come forward to block her retreat, but their gazes were enough to keep Nadia in her place. And for her to desperately wish that she was somewhere else.

A cry went up from one of the lads who'd shimmied up a tree that offered a view to the back. The ground shook as the men and horses raced from the swath between the trees and the house, turf flying from the shod hooves.

A black was the first across the line, quickly followed by a host of others, all foaming flanks and heaving sides. A gray was the last across. His rider pulled back hard on the reins, causing the horse to whinny before the man jumped off. His eyes flashed in anger as he threw the reins to a squire who ran up.

Nadia turned her gaze to the ground, only raising it when Elsbeth joined her, a mask of satisfaction on her face.

"Well ridden, my Lord Gilroy," Elsbeth purred to the tall man who stepped forward. He knelt at Elsbeth's feet. She cradled his head in her hands and kissed his brow.

Next, she turned to the dark-haired man who had lost the race. "Now, my Lord Harris, you may claim your prize."

Nadia's lord did not kneel at her feet. He gave her an angry smile and then pulled her to him. His mouth came down on Nadia's, and he crushed her against him, bending her, until they were as one. As laughter rang out, Nadia felt him go hard.

He released her with a "milady" and cheers rang out once more. Nadia's chin wobbled as she dipped a small curtsy. Blinking, she wove her way back to the kegs and picked up her task.

Like clockwork once more, she filled stein after stein. Lamps were lit, and moths came out, batting against the glass, and still Nadia worked on.

Eating turned to dancing, and though the musicians played the same songs from the formal ball just days before, there was wildness in the air and in the movements of the dancers.

A giggle from somewhere behind the tent interrupted Nadia's labors. The memory of the hot kiss and sweaty body that had been pressed against her was more than she could bear. Nadia knew well enough what happened when men were drunk or bored. And since she was no lady...

With shaking hands, Nadia set the last stein on the table behind her, then she gathered up her skirts and melted into the night.

two

Nadia pressed her back into the rough bark of the gnarled, old tree. The ones that dared to grow on the fairy fort were scrubby and short, almost as if the hill mocked them for trying to attempt life upon it. Even the villagers mocked the trees. "Fairies are death," they would say to each other, nodding as they contemplated the foolishness of anything willing to venture near the forbidden realm. For while beautiful and full of magic, fairies were also nasty creatures with sharp claws and teeth who would rip to shreds those who ventured into their protected places.

Nadia wasn't so sure the stories were true. When she was ten, she had purposely spent the night on the fairy fort, hoping the fairies would find her and kill her. Cook had beaten her for dropping a cup, beaten her until her ears had rung and all she looked at appeared as two. It wouldn't be so bad, Nadia had thought, to gaze at the fairies' unparalleled beauty as they ended her suffering.

But they hadn't. Nothing had come but cold and damp, and a large old owl that had settled itself on a branch above her and asked its eternal question until Nadia fell asleep. She had awakened, alone and alive, the next morning and crept back to her place at the manor house while the stars were still bright and dawn was just a thread of azure at the horizon.

And so she would creep back in the morning this time, though Cook would be sure to have noticed her absence. But she'd be safe here. No one would venture here at night. No one to find her and complete what the rider had started this morning.

Nadia shivered and tried to wiggle herself further against the tree. While the days of September were still warm, the nights were not. Soon, the last of the harvest would be brought in. There'd be fields full of fat sheaves of wheat and piles of hay. Basket upon basket of apples would be laid into the cellars. Carrots into barrels of sand. Pumpkins and turnips and parsnips. Only the sheep, their coats thickening for the winter ahead, would be left on the hills. And the villagers would gather and celebrate and congratulate themselves on how their hard work had provided them with such a bounty.

There was a whisper on the wind and a dark figure alighted on a branch above Nadia.

"Who whoo? Who whoo?"

Who whoo, indeed? thought Nadia as she curled up, settling her head on a root as a pillow. *Who whoo, indeed?*

The ladle Cook hit her with when she returned was hot with soup.

"How dare you run off and leave me with the work!" Cook swung the ladle again, connecting with Nadia's upper arms as she tried to shield herself from the blow. The woman gritted her teeth and whapped Nadia two more times. "I had Henry set up the rest of the washing out by the well. No warm water for you today, missy. You want to wait until the work's gone cold then so be it."

Nadia stifled a groan. Not only would the cold water stiffen her hands, the dishes would be much more reluctant to give up their grease. She would have at least twice the work and be much more miserable doing it. Nadia turned and trudged out to the well.

She groaned aloud at what greeted her. Nothing had been done, nothing except to move everything from the festival site to here.

A tear ran down her cheek as she surveyed the mountain. It was like something from the fairy stories. Towering piles surrounded the tub of sudsy water. Stacks of plates. Knobby spires of nesting kettles. And bucket after bucket of steins the villagers hadn't carted off. Only there wouldn't be any fairies or kind animals or magical wizards to do the dishes for her. And Henry had placed the dish tub on the flagstone pavers. She would have to do the dishes on her knees. There was only one small towel laid out for her to dry them with. It would soon be as wet as the ancient rag floating in the water.

Nadia collected a stack of plates and knelt in front of the tub. She dunked the first one in. It wasn't long before her fingers ached from the cold. The rag merely smeared around the grease clinging to the plate. She lifted it out of the water and rubbed vigorously, hoping friction would build up some heat. The grease finally started to lift.

One plate finished, Nadia paused to stretch out her aching shoulder. An old-fashioned sandbox would have worked better than the tools she currently had. She glanced over her shoulder then ran her fingers along the joints of the pavers, collecting up traces of sand. She worked the grit into the washcloth then dunked a plate into the tub, wetting it. The sand ate the traces left on the plate, lifting them better than the cold water. Nadia smiled.

The sun broke over the coppices, warming her face. The water would be warmed too, in an hour or so. Nadia settled her feet more comfortably under her and set about finishing her task.

A week later, the fields and larders were just as Nadia had envisioned, fat with the fruit of the town's labors. Fat with the expectations of an easy winter. Fat developed on the villagers, too, as all ate well. All, except for Nadia.

Elsbeth was now engaged and plans were underway for a spring wedding. The winter would be spent sewing now that the women's hands were no longer needed in the fields. Everyone had worked hard and all had been provided for.

Except for Nadia, who had done her very best and it still hadn't been good enough. She tried to be thankful for what she had, a bed and some bread. But winter was bone chilling next to the fish tank and, unlike the girl in the fairy story, Nadia was not allowed to creep up next to the fire. Everyone else would be tucked up nice and comfy above the stairs where it was warmer.

It was hard to keep the longing out of her heart, especially as she watched the other servants stuff themselves on the leftovers of the bounty sent to Lord Braemoor's table—stews and roast meats and puddings and pies—while she stood at the tub and washed up the dishes and ate the hunk of bread that had been left for her on the counter.

It was at the dish tub that Nadia stood when the roars first echoed through the valley. Daisy dropped the plates she had been holding, ready to place them back on their shelf.

"Saints preserve us!" Cook said, crossing herself. "What was that?"

A shared glance told Nadia that they all feared the same thing, and they streamed out the door to get a better look. The three of them stood there in a cluster in the kitchen courtyard—Cook with her ladle, Nadia with her dish cloth, Daisy with empty hands—and stared off at the smoke rising from the nearby field. Henry and Oliver tumbled out the door and joined them.

A mighty roar shook the air as an enormous dragon passed by, its black scales shining like polished steel, huge leathery wings fully open. Then fire streamed out of its mouth, adding to the blaze dancing across the field where the sheaves of wheat still sat, ripening. It roared again and turned toward the sheep field.

"I hope it eats them and doesn't roast them," Henry said.

"Why would it matter?" Oliver asked.

Cook hit him with her ladle. "Addlebrain! The beast would only eat one or two, but if it does to them as it did to the wheat, they'll all be lost."

They could hear the frantic baaing from where they stood. A thunder of hooves sounded from the other side of the manor and dust flew up from the road.

"Going to their deaths more like," Cook said.

But before the party of knights came anywhere close to the sheepfold, the dragon rose in the air, a fluffy white object held in the talons of one fearsome paw, and flew off to the west, roaring once again.

Cook looked to the wheat field. "Grab a bucket, every one of you. We need to get that fire out."

"Buckets and sacks," Henry said. "We'll need to beat that fire out."

Nadia ran to the well and had the first full bucket up by the time Henry appeared with several of his own in his hands. He grabbed the well's bucket from Nadia, filled the ones at his feet, and dropped it back in. "Leave them!" he yelled at Nadia when she bent to grab a couple. "Oliver's stronger than you. Get the sacks and get them soaking."

Nadia rolled her eyes as she turned back to the manor. Who did he think usually fetched the water around here?

She passed Oliver on her way to the kitchen and then Daisy with the sacks. "What do you think you're doing?" Cook shouted at her, trundling along behind them, four buckets in her fat grip. "Get to work!"

"But Henry—"

Cook smacked Nadia with one of the buckets. "There will be no dinner for you tonight if you don't get to work."

Nadia ran back to the kitchen. The buckets she usually used were gone. She dashed into the larder. No sacks.

She stood, hands on her hips, lips twitching as she thought about what to do next.

The mop closet!

Halfway up the stairs, she ran into Molly, the chambermaid, on her way down. Nadia grabbed the buckets from the girl's hands.

"I got these! Go find others!" Nadia dashed back down the stairs with her find, agog at her audacity.

Back outside, a stream of people had appeared at the well. The flagstones were littered with puddles spilled from the buckets of people unused to carrying water. Nadia dropped her two empty buckets by Henry and hoisted up two of the full ones. His eyes bugged. She trotted off, shaking her head.

At the field, men raced, the sheaves bouncing on their shoulders as they desperately tried to save the grain from the flames. At least it was still somewhat green. A few more days and a quarter of what they were trying to save would have simply fallen into the field. Women and boys beat at the flames with the damp grain sacks. Buckets of water dotted the field, not to be poured on the burning stubble but used for rewetting the sacks.

Nadia had one pressed into her hands and went to work, smothering the red-orange flames as they crawled toward the sheaves. It was somewhat ironic, beating out what was due to be burned anyway once the sheaves had been moved to the threshing floor, turning the stubble into fertilizer for next year's crop. But she kept at it, swinging the damp, sooty bag over and over, perspiration running down her face.

Slowly, she became as black as the field. Slowly, the crowd of beating sacks overwhelmed the fiery intruder and the village reclaimed the field. Lord Braemoor commanded that beer and sausages be brought out, and Nadia was sent back to the kitchen.

Cook, smudged and sooty, clicked her tongue as she surveyed Nadia. "Whatever are we to do with you?" Then she gave Daisy the kitchen scrub brush and sent her to the well, Nadia trailing along behind. Daisy scrubbed while Oliver dunked bucket after bucket of cold water on Nadia and leered as her wet dress clung to her.

Daisy eventually threw down the brush. "There. I can't do better."

Oliver tossed one more bucket on Nadia and then draped an arm around Daisy. "We've certainly earned our beer today, Daisy, my girl. Let's go drink our reward."

Nadia gathered up the skirt of her only dress and tried to wring the water out. Without soap, Daisy's scrubbing hadn't done much but leave Nadia's skin red and raw. Tonight, after the others had gone to bed, she'd put on a flour sack and scrub her dress in the kitchen sink. For now, she stood by the well and waited for the dripping to stop.

The sky flamed with sunset, its color an echo of the earlier fields. In the east, inky fingers of night crept toward the sky, as dark as the dragon. If the legends were true, the creature would be back again.

Nadia almost hoped it would.

Oliver updated Cook the next morning with the damage. "A third of the wheat from that field, three ewes, and the beast carried off the prize ram." Cook tutted as she poured water into a painted china tea pot. "They've stationed buckets with water and grain sacks at the remaining fields and are going to move the livestock later today, spread them out so there's only a few per paddock."

Cook shook her head and handed Oliver Lord Braemoor's breakfast tray. "Never thought I'd live to see something like this. Yesterday was only the beginning. You mark my words."

"Gorn!" Oliver exclaimed. "Why choo go and jinx us like that?"

Cook flapped her hands at Oliver, shooing him toward the stairs. "I know the stories. It will be back. And it will keep coming back until it's appeased."

Nadia turned her attention back to the potatoes she was peeling. Cook was right, if the stories were to be believed. Eventually, they'd need to offer something of value to the dragon, though it *had* taken off with the prize ram. Maybe that would be sacrifice enough. But Cook thought it would be back. Nadia sighed.

"Enough of that, missy!" Cook said. "You just do your work or the dragon won't be the only thing needing to be appeased."

Nadia picked another potato off the giant pile to her left. As far as she could see, you really couldn't appease a dragon.

It returned that afternoon, this time to a field north of town. Nadia couldn't see it from the manor, but its terrible roar could be heard even inside the kitchen.

The men and boys had been sent out to fight the fire. The women stayed behind this time, preparing food for the weary men when they returned. Lord Braemoor's men at arms mounted up again, though Hazel had heard them muttering complaints before they left.

"They were whispering that it was all well and good losing sheep or cattle but their horses were much more valuable. And their armor! They were saying they'd be roasted alive if the beast turned its breath on them. Not that they'd actually complain to Lord Braemoor. They weren't very happy when they saw me standing there, but I just put down my stack of extra grain sacks and pretended I hadn't heard anything."

They did have a point. What were mere men to do? Supposedly arrows couldn't pierce the beast's hide, and what use were swords against a creature that could fly?

Cook chopped up the carrots with a little more vigor. "There's only one thing that stops a dragon," she said, ominously. "At least I'm past my prime."

Daisy's eyes grew so large that Nadia was surprised they didn't pop out of her head. "They don't really do that?" she breathed.

"Just you wait." Cook's head bobbed as she talked. "They'll do it. They'll have to."

And with that, Daisy fainted dead away.

Unlike the previous day, they lost most of the field. People weren't sure which to mourn more, the wheat or the six dairy cows that gave more cream than milk and were one of the reasons Westfold's cheeses were so famous.

Lord Braemoor sent a rider to the king, begging for help. In the meantime, a debate raged as whether to pull the sheaves into the barns or leave them in the fields. The grain would be safe under shelter. As long as the barns didn't burn.

They talked about stuffing as much as they could into the church, since its stone walls and slate roof made it the most fireproof building in town, but, as the priest had pointed out, that would only save a portion of the harvest and would surely give the beast more reason to go after the livestock. Oliver thought it more likely the man was afraid it would make his building a target.

The sun set that evening a brilliant scarlet due to the smoke, and there were those who feared the sky was a portent to what awaited them on the morrow.

By morning, the villagers had learned what Nadia already knew — there weren't that many places to hide. The lush fields and low hills made agriculture easy but offered few places in which to conceal things. If they brought the prize livestock inside, would the dragon smell them? And would it simply tear a house apart to get at them? The trees in the coppices were too thin to really conceal much more than a rabbit, and if the dragon went after them then there'd be no firewood for winter. What to do? What to do?

Two times, riders on sweat-soaked horses stormed up to the manor house before the family had finished breakfast, nary half an hour between them. The first rider had left Lord Braemoor in a rage, Henry reported.

"He tore it open, trembling hands and everything. It had a big wax seal on it and the messenger was in the royal livery, so I'm guessing it was from the king. Lord Braemoor reads it and turns as red as a beet. He tore the letter into pieces and threw them into the air, shouting 'Thanks for nothing!' I think he would have tossed the man out but Lady Margaret jumped up from her seat and, you know how she has that kind way about her—" Nadia rolled her eyes. "—walked the man to the door, apologizing all the way."

Cook unrolled a pie crust along the top of one of the twelve beef pies she was making with what was left of the six cows. They had butchered everything that wasn't charred. "That's that then. We're on our own." A whine erupted from Daisy's throat, making her sound like one of Lord Braemoor's hunting dogs. "Who was the other visitor?" Cook asked, shaking out flour to roll out another crust.

Henry sat down. Daisy and Hazel looked at each other and then sank down at the table, too. Cook clutched her rolling pin to her massive chest. Nadia would have sunk down, too, but she feared what Cook would do with the rolling pin if she tried and chose to be motionless instead.

Henry swallowed heavily. "It was from Lord Gilroy."

"Isn't that who Elsebeth is marrying?" Hazel asked.

"Um, I'm not sure," Henry answered slowly.

"That's him," Daisy said.

"Oh, that's his name all right. It's just..." Henry swallowed again. "Lord Braemoor tore up that letter, too."

Nadia braced herself on the back of a chair.

"Do you know what it said?" Hazel asked.

"He yelled something about, 'Wait. Now he wants to wait.'"

"That poor lass," Cook said, shaking her head. She flattened a ball of dough with her hands and began to run the rolling pin across it. "I'd have expected them to send Elsbeth to him."

"Why would he have said 'wait'?" Daisy asked.

"Because he wants to see if there's anything left after the dragon," Henry said. "And at this point, who can tell?"

The dragon came again. This time they lost a shed of pigs and a hay barn. With all the fuel inside, the villagers had been able to do nothing but watch the barn burn. Everyone had pig that night for dinner. Most people had only been able to choke down a few bites. But Nadia, who'd actually gotten some as everyone had been too busy to bake and so there was no bread, thought it was the best thing she'd ever eaten and was secretly glad that the dragon had come, though she'd been careful to look mournful like everyone else.

The village elders arrived at sundown and spent hours locked up in Lord Braemoor's study. There'd been much shouting and then, more ominously, hushed tones, and finally they'd filed out, hats in their hands, and Lord Braemoor shouted for a bottle of his best Westphalian wine to be brought up.

The study door had been closed again and locked as soon as Oliver handed it over, and there Lord Braemoor stayed the rest of the night. A grim-faced master tailor arrived shortly before the sun. He handed a rolled and sealed piece of parchment to Jonah, the master at arms, and declined an offer to break the fast.

The house sat in a state of quiet waiting that morning. No one went in or out. No one made any preparations. No one but Nadia and Cook. There was still water to be fetched and food to be prepared.

So it was Nadia alone who was outside when the dragon came, black and shining and loud as thunder. She set down her bucket and shaded her eyes against the sun. He was the most magnificent thing she had ever seen.

The dragon turned his head and their gazes locked. She had been expecting to see green or yellow, but its eyes were fiery orange and pierced Nadia like the point of a pike.

Her heart matched beat with every stroke of its wings. Then it turned its head to the sky and roared before flapping off to the south. Nadia picked up her bucket and watched it go, taking a piece of her soul with it.

three

Daisy's worst fear had come true. The men had decided, shut up in Lord Braemoor's study, that there was only one thing to do. The king had offered no help and the neighboring towns were too afraid to do anything lest they anger the dragon and have it come visit them next.

"Tom got it from the tanner this afternoon," Oliver told them at dinner, though it was a very mournful dinner. "They don't know how to kill it without knowing where it roosts, so in the end they agreed this was the only way."

The "only way" being to offer it a sacrifice. A list of all the maidens had been drawn up and tonight Lord Braemoor would pull the name of the sacrifice written on a piece of paper from a jar. A lottery.

Nadia moped around with the rest of the girls but for a very different reason. While Daisy and Hazel and Molly were sure theirs would be the name drawn tonight, Nadia was sure hers wouldn't. After years of wanting death, it had finally come visiting. And while she'd never have sought it out—too afraid to be roasted and, with her luck, survive to be in even more pain and torment—being eaten alive would be quick.

Nadia actually envied the lucky girl.

The girls all walked to town together. Even Elsbeth joined them, riding horseback. Though, as Daisy pointed out, "Like her name would actually be in there."

There had been several men who had knocked on Lord Braemoor's door during the day. "Pockets jingling," Oliver had said. "On their way in but not their way out." Which had managed to depress Hazel and Molly and Daisy even more.

Nadia had two minds about it. Fewer names meant a better chance for her, but the unfairness of it bothered her. And what if it wasn't fewer? What if it meant that Daisy and the others were written down twice? Or even three times?

Nadia watched Elsbeth's proud seat as she rode ahead of her. Elsbeth certainly wasn't afraid. Nadia was sure Elsbeth's name was missing from the jar.

They gathered in the town square, ablaze from the light of a hundred torches. Lord Braemoor's men at arms herded the girls into a roped-off area. Several of the girls cried so furiously that they had to be picked up and deposited behind the ropes. Elsbeth took her place, head held high, her golden curls shining in the flickering light.

The jar was placed on a stand, and then Lord Braemoor gave a little speech. Nadia wished they would just get on with it.

"Difficult times call for sacrifice. In times of want, it is the sacrifice of our desires. In times of war, it is the sacrifice of brave men. For this ancient foe, it is our most precious that must be sacrificed—an innocent that holds within them the possibility of life. It is the future that must be sacrificed so that we may survive the present.

"We do not take this lightly. It will cut us deeply to lose one of our own, but this is a war. A war that no man can fight." Lord Braemoor turned to face the girls. "And it is you who must step forward to save us."

A round of applause broke out from the villagers. Nadia couldn't blame them. It was the kind of inspiring speech that would have made them proud to offer up their sons. This time, they were offering up their daughters.

As she stopped to think about it, it was a fairer bargain. Instead of twenty men, twenty sons to lose and leave them potentially destitute, all that was required this time was one loved but expendable daughter. They should have been cheering.

"And now our champion will be chosen by lottery."

Lord Braemoor made a big show of throwing back his cloak and pushing his shirt up to the elbow. *Look! Nothing up my sleeve!* He rolled his fingers several times and then plunged his hand deep into the slips. It emerged, one folded piece held tightly in his fingers. Slowly, he opened it and read the name aloud.

"Nadia Crofton!"

Time stopped. When she later thought back to the moment, there was the echo of a cheer that played, but Nadia couldn't recall if it had actually happened or if she had added in the sound. One moment she stood staring at the slip of paper raised in Lord Braemoor's hand and the next she was on the other side of the ropes, standing beside him, her hand raised in his. Joy shown on the faces of the crowd, but it was different from the look they gave her when they'd made her the butt of some joke. There was hope, too. They were looking at her as if she were a savior.

Nadia's heart swelled. She was needed. She was finally needed. The village would get a savior, and she would get the death she had so longed for. A perfect happy ending, just like in a fairytale.

The rest of the night was like a dream. Nadia was whisked away and, for the first time in her life, given a proper bath with warm water and rose-scented soap. The women scrubbed her so hard that she bled, but Nadia didn't mind. The dragon was sure to prefer the scent of blood to that of roses.

They shampooed her hair and dried it by the fire, then took an iron to her mousy locks and curled it into ringlets. A filmy white dress was slipped over her head and little, white slippers put on her feet. The last thing they added was a crown of pink roses while singing a song that Nadia finally recognized as the one women sang to tuck a bride into her wedding bed.

She touched the crown in wonder. Its petals were the softest thing she had ever felt. It was more than she had ever dreamed possible. A bride. She was a bride.

They gathered around her again, still singing, and offered her a cup of wine. It was sweeter than she expected. A thick, sticky taste she'd never smelled on the cups she washed. She managed just a couple of large swallows before it became too cloying, and she handed it back to them.

The room grew fuzzy, and her head began to droop.

Nadia moved her mouth. The taste coated her tongue, but no moisture came to her aid. She tried to open her eyes, but her lids were heavy. Oh, so heavy. And her arms ached. She moaned and tried to lift them. Her head flopped against her arm.

Against her arm? Nadia forced her eyes open. The limb came into view, just in front of her nose, like a small tree reaching for the sky. Nadia followed it.

Above her head, her wrists came together, tied with rope. Nadia blinked and willed her surroundings into focus. She was atop the fairy fort and it was morning. Two upright beams supported a crossbar to which she'd been tied. An empty doorway on a place that was itself a crossroads. Her lips lifted a smile. All the times she had wanted to meet Death, had lain on this very hill and hoped to find him. She was finally getting her wish.

Nadia squinted at the sun and tried to judge the time. The sun was well over the horizon and climbing. When did the dragon usually come?

Her back ached and her arms prickled, beginning to go numb. Using the small amount of slack in the rope tying her hands to the post, she moved from side to side, trying to ease the discomfort. A chilly breeze ruffled the grass at her feet and lifted a strand of hair, depositing it across her eyes. Nadia blew at it. It lifted and fell, still stuck on her eyelashes. Two more tries and still the confounded strand remained where it was. It took a frustrated shake of her head before it finally floated free.

A fat bumblebee alighted on the last of the daisies of the year at her feet. Nadia watched it hasten from flower to flower. She glanced occasionally into the sky, praying for the expected black dot. But it didn't come.

The sun climbed higher. Nadia alternatively basked in the warm sunshine or shivered in the icy breeze, mortified that the flimsy fabric of her dress offered little protection from the cold and so her nipples had hardened into peaks.

Time crept on. It was a good thing, she decided that they had given her the drugged wine. She would have died of boredom if she'd had to wait, conscious, all the hours since they had tied her there and left her. As far back as she could remember, there had always been some work that needed attending to. This endless waiting...it was a slow death. And she'd had enough of the long slow death of her twenty-three years. It would be her luck that the dragon wouldn't come and death would still elude her.

Nadia yawned and watched the swaying daisies at her feet. They drifted in and out of focus and finally faded from view.

A muffled roar woke her. The sun had risen higher, though it was not yet noon. A shining black dot in the sky was drawing closer. Wings flapped, and another roar rumbled across the plains.

The dragon circled once and then drifted lower. Her dress ruffled with the breeze, and the dragon changed course, tipping to its side and gliding toward the hill. It landed hind feet first, wings beating backward before folding them and tucking them against its shiny body.

The beast was even larger than she had imagined. She'd seen it carry off sheep, but they must have been no more than a snack. Surely the thing would swallow her whole.

The dragon gave a snort, bathing Nadia in the first true warmth she'd had all day. Its orange eyes were like that of the eagle owl that lived out in the coppices, but with the slitted irises of a snake. The dragon's trailing black whiskers twitched. It drew its head back, meeting her gaze.

The ground beneath her feet rumbled. The creature twitched on its haunches, flipping its tail behind it like an irritated cat. The rumble grew, turned into a growl. Then the dragon lifted its head and let out a roar that popped Nadia's ears. She squinched her eyes shut and waited for death to come.

There was a tug as the rope holding her hands aloft broke free, and then claws like razors ripped into her dress as the dragon gathered her into its massive paw. With a lurch, Nadia was airborne.

But death did not come.

Its wings flapped, cracking like flags in a strong breeze. The dragon let out another roar. Nadia opened one eye. And then quickly closed it again, her insides lurching with the sight of the ground speeding by far below them. She shivered in the thin air, and the dragon tightened its grip around her.

Her hands and arms became even more painful as her circulation returned. Prickles like an army of fiery ants raced across them. The rushing wind was like ice against her skin. Nadia's stomach roiled until she gagged. Perhaps it was a good thing that it was empty? And now her eyes ached from squeezing them shut. Why hadn't the stupid thing just eaten her?

Eventually, it became too difficult to keep her eyes closed. One look at the ground so, so far away, and her stomach leaped into her throat. As it fell back down, the world went dark again.

four

A roar woke Nadia, though she was past the point of caring. Her death was definitely imminent. Roasting wouldn't be such a bad way to go. It would warm up her convulsing muscles and end the painful chattering of her teeth.

Unless she was to be torn apart by hatchlings. That would not be a pleasant end.

The dragon's leathery wings snapped as it landed. Cold, hard stone met her body as the talons released her. She kept her eyes screwed shut and offered up a silent prayer.

Instead of the scramble of claws, the click of boots drew near.

"What have you here, Uro?" a silky voice crooned.

Nadia opened her eyes. A figure dressed in black bent over her. Pale yellow eyes, the color of hard cider, searched her face. They were framed by dark ash-brown hair, adding to the impression that she was gazing at an oversized owl.

A muscle twitched in the man's cheek. If he was a man. The figure was the most handsome, most terrifying thing she had ever seen, dragon included.

He tutted, clicking his tongue as he turned away from her and stroked the dragon's muzzle. "I'm afraid I'm going to have to send you out again, Uro." He glanced back at Nadia, his eyes flashing, his jaw hard. "*She* is no sacrifice." The man retreated a couple of steps. "Make sure you make it worth your while."

The dragon growled, a deep, throaty sound, almost a purr, and launched itself back into the air.

Nadia pushed herself up. Tears filled her eyes. She had failed.

The muscle continued to twitch on the dragon master's jaw as he watched its receding form. Then with a snap of his cape, he turned to go.

"What about me?" Nadia asked. Her voice trembled.

The man halted. His hand traveled to the knife on his belt. Nadia gulped and squeezed her eyes shut again. The man jerked her roughly to her feet. The cold blade of the knife rested against her skin. Then, with a jerk, the ropes binding her hands fell away. Cautiously, Nadia opened her eyes.

The pale yellow eyes traveled up the length of her. "You might want to find something else to wear, dearie." A sneer curled his lip. "The holes are in all the wrong places."

And with that, he dropped Nadia's arm and strode away, his black cape billowing out behind him.

Nadia glanced around the empty courtyard. The dragon's master had stalked off toward the gardens, but she was of no mind to follow him.

She had failed. She had failed at the one thing she'd truly thought she could do for the town. And she had failed at finding death. The dragon hadn't eaten her, and its master hadn't stabbed her.

A breeze ruffled Nadia's skirts. *Holes in all the wrong places.* She examined the damage to the dress. Great slashes revealed the lengths of her calves and thighs, and there was a tear at her waist. So much damage and yet not a single prick to her skin. Why did she have to be so unlucky?

Nadia stumbled toward the stone fence at the edge of the courtyard, half blind with tears. And leapt back as the view was revealed. Surely, she had been mistaken.

Nadia inched her way forward. She braced a trembling hand against the railing and cautiously peered over it. There was nothing below, nothing but drifting, white clouds.

Straightening up, Nadia scooted back a couple of feet. After a lifetime of never being higher than the manor's second, and highest, floor, the height was dizzying. How many times had she wished the buildings in Westfold were taller? Or that their flat and quiet valley had mountain cliffs? Death was just two feet away, for if she hurled herself over the edge there was no way she'd survive the fall.

Her feet seemed to have come to the same conclusion for they now refused to move though her knees had no trouble shaking. The longer she stood there, the more she wanted to be anywhere but this close to the edge.

A sigh escaped her lips. Another failure. She couldn't even throw herself to her death.

Nadia backed away from the fence and its dizzying view and turned to survey the courtyard. The castle to her right was huge, with spires that reached far upward. Store rooms and stables lay off to her left. Before her were the gardens. This was truly a place fit for a king, and yet, unlike the hive of activity at the manor, there was no one around. No stable hands, no pages, no washerwomen, no nobles. No one but her.

The breeze ruffled her skirts again, and Nadia shivered. She had better change. Her dress was not only flimsy and torn, it was an invitation. She stepped to the huge wooden doors at the entrance to the castle. They swung open easily despite their size.

Nadia's jaw dropped open. Gilded columns held up a vaulted ceiling decorated in alternating panels of carved fruitwood and painted heraldic scenes. A swirl of mosaic tiles covered the floor leading to a wide, sweeping staircase of marble. Carved wooden banisters bracketed the treads. Panels of stained glass illuminated the space, casting patches of color on the floors and walls. Nadia stepped into the hall and turned in a slow circle. So much splendor.

But her place was below stairs.

She crossed the mosaic floor and ducked into one of the passageways behind the stairs. A series of doors lined the hall. Fron her experience at Westpark, Nadia knew that the servants' closets would be tucked away at the back.

A glass-paneled doorway lay at the very end of the hall, through which she spied a butler's pantry. Nadia reached out a hand to the knob.

And closed around nothing.

Snapping back as though she'd touched fire and not air, Nadia stared at the aged brass handle. It looked solid enough. Slowly, she reached out a hesitant hand. Fascination mixed with horror as, once again, the handle proved phantom. Was it an illusion or perhaps enchanted?

Nadia turned to the other doors along the hallway. Each knob looked solid enough, but her attempts to turn them met with the same results. The doors themselves were solid, for she could place her hand on them easily enough, but she could not open them.

She tried every door along the passageway until she found herself back at the entrance hall. Skirting the staircase, she went down the hallway on the other side but met with no better luck than the other.

Finally, there was nowhere to go but up.

Heart pounding, Nadia mounted the steps. She did not belong on these stairs. Never had she been allowed to use the main staircase at Westpark the few times she'd had cause to go upstairs. Someone was certain to see her now and make her stop. Which would actually make it easier to find her way. She would even be glad to face the dragon's master again if only he would tell her what to do.

Nadia's knee poked through one of the holes in her dress. *Maybe not.* At least, not until she'd changed.

The doors on this floor were all raised wood and gilding. No use in attempting the handles. They were sure to be ballrooms and the like. Up another staircase she went.

The walls on this one were painted with various plants and animals. Surely, they were family or guest rooms. Again, she left the doors untouched and went up another set of stairs. This floor had frescos depicting scenes from mythology. She had heard the stories often enough. There was Pan. And over there was Venus rising from the sea. She looked a little like Elsbeth.

Nadia's breath caught in her throat. Elsbeth. And Daisy. And Hazel. The dragon had rejected her, but its master still wanted a sacrifice. Someone else would be offered to it.

Though Elsbeth was spoiled and proud, Nadia did not wish her dead. Or Daisy and Hazel, even though they were unkind to her.

Her knees went weak. Nadia braced herself against the wall. If only she had been worth more, worth something, then her sacrifice would have counted. Someone else would now die because she wasn't even good enough to be a sacrifice.

Tears rolled down her face until there was nothing left but salt and thirst. Drying her eyes, Nadia made her way down the hall. She passed an image of Persephone and the pomegranate. Hades. Maybe she was in hell.

Nadia tried a doorknob. Again, her hand passed right through it. Maybe she was dead. Maybe the dragon had killed her and she was in hell, her torment being a task she could never accomplish because she was not allowed to open any door.

Or, she thought, trying to be practical. *These are simply doors I'm not allowed to open.*

She continued to wander, finding no more luck than she'd had. Her feet hurt, her head ached, her tongue became parched, and her stomach growled with hunger.

"Is there no door I'm allowed to open?" she yelled in frustration and slid down a wall. As she buried her face in her hands, Nadia heard a click.

"Hello?" she called, getting to her feet.

There it was again. Nadia went in search of it. The sound of footsteps led her down two flights. As she peeked into a hall paneled in light blue silk, she noticed a door standing ajar.

"Hello?" Nadia gently pushed it open.

A large bedroom stood before her. Turquoise silk paneled the walls. The bed was piled high with pillows, and three wardrobes stood along one wall.

Nadia opened the first one. Silky, sheer nightgowns draped from the hangers. She lifted one out. Heat blossomed across her face. It was worse than wearing nothing at all. What it did leave to the imagination was so suggestive, she nearly dropped it. Nadia put it back and peeked at the others. They were all like that. Some with holes...

A shiver ran through her body. *In all the wrong places.* Had he expected her to put on one of these? Nadia slammed the door shut and tried the next one.

Her breath left her at the sight. Not even Elsbeth had dresses so fine. But they all laced up the back, and some had separate sleeves. She'd never be able to put them on by herself. And the dragon's master would be more likely to help her out of them than into one.

She opened the doors on the last wardrobe. Finally, day dresses. The lightweight wool one in loden green would suit her well. Nadia lifted the torn, white dress over her head and tossed it on the floor. As she stood there naked and shivering, it occurred to her to look for underwear. Something she usually went without, unless she was having her monthly flows, for while the manor allowed her a basic, castoff shift, the other girls tended to keep rags for their own use, leaving her to scrounge for the rest.

Pulling open the bottom drawer of the wardrobe, she discovered underthings of cotton so fine they were like silk to the touch. In the drawer of another, she found shoes. Blue silk high heels with pink bows, another pair covered in a tapestry-like fabric of green silk, satin slippers similar to the ones on her feet but with buckles of diamond, short-heeled boots in bright red leather, and, finally, a pair of slippers in the softest kidskin, like butter beneath her fingers. Nadia kicked off her slippers and put on the soft, black shoes.

She picked up the green dress and pulled it over her head, curious as to how would it look on her. Not that she knew what she usually looked like, but her hair was sure to be a mess. A mirror hung over a dressing table set with brushes and what looked to be boxes of hair pins. Sitting down on the small stool, Nadia lifted her eyes to her reflection.

Her hair was in knots. At least her face was clean. The green of the dress made the brown in her hazel eyes recede, leaving her eyes a clear, bright green. Did she look pretty? Not that it mattered.

Nadia fingered the mother-of-pearl brush, debating her courage. Did she dare use it? At the manor, she'd only had her fingers. Maybe she should just put her hair up.

She opened the lid to the first pin box. Shock sent it slipping out of her hand. The lid clattered onto the dresser. Gold pins studded with diamonds winked in the light. More cautiously, she opened the next. These proved to be silver, decorated with flowers of pearl and diamond.

Folding her hands in her lap, Nadia considered. The pins and the brush were too fine for her. But she didn't dare walk around with her hair down, like a child.

She reached a shaking hand for the brush and worked the knots from her hair. Which pins to choose? The gold. They were the plainer of the two.

Nadia's stomach grumbled as she secured the last pin, and she tried to recall when she had last eaten. Two days ago? Would she be able to find food? Perhaps there was something in the garden, some berries or vegetables.

Nadia met her gaze in the mirror. Frightened eyes stared back at her. Her stomach gave a noisy growl, demanding it be fed. Unless she intended to starve, she would have to leave the room. Rising from the table, Nadia set off to explore.

five

Nadia left the door to her room ajar. Though the handle had been solid when she grasped it, she didn't trust the house. The enchantment could change, allow her access one time and bar her the next. And even if it didn't change, she wasn't sure she could find her way back to it without some kind of marker.

Counting the floors as she went down the stairs, Nadia debated what to do. Lord Braemoor had always taken meals in the dining room. This enormous castle must have at least one. Would the dragon's master use one though? He didn't seem quite human.

As her stomach continued to voice its displeasure, Nadia determined the first floor would make the most sense on which to begin her search. The kitchen was one level down from it, the gardens even farther. Might as well begin with the closest.

The first few handles she tried were just as they'd been the first time, solid looking but nothing but vapor beneath her hand. Then she spied a door partway open down the hall. Inching up to it, Nadia peered around the frame. The dragon's master sat at a large dining table, drinking a glass of wine.

"There you are, my dear. Come in. You must be famished."

Aromas assaulted her nose. Ham. Roasted vegetables. Steaming cheese pies. Fruit layered with cake and cream.

Her stomach grumbled loudly. Loudly enough that the master chuckled. He rose from his chair, pulled out the one next to his left, and waited. Knees shaking, Nadia crossed the room and sat, placing her hands in her lap as he pushed her in.

"Wine?" he asked.

"Um..." Nadia paused. She'd never been offered any before. Except last night. And that had been drugged. "Please?"

The master leaned in around her as he filled her glass, so close she could feel the warmth from his body. "Thank you," she whispered. He set the decanter down and took his seat again. Her muscles relaxed a fraction as the space became hers again.

The dark figure across from her picked up his wine.

Gregson's reprimand replayed in her brain. *"You're moving as fast as the keg is—sir!"*

"I'm afraid I don't know who you are," Nadia said. "Or what I should call you."

"There are few who know me," the dragon's master said with a twinkle in his eye. "And as for my name, you can call me 'my Lord.'"

"My lord, what?" Nadia asked.

A merry smile crept up the man's lips. "Oh, just 'my Lord.'"

"You have no name?"

He chuckled lightly. "I have a name. But knowing someone's, or something's, name gives you power over them. It's why my cousin is simply known as The Doctor." He gave his head a shake of amusement and drank deeply from his wine.

Her brows pinched in confusion. "But your dragon has a name."

The Lord laughed. "Yes, Uro. But good luck controlling him."

Nadia heaved an inward sigh. The master...the Lord, as she supposed she would have to call him, was certainly one for puzzles.

Much like the plates and cutlery in front of her. Why were two plates stacked on top of each other? And what exactly did one do with four forks and three spoons?

"Pie?" The Lord held the platter out to her.

Her mouth watered at the sight and aroma. "Yes, please."

The platter remained extended. The Lord's eyebrows rose. He put a slice on Nadia's plate before serving himself. "I see you're not into formal dress for dinner."

Nadia glanced over at him. He was no longer wearing the cape but was still dressed in black. The white shirt under his quilted vest was the only splash of color. A relaxed yet elegant look.

The loden green dress was the finest thing that she had ever worn. If you didn't count the bridal gown she'd been sacrificed in. But now her choice seemed too casual for the setting.

"There were some finer gowns in one of the wardrobes, but I'd never get into them on my own," Nadia explained. "There was no one to help me."

His eyes narrowed. "No one?"

Nadia bowed her head under the intensity of his gaze. "No, sir."

Breath rushed in through the Lord's nose. It stayed in his lungs so long that she glanced up. With a huff, the air rushed out again.

"I'd be more than willing to assist you. I'm rather an expert at ladies' lacings. Unlacing mainly, but I'm sure I could figure out the reverse."

Heat flamed her cheeks. "If I'm not dressed appropriately, I can always eat in the kitchen."

"You're fine." The Lord picked up his fork. "Do eat your pie before it gets cold."

Which fork had he picked up? Her angle blocked her view. And he wasn't holding his fork like any of the servants. It was somehow balanced in his fingers, not wrapped in his grip.

"Pie not to your taste?" he asked. "I know it's not the lowland cheddar you're used to, but it does have a nice tang that I find enhances the flavor of the ham."

The smell wafting up from her slice caressed her nose. Drool filled her mouth, and she had to swallow. With a grumble, her stomach complained at her delay.

The Lord gave her another sharp look. "You're obviously hungry. What's the problem? Think it's poisoned?"

She hadn't thought of that. "No, it's just..." Nadia squinched her eyes closed as warmth marched across her face once more. Should she just admit that she didn't know what to do? Would he throw her from the table?

Her eyes stung, threatening tears. She really didn't belong here. She belonged at the back of the kitchen where she knew what to do.

With a sigh, she confessed. "I don't know how to use a fork. I've never really used one."

A surge of power washed over her, lifting the hairs on her arms. Whatever he was, the Lord wasn't human. Something infinitely more terrifying.

"Never?" The ice in his voice sharpened each sound in the word.

"No."

A muscle in his cheek twitched. And then, in an instant, his countenance changed. The corners of his mouth curled up in a smile. The Lord set his fork down and pushed back his chair. "Then I'll just need to teach you."

Nadia pushed at her chair, ready to bolt, but before she could move the heavy seat, the Lord stood behind her. He picked up the outmost fork. Bending around her, he placed the fork in her hand and curled her fingers, tucking the fork beneath her thumb. His hand came down on her shoulder as he breathed his next instructions in her ear.

"It's just a very efficient extension of your finger. Surely you've run your finger along the inside of a bowl, collecting those last delicious traces?"

"No," Nadia whispered. "I've never been allowed." Even if there had been traces left in the bowls she washed, Cook surely would have beaten her for tasting them.

The Lord's fingers dug into her shoulder. "Well," he said, the word all breath. "We'll have to remedy that." He removed his hand.

Nadia stared at the fork in her grip. The Lord took his seat again and gave her a tight smile of encouragement. When she remained motionless, he took his own fork, turned it to the side, and cut off a piece of his pie. He stabbed the piece with the prongs and brought it to his lips.

Her stomach pleaded with her to try. She followed his example, turning her fork on its edge. It cut easily through the cheesy custard and flaky crust. Stabbing it, Nadia lifted it to her mouth. A moan escaped her as the pie melted on her tongue. She could die right now. Never had she imagined that anything could taste like this.

And then a throaty chuckle broke her out of her reverie.

"That's just the appetizer," he purred. "Imagine what you'll be like by dessert."

Nadia swallowed, forcing the bite down where it hit her stomach like a stone. She pushed the heavy chair back.

"Thank you. I think I'm finished now."

The tic appeared again in the Lord's cheek though his lips held their smile. "Don't know what you're missing."

Bobbing a curtsy, Nadia fled from the room.

Practice kept the sobs filling her throat from release until she was out the heavy main doors. She was to have died today, not end up as a courtesan to some...whatever he was.

Nadia stumbled in the direction of the fence with every intention of throwing herself over it. But as soon as her eyes caught sight of the swirling clouds, now lit from underneath by the setting sun, her legs gave.

Turning onto her hands and knees, Nadia crawled away from it. There had to be some way.

The dragon! Leaping to her feet, she ran for the stables.

Pushing open the door, Nadia stopped short. No partitions broke the huge expanse. No stalls. No tack rooms. Just the enormous dragon, curled into a ball, resting on the flagstones, faint curls of steam rising from its nostrils. It lifted its head at her approach.

Convincing it to eat her shouldn't be that difficult. Nadia gathered her courage and walked straight up to it, placing her hands on its muzzle. She pulled at the dragon's lips, growling in frustration when the jaws refused to part.

"Come on, you stupid creature!" Nadia cried, continuing her attempt to open its mouth. "You're supposed to eat me." With a puzzled look, the dragon tilted its head to the side. Finally, she managed to slide one hand between its lips. But no farther. Screaming in frustration, Nadia hit it on the nose.

With a snort, the dragon sat up, lifting its head out of reach. Nadia continued to pummel it.

"Eat me! You're supposed to eat me!" Her fists slammed, hammering against its neck. Her feet lashed out, connecting with its upper chest.

A throaty grumble shook the flagstones. Nadia closed her eyes as the dragon's chest rose in the air.

A tremendous thud rocked her on her feet. The long neck of the dragon curled around her, sending shivers along her skin. Nadia held her breath, offering up a quick prayer that death wouldn't be painful.

But it didn't come.

An impatient snort bathed her in warmth. Cautiously, Nadia opened one eye. The dragon had rolled onto its back, all four legs in the air. It nudged her toward its massive underside, like a giant dog waiting to have its belly rubbed.

Her breath hitched. Pain flooded her body. She'd failed again.

"Why won't you eat me?" The weight of her defeat pushed Nadia to her knees. "Why won't you eat me?" she asked again, as her body slipped farther, coming to rest alongside the hard leather-like scales. Her breathing staggered as sobs took control of her lungs.

The dragon whined, rolling carefully back over. It curled around her, warm and solid. Worn out from the long, eventful day, Nadia huddled alongside it and cried herself to sleep.

"He's warm, but he's not that comfortable."

Nadia's eyes jerked open. She lay on the flagstones, partially tucked under one of the dragon's wings. The Lord's black boots glinted in front of her. She raised her eyes to his face. His mouth twitched with amusement.

"The bed upstairs is infinitely more comfortable. Or were you looking for someone to share it?"

Nadia scrambled to her feet, her cheeks burning. "No, I hadn't planned…It had been a long day." She bowed her head and brushed her hands on her dress.

"Death wish?"

"Something like that," she said to the flagstones.

The soft sound of a mouth opening and closing met her ears, and she glanced up. The Lord's eyes closed. A smile twisted his mouth as his lids raised. "Well, you're not dying today. Uro, you're going to have to leave her alone. You have other work to do."

The dragon gave the Lord a nod and shifted to its feet. A strange mixture of gratitude and horror rippled through her as the dragon slunk out the massive open door and disappeared.

"Someone is dying today," Nadia said, watching him go.

"Oh, yes."

Bile rose in her throat, and she struggled to choke it back down. It was her fault. She hadn't been good enough. "Why?" she asked.

"Because the hearts of your villagers are full of themselves and they have become lazy." Nadia opened her mouth to protest, but he cut her off. "They're not lazy in their work, but lazy in their expectations. They are sure of themselves. Their hearts are not thankful."

Nadia stared at him. "Who are you?"

The Lord chuckled. "I've answered that one already. Don't you think the question should be, '*What* am I?'" His strange eyes glinted, daring her to guess.

He definitely wasn't human. More like something out of the fairy stories. With that, a memory surfaced. Elsbeth, playing with her dolls, acting out the fables her tutor had made her memorize as she watched Nadia working in the kitchen courtyard.

"You're like the creature in the story of Psyche. The drag-on-like beast who harasses the world with fire."

A triumphant smile lit the Lord's face. "Very good. Though—" His head bobbled. "I'm not the dragon. Uro is. I am—"

The last piece of the story clicked into place. "A god," Nadia finished breathlessly, instinctively shrinking from him. Psyche had been left for a dragon but had been taken by a god instead.

The Lord dipped a tight, tidy bow.

"So am I...?" Her throat closed up before she could get the word out.

"Dead?" he finished for her. "What do you think?"

"I don't know." Her head moved back and forth as she thought. "My hand goes right through the doorknobs."

The Lord reached out, placed one finger under her chin, and raised her head. His eyes searched hers, narrowing before he released her. "I can fix a few of them, but—" Abruptly, he broke off. The fingers of one hand came together, rubbing against each other in a jerky motion, as if they wanted to do something, but he was fighting against it. They curled into a fist which he pressed against his mouth. With a deep inhale, his manner transformed.

"You can make it a game," he said with a flourish, all smiles. "You like games, don't you, Nadia." Her name rippled off his tongue, all foreign sounding with some strange accent.

Games. She had never had time for games. She wasn't sure she wanted to start now but...

"Is that what I'm here for? Games?"

His shoulders raised and lowered in a slow shrug. "What would you like to do?"

Nadia swallowed nervously. "I've always been a servant."

He waved his hand dismissively. "I don't need another servant. I already have all the help I need."

Nadia's eyebrows inched together. Help? What help? The castle was completely empty. "Then why am I here?"

"You know why you're here."

Her mouth moved, attempting to push the words beyond her lips. "Because I was the sacrifice."

Muscles rippled in the Lord's face as he wrestled some emotion. A smile broke free and curled his lips. "Yes, and as your reward, you will not work for me." He took a shaky breath. "I'm sure you'll figure it out." He gave her a sharp nod. "Good day." Then he strode away, his cape snapping behind him.

Nadia's stomach growled. All she'd had to eat the day before was one bite of cheese pie. She wiped her sweaty palms on her dress and departed the stable. Mounting the steps to the castle, she pulled open one of the large, ornate doors. Dust motes danced on the air in the otherwise empty entry hall.

Crossing the mosaic tiles, Nadia made her way down the hall to the kitchen, halting at the door that had failed her previously. Would this be one of the handles that the Lord had "fixed?" Gathering her courage, she reached out a tremulous hand. And touched brass. Relief flooded her as Nadia gave it a turn and pushed the door open.

Three butler's pantries lay along the passage, each with a different pattern of china. Next, came a room lined with shelves of gleaming tureens, platters, and cruet sets made of silver. Finally, the main kitchen came into view. And, oh, what a kitchen! Never had she imagined that a place not seen by guests could be so fine. Nadia ran her fingers along the soapstone sink with its three basins. Nearby stood a stove as large as an ox. Above it, shelves of pots and pans and a rack of roasting forks.

On the harvest table beside the stove, a plate of toast with a wedge of cheese sat beside a steaming mug of warm, brown liquid. Nadia raised the cup to her nose. Chocolate!

But who had made these? Glancing around, Nadia found no one lurking in the corners or standing inside the pantry. Even the sink was empty. Any cooking utensils had either already been washed or the meal had appeared out of thin air.

Nerves prickled the back of her neck as Nadia pulled out one of the stools from beneath the table and lowered herself onto it, ready to jump up again when the meal's owner appeared. As the seconds ticked past, a giggle escaped. Heaven help her. She sat. In a kitchen, of all places.

Her heart filled with glee as she tucked into breakfast. She had indeed died and, while not in heaven, had landed somewhere close.

Tense as a cat, Nadia washed her meager two dishes. The Lord was sure to appear out of nowhere and stop her. But all the years of staying up late, working until everything had been cleaned and put away, made it impossible for her to simply leave them in the sink and walk away. Though, for all she knew, it was a magic sink and the dishes would have washed themselves.

Nadia dried her hands on the dish towel and swept the table for crumbs one more time, surveying the empty kitchen. She sighed. Clearly the Lord was correct in his assertion that he had no use for a maid.

She placed the towel on the apron of the sink and left the massive chambers, pulling the door closed behind her. Leaning against it, she collected herself for the trek back up the staircase and the endless wandering that awaited her. The endless trying doors that would not open.

A few of them. The Lord had said he could only fix a few of those infernal handles that refused her grasp. Her body went stiff as a sudden thought pierced her. Perhaps he was not master of this place.

But he was a god.

Nadia pushed herself off the door. Upstairs was a labyrinth, a puzzle that she had no patience for today. Perhaps the grounds would be more welcoming.

Outside, the autumn sun shone brightly. The air was crisp, but she would do fine without a sweater. Nadia crossed the courtyard, passing the stables. Uro, the dragon was out, eating someone she knew. A shiver jolted down her spine, and her feet picked up their pace, anxious to put some space between her and the reminder.

The weight in her heart lightened as her feet touched the soil of the gardens. She wandered through a series of boxwood hedges and geometrical beds with short, colorful mixes of flowers. The wide-open park with its tall sheltering trees called to her to come explore, but Nadia left it alone and set out toward the herb garden. Beyond it, she found an area with fresh, turned soil. A shed stood off to the side, its door ajar.

Nadia poked her head in. "Hello?"

Her quiet voice barely cut the air. Spider webs hung in the unused and neglected corners. Shelves of empty pots ran up to the ceiling. On a tall bench, paper sacks tied with string and sporting tidy labels sat in a pile. Nadia turned one of the papers toward her, but there was no use in trying to decipher the script.

She opened one of the bags. Fat flower bulbs sat nestled within. A trowel lay next to the stack of bags. Nadia peered out of the dusty window. The Lord might not need a maid but he apparently needed a gardener. The work was half-done and who else was there to do it? Certainly not the Lord or his dragon.

The dress she had on was the best she had ever worn, but it was a work dress, even if it had not originally been intended for work in a garden. Nadia picked up the trowel and a bag of bulbs. She might no longer be a maid, but today she would be a gardener.

SIX

Nadia retreated back to the castle as the sun began to dip behind it, casting shadows that seemed to go on forever. Her knees ached, unused to the time spent upon them, but she had managed to plant every bag of bulbs. Grime covered her hands, darkening her fingernails, and smudges stained her dress, but both were easily washed. She might not be used to cleaning fine wool but the principle had to be the same as the rough fabric she had always worn. And if she made a mess of it, there were a multitude of others in her bedroom.

Nadia crossed the lawns, picking the golden pins from her hair and tucking them along the front of her dress, allowing her hair to blow in the breeze. She shrugged her shoulders and stretched her neck, working out the knots that had developed from using her muscles in an unfamiliar task.

A hint of sweet perfume caused her to change direction. Nadia followed the scent to a rose garden she had not noticed on the way in. Brilliant coral, velvety red, soft pink, and snow white blooms bent the long green canes. A lush last effort by the plants before the crispness of fall caused the plants to stop flowering and drop their leaves. A maze of copper beeches lay beyond.

It was too late to explore it. Fear rose at the thought of getting lost and then trapped there in the dark. If this place had a dragon, what other sorts of creatures might roam the grounds? Nadia quickened her pace, not wanting to get caught in the gardens after sunset.

The foyer was empty, and Nadia encountered not a soul on her journey upstairs. The door to her room still stood open a crack. Cautiously, she pushed it open. No one was there.

But a panel she had thought to be just another part of the wall hung inward a good six inches, revealing itself to be a door. Nadia crossed the room and pushed it open the rest of the way.

A large copper bathtub stood in the center of the room. Filled with warm water, she found when she tested it. A sheen of rose-scented oil lay on the surface. A brand new bar of soap, also scented with rose, sat on a tray along with a soft cloth and a scrub brush backed with mother-of-pearl. A fluffy white towel hung on a rack next to the tub.

Warmth filled the room from a fire lit in the tile-covered stove. Nadia quickly twisted her hair back up and secured it with pins from her bodice. It was too close to dinner to wash her hair and have it dry. Besides, how dirty could it have gotten in the two days since they had scrubbed her clean?

Nadia pulled the green dress over her head and shucked off her underwear. A moan of pleasure escaped as she lowered herself into the water. She closed her eyes and leaned back. This place was truly enchanted.

Unless the Lord prepared the bath for you.

Water sloshed over the rim as she sat up with a start. The door to the bathroom was open, as well as the one to her room. She had been too distracted to think of closing them.

Nadia hugged her knees and listened close. Nothing. But for how long? And how had he or the castle known she would need a bath? Had someone been watching?

Holding herself perfectly still, Nadia lost track of her heartbeats as her ears searched for the hint of any sound. Only her breathing filled the silence. Finally, she picked up the bar of soap and, keeping her knees close against her chest, soaped down her arms. She picked up the brush and scrubbed at the dirt embedded around her fingernails. When her hands were clean, Nadia dipped the cloth into the water and quickly ran it over the rest of her, keeping as much of her modest pose as possible.

As soon as she could, Nadia pulled the towel to her and held it up as a screen as she stood and stepped from the tub. She wrapped it around and padded across both rooms to the bedroom door. A quick glance up and down the hall and she pulled it shut, turning the lock, ensuring that she could dress unobserved.

Nadia paused at the entrance to the dining room. The Lord sat slouched in his chair, a glass of wine in one hand, his eyes closed, softly humming a tune. Unsure of whether to knock or clear her throat, Nadia just stood there, hesitant to break his reverie.

But he must have sensed her presence. His eyes flew open, and he set down his wine.

"Don't stand there lollygagging." The Lord rose from his chair. "Don't want dinner to get cold, do you?"

Amazing smells wafted toward her. The food looked as mouthwatering as the night before. Tonight, there was a fish course instead of pie, asparagus in a butter sauce, roast beef, and a pudding studded with candied violets.

Nadia scowled at her place setting as she lowered herself into her chair. The table had been set with as many plates and sets of knives and forks and spoons as the night before.

The Lord bent close and inhaled as he pushed her chair in. "Roses?"

It must not have been him then that had left the bath for her. "I washed before dinner," Nadia murmured.

His attention shifted from her to a place along the wall, though why that particular set of swirls in the wallpaper was so compelling, she couldn't fathom. A laugh escaped his lips.

"Well, I guess as you spent the day in the garden, you must have needed it." He sat back down, biting his lips to hold back some mirth.

"Have I amused you in some way?" Nadia asked.

"No," he said, choking back laughter. "Not at all."

Nadia placed her hands in her lap and bowed her head. "If I have done something wrong, I wish you would tell me." Tendrils of pain blossomed in her heart.

The Lord held up a hand. "No. You must excuse me. It's my fault. I had no idea you had such a compulsion to work." His mouth began to quiver. "I'm sure the gardens will look lovely come spring." His lips rolled inward and clamped between his teeth.

She had erred in some way. "What did I do wrong?"

"Nothing. You...you've...simply added your own flair to the garden." He offered her an encouraging smile. "So I'm sure you've worked up an appetite. We'll start with this white wine with the fish." He poured some into one of the three glasses in front of her. "And I've decanted a red that will do just magical things to the roast. Do drink up."

Nadia lifted the glass to her lips. A fresh, clean aroma filled her nose.

But the liquid that spilled across her tongue was surprisingly sour. Conscious of the Lord's watchful eyes, Nadia forced herself to swallow. A grimace twisted her face.

"It can be an acquired taste," he said. "The fish will help even out the flavor." The Lord placed a portion on her plate and poured some sauce over it before serving himself. "Remember, you work from the outside in." He picked up the leftmost fork and a knife from the top of his place setting. "For the bones. Do be careful. Don't want you choking."

Nadia watched him. Great. He was holding the fork in his left hand and the knife in his right. The Lord separated the meat from the bones and then switched hands, the fork now in his right as he brought a piece to his mouth.

But she couldn't move. The Lord wiped his mouth on his napkin and came to stand behind her. "The principle is the same," he said, picking up her silverware. "They're extensions of your fingers. One to hold down the meat—" He curled Nadia's left hand around her fork, placing her index finger on the back. "One to flick the bones away." His fingers wrapped hers around the knife.

The blade truly became an extension of her finger. Hand-over-hand, he guided Nadia in securing the first piece and then returned the fork to her right.

"I'd feed you, too, but I fear there'd be a repeat of last night." The Lord returned to his spot, a smile curling the corners of his mouth.

Nadia raised the fish to her mouth. Flavors burst upon her tongue. Her eyes closed. She had definitely died and was now in some strange limbo. Never had she imagined that food could taste like this.

"Now try the wine."

The flavors of both blended on her tongue. The essence of the fish was still there, but now the wine came alive with hints of apricot, rose, and pear.

"Yes, much better," she agreed.

The Lord smiled at her, and silence fell, broken only by the quiet scraping of silverware against plates. Nadia had nearly finished her fillet when the Lord finally spoke.

"They say curiosity killed the cat, and in this case, it will probably kill dinner, but I must ask. What has been your prior culinary experience? I mean, your food experience," he amended as Nadia frowned with her confusion.

She put down her knife and fork. "I don't belong here."

"Yes, you do. You're in my house."

Bowing her head, Nadia placed her hands in her lap. "I'm a scullery maid. I ate bread and cheese and drank only water."

"And did all the servants in your house eat as you did?"

Nadia blinked, willing away the tears gathering in her eyes. "No."

"I thought not." The Lord reached for his wine glass but withdrew his hand before grasping it. "Well, I doubt tonight they are feasting on trout à la meunière and washing it down with Riesling. And that's just the starter course." He gave her an encouraging smile. "So enjoy it."

She tried. She ate all of the lime sorbet that came as a palate cleanser between the fish and the main portion of the meal. Of that, she managed just one spear of asparagus and a piece of roast so small she could have hidden it in her hand. The pudding sample was so tiny that the Lord protested it was no taste at all. But she knew what happened to people who had been starving, how they gorged themselves and then were sick. She drank little of the wine. What if it made her tipsy? She might wake to find the Lord in her bed. Or she in his.

He took her hand at the end of the meal. Nadia gulped. Would he draw her close and kiss her? Did he believe she'd had more to drink than she had?

Bending at his waist, the Lord bowed deeply. "Goodnight, Nadia."

Flustered, Nadia made her knees move and wobbled a curtsy. Then her hand was hers again. His back straightened, and the hands that had grasped her went behind him. Nadia darted out the door, alone, hardly breathing until she had safely returned to her room, closed the door firmly, and slammed home the lock.

As her breath settled, Nadia peered about. Where was the green dress? It was nowhere to be seen. Pushing open the bathroom door, she found the water and implements from her bath had gone, though the tub remained. Nadia worried at her lip. Too many things were vanishing or appearing out of thin air. Like the sorbet at dinner. She was certain it hadn't been on the buffet until her host rose to get it. One more annoying mystery.

With a sigh, Nadia plopped down onto the bed. The mattress cushioned around her backside. What heaven. It was like sitting on a cloud. She fell back into the comforting embrace, longing to stretch out on the downy bolster beneath her. But not in this dress. She would not treat the rose silk as a nightgown. Nadia pushed herself up. Perhaps something new had appeared in the wardrobe. The house seemed to anticipate her in other matters.

She crossed to the one that had held all the lacy nightgowns. Gathering her resolve, she flung it open, only to be met by the rack of obscene garments.

However, the one hanging on the very end on the right was new. And next to it, a dressing gown in swirling patterns of paisley that she could swear had not been there the night before. Nadia pulled the hanger from the cabinet. The new nightdress was simple and modest. She tugged the rose silk over her head and slipped on the cool, white cotton.

After placing the evening gown safely back in the wardrobe, Nadia padded back to the bed, turned back the covers, and climbed in. The sheets caressed her skin like the petals of a rose, soft as the silk dress though made of cotton. The pillows and mattress top had been stuffed with feathers or down. Nadia curled onto her side and wiggled into the fluffy nest.

It had been fifteen years since she had slept in a proper bed. Fifteen years since her mother had tossed her out. The bed had been smaller and its cover only one thin, threadbare blanket, but she'd had four brothers to help keep her warm.

Until her mother had needed space for her youngest brother, James. His cradle would soon be needed for the newest Crofton swelling her mother's belly. Nearly one a year. And since girls couldn't work the farm as well as boys and she'd eventually cost her father a dowry, they had turned her out.

Nadia threw back the bed covers, their weight now unbearable. She did not belong here, in this bed, in this place.

Her fingers shook as she pulled the nightgown over her head and put on the damask dress again. Best not to wander the castle in a nightgown, for she had no intention of sleeping in this room. She needed to find her true place, and it was not upstairs.

The knob on the kitchen door passed right through her hand when she tried it. A howl rose in her throat, refusing her attempts to stifle it as she slid down the door, landing in a puddle on the floor. Why was the castle so intent on keeping her from her rightful place?

Nadia pushed to her feet and staggered out to the stables. She was sure to find failure there, too, but she had at least to try. The dragon lifted its head at her approach.

"Please?" The dragon gave her a questioning whine. "Please?" she asked again. She couldn't do this anymore. It was better to end it now. Her agony became too much to bear. Tears overflowed and ran down her face. With a whine, the dragon nudged her with its muzzle.

His kindness erased the last of her control. Her knees collapsed. Nadia pushed herself up from the floor and huddled against the creature's massive paws, with their thick, black talons that curved into the flagstones. She had huddled this way in the market after her mother had tossed her out. Starving and cold, sure that she would die.

Until Cook found her. And brought her back. She hadn't cared a whit that she wasn't paid or actually part of the staff. Cook had brought home a stray that was thankful for its bed and the scraps they gave it. And in the end, for no cost at all, they had someone to do the worst of the chores.

For the first time since that day, Nadia wished that Cook had never brought her home. Being here, in this place, had shown her just how unloved she truly was. She had been better off in ignorance.

The dragon whined again and lowered its head to the floor. It fixed one bright orange-red eye on Nadia.

"Please," she said. "Eat me."

The dragon blinked and simply stared at her and, for the second night in a row, Nadia cried herself to sleep against its dark, warm body.

♪♪♪♪♪♪♪♪♪♪

"If you wanted a companion for your bed, all you needed to do was ask."

The Lord's voice trickled into Nadia's consciousness. Bolting upright, she teetered and placed a hand against the dragon's chest to keep from falling over.

The Lord's eyes danced their merriment. "I would be happy to oblige."

"No, thank you."

"Why else would you have left your perfectly lovely bed inside to sleep on the ground with a dragon?" the Lord asked. Nadia lowered her gaze and didn't answer. "Next time I find you here, I'll carry you to bed myself."

"So I am here as some bedmate for you?"

The Lord's mouth twitched with a smile. "Do you want to be?"

Nadia shrank back with the idea. "No."

"The choice is yours," he said.

"So why am I here?"

The Lord clasped his hands behind him and strolled around the dragon. "Because you were offered as a sacrifice."

"But you said I was no sacrifice," she called to his back.

"Because you weren't."

With a growl of frustration, Nadia threw her hands into the air. "You're speaking in riddles!"

The Lord halted his meandering. "Hm. I guess I am." He ran a hand along the dragon's tail and continued around the beast. It closed its eyes and gurgled in contentment.

"That creature is an oversized dog," Nadia remarked.

The Lord patted the dragon's side as he continued around the beast. "He is rather. Though most people don't discover that. Too much running and screaming."

"And burning and dying," Nadia muttered.

The Lord stopped at the dragon's head and scratched its jaw. "That is what dragons do."

"On your orders."

"Oh, yes."

Revulsion coiled in Nadia's gut. "You're a monster."

"Interesting choice of words," the Lord mused. "I've not heard you utter one word against the people who offered you up, yet I'm the monster."

"It was a lottery!" Nadia took a step toward him. "A lottery that you necessitated."

The Lord had the gall to look affronted. "Not me. I'm not the one who broke the rules."

Nadia's brows pinched together. "The rules?"

An indulgent hum escaped his lips. "I explained that yesterday—fat and lazy."

A grumble rose in Nadia's throat, but she bit it down. "And you're the one who sits in judgement."

The Lord closed the distance between them and tapped her forehead with a finger. "You were paying attention. Though you did work for me yesterday. I don't need a gardener, either."

Exasperation filled her. "Who was going to plant those bulbs? You?"

He chuckled. "I have a job and it's not gardener."

"Then who?" Nadia asked. "There's no one else here."

A muscle in the Lord's cheek twitched. "You'll eventually figure it out."

Nadia growled, something she usually saved for burnt on grease, and even then, only when she was alone and couldn't be punished for it.

"That's better," the Lord said with a smile. "I like a show of some spirit."

Nadia shrank back. "I'm sorry."

"Nothing to be sorry about." His gaze traveled over her. "Other than maybe wrinkling that dress. "There *are* nightgowns in your wardrobe, you know."

Her cheeks flamed with their mention. "I thought you said the choice was mine."

Merriment lit his eyes. "It is. But, you know, the god thing. Most women can't resist me." He leaned closer and whispered in her ear. "Can't wait to please me." The Lord straightened. "But if you don't want them—"

"No, thank you," she said, quickly.

His playful attitude vanished away. "What do you want, Nadia?"

An ache so strong filled her, her eyes stung. "I want to die," she whispered.

The tic appeared again in his cheek. "Sorry," he answered coldly. "I'm not going to help you with that."

Tears clung to her lashes, clouding her vision. "Then what are you going to help me with?"

His voice became like honey. "Things you never dreamed of." He studied her for a moment. "I'll take them away, the nightgowns. Most of them, anyway," he amended. "Women are known for changing their minds. In the meantime, explore."

"I can't open the doors."

"You can open the ones that matter to you. So think. What have you always wanted to do? Dance?" He took Nadia's hand and spun her under his arm. Her skirts twirled around her ankles. "There's several ballrooms, though—" He put a hand on her waist, stopping both her and, momentarily, her heart. "I don't suppose you have heard any music at dinner?"

Nadia gave a breathless shake of her head.

"Um, thought not. I'd have to hum." He dropped her hands and tapped a finger against his lips. "Read? The library is enormous. Books from all over the world. You could spend a lifetime curled up in a comfortable window seat and never finish them all."

Nadia swallowed and turned her gaze to the floor. "No, thank you."

"Music? Do you play an instrument?"

"I'm a scullery maid," she bit out. Did the man ever listen?

"Not anymore." He raised Nadia's chin and stared into her eyes. The tic in his cheek transformed into a snarl. Nadia shrank back. His eyes softened, filled with something almost sad. He dropped her chin and then ran his hand along the dragon's snout. Bending close to the dragon's ear, the Lord whispered something to it that she couldn't hear.

The creature nodded, rose to its feet, and curled away in a motion that had earned its kind the ancient name of wyrm.

Nadia watched it go. "You're a dealer of death, so why not take mine?"

"You're not yet ready to give me what you need to," he replied without a glance at her.

A cry of horror erupted from her throat, and she raced from the stables.

The bolt of the lock slammed home, easing some of her panic. She had died. The dragon had actually eaten her, and she had died. And landed in hell.

Sobs gurgled up, and her knees went weak. Nadia slid down the door and landed in a puddle of salt and wool. *Give him what he wants.* The thought bent her farther. Her cheek came to rest on the floor. Tears slid across her nose and dripped onto the wood.

She lay there, weeping, until her eyes refused to offer up any more tears. Too drained to lift her head, Nadia stared at the base of the bed, both too close and too far away. It was her destiny, it seemed.

Nadia blinked and then scrambled upright. No longer did the bed appear solid. The rest of the room was as always, but the bed had become an apparition, a ghost of what it once was.

She inched away from it, keeping her back against the wall, eyes fixed on the shadowy form.

What kind of place was this?

Nadia flinched, startled by a hammering knock on her door.

"Your presence is required at dinner." The Lord's voice was barely muffled by the wood. Nadia pressed herself further into the corner. All day, she had stared at the dust motes swirling through the space that was somehow the bed and yet not.

The door handle rattled. "Locks won't keep me out, Nadia. Open this door."

But she couldn't. She couldn't even move.

The door creaked open. Nadia closed her eyes, desperately wishing she could disappear.

"Nadia—" The rest of his words faded away. Footsteps drew closer to her, and then the Lord took her hand. "Nadia, look at me."

She tucked her chin against her chest and pressed tighter to the wall. If only she were like the bed and could fade away.

The Lord's fingers caressed her hand. "Nadia...Nadia, I am sorry."

Raising her eyes, she found genuine regret on the Lord's face. "I have frightened you, and I am sorry."

Nadia slipped her hand from his grip and glanced behind him. The bed remained a shadow of its former existence. The Lord followed her gaze.

"For it to come back, you have to want it."

"I don't want it," Nadia whispered.

"I can tell. But you should."

Nadia shook her head. "No."

"Make the bed come back," he entreated. "You deserve someplace warm and safe. A place to dream."

"I don't want to dream."

"I know," the Lord said gently. "You've had a lifetime of nightmares, but wishing the bed away won't change that."

Was that what she had done? Nadia's gaze traveled over the wood with its hangings and linens. It appeared even less solid than it had during the day.

"What if I can't?" she whispered.

"We'll settle you in another room. There are plenty of beds in this place."

Plenty of doors she couldn't open. Nadia's gaze fell to her hand. She flexed her fingers and studied their movement.

"Want it, Nadia."

A good kick. That's what you deserve. Cook's voice repeated in her mind.

Cook was right. She didn't deserve it.

Nadia glanced at the bed, blinked once, and it was gone.

The Lord gave a heavy sigh. "No matter. Lots of others here."

"In rooms I can't open," Nadia lamented.

He picked up her hand and kissed it. "Have a little faith. And now—" The Lord got to his feet. "Dinner."

Gently, he raised her to her feet and then led her down three flights of stairs. Nadia trailed meekly behind. There didn't seem to be any point in arguing, and the last thing she wanted to do was give him an excuse to carry her. Over his shoulder like a sack of potatoes, most likely. His arm clamped around her thighs. A shudder rippled through her at the thought.

Into the dining room, the Lord led her. He pushed in her chair and handed her a glass of wine. "Drink it. You've had a shock."

"No—"

"I won't take no for an answer," he said, cutting her off.

Nadia brought the glass to her lips and managed a couple of swallows. It burned its way down to her empty stomach.

"A few more," he commanded.

She managed one more while the Lord dished up some soup and placed it in front of her. He picked up a spoon and wrapped her fingers around it. "Eat."

A smooth velvet of pureed bean filled the bowl, dotted with small chunks of meat. Nadia's stomach gurgled at the salty, savory smell.

The Lord took his seat and served himself. He began to chatter on about something. She stared at the soup but couldn't bring herself to try it. An ache had blossomed—

No, that wasn't right. Something had made her more aware of the pain. The wine? Her gaze shifted to the glass. Did it contain poison?

"You need to eat, Nadia. Unless, of course, you want me to feed you." A roguish smile lit his face.

Nadia pressed a hand to her chest. It felt as if there was a hole in her heart. A hole, and as if something was burning.

"Here." The Lord passed her a slice of crusty bread, smeared with butter. "We won't stand on ceremony tonight. Skip the spoon and use this instead." He tore a strip from his piece and ran it through his soup, scooping up the broth. His eyes twinkled as he brought it to his mouth for a bite.

Nadia did the same. Flakes fell from the crust and dotted the surface of the soup. Like the crackers Cook would put in Elsbeth's soup when she was young. Nadia brought it to her mouth, moaning when she tasted it.

Heat ran up her cheeks, and she braced herself for the Lord's comments. But he was silent, his attention on the tangerine now in his hands. The sharp, citrus smell drifted over and caressed her nose.

The bread in her hands was the best she had ever eaten and yet...it could hold only traces of the soup. She picked up her spoon, carefully closing her fingers around it, and brought it to the bowl. Her hand shook as she lifted it. It took her entire focus to still it, but the reward...

The warm liquid spilled over her tongue and down her throat, dispelling some of the ache in her heart. The Lord chattered away as she ate and carefully mopped up the traces with her bread. He rose to clear the bowl away when she finished, returning with a plate topped with crumbly cake sandwiched with cream. He plucked a smaller fork from the top of her place setting and handed to her.

"Coffee?" he asked.

Nadia took the implement from him. "No, thank you." It was only then that she noticed the serving dishes on the table. A soup tureen, a bowl of fruit, a plate of bread, another of cake, wine, coffee, cream, sugar, salt, and pepper. A decent supper, but not the previous feasts. Had she been so blinded by the usual myriad of items at her place setting and the, what? Grief? That had overcome her that she had failed to look?

The spot in her chest began to ache again.

The Lord poured a cup of coffee. "Have you tried it with cream and sugar? Takes away the bitter and mellows it out to a balm that will sooth your heart."

Nadia flashed him a panicked glance. Had he sensed her distress? The Lord simply gave her a warm smile and stirred a cup which he then extended to her. "Cake and coffee are the perfect way to end a meal."

Nadia took it from him with a whispered, "Thank you."

The rich, earthy aroma rising from the cup proved a soothing balm. So unlike the sharp, bitter stuff Cook usually brewed. Warm and gentle on her tongue, it worked in similar fashion to the sorbet the night before, washing away the saltiness of the meal.

"Now the cake," he commanded.

Reluctantly, Nadia put down the warm cup and picked up her fork. The cake resembled the morning one that Cook sometimes made, but was denser and without traces of cinnamon. Powdery chunks crumbled off as she cut it with her fork. It smelled sharp and tangy and tasted, surprisingly, of lemon.

The Lord gave her a triumphant smile. "Yes, coffee and lemon. The people who dwell in the southern lands have figured out how to capture sunshine in a meal."

It did feel as if she had taken a piece of summer inside her. It sat by her heart and wove little, warm fingers into the ache. A warmth that soon had her eyes closing with sleep.

"Hmm," the Lord hummed as Nadia jerked up her drooping chin. "I can see we need to find you a new bedroom." He rose from the table, pulled out Nadia's chair for her, and then gathered one of the candelabras from the table. "Shall we?"

She followed him to the staircase, her feet so heavy they required her complete concentration to simply lift them.

"Not so high this time, I think," he said. "Closer to the kitchens. You're too thin."

They only went up one flight and down the hallway with the fresco of a unicorn hunt. The Lord stopped by one of the doors. "This should do. Go ahead. Open it."

She had tried this door before. Nadia didn't see what could have possibly changed in three days, but it opened easily.

Nadia gasped as the ability to move fled from her body. Dumb with shock, she stood stiffly in the doorway as the Lord strode into the room. Not even the family bedrooms at Westpark were this grand. Or this large. The entire manor kitchen would easily fit in the cavernous space.

Watery-blue silk covered the walls. White furniture edged with gilt trim defined separate areas of the room. Darker blue silk fell from a crown above the bed, screening the side of the bed while offering its occupant a view of the apartment.

The Lord set the candelabra down on a table. "Lots of choices for where to sleep. The bed, of course, which would be my choice. The chaise lounge, the window seat, and the floor, if you really insist."

The outer edges of the room revealed a pattern of inter-locking wooden figures. The rest was covered by a thick carpet patterned with pastel flowers.

"Silk," the Lord informed her. "So it's not really like sleeping on the floor."

Nadia finally stepped in. Five wardrobes stood like sentries along one wall. Bookcases sat between the diamond-paned windows on the one opposite. An alcove containing a window seat lined with satin cushions had been tucked between them.

The carpet was like thick moss beneath Nadia's feet. She wanted to sink down into it but chose the chaise lounge instead.

The Lord fixed his gaze on her. "No excuse to be sleeping with Uro. If you decide that you can't sleep here, then you can sleep with me." A wolfish grin crept across his face. "And I know how appealing you'd find that."

Nadia managed a small smile before it turned into a yawn she needed to hide with her hand. The Lord retrieved a pillow and throw from the window seat.

"Best to settle you here tonight," he said, unfolding the blanket and tucking it around her. "Any more effort and you'll be testing my floor theory." He blew out the candles and left Nadia in the dim moonlight that fought to be seen from behind a veil of clouds. "Try not to wish this one away."

There came the whisper of footfalls on carpet, and then the soft click of the door closing. Nadia settled the pillow behind her head and watched the clouds drifting across the moon.

Had she really wished the bed away? Did she truly have that kind of power in this place?

A wide yawn interrupted her musings. Eventually, her jaw closed, but her eyes refused her command to open. *Tomorrow.* She could think about it some more tomorrow.

seven

Rain pounded on the windows. Nadia opened her eyes to a room bathed in shades of gray. Wrapped up in the warm blanket, she watched the drops gather until they gained enough weight to run down one of the diamond panes, only to be thwarted by the point and have the process begin all over again. Snatches of a half-forgotten rhyme came to mind, told to her by a woman she had once thought kind, a long time ago. But the kindness had been short-lived. And Nadia was lucky the woman's actions hadn't shortened her life.

Or was she?

Her current fate was not something that Nadia could pin down. Had the dragon and its master brought her blessings? Or curses? She flexed her fingers, watched them ripple, wondering at the magic of this place. Magic that had, apparently, allowed her to make the bed disappear.

She had somehow known, even before she'd asked the question, even before the Lord had confirmed it, that she had made the bed less than it had been. She had wanted it gone—because she did not deserve it, because it was a reminder of what the Lord could do to her and a place in which to do it. She had wanted it gone. And it had gone.

With no idea of how to get it back.

Was it truly gone? Was that why the Lord had moved her to this room?

Or is it closer to him?

Nadia bolted upright.

She had not been able to open the door earlier to this room, so obviously family quarters. She had been moved from a basic guest room into this palatial space that was fit for a lady. A lady of much more importance than Elsbeth's mother. A queen? The wife of a god?

The blanket slithered to the floor as she sprung from the chaise.

But she had to stay here. The Lord had promised her that it was here or in his bed, and she did not want his bed. And he'd proved yesterday that locks wouldn't keep him out.

Heart pounding, Nadia began to pace the room.

He wanted her closer to the kitchens.

Kitchens. Breakfast.

Her stomach tugged her toward the door, begging to be filled. Downstairs, just a floor or two away, lay the best food she had ever eaten and as much of it as she wanted.

Passing a mirror, she halted her steps. The rose dress was hopelessly wrinkled at this point. She should probably change. But who was there to notice? The Lord never seemed to appear unless it was time for dinner or she was doing something she was not supposed to. Besides, she was only following his instructions.

Striding across the room, her hand faltered as she reached out for the door. *You're too thin.* Too thin for what? Nadia glanced back over her shoulder at the bed. No, she would not think about that. With a burst of determination, she pulled the door open and marched down the hall before she could make the new one disappear as well.

But the question would not leave her alone. The Lord was trying to fatten her up. For what purpose? The story of the witch with the candy house offered one explanation. Was that why the dragon wouldn't eat her?

Now you're just being silly girl, Cook's voice said, and Nadia could practically feel the smack Cook would have given her.

A table with a bowl of flowers sat at the bend in the hall. Above it was a mirror. Nadia stepped forward and took a good look at herself. Her hair was mussed, nearly a mouse nest. Dark circles framed her eyes, which had a sunken look to them. Her cheekbones were sharp, not soft and full like Elsbeth's, and her collar bones stuck out like broken wings.

Nadia shifted her inspection to her arms. They were thin and muscular, her hands red and cracked from years of hard work. Her eyes drifted back to her reflection. If she were a cow in the market, what would she think of it?

That it was sick. Too thin.

Nadia reached out, gripping the edge of the table for support. They had made her like this. Lord Braemoor and Cook and all the rest had made her like this. The cows at the manor were treated better than she had been, and she produced, just as they did. She had cleaned and scrubbed and fetched. And they had barely kept her alive.

I've not heard you utter one word against the people who offered you up...

Pressing her teeth together, Nadia felt her cheek tic, much like the one she had noticed on the Lord. She still wouldn't.

Utter one word. But she would certainly march downstairs and eat all the breakfast she desired.

♩♪♭♪♭♫♪♪♭♫♪♪

Someone had been frying sausages. And mushrooms. With onions. Nadia let her nose lead her to her plate. A pile of toast sat next to it, spread with fig jam. And a cup of coffee with cream to wash it down.

Nadia picked up the fork and forced herself to use the table manners she had learned dining with the Lord, rather than the hungry farmhand ones she was tempted to—shovel it in like there was little day and too much to do.

The sausages had been cut into pennies and mixed with the mushrooms and onions, creating something like a hash. Tender and flavorful, she nearly swooned with the first mouthful. Then swooned again when she took a bite of toast. Fig had seemed like an odd choice for jam. They usually had strawberry or marmalade with breakfast at the manor. But the sweet earthiness of the figs blended with the savory flavors of the hash, creating a new magic on her tongue. The coffee was perfect, too. Unsweetened and bold enough to stand up to the other flavors of her breakfast.

The debate took up in her brain again, drawing a sigh from her lungs. *Dead or alive? Heaven or hell?* She gave her head a little shake. At this point, she truly didn't care.

♩♪♭♪♭♫♪♪♭♫♪

The strangest thing happened when she went to wash the dishes. Nadia put them in the first of the sink's three basins, turned to look for soap, and then had to stop and blink. The dishes had vanished. That hadn't happened the first morning.

Hands on her hips, Nadia surveyed the sink. Perhaps she had made the dishes disappear, too?

"But I didn't want them to go away," she said, voicing her frustration aloud. And then clapped her hands over her mouth. "Great! Now I'm talking to myself," she muttered.

She stood by the sink, waiting to see if the dishes would reappear. As the seconds turned to minutes, she had to conclude that their vanishing probably had more to do with the Lord's "no work" policy rather than her newfound abilities and went to change her dress.

A proper autumn storm full of screeching winds and slashing rains had the castle in its grip. "I guess I'm spending the day in," she said with a sigh. There was certainly enough to keep her busy. The spire at the castle's peak had appeared to go on forever, reaching far into the heavens. She'd start at the top and work her way down, skipping floors and returning to her room if she needed a rest. That way she'd be able to work from what she didn't know to what she did.

After pulling on a soft dove-gray dress to hide the layers of dust she expected to find, Nadia stepped down the hall to the staircase and began to climb. Up. And up. And up. Eventually, she found herself on a spiral staircase, climbing in a twist of never-ending circles. Though no windows had been cut into the walls, a twilight glow illuminated the space. She searched for the source of the light but could not discern it.

Her legs became heavy. Holding up her skirts with one hand, Nadia braced herself against the outer wall and forced her feet up each step. Her lungs burned with the effort of simply drawing air by the time she reached the final step. A heavy wooden door, dark with age, curved and pointed at the top, barred the way at the end of the small landing. Nadia extended her hand toward its brass knob and, with a surge of determination, turned it. The door clicked open.

A small, circular room stood before her. Narrow windows, hardly more than arrow slits, let light into the room.

Only one thing sat in the otherwise empty space. A spinning wheel.

Nadia stepped closer. Familiar with the stories, she knew better than to touch it. The stone floor bore no trace of wool, no linen fibers, or tufts of cotton. What could it have been used for?

There's a princess
In a tower...

The lines of the old song sent her heart racing. Nadia dashed for the door, open and waiting, just as she had left it, but still...

Lightning flashed, drawing her attention back into the room. For a moment, the spindle gleamed with the light. Best not to chance it. Drawing in a bracing breath, she began the long trek back down the stairs.

Once she reached the bottom, Nadia sat down to catch her breath and to think. Why was there a spinning wheel in the topmost tower? Sketches of thought zigzagged through her mind like dragonflies, hovering, then zooming just out of reach when she turned to look at them. Foreign and familiar. Impossible and yet somehow entirely probable.

Dragon. Tower. Spinning wheel.

Did she really want to know what else the castle contained?

Yes. Best to know what she was dealing with. If fairytales were real, she had better figure out which one she was in.

Nadia discovered that the doors on the upper floors were far more likely to open for her. Not that she found anything use-ful up there. Many were completely empty except for the dust of centuries. One small room had been completely covered in mirrors of all sizes and lined with dressing tables, each having a set of silver-backed hairbrushes. What she had initially taken to be a spider web turned out to be an impossibly long hair so covered with dust that she could not begin to determine its color.

One room had a window that stood ajar. Chest height, she felt secure enough to push it open and peer down. The rain had stilled, and the wind had calmed into a stiff breeze. As before, there was nothing to see but clouds.

Nadia reached out and pulled it closed, glancing down when a dancing patch of white at her feet caught her eye. A feather hopped on the air kicked up by her feet. Nadia bent down to pick it up and spied something glinting against the baseboard by her toes. A gold coin. She took it in her hand and squinted at the markings but could not read them.

Her fist closed around the treasure. Never had she held so much as a penny before.

Unfurling her fingers, Nadia glanced from the coin to her feet. The feather continued its slow dance. If the stories were true, there was only one reason for the feather and the coin. Nadia opened the window and tossed it out. She closed it again, a smile lighting her face. Someone would be truly lucky today because of her.

Unless it hit them. From this height...

She flung the window open again and shouted. "Sorry!" Hopefully, it wouldn't strike someone in the head.

The day whittled away as she explored, not even bothering to break for lunch. Her stomach was accustomed to two meager meals a day and there was so much to see. She worked her way from room to room until the sky began to darken again, heralding the approaching sunset. As predicted, she had become covered with dust. It was time to return to her room to wash for dinner.

♪♫♪♫♪

"Something on your mind?" the Lord asked Nadia.

Tonight's dinner consisted of a spicy stew of beef, sweet potatoes, apricots, and chick peas, sweetened with cinnamon yet savory with some spice she could not remember having smelled or tasted before. The wine was rich and hearty, bold, and exploded with flavor on her tongue each time she took a sip. Nadia set her fork down and picked up her glass, both for fortification and for time to formulate an answer.

"I found something curious today."

"Did you?" The Lord's eyes winked with amusement.

"At the top of the highest tower."

"Ah." He covered his mouth with his hand, but it didn't hide the upturned corners of his smile.

"And I was wondering why it was there."

"No, you weren't."

"Pardon?" Nadia blinked.

"You are hoping I'll confirm your suspicions of why it was there." His observation was so on point that she squirmed. "Or lay them to rest," he added.

"And?" Nadia's heart quickened its pace.

The Lord carefully wiped his mouth on his napkin. He picked up his wine. "Are you sure you want the truth? It can be a dangerous thing. More powerful than you can imagine."

Her heart twisted like a weathervane in a gale. What if her fears were correct? What if fairytales were real? What if she were now where they had all taken place? What then would be her fate?

The Lord was either toying with her or she was in more danger than she had imagined. What could be worse than that?

"So ask," the Lord said.

"Did...Is...Was...?" The words to her question kept changing. What did she really want to know? What question could she ask that he wouldn't laugh at? Perhaps she should just be ridiculous, ask something that even she could laugh at when he replied that she was foolish.

"Was that Aurora's spinning wheel?"

The Lord set his wine down and folded his hands. "Yes."

His answer hit her like a bolt from the sky, piercing through her, pinning her to her chair. "Y-y-yes?" The word didn't want to leave her lips, as if speaking it would make the impossible real.

The Lord laughed. "I did warn you. Dangerous." Glee danced in his eyes.

Nadia's mouth flapped wordlessly for a moment. "Tower... dragon guarded...you?" she managed to stammer.

The Lord's mouth pinched with thought. "Tower—yes. Dragon guarded—Uro doesn't guard. Me—yes."

Her thoughts ran in circles, not quite matching up. Creases tugged at her brow. "So you're the witch?"

The Lord rolled his eyes. "Really? Me a magnificent maliciousness? Do be more creative."

Nadia frowned. "But there's a witch in all those stories."

He smiled. "Very true. But they have something else in common."

"Poison?" she said, wracking her brains. "Curse?"

"Yes," he said. "Again, not me...exactly. Or my fault anyway."

It was too much. Grabbing her glass, Nadia downed a large gulp of her wine. Rendered mute from her shock, silence fell.

The Lord broke it with a dramatic sigh. "Really! Is it that big a stretch? Who else is the common thread in all those stories?"

"The handsome prince," Nadia said, dismissing the notion with a tight shake of her head. Then her eyes narrowed, creating a furrow between them. "The handsome prince?"

"At your service," the Lord said, extending his hand with a flourish.

Nadia harnessed a snort. Prince of Darkness more likely. "Why would you be the handsome prince?"

"What does the handsome prince do?"

"Rescues the princess," Nadia said automatically.

A wide smile crept across his face.

"I'm no princess," she reminded him.

He snorted. "Who says they were?"

"Everyone. Once upon a time there was a princess..."

Incredulity crossed his face. "And you believe everything that people say? What do they say about you?"

His question was an arrow that hit the mark of her heart. Moisture filled her eyes with the pain of it. "That's not fair."

"No," he whispered. "It's not."

Despite her efforts, a tear slipped down her cheek. The Lord reached out and captured it with a finger. "There's truth in everything, but sometimes...sometimes it's hidden by honest mistake, and sometimes it's hidden by lies." He rubbed the tear between his fingers, before erasing the traces on his napkin. "And things do get tangled up after a thousand years."

Her eyes widened. He'd been here a thousand years? "So what is the truth?"

The Lord drank from his wine, considering her over the rim. "You're not ready," he said as he placed it back down. "You have to be ready to hear the truth or it can kill you instead of heal you."

Nadia's mouth dropped open. "So I'm ready to hear that I'm trapped in some fairytale but not ready to hear why?"

Triumph flashed in his eyes. "Exactly."

Flinging her napkin on the table, Nadia shoved back her chair. Its legs gave an agonizing screech along the parquet floor as she leapt to her feet. "I...!" But the words wouldn't come. With a howl of exasperation, Nadia turned and strode from the room.

"Perfect example!" the Lord called after her.

Her feet found their usual path down the stairs, out of the castle, and into the stables. What had started as tears of frustration soon turned to tears of pain.

Good for nothing.

Unwanted.

Uncherished.

Truth in everything.

Nadia gasped against the pain boiling away in her chest. She skidded to a stop and clenched at it, bent over with the burn. The ground rumbled beneath her feet and echoed in her ears as the dragon rearranged itself. Putting a hand on her hip, Nadia forced herself forward. A rush of air buffeted her skirts as the dragon inhaled. Reaching its towering, steel-like side, she fell against him.

"Why? Why did you bring me back?"

The dragon sniffed her, but Nadia had abandoned any hope that it would eat her.

"Why?" she asked again.

The creature butted her with its head and then lowered its nose to the ground. Nadia stood there, unsure what it wanted.

Warm air rushed over her as it snorted. It butted her again, this time rocking her on her feet. Its eyes nearly crossed as it peered at Nadia over its snout. Cautiously, she lifted a hand and ran her fingernails over the long bridge of its nose. The dragon's inner eyelid closed and a contented purr burbled in its throat. He was lucky she had nails. The fashion was to keep them short, even with the tips of the fingers, but she had found it useful to grow them out a little longer, giving her something to help scrape the stubborn bits off of the dishes.

Its outer lids closed as well, and the dragon gurgled in pleasure. "Surely you didn't bring me back as a pet?" she asked.

The dragon didn't answer. Nadia kept scratching. She worked her way up and around the bridge of its eye.

And what if it had brought her back as a pet? It, and its master, had been kinder to her than anyone ever had.

Unless they're fattening you up.

Nadia's hands stopped their scratching. She *was* horribly thin. Hadn't the witch fattened Hansel up before she tried to cook him?

The dragon's lids scrolled back open, first the hard one and then the clear, revealing its fire-colored eye. The slitted pupils contracted. Nadia resumed her scratching and gave her head a small shake. Now she was worried about dying? Hadn't that been her goal all along?

She left the head and trailed her fingers along the dragon's long neck. A neck that had swallowed or burned up someone else in her place. Because she had been no sacrifice. Why hadn't she been a sacrifice?

Her hands froze. Why hadn't she been a sacrifice?

She began to stroke the creature's neck, her eyes unseeing.

The Lord fed her. And housed her. And clothed her. Above her status. Wouldn't let her work. She was the sacrifice that wasn't a sacrifice.

Thinking about it made her head hurt. Nadia let her hands drop. The dragon opened its eyes and turned its head to look at her.

"Still not going to eat me?" she asked, more out of habit than expectation. The dragon blinked. "Then I guess I'd best be off to my own bed. Don't want to end up in his."

eight

Nadia stirred under the covers, the gray behind her eyelids alerting her that it was morning. Years of being conscious to the dim light that heralded the dawn worked like a cockcrow even now that there was no work to wake for.

She curled the covers under her chin and snuggled deeper. How could she have waited three days to sleep in a real bed?

Again, whispered a little voice in her head.

Nadia's eyes snapped open. "Not like this," she whispered, a bead of guilt growing in her stomach. "It was never like this." Four cherubic younger brothers nestled against her. All of them huddled together under the thin, worn blanket for comfort. Nadia managed a ragged smile before it slipped away.

It hadn't lasted. The bed or her brothers' devotion. They were as bad as the rest, had laughed raucously as she had been mauled as the consolation prize.

Nadia burrowed deeper into the cushions of down beneath her. No one to laugh at her anymore.

The thought struck like lightning. The Lord had never laughed at her. Teased her, yes. But never belittled her. Never told her she counted as nothing.

Except as a sacrifice. Why was that?

Pushing herself up, Nadia glanced around. This was a room fit for a princess. Could the Lord have been telling the truth last night? Had those stories happened here?

She tossed back the covers and scrambled out of bed. There was only one way to find out.

Breakfast was a distracted meal of toast and some sort of thinly sliced ham, hard like a sausage yet clear and obviously sliced off from a full shank. She munched while her thoughts churned, washing it down with a cup of coffee. When she finished, she stacked the dishes in the sink and left them there, unwashed, all the better to start exploring again. Besides, the magic sink would clean them.

Nearly all the doors of the upper levels had opened for her, so she continued her exploration there. Her task today was to see if she could find more evidence that the old stories had happened in this place.

Most of the rooms were empty except for layers of dust and lacy cobwebs. One chamber contained a collection of birdcages. Another, nothing but a swan feather and a shriveled nettle that crumbled at her touch.

There was one, though, that took her breath away. After opening door after door to find nothing but dusty emptiness, Nadia gasped when one revealed a room edged in exquisite mosaic tile. When she stepped in, the tiles revealed themselves to be white pebbles. The pebbles, each about the size of the pad on her thumb, had been laid out in a pattern that swirled and flowed like a river around the room. A river that glowed, for in the dim light, the pebbles shone like the moon.

Nadia dropped to the floor and traced her fingers along the smooth yet bumpy path. She searched her pockets for a scrap of paper, wanting to fashion a boat, but found them empty. Humming a tune, she crawled along, using her imagination instead. When her knees grew tired, she sat down and clasped her arms around them, closing her eyes and soaking up the peace that permeated the room.

It was only when her butt began to tingle that she realized she had been there for hours. Pushing herself up, Nadia shook the feeling back into her legs. But still the room pulled at her. The river needed a boat. She needed to come back with a boat so that the pebbles could show her the way home.

Nadia forced her foot back one step. Then another. Her eyes continued to trace the patterns. Her fingers itched to caress the softness of the pebbles.

Inch by inch, she willed her feet backward until she stepped over the threshold and into the hall. A shiver racked her body as the compulsion fell away. Fear rose in her throat. Dusk shown through the windows. It had been mid-morning when she'd entered the room and now dark was falling, but the light in the room she'd just left had never changed.

With a click, Nadia firmly shut the door. That was a room she had best not visit again.

"You're distracted tonight," the Lord said to her. Nadia held back a snort. He was one to talk, slouched in his chair, tossing his knife end-over-end, catching it by the blade. The rhythmic, soft *thwap...thwap...thwap* had lulled her into an introspection of her own. She merely hummed her response.

"What did you do today?" he asked, continuing his tossing.

"Wandered the house."

He gave an amused huff. "Well, at least you're not working." He tossed the knife higher this time and caught it by the hilt. "But it won't do for the long term."

Nadia poked at her food. "How long am I to be here?"

"Depends," he answered. "For you—" The Lord eyed her, his nose wrinkling as the thought. "Probably months."

A groan she couldn't control slipped free. "And then what?"

"That will be up to you." He gave her a grin. "It's all up to you."

"A truth I'm ready to hear or another riddle?" she asked.

His eyes twinkled. "Yes."

Nadia gave her head a small shake and rolled her eyes before turning her attention back to her dinner—trout with almonds, tonight. Almonds that she carefully slid to the edge of her plate. Their crunch reminded her too much of biting down on bones.

Thwap. Thwap. Thwap. Silence.

It was a moment before she noticed it and looked up. The Lord sat frozen, the raised blade held between his fingers, his eyes trained on some spot on the table. Or rather, beyond it.

Her attention focused on the knife poised in his hand. He hadn't eaten tonight, just drank his wine, pulling the knife from his belt after serving her portion of the main course. His behavior had been odd, rude even, though welcome as it had left her time for her own thoughts.

Like the ones that still swirled about the room with the pebbles. In a place of oddities, it stood out. Sure, the door-knobs were not always what they seemed to be. And she had made the bed vanish. But the dragon was harmless, and she had even begun to think that the Lord posed no immediate threat. The place had begun to feel somewhat safe. Until that room. Until this odd mood that had taken hold of the Lord.

Her eyes widened, and she nearly dropped her fork. What if she had brought something back with her from that room? Something unseen. Or some dark magic.

Nadia cleared her throat. "I came across a strange room today."

"Hm?" The Lord blinked and raised his head. "Did you?"

It was harder to speak with his gaze on her. "A room filled with pebbles. It...I somehow lost track of time in there, the way you do on a summer afternoon." It was the best she could do to explain the compulsion she had felt in there. "It was only after I left, hours and hours later, that I realized the room must be enchanted." The Lord's brow crinkled with puzzlement. "Thought you should know," she finished softly.

"One of our previous guests must have been playing up there." The Lord frowned. "Thank you. I'll have to take a look."

Though the sun shone brightly the next morning, Nadia still felt as though a shadow followed her. All traces of rain and clouds had gone from the sky. She sorted through the wardrobes until she found a cloak. Fresh air was what she needed, not more dust.

Or more places to get lost, a little voice whispered in her head.

Nadia stopped first at the stables but found them empty. The Lord must have sent Uro out on an errand. She didn't want to think too closely about the dragon's task.

She wandered past the cypress hedges and down the path through the garden, the gravel crunching beneath her feet. The morning air was cool and crisp. Nadia formed her mouth into an "O" and breathed out a stream of air, hoping it would condense. But no, there were no dragons to be found this morning. Though the seasons were changing, it was not yet cool enough despite their elevation.

Her stomach pitched at the thought. She didn't think the castle was on a mountain. Though, if it wasn't, that would mean they were on a cloud. Her stomach rose, taking all her concentration to swallow it back down.

Well, wherever she was, the ground felt solid. And large enough to fit several gardens—the wide parkland she now found herself in, the formal gardens, and a rose garden.

Nadia skirted the formal gardens, the last of the flowers now battered and trampled by two days of heavy storms. The rose garden had not fared much better. The petals of the blossoms she had admired had been blown away, leaving only fuzzy centers. Leaves were torn and hung at odd angles. The gazebo was now a tangle of thorny skeletons. Even the bee skeps on their platform not far from the northernmost bed were water laden and looked ready for a nap.

She sank down on one of the stone benches inside the white lattice, imaging the place in summer—a riot of green and color, perfume heavy on the air, the hum of bees.

A breeze batted at the last of the foliage clinging to the copper beeches, bringing her back to the present. The leaves fluttered like birds, arranging themselves on a branch for the night, calling to her to come and explore. The day was only just beginning, and should she become lost in the maze, she could always push through the spindle-like branches and make her own exit.

Entering the avenue, she chose the path to the left. It soon came to an end, and she needed to reverse her course. Right, right, dead end. Reverse, right, straight.

After about twenty minutes, she turned a corner and found herself in the center of the maze. A tiered fountain with scalloped bowls occupied the middle of the space. Water still splashed even though it was late in the season. Unless it was drained before the freeze came, the bowls would crack.

Nadia wandered closer, glad to have found it before it was turned off for the season. A sharp yet sweet scent perfumed the air. The falling water made a merry sound, and yet…

Something tugged inside her heart…something that was both a joy and an ache, longing and fear.

Nadia came to stand next to the fountain; its lowest bowl hip-high. Water spouted at the top and ran through four tiers, slipping down between the scallops to pool in the largest one. Beech leaves swirled at her feet, but there was not a single one in the fountain. That was odd.

The water was strange as well, luminous and flowing like hot jelly. Not exactly sticky, but as if the drops were determined to stay together.

She reached out a finger toward the liquid where it ran between two scallops.

"I wouldn't."

With a shriek, her feet left the ground, her heart banging so fiercely against her ribs, she could have sworn she felt one crack.

"It's poison," the Lord said from behind her.

"You keep a fountain of poison?" Nadia croaked out, her heart still taking up too much space to draw breath. She turned, ready to rant at him but, as her gaze met his, her heart clenched so tightly that she was bent in two. A ragged cry tore from her throat.

"Move away from the poison, Nadia."

Tears pricked her eyes as she forced her feet away, one hand pressed against the crushing tightness in her chest. As she blinked, a tear rolled down her cheek and landed in the grass.

"Something happy," the Lord said. "Think of something happy."

"I can't," she whispered, unable to catch her breath.

"Cotton sheets. Hot chocolate," he said, tossing out suggestions. "Sausages frying." Nadia managed a weak smile. The Lord took a step closer. "The silly way Uro asks to be scratched," he said, close to her ear. A single hum of laughter ran from her belly and out her nose. "Especially his underside—rolled over, paws in the air." The corners of her mouth curled up.

"Better now?" he asked.

Fear and pain still tumbled about in her heart, but the laughter had softened their edges. "A little." Nadia straightened up, exhaling slowly. "You startled me. I didn't expect to find you out here."

"I'm usually where I need to be."

Nadia rubbed at her heart. "Come to save me from the poison?" The Lord didn't answer, and Nadia couldn't read his expression. "Why is it here?"

"Because it needs to be."

"You need a fountain of poison?"

"Every place has something beautiful and poisonous. And it's not like it's out in the open. You have to come looking for it."

Nadia shivered and turned for the exit. As did the Lord, based on the sound of leaves crunching behind her. With her mind focused on the sound, she didn't realize she had missed the turn until faced with a wall of branches. She stood staring at it, rather than turn around. Especially after his amused chuckle.

"Wouldn't you rather walk with me?" he asked, laughter still lacing his voice. "I'm more than willing to watch you find your own way out, but it might be more expedient."

Nadia clenched her jaw. Her entire life could be summed up in this one moment—a dead end with nothing but obstacles to face. She closed her eyes, trying to find the strength to do it.

It's just a walk, a voice of sensibility whispered.

But to where? another one countered.

A jumble of questions crowded her thoughts, each fighting for attention, creating such a cacophony that she pressed her hands to her ears. The voices raged, consuming her so thoroughly that a touch to her shoulder sent her skittering into the trees.

"My apologies," the Lord said.

Nadia plucked her way out of the branches. "No mine," she said with the little breath her lungs would allow. "You just startled me."

A smiled tugged at the corner of his mouth. "So I'd surmised. Would you like me to leave you?"

She did. She wanted no witness to her folly, how she never got anything right. But this was his home. And he was her better. Nadia smoothed her coat around her. "Perhaps you could just lead?"

He took a step toward her. "Are you refusing to walk with me?"

Nadia looked away, taking sudden interest in the buttons on her coat. "No," she offered with a small shake of her head.

The Lord closed the remaining distance between them. "Where would you like to be, Nadia?"

Nadia turned, desperate to retreat, but the bare arms of the trees blocked her way. She was trapped. This time between the trees and the master of this place. "Wherever you would like me to be," she answered automatically. Realizing how her words could be construed, her eyes widened, and she quickly added, "Except your bed."

"Who would you like to be?" he whispered in her ear.

"I..." But the question puzzled her. Nadia frowned. "I...I don't understand."

"You've been rescued. You are no longer the scullery maid forced to sleep with the fish." Her mouth dropped open. "By the fish, with the fish. Same thing," the Lord said with a dismissive wave of his hand. "You can be the girl who walks with a gentleman, though even I admit I'm using the term loosely. You don't need to walk a step behind."

"How did you know?" Nadia whispered, as startled as the rabbit she'd surprise in the lettuce patch. Her eyes were probably just as wide, too. "How did you know where I slept?"

His body shook with his amused chuckle. "Have you not been paying attention? I'm a god. I know all sorts of things."

Her discomfort shifted from rabbit to bug, one who was under an enlarging glass. "Why me?"

"Because you were the one they offered."

She shook her head. "But you said I wasn't good enough."

"Exactly!"

His words were making her head hurt. He was speaking in riddles again.

"Who would you like to be?" the Lord asked again.

"Just me," she whispered.

"And what does 'just you' look like?"

For one brief moment, Nadia left herself imagine. But then the words crept out of her heart. *Good for nothing. Worthless.*

"I'm nothing," she answered.

"No, you're not."

Nadia pressed her teeth together and nodded. She forced the wobble that played on her lower lip to stop. "Yes, I am. Even my name says so. I am Nadia. Nothing."

The air crackled around them with a sudden surge of power. "You are most certainly not nothing." The Lord clenched his jaw. His head moved slowly from side to side. "They've corrupted even your name. In the language your name originated in, Nadia doesn't mean 'nothing.' It means 'hope.' That is what you are. Hope." His hand reached toward her face. The movement was arrested, his fingers curled and drawn back before they touched. "Won't you claim it?"

Nadia swallowed the lump of emotion that had risen with his kind words. "You're just saying that because you can."

"True." A small smirk twisted his lip. "But in this case, it also happens to be the truth. One I'm hoping will heal you. Lies have already caused a thousand small deaths."

And hadn't they? The pain from every beating, every unkind word rose like a ghost from her skin. Her eyes pricked with the ache of it, sending tears down her face when she blinked.

The Lord made a melodramatic roll of his eyes and head and extended his arm. "So come walk with a god. Think about who you want to be. Trust your heart. Never mind, scratch that. Trust your dreams. Surely you made some wish in childhood, a vision of who you'd like to be?"

Nadia searched, but a lifetime of kicks and rebukes greeted her instead. There was something there, something she hadn't looked at in years, but it was unreachable beyond the abuse. Silently, she met the Lord's eyes and managed a weak smile before taking his offered arm.

He patted her hand. "No matter. I'm sure it will come."

Nadia took a tentative step by his side. "Handsome prince?"

"It's my ravishing good looks." His eyes twinkled. He leaned closer and whispered in her ear. "Even if I am the feared Dragon Lord."

He was certainly that. But, at this moment, she could see how he could be thought of as Prince Charming.

nine

N adia didn't go down for dinner. Her encounter with the Lord had left her so full of questions, she had no room for food. And he left her alone, did not come to fetch her. Restless, she had tried the chaise and then the window seat and then the padded chair but had abandoned each one, finding them too confining. Now she sat in the center of the room, her chin balanced on her knees, running her fingers through the carpet, her eyes following the tracks they created in the silky piles.

It was a mystery, that question of who she was. She had thought she had known. She was Nadia Crofton, a scullery maid who wore rags and slept on a pallet by the fish. Then she had become the sacrifice that wasn't a sacrifice. Her head shook, moving from side to side, unable to tease out why Uro hadn't eaten her. Why the Lord had been so surprised, angry even, that Uro had brought her back.

Nadia glanced around the room, taking in its furnishings. She sat in a room fit for a princess, filled with wardrobes of beautiful clothes, was allowed to eat as much as she wanted, and forbidden to work. There was the proof she was no longer who she had been.

All because she had been rescued. Her lips curled into a smile. Joy bubbled up until she was nearly giddy with it. She could become anything she wanted to be, for she had been rescued.

A pang akin to hunger curled her insides. Nadia ignored it. She was used to going without. Why take the time to eat when she had the opportunity to figure out who she wanted to be?

The pain changed, unfurling like a snake, wrapping coil after coil around her heart. And then it squeezed. Nadia gasped, and voices filled her head.

Worthless wretch.

Good for nothing.

You need a swift kick.

There's no room for you.

Nadia struggled against the words. She would push them away, drown them out. But the more she wrestled with them, the louder they became. They swirled around her head, becoming a jumble, then twisted into laughter that grew and grew. Nadia clapped her hands over her ears, and began to rock back and forth. "Stop. Please make it stop." Her whispered words ended in a whine.

But it didn't stop. The cacophony rang in her head until she gave up and let it have its way. Let it claim her heart.

But wait. The Lord had told her to skip her heart and trust her dreams. Nadia lifted her hands from her ears as the voices faded away. But she'd gotten it wrong. He'd gotten it wrong. The saying was, "Trust your heart, not your head." Why had he told her the opposite?

Hope. Your name means hope.

Nadia snorted. What would her mother have had to hope for with her? The local term—nada—was surely what her mother had meant when she had given Nadia her name, for Nadia was no son to help work the farm. She was nothing but a mouth to feed, and so easily turned out when they needed more space for the sons that had followed.

But her mother *had* named her "Hope," intentionally or unintentionally. And the Lord wanted her to claim who she really was. He wanted her to hope. He wanted her to dream.

Nadia pushed up from the floor and went to put on her nightgown. She doubted that the Lord had meant her to take his command so literally, but she was tired of thinking. Perhaps in her dreams she would find some answers.

Her stomach rumbled, rousing Nadia from sleep. Just a few days, and it had already decided it deserved to be fed. She threw back the covers and crossed the room, opening the door to the wardrobe containing day dresses. So many choices, but what to wear? How much her life had changed in a week. Here she was procrastinating because she now had choices. In some ways, life was easier when you had none.

She slipped the dove gray one from its hanger. No sense coming back to change if she decided to explore upstairs again.

An assortment of cheeses and a slice of apple cake had been set out for her in the kitchen. Nadia nearly swooned with the first bite of cake. The apples were perfectly tender and spiced, and the crumb topping offered a nice crunch while the cake itself was moist and delicate.

Nadia pressed her fork against the errant crumbs, picking them up as she would have once done with her finger, in secret, when she was supposed to be brushing them away. She had always wished that Cook had taught her to bake. The woman had shown Daisy and Hazel how to prepare things. The only things she had shown Nadia were how to stir and scrub and fetch. But Nadia *had* spent fifteen years watching.

Her teeth caught at her lip as a spark of desire grew. Hadn't she dreamed of being Cook? How hard could cooking be?

Nadia fanned her apron, hoping the movement would encourage the smoke to seek the outside. At least her eyes weren't watering as much in the fresh air. Cooking, it turned out, was actually rather hard. Especially baking. How did one know when things in the oven were finished?

She knew better than to open the door too often to check for she had heard Cook countless times yelling at Daisy to not "leave the door open like a stupid cow and let all the heat out!" The cake had seemed fine the first time Nadia had checked, rising nicely, and then this! And after all the time she had spent fiddling with the batter, getting it to taste right.

The burned-up lump still smoked in the pan she had tossed out the door after hoisting it from the oven. Her deep coughs had filled the kitchen along with the smoke and echoed more than she would have expected for they had seemed to come from everywhere.

Nadia ducked back inside to open the two windows as well. She rescued the cup of tea she had made and the piece of bread and jam she had been munching on until she had smelled the smoke. Outside, she leaned up against the wall, just beyond the door, and savored the knowledge that: one, she wouldn't need to scrub the burned pan or its contents, the magic sink would do that; two, most cooks burned things when they were learning how to cook; and three, even if she had failed, she was able to sit and enjoy a treat while the smoke literally cleared.

She bit into the soft bread spread with salty, creamy butter and sweet strawberry jam. What heaven. An advantage to all those years of depravation was that small things were easy to count as blessings—her new bed, the clothes, the food, and even the smoke for there was no one here to curse her for her mistakes. Or beat her for them.

Nadia finished off the last bite of bread and took a sip of tea. She lifted her face to the sun, drinking in its warmth in the cool air, and let the cup come to rest in her lap. No chores to do. Nowhere to be. She was almost like Elsbeth.

Elsbeth. Nadia's eyes opened. There was something familiar, just out of reach. She was half-afraid to chase it; both for fear it would fade away and for fear the voices would start up again.

And then Nadia recognized it. When she had been young, when Cook had first brought her to the manor, Nadia had watched Elsbeth playing in the garden while she lugged the water bucket down to the well. Nadia had never seen anyone so lovely. Thick blond hair with a beautiful curl to it. A purple bow in her hair to match the dark lavender dress that Elsbeth wore. A rufflely, white petticoat edged with scalloped lace peeking from beneath the hem. Elsbeth had her dolls and a stuffed bunny arranged on a scarf, playing tea with a real china tea set. Cook had supplied her with some miniature cakes.

Nadia would have given anything to have sat and played with her. And though sometimes the children of servants played with the master's children, Nadia might as well have been invisible. Which was a good thing, she later thought, for it would never have been allowed.

She would have given anything to be Elsbeth—beautiful, cared for, given every opportunity. It was only later she learned that cruelty often lay behind beauty, for beauty usually wants for nothing and learns to despise, and then she no longer yearned to be Elsbeth.

Bringing the cup to her lips, Nadia sipped her tea and mulled on that long-forgotten wish. *Who would you be?* the Lord had asked.

Elsbeth, Nadia thought. *I'd be a better Elsbeth.*

Nadia pulled the cake from the tin and scattered it for the birds before she returned to the kitchen and placed the pan in the sink to soak. Even though she didn't need to, she wiped down the table and counters and set things to rights before departing.

Returning upstairs, Nadia slipped on her coat. The dusty upstairs held no appeal after the spell outside. Instead, the gardens beckoned and, while the sun had been warm enough outside the kitchen, the sheltered areas would be chilly. It wouldn't be long before she'd find frost on the windows and decorating the ground in the morning.

Dew still lay heavy in the shaded areas under the trees. A tangy crispness scented the breeze. Across the lawn, ground daisies threw up their last blossoms. Nadia knelt down among them and began to fashion a chain. A bittersweet smile rose on her face as she recalled the last one she had made, placing it on the cherubic head of then three-year-old Albert. Back before he had learned to taunt her like the rest.

Over and under. Over and under. The chain grew beneath Nadia's fingers.

These had always been her favorite daisies. Pink fingers spreading out from the center along the white petals, without the bitter scent of the tall yellow ones. Those were cheerful to look at, but not something you'd want under your nose.

Nadia knotted the tail of the last around the stem of the first and slipped the completed necklace over her head. Just a week ago, this simple chain would have been a luxury.

She slid her fingers along the blossoms. There was a golden chain set with pink rubies in her room. A necklace for a princess. Not that she had been brave enough to try it on. Maybe she didn't want to be Elsbeth. If someone held out both necklaces and asked her to choose, she would pick the daisies every time. Elsbeth wouldn't even consider the daisies a necklace. At least, not any more.

Beautiful. Cared for. Given every opportunity.

She might not be beautiful, but at least here she was cared for. As for opportunity...

Nadia gave a small sigh of frustration. How was she supposed to figure out who she wanted to be if there was no one to help her? Not that she expected the Lord to follow her around. A shudder racked her frame at the idea. He might not be as horrible as she had first thought, but that didn't mean she trusted him. He may have saved her from the poison yesterday and helped her when she had that odd attack, but people who were nice to you usually wanted something in return.

Goosebumps rose on her arms. How could she have been so stupid? She had thought herself "rescued," but she didn't even know where she was. For all she knew, she was now a prisoner.

Nadia pushed herself to her feet. Behind the castle was the sheer drop off and clouds. Before her lay the gardens and woods. Did they lead anywhere? Anywhere useful, that was. Could she leave this place if she wanted to?

Wrapping her arms around herself, Nadia took a deep breath and set off to see.

Her stomach had begun to growl, protesting the meal she had missed at midday. She had walked as far as she could through the park, past groves of trees until she came to solid rock, the face of a mountain. Confronted with that, she had turned right and followed the rock face until her feet had begun to ache, her heart sinking when she came to another fenced off edge. Turning around, she had walked along it in the other direction so long that dusk was beginning to set in.

Her feet slowed. The trees up ahead looked strangely familiar. Nadia closed her eyes against the sight. She was back at the edge of the park. The roof of Uro's stable was visible above the tall cypress hedges and the spires of the castle beyond that.

Hot tears began to drip down her face. In Westfold, it had been circumstance that trapped her. If she left the manor, set off for a different life somewhere else, she would have ended up a beggar—or worse—for who would have taken her in? Her existence might be better here, but there was no way to leave except the way she had arrived. So much for being rescued.

Her knees crumpled. She faced a lifetime with nothing to do but wander empty corridors. No one to talk to except the Lord at dinner. Would she eventually become so lonely that she would welcome his bed? Was that why he hadn't pressed her? He knew she would eventually pursue him? Like all the others.

A familiar hopelessness drifted over her. Nadia brushed the tears from her face. She might not be much better off than she had been, but she did have a place to sleep and food to eat and a master who did not work her to exhaustion. Pushing herself to her feet, Nadia gathered her determination. She would figure out how to do this.

Nadia drew the rose-colored dress from the closet. She hung the daisy chain on the corner of the dressing table mirror and put her hair up using the silver pins with the pearl and diamond daisies.

A glance in the mirror proved her to be pale, even by her standards. She pinched her cheeks to add some color. The haunted look in her eyes and their red rims were things she didn't know how to change. Things the Lord would be sure to comment on.

Nadia sighed and went out to face him.

"Not brooding over burnt cake?" the Lord asked as Nadia picked at her food.

"You heard about that?" she asked, glancing up. There had been no one to tell him about her experience this morning, yet he did know. As he seemed to know everything.

A smile tugged at the corners of his mouth. "Yes. I did. Have you always wanted to be a cook?"

Nadia pushed the peas around her plate and gave a small shrug. "I was always amazed at the dishes our cook turned out. It seemed a useful wish." A more useful one than being Elsbeth.

"You'll just have to try again," the Lord said. "I'm told most cooks practically burn down the kitchen before they learn to succeed."

Nadia bit back the sigh that rose. "It's a little daunting without a teacher."

"Ah, yes. There is that." His smile faded.

She stabbed a couple of the peas but, as soon as she turned her fork, they slid off. Nadia set her fork on her plate. "May I please be excused? I guess I'm more tired than I realized."

The Lord rose as Nadia placed her napkin on the table. He grasped her chair, his hands inches from her waist, and pulled it out for her, so near that his breath warmed her neck. "Thank you," she said to the floor as she stood, turning her face from the closeness.

"Good night, Nadia." Her name rippled off this tongue in that strange accent that made it sound exotic.

She bobbed a curtsy and hurried out of the dining room.

Nadia snuggled down into the mattress. It curved around her in a soft embrace. The bed was more than she could ever have wished for, but she couldn't shake the feeling of hopelessness that had pursued her all day.

How many others had slept here? How many others had wandered the halls. The scenario must have played out countless times. According to legend, and the Lord, those princesses had lived happily ever after. But if that was true, where were they? Where was the evidence that they had lived, yet alone ended up happy? She had found nothing but a spinning wheel and a long hair.

And the room of pebbles that had made her want to forget. Could Gretel have been their creator? If so, what had happened to Hansel? What if Uro had eaten Hansel and the pebbles were all the Gretel had had left? With no way to find her way home, she would surely have wanted to forget and poured out her longing into the room.

If that was the case, then the Lord was the witch, despite his protests otherwise. Which would mean that he had lied to her. Maybe about everything.

Even her name.

A false hope. Why would he give her a false hope?

So it's easier for you to end up in his bed, whispered the insidious little voice in her head. *You'd be ever so grateful for everything he's done for you.*

The covers twisted in her hands. It was right, the voice. He was so handsome, and he had made her feel so free. She could see how she could grow to want him.

And then what? Did Uro just eat them when the Lord got tired of them? Toss them over the side of the mountain? Just what was going to happen to her?

ten

As soon as she had dressed in the morning, Nadia headed upstairs. She could not face the kitchen after the fears she had wrestled with all night. Up and up she climbed, all the way to Aurora's tower. Unlike so many of the other rooms, the spinning wheel lay free from a cover of dust.

Settling herself on the stool, Nadia stretched out her hand and gave the wheel a turn. She had watched her mother spin—foot tapping the pedal, hands pulling and feeding the wool, humming a tune. At all other times, her mother was like an overwhelmed whirlwind; five children underfoot and too many chores to do. But at the spinning wheel, her mother entered into some other world. One that allowed her to sit and sing.

Nadia reached out again and watched the wheel as it spun. If only she had some wool. If only Aurora had left the wheel's task half-finished so that she could at least have a try at a task that captivated your hands but left your mind free. Something like the last of the dishes—a warm sink, low lights, everyone else in bed. But without the hot water cracking her hands or the need to think about how to get the stubborn bits up.

Maybe that was what was meant by Aurora's slumber. If she had truly not been a princess, if things had not happened exactly like the stories, maybe someone had been trying to keep her from the peace and thoughtfulness of spinning. And then Uro took her. And she spent her time up here. Time away from the rest of the world, following her heart's desire until...

Until what? She was rescued by the handsome prince?

A huff of laughter burst free as she pictured the Lord in that role. No, he was no prince. Rumplestiltchen more likely. Teaching Aurora how to spin straw into gold. Maybe the stories had gotten mixed up.

But...that did not explain what happened next. Nadia frowned and gave the wheel one last turn. So many questions. But the answers wouldn't be found here.

Trailing her hand along the stones, Nadia descended the stairs. If only she had Aurora's ghost to talk to. As frightening as it would be to face an apparition, she would have someone other than the Lord to converse with. Someone who would not answer all her questions in riddles. Someone to tell her what to do, to tell her what came next.

Nadia stepped off the last riser and faced the empty corridor. So many doors. So much emptiness.

Rapunzel was here, behind one of the doors on her right. Where she had stared into the mirrors and, what? Brushed her hair?

Nadia lowered herself to the step. What was she hoping to find? A story that matched her own?

But there was no story like hers. In all the fairytales, someone had loved the girl, someone had been there to care. She had no one.

Her mother's gentle humming drifted through her mind and then took form, becoming the lively but haunting tune Daisy and Hazel liked to sing when they were chopping vegetables or shelling peas. Nadia joined the voices in her head, humming when her tongue stumbled over the words, embracing the melancholy tune.

Hey, ho nobody home
Meat nor drink nor money have I none
Still I will be merry, very merry...

Around and around her thoughts traveled, just like the song. Nobody home. Have none. Still be merry.

She had nothing, not even her freedom. But it was her decision how she faced this. She could let the hopelessness overtake her. Or she could choose to be...not merry, but positive. Uro *had* rescued her from the conditions she'd been forced to live in at Westpark. And even though the conditions had been deplorable, she had made the best of them. She could do the same here. She might not know what the Lord's plan for her was, but at least he had offered her some freedom.

As much as he has, whispered the little voice in her head.

Nadia sucked in a breath. Surely not? He could not have been stuck here for a thousand years?

How's he to leave if you can't?

"But he's a god," she said aloud, her voice echoing in the empty hallway. He had to have some way of leaving. Otherwise, that would make this place a prison.

Shivers ran down her back and shook loose an even more terrifying thought—why would someone imprison a god?

Her heart took on the pace of a jackrabbit's thumping warning. Nadia shot to her feet and circled the floor, trying to slow her gasping breaths. Fainting would do her no good.

As she worked off the adrenaline, her thoughts began to clear. Whether or not this was a prison for her or one for the Lord, it did not change the fact that she couldn't leave. Or that she was here for the foreseeable future. With nothing to do. Nothing but explore the castle and try to figure out what came next. To do that, she needed to be as familiar with the castle as possible. And to do that, she needed to eat.

No more skipping meals. It was time to take full advantage of the unlimited supply of food. And time to humor the Lord and figure out what he was up to.

A sandwich of meat and cheese and an apple tart waited for her in the kitchen. Nadia washed it down with a draught of ale pulled from the keg by the larder and then headed back upstairs. Starting from the base of Aurora's tower, she worked her way down the corridor, noting which rooms were unlocked and what they contained. No new doors opened under her touch. The previous rooms offered no new surprises, but she marked them just the same.

Down another floor and repeat.

And found a room that she had missed. Or, at least, this time it opened to her grasp. A workroom full of leathers, tools, and fabrics. A pair of peacock blue high-heeled shoes rested on the workbench; its bows embellished with the eye-like feathers. The wardrobes in her room contained many beautiful shoes, but the sight of these stole her breath.

Nadia crossed the room and picked them up.

Just try them. Who's to know? whispered the little voice. It was right.

Nadia kicked off the black kid slippers and slid them on. The peacock shoes fit like they had been made just for her. She twisted first one foot and then the other, admiring the workmanship. They made her feet look delicate yet elegant. Like she was going to a ball.

Nadia took a few steps and imagined that she was dancing. There had been no time to learn any actual steps. But she had watched Lord Braemoor's guests at the summer galas, usually held outdoors, for Elsbeth had liked to dance under the stars. Working in the shadows, she had watched the skirts swinging, feet flashing, and the joy on the faces of the dancers. Nadia drew to a standstill, a sick feeling growing in her gut. Such things were not for her. She had no right.

Nadia removed the shoes, placing them back on the bench, and slid her more practical ones back on. As she snugged the slipper to her heel, her eyes were drawn to the waste bin at the end of the workbench. Scraps of leather hung over the edge. She might not have the skills of a cobbler, but it would be fun to try. Maybe this would be her calling—someone who created beautiful shoes.

Nadia drew a scrap from the waste bin and picked up the embossing tool, fingering the hollow space of the feather cut in relief on its tip. Turning it over, she positioned it on the leather, and hit it with the hammer. Not hard enough, it turned out, for when she lifted the tool, there was only the barest impression on the leather. She repositioned it and struck again. With too much force. The frame of the tool had been pressed in, creating an outline around the image. Another strike, softer than the last, more strength than the first, revealed a perfect raised, ridged feather.

Her fingers traced the impression. This would be something she would like to do. Her gaze traveled over the leathers and tools, colorful spools of thread, odd shaped needles. If only she had a teacher.

Who would you be?

What was the point in wondering? How could she become anything other than what she already was—someone who knew only how to fetch and clean. Things the Lord no longer allowed her to do.

Nadia let the tools fall onto the bench. She knew who she was. And dreams got you nothing.

Lies...all lies, said her head. And then the voices started from her heart.

Shouldn't you be figuring out who he is? How do you know he's not the witch who will kill you? Does an honorable person keep a dragon and a fountain of poison? What else is he hiding?

Her hands gripped the edge of the bench. Nadia swallowed heavily as an icy chill settled around her heart. It was one thing to seek death. It was another to have someone seek yours.

She was cooped up here. Being fattened up.

Just like Hansel, whispered the voice.

Nadia shook her head. Never. She would jump over the side first.

If you knew it was coming.

"Stop it!" Nadia clapped her hands over her ears. The voices receded, leaving a tendril of satisfaction curled in her heart. The rest of her ached with misery.

Everything in her life went bad. Why should this be any different? Nadia groaned. Dinner. She would have to share dinner with him tonight. The Lord had given her the previous night off, but she doubted he would give her another. Her head moved from side to side as if the motion could deny the truth.

The truth can kill.

Yes. It certainly could.

Nadia pulled the door closed, leaving the peacock shoes on the workbench. She could have rescued them from a future of dust, but they were now too much like candy and she was too much like Gretel. The door clicked shut with a satisfying *snick*. The room had robbed her of the spark of hope, the tiny sense of freedom, that she had held on to.

She returned to her room to dress for dinner. A gown of forget-me-not blue soothed the raw ache that had settled into her soul. Avoiding the mirror, she put her hair up as simply as possible.

The Lord rose as she entered the dining room. Nadia tried to return his smile but feared she was not successful. The graciousness slipped from his face to be replaced with a frown.

He pushed her chair in for her. "I'm afraid to ask what you did today."

Nadia shook out her napkin, averting her eyes as the Lord moved back around the table. "Just wandered the upper floors. I wanted to make sure I could find my way around."

His continued gaze pricked her skin. He lifted his napkin and dipped it into his water glass. Nadia shrank against her chair as he stepped toward her.

The Lord took her chin and raised it. "You've been listening to your heart," he said, and gently rubbed the napkin across her face, washing away the traces of tears she had shed after leaving the workroom.

"I guess I have," she replied once he removed his hand. "It reminded me that I'm alone here."

He picked up the carafe and poured her a glass of wine. "They say to listen to your heart, that it won't steer you wrong. But that depends on what's in your heart. Yours, I think, has too much…fear, shall we say? It isn't entirely trustworthy."

Nadia tipped up her chin. "And you'd have me trust you instead?"

The Lord flipped the ends of his coat aside as he took his seat. "Trust takes time, and I'm not so foolish as to think that you trust me." He picked up his wine. "But I have not lied to you. You are hope, and I'm going to trust that. So should you."

Nadia scowled. "Hope only results in disappointment."

"You are wrong," he said. "Hope is everything. Hope is life." A pained expression crossed his face. "And there are times I would do well to remember that myself."

How do you know? How do you know?

The question filled Nadia's thoughts as she drifted to sleep and again as she woke. She must have asked it in her dreams as well, for there was something...

But like most dreams, the details were lost with the sun and slipped away until she began to question whether she had even dreamed at all. Answers just out of reach.

Answers that were somewhere downstairs.

Today was a day to explore the family rooms, the rooms that the Lord would be more likely to use on an everyday basis. Unless he had some way of leaving that she didn't know about, he had to spend his days here in the castle doing...whatever he did. Should she come across him in one of them, she had the perfect excuse—she was trying to figure out who the new her was. She was simply doing what he had asked.

Nadia dressed, ate her breakfast, and climbed back up the great staircase to the rooms the family would have set aside to greet and entertain visitors. Westpark had a breakfast room, day room, sewing room, study, library, two reception rooms, dining room, and a ballroom all on its ground floor. The Lord's castle was at least ten times the size of the manor.

His study would be the most useful for figuring out who he was, but she didn't relish finding him. The other rooms would suffice. If she could gain access.

Her luck was sparse. Only one door on the first floor gave her admittance—a ladies' drawing room of some sort. Painted a lovely soft blue, wide windows offered a view to the garden.

A cushioned window seat had been tucked into one, a book sitting forgotten upon it.

Nadia picked up the book and rifled through the pages. Who had left it here?

She placed it back on the velvet seat and turned her attention to the writing table, quills and ink laid out and waiting. She had rarely ventured upstairs at the manor, but she imagined that Elsbeth would spend her days in a room such as this. When she was not out riding.

There was nothing for her here. Nadia went out again and up the stairs. The fourth door opened for her. A library. Never had she seen so many books in one place. Nadia wandered between the shelves, trailing her fingers along the spines. A gentle light filled the room, illuminating the swirling dust motes. A crisp yet calming scent hung in the air. Nadia breathed deep, drawing it into her lungs.

"I can help you find some—"

The unexpected words drew her breath back out in a scream that drowned out the rest. The Lord chuckled from an alcove to her left as Nadia gulped lungfuls of air, a hand pressed against her pounding heart. He slid a purple ribbon between the pages of a book open in his hand.

"Let me try that again. Is there something in particular you were looking for?"

Nadia edged her way back toward the door. "No...I...uh, was just looking."

The Lord waved a hand. "Well, don't let me stop your search. Most of the shelves aren't labeled but, as I said, I could help you find anything you might be looking for."

Of course he had to be here. "No. My mistake," Nadia said. She turned to leave.

The Lord's hand closed over her wrist. "What's the matter, Nadia?"

Nadia screwed her eyes shut and sighed, hating that she was going to have to confess to him just how stupid she was. He would not release her until she did. "I can't read."

He let go of her. "Of course not." Anger tinged his voice. "Well, if you'd like...I could teach you." Nadia turned. "I have primers. You see—" His jaw clenched. "—sometimes they send me children."

Her stomach gave a horrible flip.

"People are so kind, aren't they?" He fell silent, all too obviously wrestling with his anger. When his control was better, he spoke again. "So if you'd like to learn, I could teach you." A real smile worked its way across his face. "The worlds that are within these walls would amaze you. Maybe inspire you." His shoulders raised and lowered in a small shrug. "Maybe help you figure out who you'd like to be. You have complained about a lack of teachers. I'm offering you my services."

His eyes held a tired sadness. She had gone looking for who he was—prince or witch—however, standing there, he simply looked like a man weighed down by too much responsibility. He'd come here to escape, and she had interrupted his peace.

Nadia twisted her hands. She didn't want to intrude, but the carrot he was dangling...

"One thing I have learned, being here for a thousand years," he added as she hesitated, "is patience. In case you were worried."

Nadia hung her head. "I was more worried with being a bother."

"Was?"

She lifted her gaze. "Am?" she corrected, and swallowed against the lump that had risen in her throat.

The Lord offered her a gentle smile. "Not a bother. A welcome distraction."

A tiny flutter stirred deep inside her. Nadia looked around. Books everywhere. Books she would eventually be able to read. In the drawing room downstairs, curled up in the window seat.

A better Elsbeth.

"Then yes. I'd like that very much."

The Lord extended his arm. "Right this way. I'll pull out what we're going to need."

As she drifted off to sleep that night, the rhyme still caroled through her thoughts.

A is for apple
B is for ball
C is for cat
D is for doll

She didn't remember her dreams the next morning either, but she was sure that the Lord had figured in them, as well. Just not in the same way as the night before.

eleven

Autumn eased. Snow began to fall and blanketed the castle and its grounds in fluffy white drifts. Nadia didn't mind. She had mastered the alphabet and its sounds and had graduated from easy stories about a mouse who lived in a house to longer ones recounting the adventures of Lucky Hans, who was definitely more foolish than his name implied.

Mornings she spent in the window seat of what she now considered her morning room or curled against Uro's warm side after having smuggled some meat, usually a ham, from the kitchen. After swallowing the treat, he often demanded to be scratched before rolling back over so that Nadia could use him as a rather hard and scaly cushion for her back.

After lunch, she'd meet the Lord in the library where he'd have her read aloud to him, correcting her pronunciation as necessary. She had always imagined school as a chore. Elsbeth had certainly complained about her lessons. Especially the ones in Latin.

When she'd asked the Lord if she'd have to learn that as well, his eyebrows rose. "Do you want to?" he'd asked.

Nadia had sunk back into her chair. "Aren't most books in Latin?"

"If you're a scholar. I'd be more than willing to teach you but, don't you think, one language at a time?"

She'd given a small smile and nodded and they'd carried on with the story of *The Traveling Musicians*.

She hadn't been as happy when he determined she was ready for writing.

"Despite what so many kings and their learned advisors think," the Lord had said to her. "Reading and writing are not separate disciplines. If you can read, you can scribe. If you can write, you can read. The thinking of humans never fails to amaze me."

Paper was a precious item, but he had covered sheets with examples of both the upper and lowercase letters in his own hand. Solid for her to see, dotted for her to trace, and blank lines for her to attempt on her own.

"The only way to teach your body anything is to create muscle memory, and that only comes through practice. Think of it as swordplay for your hand." The Lord chuckled. "Apro pros since the pen is mightier, they say." Then he shooed her out of the library.

Well, the "swordplay" had made her hand tired. She was also tired of Hans. Nadia flexed her fingers and sighed. Maybe there was something else in the library, some other book. Flora, fauna, history of the kingdoms. Something other than Hans trading his lump of silver for a rock and feeling lucky.

Isn't that you? whispered the little voice. *Trading safety for a dragon and its master. How foolish you have been...Gretel!*

Nadia wrestled with the voice, attempting to stuff it back in its box somewhere inside her. It had become nasty over the last few weeks. Imagining it as an entity she could control helped, though it did not silence it.

She set the pen down and retrieved her book from the window seat. Time to trade it in for something she could get lost in.

The library was empty, as usual. Too early for the Lord to be there. Nadia set the book on the large reading table and began to browse the shelves. *The Consolation of Philosophy. Divine Love. The Letters of Abelard and Heloise.* The next case sported titles in a language other than hers.

As she rounded the corner, Nadia came across the alcove the Lord had been sitting in when she'd first found the place. A book with a purple ribbon between its pages lay on the table. What had he been reading?

Nadia picked it up. There was no title on the cover of the thin tome. She flipped it open to the place the Lord had marked. The words were handwritten, not printed.

My beloved, I ache for your love.
Alone, in the darkness of night
I turn but you are not there.
No lips, soft as roses, to caress
No hair, soft as silk, to get lost in.
Your eyes like stars to match my own.
I long to bend your curves against mine
　　　Once more.

Her hands shook as she snapped the book shut and tossed it onto the table. Then scrambled to pick it up again and check that the ribbon still marked the correct place. It did. The book wobbled violently in her hand when she set it down again. Nadia backed up three paces and tried to still her hands, finally noticing that her heart shook just as much.

Nadia swallowed. She was not meant to have seen that.

Love poetry. The Lord had been reading love poetry. Handwritten love poetry. Though she was unsure if the hand had been his. She'd been lost in the words.

The book seemed to stare at her from the table. Nadia backed up farther, bumping into a bookcase.

She could check. She'd been staring at, trying to copy, his writing for weeks. She knew his hand. Or thought she did.

But, no. She already felt like she'd walked in on a pair of lovers. And one who was as good as her host. Whom she was alone with.

Her eyes widened. Heat rushed to her cheeks. The Lord's stunning good looks had lost some of their splendor and become almost ordinary. Just as the castle had slowly lost its ability to astound her, unless she stopped to compare. But the image of that face, those eyes, filled with love, staring...at her. Nadia swallowed. Oh, why had she ever picked up that book?

Lips to caress...

Hair to get lost in...

Nadia turned and fled from the library. A walk in the cold winter air would do her some good.

She had always avoided snow. Other than the trek to the well, once flakes had blanketed the ground, she stayed inside. Better to avoid frostbite than court it. But with fur-lined boots and a hooded wool coat, she could see why others might call it a "winter wonderland."

Nadia shredded a hunk of bread she'd taken from the kitchen and scattered it under the trees. The snow inside the courtyard had been shoveled or melted under Uro's fiery breath. Most likely Uro, for Nadia couldn't see the Lord shoveling. But here in the park, the snow lay in virgin drifts.

Undisturbed drifts, Nadia corrected. Such thoughts wouldn't help her forget the poetry. Activity was what she needed.

She had played in the snow only once before. Her mother, tired of three rambunctious boys underfoot, had stuffed Nadia and her three oldest brothers into their parents' sweaters and socks and pushed them out the door. Her father had heard the commotion from the barn and came out to play with them, helping them create first a snowman and then opposing forts for a snowball fight. When he'd flopped down to make a snow angel, the four of them had piled on top of him like the pack of puppies her mother usually compared them to.

Nadia trod into an open area and gently fell backwards. She swung her arms and legs before carefully pushing herself up. The impression did look like the angels in the stained glass windows of the village church. Unlike the messy depression that had resulted from her father wrestling with four squirmy children.

She reached down and scooped up a handful of snow, her attention drifting back to the past as she packed it between her hands. She hadn't thought about her father in years. It had been her mother who had turned her out. Had it been with his blessing or had he simply avoided standing up to his wife? He'd treated Nadia with the same playfulness that he'd treated his sons...and then he just let her go. At eight years old.

Hot tears pricked her eyes, threatening to drip down her face and melt the snow. She was sure if George or Albert or John or any of her other brothers had not come home that her father would have searched the countryside until they'd been found. She had been hanging around the village for two days before Cook took her. Two days of sleeping alone in the streets, hunting through garbage heaps when she grew hungry.

Nadia placed the ball at her feet and pushed it along until it grew taller than her knees. Then she began again, scooping up the snow, packing it together, rolling it along. When this one had grown almost as large as the first, she changed direction and rolled it up to the first. And discovered that she was totally unable to lift it. After several minutes of sweaty trying, she constructed a ramp of snow and managed to push the ball up it. Undaunted, she started on the head.

She was struggling to lift it into place when a voice sounded behind her. "Playing truant, I see."

Nadia braced the heavy snowball against the rest of the figure. "Is it already that time?" she asked, huffing with the effort.

"Well past. Here, let me help you with that." The Lord easily lifted it into place.

"Thanks," Nadia said, still breathless. She brushed her snowy mittens against her coat.

The Lord centered the head and packed some snow around it to keep it from falling off. "I think he's ready for his face."

"Um...I hadn't really planned on building a snowman," Nadia said. "So I didn't bring anything with me."

"We can't have that." The Lord's eyes twinkled. He began to search the contents of his pockets. He drew out a white handkerchief. "That won't work." He stuffed it back in and kept looking, never satisfied with what he found.

Eventually, he drew his knife from his belt and grasped one of the buttons of his coat between his fingers.

"You're not going to spoil your coat?" Nadia exclaimed.

He sliced through the thread holding it and handed the button to her. "They can be sewn back on later. Your snowman needs a face." The Lord gestured with his knife toward the base of an oak tree. "Why don't you see if you can find some leaves or acorns to use. I only have three buttons and your snowman will still need a mouth."

Nadia tromped over and shoveled through the snow under the oak with her hands. Two feet down, she finally came to the bed of leaves it had dropped in the fall. She set several of them off to the side and dug around for acorns. She didn't remember seeing squirrels hopping around, and there must not have been any, for she soon found six acorns. Nadia brought them back to the Lord who was placing his third button as a nose.

"Shall we set them in lengthwise to give him teeth or pointy side out?" he asked, taking one from her.

"Pointy side out," she replied. A mouth full of fangs would make the snowman look like something out of a nightmare.

The Lord set them in a curving smile and stepped back to admire his work. The large silver buttons shimmered with the light reflected by the snow.

"Not bad, if I do say so myself," he mused. "Might change his nose out for a carrot later."

"And his eyes for lumps of coal," Nadia added. "Would you like me to sew your buttons back on?"

The Lord brushed the last traces of snow from his hands. "No need." He gave Nadia a smile. "But you, my dear, now need to get some lunch and then join me in the library."

He turned and headed back to the castle, his coat drooping at odd angles due to the loss of the buttons. Nadia looked at the now merry face of the snowman. Without the Lord's efforts, it would have been blank and unseeing. In his own way, he had given it life.

twelve

Nadia tossed down the pen and flexed her fingers. How did scribes spend all day writing? Her eyes felt gritty, too. She rubbed them and sat back with a groan. A cup of tea was what she needed to restore her.

Nadia headed down the hall, stretching as she went. As she turned the corner, a resounding thump shook the wall to her right, followed by the sound of breaking glass. The wall shuddered again as something else was hurled against it. She quickened her pace, anxious to put some space between her and the violence occurring on the other side. The door crashed open behind her and then slammed shut. Sparing a glance over her shoulder, Nadia prepared to run.

The Lord planted two swift kicks against the door, bent his leg to deliver another, and then slowed, becoming aware of her presence. His face was twisted and colored with rage. As his eyes met hers, the corners of his mouth attempted to raise a smile but only accomplished a tic.

He spun on his heel, whirling away from her, and marched off in the direction she had come. Moments later, there came a twang of metal being hit, followed by the cascading crash of a suit of armor as it fell.

Nadia crept to the door the Lord had emerged from. Her hand reached out, her fingers flexing, uncertain. They closed around a knob that was solid. Surely, this was his study, the place in which he spent most of his day.

Did she truly want to see what had upset him so? She had her suspicions, but did she want them confirmed? To see the evidence? She had already gotten more than she'd bargained for when she read his book. Nadia let her hand fall away.

Stepping away from the door, she continued her trek to the kitchen. As she was pouring the water for her tea, Uro's roar broke through the silence. With a sigh, Nadia set the kettle back on the stove. A heaviness settled around her heart, and she wasn't even the one who had sent out the dragon.

Why does he do it? she wondered. *Why does he do something that's such a burden?*

There was no roar when Uro returned. No third place setting at dinner, though she had wondered. Only the Lord with a look of apology on his face. He pushed Nadia's chair in and poured her some wine.

"I must apologize for scaring you this morning."

"You didn't scare me," Nadia countered. "Startle, yes. But not frighten."

His hand hovered in the air, still holding the decanter. "You weren't at all concerned?"

"Thank you," she said, and picked up her wine. "For you, yes. For me, no." She lifted a sympathetic smile and explained. "Nothing was being tossed at me. No kicks, no blows, came my direction. But you...you were in agony."

Nadia carefully considered whether or not to add the next words and decided they mattered. "You didn't want to send out Uro."

The Lord froze again, this time in the act of scooting in his chair. He stared at Nadia in astonishment.

She picked up her fork and started in on the stew of beef, apricots, and sweet spices. "Why do you? If it bothers you so much, why do you do it?"

Nadia kept her gaze to her plate and focused on spearing one of the apricots. If he was now going to rage at her, at least she wouldn't have to see it.

At first, her words were met with silence. "It's a role I'm meant to play," he finally answered. "Sometimes it's easier than others."

"Like when they send you children."

The glass in the Lord's hand shattered, spraying shards and wine across the table. There was a brief moment where he stared at the empty space in his hand, at the mess, and then his other hand flew up in a "stop" motion.

"I apologize again," he said, and began to collect the larger shards. He stacked them and reached over, lifting and removing Nadia's plate. "We'll find something else. I don't want to risk you eating glass." As he set her plate by his, his head bobbed sharply. A gesture of silent acknowledgement. It gave her the impression that they were not alone and, yet, there was no one there. "Let's just get this situated, and we'll adjourn to a smaller dining room I sometimes use."

The Lord scraped and stacked their plates, brushed the glass onto a bread plate with a knife, took his time cleaning up. There was a barely perceptible moment, one she would have given no notice to if she hadn't been looking for it, where the Lord's mouth twitched. Twitched in the same way his head had nodded a short time before. It was as if the house was talking to him, for he left off cleaning the table and extended an arm to her.

"Shall we?"

His arm was steady and contained the muscles of one used to exercise. Which surprised her. She had come to the conclusion he was one who spent his days locked up in some room. Of course, he was a god so maybe he was just naturally fit. Or the castle was large enough to contain an exercise room or rooms she hadn't yet come across. Whatever the reason, that simple gesture made her feel more like a princess than anything else since she'd arrived. She was walking to dinner on the arm of a prince.

The room was just down the hall from the Lord's study. A dark paper patterned with fruits and birds covered the walls. The wood of the wainscoting and mantel had aged to a deep cinnamon and been oiled until they shone. Dishes of the spiced stew had been set out on a small round table, along with a platter of cheese, cakes, and fruit. Fire crackled merrily in the grate. A low-slung table and couch sat in front of its warmth.

"My private dining room," the Lord explained. "I generally take my meals in here when I'm not entertaining guests."

"I'm honored you've let me into your inner sanctum," Nadia said.

A hearty laugh bent him backward. "I see all that reading is expanding your vocabulary."

"Isn't that what it's meant to do?"

"Yes. Just...I haven't had someone pick it up so quickly. Boys spend years at school to get to the level you have." He pushed in her chair and took his own seat.

"Actually—" Nadia speared a chunk of sweet potato. How could she tell him she was bored with what she was reading?

My beloved...

Her eyes flew wide at the memory. Heat warmed her cheeks.

"Is there a problem?" the Lord asked.

"No, no." Nadia tried to hoist a smile onto her face. Then fought to keep it there as she remembered that he'd come looking for her yesterday when she wasn't in the library. Where she'd left her book. On the table next to his.

"I'm just tired of Hans. I returned it yesterday but need your suggestion on what to start next."

A devilish grin crept across the Lord's face. "Do you mind something a little...racy?"

The blush on her cheeks took on a full burn. Did he know she'd been reading his poems? "What did you have in mind?"

The Lord finished his latest bite before answering. "A series of tales collected by a pilgrim on his journey. The knight's adventures are full of the time-honored trio—wine, women, and song."

Relief swept through her, though she still had to ask, "Do you consider that proper reading for a young lady?"

The Lord chuckled. "Come now, Nadia. Surely you know by now that I'm not that proper."

"I think you find joy in pushing the limits of what's proper," she said. She meant it as a jest to match his own, but it had the opposite effect she'd desired. The Lord's face clouded and then darkened. "What did I say?" she asked.

"It's not you, it's—" But he didn't finish. The Lord smiled, but it didn't reach his eyes. There was a weary weight in them.

Nadia concentrated on cutting her meat into even smaller pieces. Part of her wanted to comfort him. The other part was silent but reproachful. Nadia sighed inwardly and let that part have its way.

She was a fool whose head was easily turned by comfort and a handsome face. The man sitting across from her was not to be pitied. He was responsible for terror and death. Which had rained down only this morning!

But he doesn't want to do it, Nadia argued.

Really? Remember how he gloated when you first came that someone was going to die.

But he doesn't want to do it. Nadia snuck a glance at the Lord which he caught and offered her a small smile in return. She was certain her argument was correct, though she had no proof, nothing but the feeling that his current charm and effort were for her benefit.

You're a fool, the voice whispered.

I guess I am.

Nadia wandered down to the stables to visit Uro after dinner, her mind still full of thoughts and misgivings. The dragon lifted his head at her approach and gave her a throaty purr of welcome.

"I'm not much better than he is," she said to Uro. She ran a hand along his thick scales. Uro lowered his head and offered Nadia his brow to be scratched. She ran her nails along the ridge. "My best friend is a dragon. What kind of person makes friends with a dragon?"

One lid slid open. The fiery eye seemed to answer, *A wise one.*

"But you're death," Nadia whispered. She sighed and leaned against his snout.

Uro gurgled. *And you welcomed me.*

"That I did," she whispered. "That I did."

♪♪♪♪♪♪♪♪♪

After a restless night, Nadia couldn't bear the thought of the morning room, spending her time reading and writing like nothing had happened. Instead, she climbed the stairs to Aurora's tower and gazed out the window, consumed by the thoughts that had chased her as she'd tossed and turned on the mattress.

What was this place doing to her?

She'd heard a sermon long ago, or perhaps somewhere else, that freedom breeds sin. That people don't willingly choose to do what's right. So that, when left to their own devices, they choose themselves.

Wasn't that what she was doing now, putting herself above others? Shouldn't she be trying to find a way to stop the Lord, to stop the dragon? Someone had died yesterday and her concern had been for the Lord, not whomever he'd killed. She had supped with him and then gone out and petted the dragon. She was truly a terrible person.

Her eyes pricked. A bit of kindness, a warm bed, and food were all it took to bribe her. Nadia turned her back to the window and slowly slid down the wall. She'd been better off at Westpark, despite her treatment, where she'd been thankful for what she had and cared about others.

The spinning wheel swam in and out of focus as her eyes filled and then overflowed and filled again. This place was changing her, yet there was no way to leave. Her gaze caught on the empty stool. Where were they—Aurora, Rapunzel, and the others? What had happened to them? She tipped her head against the wall and wallowed in her misery, losing all track of time.

Until the door moved. It swung inward, revealing the Lord. He stood there, surveying where she sat crumpled against the base of the wall, and a gentle frown crossed his face.

Crossing the room, he settled himself against the wall next to her. "I've thought about permanently locking the door to this room. I find there is something about it that causes too much reflection."

"Where's Aurora?" Nadia asked. She didn't bother to dry the tears on her face.

"She got her happily ever after."

A disbelieving huff left her lips. "Is that another way to say she died?"

The Lord opened and then closed his mouth. "She didn't die here, if that's what you're asking. No one dies here." He sounded sad.

Nadia looked sideways at him. "Why is that?"

The Lord turned his head and ran his gaze over her in some assessment. He sighed. "You're not healthy. That's why Uro brought you back."

Her blood turned to ice with his words, freezing her cheeks and creating a hollow ache, as if her insides had been scooped out. Reaching over, the Lord brushed the salt from her cheeks. "I don't know that I've ever had anyone quite so...ill as you." He squeezed his eyes shut and swallowed. He opened his mouth but only managed an inhale. His head shook back and forth as if to deny some thought that lay unspoken. "You could prove to be the exception if I'm not careful. If you're faced with too much too soon."

"Too much truth?" Nadia asked.

"I hadn't realized how fragile you were until—"

Her eyes widened, and she cut him off. "Until I made the bed disappear." He'd treated her differently after that.

"Exactly."

"Why *did* it disappear?" she asked.

"Because you couldn't handle what it represented, and I am sorry for that." He shook his head again. "Most women want a charming rogue, so I oblige them." His mouth tipped up in a smile. "Which can have its rewards. If I knew then—" He stopped mid-sentence, suddenly guarded.

"What do you know?" Nadia asked.

"Sometimes more than I want to. Sometimes not enough," he answered evasively.

Nadia sighed. Riddles again. "So why am I ill? Or is that another closely guarded secret?"

The Lord tapped his finger to his nose. "For the time being, anyway. Until you're stronger."

Nadia got to her feet. "And how will you know when I'm strong enough?"

He laughed. "I have a feeling the whole castle will know when you're strong enough."

Nadia shook her head. "You are quite the joker."

The Lord got to his feet and brushed the dust off his hands. He gave Nadia a roguish smile, eyes twinkling. "Maybe. But not as much as I once was."

thirteen

Nadia stared at the shadows moving across her ceiling for hours after she'd gone to bed, too puzzled by the revelation of her illness to sleep. Initially, she'd assumed the Lord was talking about the malnutrition and overwork she'd suffered, but months of good food and little work had filled her out. She no longer cringed at the sight of her face in the mirror. Gone were the sunken, bruised-looking eyes and hollow cheeks. These days, she would have accepted that she even looked pretty. So how was she ill?

She didn't doubt it. There was something in her heart that told her it was true. Something that whispered that *she* was the reason that Uro hadn't brought back someone new. That the Lord had had to choose, and he'd chosen her, Nadia, and that choice had torn him apart.

But what could it be?

A canker wouldn't be curable, though he was a god. Didn't gods answer your prayers? She'd wished to die and yet—Nadia rolled over in frustration, punching the down in her pillow into a better bolster—she hadn't died. The dragon, Uro, hadn't eaten her. He'd rescued her.

Because she wasn't a sacrifice. And she was ill.

Around and around her thoughts flew as she watched the moonlight bend through the sundial-like opening that was her window.

How was she ill? Why was she here? Why could the Lord cure her? How would she be healthy? When would she be healthy?

Around and around until she drifted off to sleep.

And dreamed of doctors and blood lettings and Uro piercing her with his fangs to drain the illness, which shimmered like pearl as it wept from the wound. She screamed from the pain but it never seemed to end.

As her eyelids lifted with the dawn, her hand went to her throat. It ached as though she had been actually screaming. With a huff, she tossed back the covers, ready to leave behind the night. The eyes that looked back at her when she pinned up her hair were ringed with dark circles and a *why?* that felt as if it had been burned into her soul.

Nadia broke her fast, drinking only tea laced with honey to sooth her throat and eating cheese bread. She cut off the crusts that would have scraped their way down when she swallowed and tied them up in a napkin to take to the birds later.

Tucking the packet into the pocket of her gray dress, she returned to the labyrinth of doorknobs, to the top of the castle. Not as far as Aurora's tower. That, she felt, had revealed its secrets to her yesterday.

Turning her back to the spiral staircase that led to the spinning wheel, Nadia stared at the dusty hallway before her. What did she want to know? Nadia closed her eyes.

How ill she was. Despite what the Lord had said, if she knew what was wrong with her, she'd know how to proceed.

Prickles tingled across her skin as she stood there. Holding onto her want, she focused it into a wish—her desire to have some clue as to her illness. The energy gathered, forming a spark that came to rest above her heart. Nadia shivered as it passed through her skin.

She opened her eyes and walked, led by the knowledge now inside her. Down the hall, down the stairs, into a corridor that she'd only been in once before as nothing had opened under her touch previously. She stopped in front of a door, its jamb covered with little flowers that had been carved into the wood. The spark dissipated.

Her heart gave a thump of something both joyous yet wrong. The sensation slithered down and roiled in her stomach. Reaching out a shaking hand, Nadia grasped a knob that stayed solid. It turned under her grip, and the door clicked open. Putting the tips of her fingers to the wood, she pushed.

A large mirror stood against one wall; the otherwise empty room reflected in it. Every warning from every story she'd ever heard rose up in her, telling her not to look. But her desire to know was stronger than her fear.

Though her feet were reluctant to make the journey, Nadia crossed the room and centered herself before the glass. With a bracing breath, she closed her eyes and spoke her wish. "I want to know why I'm ill."

As she raised her lids, the image in the mirror swirled. Vertigo, nearly as great as when she'd been at the edge of the courtyard wall, washed over her with the spinning. Just when she thought she'd be sick, the mirror slowed and the image began to take focus. Nadia backed up in horror at the picture it revealed.

There she was. Thin and poorly dressed, clamped in the arms of the losing rider at Elsbeth's steeplechase while all around them people laughed raucously. Her thigh burned where his member had pressed against her and then, in the mirror, he let her go; his "milady" as silent as the jeers, but she could hear them anyway. A lifetime of being the butt of jokes had burned an echo into her that needed no voice to be audible.

Nadia stumbled into the wall behind her. She swallowed, trying to shut out both the image and the voices, yet hold onto the knowledge they provided.

They had done something to her. Something that had made her ill. Something that had made her unacceptable as a sacrifice. They were the reason Uro had needed to be sent out again.

Make sure you make it worth your while.

The Lord had punished them and taken her in.

With that, Nadia could bear no more and fled from the chamber.

Returning to her room, Nadia quickly donned her coat and boots. Every heartbeat shook her body. But not with blood. It was as if something vile, poisonous, was being pumped through her veins. She had intended on walking off the effects of the shock but, as soon as she entered the courtyard and saw the curling steam rising from the stables, she rushed there instead.

Uro raised his head as she entered, didn't flinch when she flung herself against his side. She pressed herself against his smooth scales, cheek and palms flat against him until she was like moss upon a stone.

"What have they done to me, Uro?" Nadia whispered.

Uro looked down at her and exhaled, bathing her in warmth. Tears gathered in her eyes as she pressed herself further against him, would have burrowed into him if she could. He gave her a questioning warble and curled his head around, tipping his eye ridge toward her, his expression not unlike Lord Braemoor's great wolfhound.

Nadia reached out and scratched. Uro closed his eyes in contentment and gurgled. So much like Fala. A true and loyal companion. Fearsome. Her champion.

The thought brought a smile to her face. She had a dragon as a champion, more fierce and greater than any terrier or wolfhound. Yesterday, she'd wondered what sort of person made friends with a dragon. Uro had said, "A wise one." But today she thought the answer was, "A lucky one."

And she had the people back in Westfold to thank for that. Whatever they had done to her, they'd meant it for harm. But she'd been rescued. The magnificent creature under her hands, blowing smoke rings from his nostrils in contentment, had saved her from a life of torment. From a life where she'd wished to die.

Nadia wrapped her arms around Uro's snout and kissed him. "Thank you. Thank you for not eating me."

Uro gave a growl of frustration. "Fine," she said, and resumed her scratching.

"So if I'm ill—" Nadia had waited for the Lord to take a bite of the stew that was for dinner before she spoke. As he shoved the bite into his cheek, she held up a hand to stop his words. "I accept your assertion that I am ill, and I accept your assessment that I am too fragile to know why I am ill. What I want to know is—what can I do to become stronger?"

The Lord swallowed the piece. "What did I ask you all those months ago?"

"I don't know," Nadia retorted. "You've pelted me with so many riddles that none of them stand out."

"I asked you who you would be. And you answered..."

"Elsbeth," Nadia said. "A better Elsbeth."

"And so you have her life. Though somewhat limited by space."

"And lack of people." For Elsbeth had never been without servants or companions or suitors. A pained expression crossed the Lord's face. Nadia clapped a hand over her mouth. Before she'd come along, he'd been alone. "I'm sorry," she whispered.

"Nothing to be sorry for," he said. "You must be very lonely."

Nadia twisted her napkin. "At first, it was frustrating, for I didn't know my way and nothing seemed to work. And then it was nice, for there were no expectations. Except your vague hints. And now—" She pulled her wine toward her and turned its base, spinning it in slow circles with her finger. "Now it's a bit lonely. Though if you can bear it, so can I."

The Lord bit his lips and looked to her as if he was desperately trying not to smile. As the grin grew, he covered it with his hand. His ribs began to shake.

Nadia rolled her eyes and returned her attention to her food. Really, he was too much. What did he think was so funny?

fourteen

Continuing her explorations of the castle, Nadia stumbled across the most unusual, breathtaking ballroom she could have ever imagined. Hardly believing her luck when the handle actually turned, she had to blink when the room was revealed. Parquet floor, as expected. Wide empty space. But instead of the usual chandeliers, a myriad of small glass globes whirled and danced across the ceiling.

Her feet crossed the floor, though she was hardly conscious that they moved. All she could do was stare at the miracle of the ceiling. Until her craning neck began to ache. Nadia stretched out on the floor to better watch them.

When she'd been small, she and her brother, George, had once lain on the small rise in the sheep fold and watched the clouds go by. But that had been a procession, a line of clouds that marched by, changing from a tree to a cat to a rabbit with long ears that was soon outpaced by the dog behind it until it had become merely shapeless vapor. This was something in between a village dance and the swirling undulations of a flock of starlings in the fall.

Despite the hard floor beneath her, time lost all meaning as the ceiling danced. Ebb and flow, to and fro. Slowly working as a lullaby, creating such a sense of peace that she didn't even notice her eyelids close.

Nadia stretched. The ceiling still danced above her heavy eyes. All was peaceful.

Until her outstretched hand connected with something soft, yet hard. A body.

Her heart leapt into her throat, pulling her up off the floor.

"I used to have cushions in here for just this reason," the Lord said as she sat and tried to calm the pounding. "But I found they encouraged…immodest behavior."

The Lord remained on the floor, his hands folded across his chest. He gave Nadia a lazy yet amused smile and returned his gaze to the dance.

She pressed a hand over her still racing heart. "What is this place?" she asked when control of her breath returned.

"A ballroom."

"I gathered that. But the ceiling…"

The Lord gave a wistful sigh and seemed to choose his words carefully. "I had it installed shortly after I came here." His head shook lightly. "The most amazing craftsman. I missed the way the stars danced where I came from. Here, their journey is slow, like condensation building on glass in cool weather. There…swirls of fireflies."

Nadia looked up. "But there aren't any lights."

"Not during the day," the Lord said. "But at night the balls glow like stars and swirl across the ceiling." Another, heavier sigh heaved his chest. "I do miss it."

The ache in his voice was raw. Nadia toyed with one of the ribbons on her dress, running it through her fingers as she gave him some space. But the loss tugged at her heart. "I get the feeling you can't return."

The Lord gritted his jaw. "No."

"Would you mind my asking why?" she ventured, though she didn't expect him to answer.

He was silent, and she thought he wouldn't tell her. Then, with a soft rush of air, he spoke.

"I was once like them, the people I send Uro after. I believed I was owed everything at no price. After all, I am a god. I was reckless, careless, and uncaring." He closed his eyes and swallowed. "My actions caused the death of someone very dear to me." He paused again. "You once called me a monster, and that is true, for I have done monstrous things." Tears shone in his eyes when they opened. "And so, I was punished. I was banished here and tasked to spend eternity teaching others the lesson I needed to learn—that everything is precious, that our actions have a cost—and to heal those most damaged, most like—" The Lord gritted his trembling jaw and did not finish. "But they're not like she was. They're oh so human, always wanting something."

His last statement was a bit like the pot calling the kettle black. An attitude close to what had gotten him sent here. "A thousand years must be like nothing to you," she mused.

A rush of air left his lungs in a huff. "No matter how you look at it, a thousand years is a long time. Though, I dare say that when the sun expands in five billion years and engulfs the planet, I will welcome the end."

Nadia's heart filled with pity. It was horrible to feel helpless, unable to change one's situation. She hugged her knees and glanced up. "It must have been beautiful. For this is just..." She trailed off, unable to find words to adequately describe the ceiling.

"Yes," he answered. "The closest you come on earth is the sea. The ebb and flow of the waves." He inhaled deeply and closed his eyes. "The smell of salt on the wind, especially when a storm is approaching. Not so peaceful then, but the waves... the waves like white hair blowing in the wind."

"Sounds lovely," Nadia said. "Though I can't imagine so much water. I used to wish—" Her teeth began to chatter. Nadia blinked, fighting back the tears that rose. "I used to wish there was enough to drown myself in."

The Lord pushed himself up. "I'm glad there wasn't. You are truly remarkable, Nadia." He shook his head. "So aptly named. So much stronger than you realize."

Her brow pinched. "I thought you said I was fragile."

"You have been made fragile, but you have survived. Not only survived, but, in many ways, you are unchanged. You are like gold. You've been beaten flat and yet you still shine."

That wasn't all that happened to gold. Fear filled her heart and rose up her throat. She tried to swallow down the lump so that her voice could find a way out. "But isn't it refined?"

The Lord's countenance became serious. "Yes. You still have some fire to face. But not yet. Not until you are stronger."

It swelled again, growing until her eyes pricked and burned with it. Not long ago, she had been ready to face a dragon, ready to embrace death, but the thought of the "fire" to come filled her with dread and twisted in her heart like a worm on the hand.

The Lord reached out a hand. It drew to a standstill near her cheek and hovered. Nadia tensed, uncertain about his intentions. Then he plucked a stray lock of her hair and tucked it behind her ear.

"Don't worry, Nadia. You still have some healing to do first." The Lord glanced up at the ceiling. "And I need to teach you to dance. But not today." He pushed to his feet. "Today I want to hear your thoughts on the trick the old hag played on the knight."

He held out a hand to help her to her feet. It closed around hers, strong and firm. Her heart trembled for a whole new reason, but she beat it down. She would not become one of those women enthralled with him.

But when he smiled at her and the light danced in his strange yellow eyes, it was easy to see why so many before her had fallen for his charms.

Despite the seemingly normal lesson—the Lord listened to Nadia's retelling of the Wife of Bath's tale and debated the hag's lesson with her—Nadia realized that the encounter in the ballroom had changed her. Changed how she viewed the Lord.

She thought on it still when they talked about the preparation of fish over dinner, though they were eating beef. And thought about it when she had slipped on her nightgown and crawled beneath the sheets on her bed. The Lord was a prisoner here. He'd done something so terrible that he had been cast out of his home.

And sentenced to relive his crime over and over.

Any fear she'd had of him had fled. Which was strange, for he was a criminal. He could probably frighten her again, if he chose, but the overwhelming feeling she had for him was pity. She knew what it was like to be cast out, to be torn from everything familiar, everyone you loved. Everyone you thought had loved you.

He'd spent a thousand years looking for his crime in others. Meting out their punishment. A thousand years of being faced with, "Guilty, guilty, guilty."

Nadia curled the covers against her chin as she stared at the dark ceiling.

How could he bear it?

She still pondered the next day. It interrupted her thoughts so frequently that she abandoned her book and decided to write instead. Nadia sat at her desk, sheets of creamy paper before her, attempts at lines that weren't half bad, but mostly just twirling the quill between her fingers.

My actions caused the death of someone very dear to me.

She suspected the someone was the beloved from the poem she'd read. Or, at least, the Lord read the poem to be reminded of her. Which made it all the more sad. He'd unintentionally brought about the death of his love, and the gods wouldn't let him forget it.

She had once wondered if she had landed in heaven or hell. Now, she realized, this place was a bit of both. It was a bit of heaven for her, and most certainly, hell for the Lord. Was that true for most places? Nadia copied the next line.

Heigh ho, the winter snow

She gave a small laugh and glanced out the window at the piles that lay everywhere, humming the next line as she wrote.

Softly, whitely dost it grow.

The Lord had begun having her scribble folk songs, now that she'd moved beyond basic letters. Writing came easier to her than reading, but then she'd built up her "fine motor skills," as the Lord called it, scrubbing stubborn bits efficiently.

Heigh ho, let us go

The pen scratched as Nadia wrote the line beneath the Lord's tidy sample.

Down to the river where the ice doth flow.

Nadia thought back to the ballroom and its wonderous ceiling. Skating on the frozen river had been a favorite pastime in the village. At night, they'd set up bonfires along its edge and skate under the stars. She had never been able to join them. At first, there'd been no money for skates, and then there'd been so little time. Winter meals were always more hearty and thus required more dishes. But she had slipped out to watch them a few times.

She'd like to dance. In that ballroom, when the globes were lit. Watch the swirl and sway and join them. But her only partner would be the Lord, and it would be too intimate to have him hold her in his arms. Just the idea of it sent a shiver down her spine. Maybe when she was stronger, she would dance there by herself.

A sigh slipped its way free. At the manor and in the village, she'd been surrounded by people, though they had excluded her unless she was needed for work or as the butt of a joke. So she hadn't minded, really, when she'd found there was no one else here but her and the Lord. But now—

Nadia put down the pen and massaged her brow. She was tired of having no one else to talk to, of having to be careful. At first, she'd been afraid to anger or disappoint the Lord. But lately, he'd been so kind. And now she feared her heart latching onto the one thing she shouldn't have.

A strange ache welled up in her chest, so strong, it brought a grimace to her face. She'd begun to suspect that her illness had something to do with her heart. As she'd grown healthy in weight and appearance, she'd started to notice it having funny fits. Not like the pains that had caused Finch, the butler, to drop to his knees, then the floor, and then took his life right there in the doorway to the kitchen two years ago. But it did ache, almost burn, from time to time, which had only begun after Uro had taken her. Maybe she should ask the Lord about it this afternoon.

All thoughts of her heart left her when the Lord presented Nadia with a new book.

"You've never seen the sea," he said. "And I thought I should remedy that." The volume he handed her was very old, its leather worn, the title rubbed away, testament to its years of use. "It's the story of a mermaid who wants to be human. It's magic. Not the kind of magic spoken of in stories, or even the kind you've experienced here. Books have transportation magic. They can take you anywhere the author would like you to go."

Nadia opened it and gasped. The pages were all handwritten and embellished with illustrations and illuminations. "It's not printed."

"No," the Lord said with a smile. "Until they developed the printing press a hundred years ago or so, all books were printed by hand. Most of my library is old enough that the books were done by a scribe." He sat next to her and pointed at one of the illustrations. "Look at the waves crashing around her. Now close your eyes. The air is full of salt and brine. The wind blows, cutting at your cheeks. The waves first crash like buckets of water splashed out to scrub the cobblestones and then whisper back like sugar being poured out of a sack; the lungs of the ocean breathing in, breathing out. The gulls wheel overhead and laugh and cry like an old crone's joke. And in the midst of it all, a young girl waits and wonders what it would be like to walk on land."

Nadia opened her eyes and touched her fingers to the white spray crashing around the rock the red-haired mermaid rested on. "Thank you. It sounds amazing."

"My pleasure."

"My Lord," Nadia said. She brushed her fingers along the page, pulling up courage. "May I ask you a question?"

His smile faltered then returned, though caution shown in his eyes. "Of course."

"My illness...does it have something to do with my heart?"

The Lord stiffened next to her. It was a moment before he spoke. "Has it been bothering you?"

Nadia turned her eyes back to the book, but her gaze passed through it. Why hadn't he just answered the question? "At times."

His finger tapped a slow beat on the back of his chair, then he drew in a breath. "Yes, it's your heart."

Her face went numb. Nadia blinked as tears filled her eyes. Hearts couldn't be fixed. Hearts were like Finch or the Baker boy with the blue lips who gasped when he walked. Hearts killed you. And for the first time in longer than she could remember, Nadia found that she didn't want to die.

A tear spilled over and slid down her cheek. The Lord reached out and caught it on his finger. The warmth and pressure of his touch against her skin ached. Nadia closed her eyes as others ran past her lids and joined it.

"Oh, Nadia. Be your name. Have hope. When you're ready, I can fix your heart."

She could hardly see him through the tears in her eyes and on her lashes, but the smile he gave her was so filled with promise that she answered him with a stiff nod. She could at least try.

The story about the mermaid had a strange effect on her. At least, she found it strange. Nadia fingered the illustrations, closed her eyes, and tried to imagine the forests of kelp, their leaves like hands waving. Back...and forth. Back....and forth. Her body swayed in tempo to the images in her head as her mind grasped for a sensation that was just out of reach.

Like Roquefort. The kitchen mouse who defied everyone, every trap, even Miss Needles, the savage barn cat Cook had once brought in and locked up for the night in the kitchen. Miss Needles had sat outside Roquefort's hole, where his beady black eyes could be seen blinking in the half-dark. She had just finished putting away the last pot when she had spied him high up on one of the shelves. He'd peered down at her and twitched his whiskers as if to say, "Really? A cat?" And then gone on his way, looking for crumbs.

The only thing Miss Needles caught that night was Nadia, jumping on her in a rage of fur and claws. After raking her arms and waking her up, Miss Needles had strutted to the kitchen door and demanded out. Cook had blamed the failure on Nadia and beat her soundly. As she took care to raise her sore arms out of the way of Cook's rolling pin, her only thought had been how unfair it was. Roquefort remained elusive. And better fed, for she began dropping crumbs for him.

Crumbs.

Crumbs hadn't helped capture Roquefort but they might help her capture the sea. Slipping down to the kitchen, Nadia set a pot of heavily salted water to boil on the stove. As she waited for the water to heat, she hunted down a paper sack and scooped some sugar into it. The grains fell with a tinkling sigh, white sand instead of beige.

Rolling the top closed, she sat on a stool. When the vapor began to rise from the pot, Nadia closed her eyes, inhaled deeply, and tilted the bag back and forth.

She could hear the sea.

Her bath was laid out differently the next night. Instead of the jar of rose oil, a clear, lidded one full of turquoise-blue crystals sat on the bench next to the tub. Flipping up the metal clasp, Nadia breathed in the most subtle, wonderfully strange fragrance that she had ever encountered. It was vaguely sweet with a hint of salt, a perfume, yet a balm. A white shell sat on top of the grains for scooping.

Nadia poured in a couple and slipped into the now silky, turquoise waters. She picked up the shell and ran her fingers over the bumps and ridges, tracing the scalloped edge. The scent soon overtook her senses.

Closing her eyes, Nadia waved her hands in the water. Back and forth. Back and forth. Arms of seaweed in her bath. She'd never swum. The boys in the village had a favorite hole they liked to paddle in, the water being too shallow to truly swim. It was the closest many of them ever got to a bath. Loud and raucous and naked, she had always stayed away from them for fear that they would throw her in, or worse, take advantage of their nakedness and have only to lift her skirt to get at her. But here, in the warm water, surrounded by the intoxicating scent, she could imagine swimming.

Nadia pointed her toes and kicked her feet, waved her arms, feeling the water slide between her fingers. Drawing a breath, she closed her eyes and slipped beneath the water.

Her hair fanned out around her, and she smiled. The book had indeed been magic. A few days ago, she had been only Nadia. Now she was a mermaid.

"What was it like?" she asked the Lord at dinner that night. "The sea?" She had found a soft blue dress in the wardrobe that was a pale, watery version of the color of the bath salts and had put up her hair with the pearl-studded pins.

He closed his eyes and drew in a deep breath. "Eternity." His face twitched as he thought, and then a smile curved his lips. "Like being curled up against a sleeping dragon. The rumble when it exhales, the rush of air that lightly moans with every inhale. A rhythm that lulls you into peace yet never lets you forget the power and danger that is at rest."

His eyes held a faraway look when he opened them. His gaze traveled over her. One corner of his mouth twitched upward. "Feeling kinship with the mermaid?"

Heat flooded her cheeks. "I guess I am," she said, turning her head from his gaze. "She always felt different from others and yet...and yet, I think it would be nice to be her."

"Why?" the Lord asked. "Because her dreams came true?"

They had in the end, though she had feared for Linette when everything the mermaid had ever valued had been swept away in pursuit of that dream. "That's part of it, I think." Nadia searched for the thread that had resonated with her, seeking to put a name to it. "But I guess it's...how she clung to her hope."

"Ah." The Lord grinned widely. "That did make all the difference. And she had some help along the way."

"Yes," Nadia said, reddening again. "She did."

"I'm glad you've been able to experience the power of transformation that lies within the pages of a book. Shall I find another exotic place for you to travel?"

Linette's watery world had been even stranger than the castle she now found herself in. Though she never knew what sort of enchantment she might encounter, the castle was like a grander Westpark, and, therefore familiar.

The call to adventure stirred in her veins. Raging storms had gripped the castle for weeks, as if winter sought the extra ice and snow to keep the coming spring at bay. A chance to travel beyond the walls, if only in her mind, gave her a thrill.

"How exotic?" Nadia asked.

"As far away from wet as there is."

Nadia spent the next morning curled up in the window seat, hungrily taking in the pictures of Linette and her world one last time. Now she understood why people had libraries. She was loath to part with the book. Giving it back would be like handing over a piece of her soul.

That must be why he keeps the book of poetry out, the little voice whispered.

Indeed, she could now sympathize with leaving it on a table instead of having it tucked away, camouflaged by the multitude, as with soldiers on a field or trees in a forest. Nadia clasped the book to her heart and sighed. It wasn't like it was going far, just upstairs, back to its home. Maybe she could ask the Lord to show her where it was kept, then it wouldn't be so far out of reach, lost like a needle in a haystack; there, but not terribly easy to find.

The Lord laughed when she asked him. "I can see I've been remiss. The library is yours for the using. Let me show you how it's laid out."

The depth of it made Nadia's head spin. Histories, biographies, treaties on politics and religion, books explaining the cultures of various countries around the world, medicine, agriculture, herdsmanship, books on flora and fauna, books in Greek and Latin and some language the Lord called Arabic but looked to her like lines of squiggles and dots, poetry, plays, and, at long last, stories. Nadia traced her finger down the spines of one row, her brow furrowing as her puzzlement grew. Was there a method to their arrangement?

"I must apologize," the Lord said, when she turned to him in silent question. "After category, they're arranged by date of acquisition." He replaced the mermaid story, made sure that Nadia could find it again, and turned to the leftmost bookcase. He pulled out one with a spine as wide as Nadia's palm. "A thousand and one nights in Arabia, where the land is filled with sand and sun and trees with branch-like leaves only at their crown. A land where women are veiled and slaves are bought and sold and magic walks among them. A thousand and one tales told by a wife to keep her royal husband from executing her on their wedding night."

"How horrible!" Nadia said.

"Very misguided," the Lord replied. He held the tome out to her with a flourish. "But wonderful, for these stories so entranced the sultan—the oriental title for king—that he kept putting off her execution." Nadia hefted the book. It was more like a brick. "But you don't have to read them all or even start at the beginning. They are, however, all interconnected so worth the while to explore every one."

Nadia opened the book and rippled the pages. They were very old, yellowed, almost brittle with age. "How long have you had this?" she asked.

"A long time," the Lord said. "Though the original is even older, by hundreds of years. A thousand and one nights. It was an expression that meant eternity. These were once tales told in coffee houses by day and around gleaming campfires at night." A weary expression crossed his face. "They fell out of favor hundreds of years ago. I...happened upon and old edition that time had not been kind to. Like the sultan, I became entranced by the tales, so I commissioned this copy."

Nadia flipped through the topmost pages again. Unlike Linette's story, there were no illustrations. The Lord read the disappointment on her face.

"The man who created this for me was a Muslim and continued his religion's stricture against graven images even after he came here." As her brow wrinkled, the Lord added, "Islam forbids the creation of images of living things so that they can't be used as idols and worshipped. Omar refused my request for illustrations for this reason, and I was willing to forgo them in order to secure the stories. I do have other books that offer pictures of the world within those pages." His breath came out in a sigh, and he gave Nadia a tired smile. "But another day, I'm afraid. I have work to attend to, and so I will leave you in Scheherazade's capable hands."

He dipped a small bow and left the library. Nadia held the book to her chest as she watched him go. He had cut short their time, but for what reason? She had her suspicions, and her heart ached because of it.

The Lord was absent from dinner. Nadia rushed through her meal, feeling like a mouse at the table, nibbling the offerings alone. She escaped back upstairs, to the company of the Genii.

He had certainly been correct in her assertion that she would find the place exotic. But as the tales progressed, Nadia began skipping ahead, disenchanted with what she found. Other than Scheherazade, the human women were all unfaithful. She started to sympathize with the sultan, for if this was the norm, who could trust them? The men weren't much better. Greedy or foolish.

Perhaps the problems were the result of the way the people entered into marriage. There wasn't much talk of love. Everyone seemed to get married for convenience. Their parents wanted the arrangement or it was a reward for some deed well done. Not unlike Elsbeth's tournament.

That was certainly not the way she would want to wed. Not that marriage had ever really been an option for her. But the idea of spending one's life bedding someone you didn't really know was abhorrent. And while the participants in Scheherazade's stories went willingly to the altar, or whatever, they all seemed to look elsewhere for actual love.

Nadia snapped the book closed. She had wished, when she let herself wish...when she thought of Elsbeth's search for a husband...she had hoped that maybe, just maybe, there was someone out there for her, too.

But now...

Now what? At some point the Lord would fix her heart, and then what? What had happened to Aurora and Rapunzel and the others?

Her heart began to churn, unleashing the voices in her head with their messages of doubt. Nadia gritted her teeth with the effort to block them out, struggled against them as tears pricked her eyes and gathered on her lashes. The more she tried to hold onto hope, the more the voices gathered strength and volume.

Don't trust him. Don't trust him. Don't trust him.
HE ONLY WANTS YOUR HEART!

Nadia released the book, dropping it as though it had caught flame, and dove under the blanket, pulling it up over her head. All her fears rushed back in. How did she know she wasn't Hansel in the witch's house? Everything the Lord did was fattening her up. What had happened to all the others? Why was he alone?

Would Uro trust him? asked a stronger voice. *Serve him?*

She pressed her hands against her head, desperate to still the warring voices inside it. Tears fell hot and fast down her nose and onto the pillow. How could she trust when everyone she had ever met had only meant her evil? Why would the Lord be any different? If he was, he wouldn't be here alone.

fifteen

Her dreams were filled with water and the Lord who plunged a hand deep inside her chest and ripped out her still beating heart. Blood blossomed from the wound, billowing out to match her hair which floated around her like a swaying wreath.

Morning brought an end to the dream, but Nadia couldn't bring herself to rise. Her body ached as if she had spent the night wrestling with the big black feasting kettles, and her eyes burned from the salt still crusting her lashes. At least there was just the two of them in the castle. The Lord didn't expect her until the afternoon, so she could just stay in bed.

Curling the covers under her chin, Nadia watched the sun creep across the bed. The little voice that whispered, *But where are the others?* continued its nagging. On and on it droned.

But then a curious thing happened. A louder, stronger voice repeated the Lord's explanation—*They got their happily ever after.*

Nadia strained to listen in the stillness that followed, but could only hear her beating heart. Her fear no longer seemed like a living thing, just fear. So what was she afraid of?

With the whispers silenced, she knew. Closing her eyes, Nadia gathered her courage to say it aloud. In her head, anyway. She didn't deserve a happily ever after.

By the light of day, her nightmares made sense. She feared the Lord would destroy her, for that's what she deserved. She feared the Lord was lying to her, for that's what people did. Especially to her.

The Arabian tales had shown her the worst of human nature, and she'd taken them into her heart. Which was not what the Lord had intended.

Releasing the covers, Nadia rolled over and picked up the book. He had given it to her as a treat, had wanted to give her someplace new and different to travel to. He'd had it for hundreds of years, so maybe he didn't remember what they were like. At the beginning, anyway.

Maybe he just remembered how they ended.

Nadia sat up and flipped to the table of contents. The last story was about Ali Baba and forty robbers who were killed by one slave. That was quite the feat. The one before it sounded intriguing, too. A story of someone named Aladdin and a wonderful lamp.

She drew in a shaky breath. Her hands trembled, but that was due to an overabundance of emotion and not her lack of breaking her fast. Besides, she was in no shape to venture out to eat. Not until she'd had a chance to put some of the night's trauma behind her.

Nadia turned to the page she sought and began to read.

In a certain town of Persia...

With a snap, Nadia closed the book. She stared at the bed-covers, her fingers tracing the raised patterns in the leather of the book. So much to love. A land where warm, spice-scented breezes blew from the sea to the desert and cooled the houses that baked under an endless sun, where people sat on cushions and ate meat and fruits.

Her fingers clenched. So much to hate. She had thought her lot at the manor had been poor, being an afterthought that no one cared for. But the people in these stories...they were liars and cheats and slaves and murderers and shared their husbands with other wives. Her head moved as if to deny it. Yes, her lot could have been worse.

Throwing back the covers, Nadia crossed to the wardrobe. She knew why the Lord loved the book. The people in the stories had triumphed in the end; their poverty replaced by riches, their hardships with ease. And maybe he had meant to give her hope, but she wanted stories of a handsome prince who rescued the princess, or at least someone worthy, like Cinderella, for love rather than status, glory, or riches. Someone who wouldn't execute his wife when she displeased him. The stories she had grown up with had their share of cruelty, but at least they had a happily ever after. Something she was just beginning to believe might be found at the end of hers.

And if the nightmare and the voices that whispered in her heart were right, if the Lord had truly lied to her and wanted to kill her...she would welcome it. Hadn't she gone to face him, face his dragon, so she could die?

But if he could heal her...

If the voices and the nightmare were wrong, if they were something to do with her illness, and he could heal her, she'd get a life. A better life.

Her hand closed around a dress of gold. She donned it quickly and did up her hair with the plain gold pins. There might still be time to find some luncheon and sneak the book back in the library before the Lord came.

Nadia set the book on the reading table and turned to face the rows of bookcases. Although she no longer desired to spend time with people who found love so dangerous, she longed to glimpse their world. Somewhere in the sea of books, the Lord had to have one that could show her. Even if it was a world where pictures were forbidden.

She straightened as he entered.

"Those looked like some serious thoughts you were thinking," he said with an amused grin.

"I was trying to remember the layout of the library." It was half the truth.

"I will draw you a map," the Lord offered. "What is it that you are seeking?"

"A book with pictures of Arabia."

He gestured for her to follow. "Enjoying the stories, then?"

Nadia hesitated by the table and dropped her gaze. "No, my Lord."

Her answer stopped him mid-stride. "No?"

She gripped the edge of the table for support. "They're cruel. And selfish."

His gaze fell to the book on the table. He picked it up and flipped through the pages, reading part of one passage before moving on to another then another and then another, a scowl growing on his face.

"I must confess that you are right. I do apologize. I loved the stories for their adventure, but I can see the reason for your aversion." He closed the book and gave her a gentle smile. "But they did arouse your curiosity." He nodded with his head for her to follow. "I think I have what you seek." Nadia trailed behind him. "And I will draw you a map so that you may browse at your leisure."

The Lord stopped in front of a bookcase and held out a finger as he scanned the titles. With a nod, he pulled one from the shelves. "An illustrated guide to Arabia and the Orient." He let it fall open in his hand and flipped to one of the colored illustrations. Strange horse-like creatures with humps on their backs stood by a pool surrounded by equally strange trees that were mostly trunk, their fringed branches only at the crown. People in long robes with flowing scarves tied around their heads held the bridles. *The ever-important oasis,* read the caption.

He flipped to another. This one showed a city of white buildings with smooth walls and arched doorways. Towers were topped by domes that looked more like onions. *The minarets of Baghdad.*

The Lord closed the book and held it out to Nadia. "All adventure, no tragedy. I promise."

Nadia spent the rest of the day curled up in the window seat of her morning room devouring the book. The strange horse-like creatures were "camels," with fat, wide feet for walking on the sand and long eyelashes to keep it and the sun out. They could go for days without water. The strange trees were "palms" and produced fruits known as "dates" that were sweet and chewy, like candy. Minarets were tall towers where a muezzin would climb and call people to prayer, his voice rising and falling like a flock of birds looking for a place to roost.

It was a magical fairyland. Rich, saturated colors, warm winds that carried the scent of spices sold in open markets, glittering bangles on the arms of the women. The perfect thing to chase away the winds of winter blowing outside the window.

"Were you ever there?" Nadia asked the Lord at dinner. "Arabia?"

"I knew you'd find it interesting." A faraway look entered his eyes. "Once." His lips thinned as he held back a smile. "Pursuing a Jinn that my brother had raved about." His eyes closed and the smile curled cat-like up his face. "She was everything and more."

His eyes opened, and he flashed Nadia a roguish smile. "A young man's adventures when I was young and foolish. Or so my father chastised me when I returned." He forked up some of the pie filled with beef and potatoes. "There are some crimes worth paying for and fruit stolen out of the orchard is one of them." His tone turned more serious. "Though that was a symptom of my recklessness, it is one of the things I don't regret. How about you? Any mischief you got into that still pleases you today?"

Nadia swallowed. Her small amusements seemed so petty by comparison. "I'd sneak things from the kitchen to offer at the fairy fort. I wanted them to look kindly on me so that—" The words dried up in her throat.

"So that?" the Lord prompted merrily. Then he glanced up from his plate and spied the look on her face.

Nadia flushed as his expression became searching. She averted her gaze, attempting to shut out the Lord and the memories. The offerings had been simple and childish but the reasons behind them had not. After the night when the fairies had failed to eat her, she would play out on the fort whenever she had a free moment. The next summer, when she'd been eleven and Lord Braemoor's brother had come to stay, the groom who had accompanied him had begun watching her. And then brushing by her. He found reasons to come into the kitchen late—Sir Errant's horse had a sore knee and needed a warm poultice. The next night, it was a special mash. The third, some tonic, just as Cook was getting ready to go to bed. Cook had complained and fussed, slamming things as she got the pots out again. The groom suggested that Nadia could mix it up; it was a simple enough brew. Another person would have welcomed his suggestion, but Cook had thrown her a withering glance and assured him that she would only "muck it up." He'd had no choice but to concede.

He had hungrily watched her as she'd washed the last of the dishes, had grudgingly gone out the door when Cook gave him the draught. Nadia had stood in the doorway and watched him head back to the stables, pouring out the brew as he went. She had nodded an acknowledgement to Cook's command to make sure that everything was scrubbed well and then darted out into the night as soon as Cook had mounted the stairs.

Secreting herself against the large old oak on the fort, she had prayed, once again, for the fairies to take her or keep her safe. They didn't come but neither did the groom. When the huge old owl flew back and settled himself on the branch above her to roost for the day, Nadia had crept back to finish her work.

At eleven, she'd still been young enough to want to sit in the garden like Elsbeth and fashion dolls and tea things from acorns, flowers, and leaves. So the next night, she had taken an offering of raspberries and a nut cap full of elderflower wine with her. For three weeks, she spent a few hours resting against the tree before creeping back to finish her work.

He finally caught her one morning as she finished the dishes, backed her up against the sink and tried to raise her skirts, but

Cook rose early to begin preparations for Sir Errant's going away feast and her footsteps on the stairs had stopped him.

The last night, she risked a beating by creeping upstairs and sleeping on the landing of the servant's quarters. Something had told her that the groom was drunk and waiting for her out by the path. Her heart knew that it was a warning from the fairies, so she had repeated the offering every night that summer, thanking them for their protection, even though she would return to her pallet by the fish tank to sleep.

It was the closest she'd come to Elsbeth's garden play. As the years went on, she thought that she had been fanciful, reckless even, because of the beating she would have caught for the theft. The fruit and wine weren't hers to give.

Nadia raised her head and tried to hoist a smile onto her face as she confessed, "They were offerings of thanksgiving for keeping me safe." The last word caught in her throat. Her lips trembled.

An action mirrored by the tic in the Lord's jaw. He had realized there was more to the story. But his voice was calm when he asked, "What were your offerings?" before raising his wine glass and taking a large swallow.

Nadia dropped her gaze. "Raspberries and elderflower wine." When she glanced back up, he was smiling.

The Lord set his glass down. "Very wise of you. Your gifts were definitely met with welcome."

Nadia goggled at him. "You make it sound like they're real."

A very undignified laugh burst from him. "Of course fairies are real. Though dangerous. Some will clean the meat right off your bones. You must have had great need of them and then rewarded their care aptly. Definitely not a theft to regret." His expression became strained, and he changed the subject. "Have you come to the part in the book yet where they list the local curses? My favorite, though it's not really dinner appropriate, so do forgive me, is, 'May the fleas of a thousand camels infest your armpits.'"

Nadia snorted, immensely thankful she'd not been sipping her wine. "That would definitely be painful," she said. He smiled widely, but it didn't reach his eyes. Something was bothering him. "Do tell me some others," she asked, hoping to distract him.

Uro's roar broke through the night as Nadia brushed out her hair before bed. She crossed to the window and peered out. His dark form created a shadow in the moonlight sky. A burst of flame lit up the dark night like fireworks, yellow and orange with shooting sparks. The only time she had seen him breathe fire was in her village. And he'd never before left for some task at night.

As she turned, a dark form exited the stables and crossed the cobblestones to the castle. There was an angry purpose to the Lord's stride, one she had seen before—just before he knocked over the suit of armor. What had filled the Lord and his dragon with such anger?

That night, she dreamed she was back on the fairy hill, curled against the tree, the great owl watching the dark with his bright, yellow eyes. When she woke the next morning, Nadia couldn't shake the feeling that someone had indeed been watching her sleep.

sixteen

A dress of rose-colored silk hung on the door of one of her wardrobes two days later. Its columnar shape made it look more nightgown than ballgown, but she had seen its like in the book on Arabia that the Lord had lent her. Nadia ran her fingers over the gold embroidery that scrolled around the bodice and edge of the sleeves and down onto the skirt, ruffling the scattering of small gold discs like fish scales.

A note had been pinned to the hem. *Wear this for dinner. I will collect you at seven.*

Collect her? The hairs on Nadia's arms rose. In the six months since she'd come to the castle, he'd never collected her for dinner. Other than the time she'd made the bed disappear. And he'd never picked out clothes for her. But now he'd left her a dress. And a note. Instead of speaking to her about it when they'd met this afternoon.

Nadia sat down on the bed and touched a shaking hand to her mouth. The Lord had provided her with a gown he wanted her to wear. One that, at first glance, was similar to the nightgowns she'd found in the wardrobe in her first room. But there was nothing immodest about this gown, other than a lack of volume, though she didn't think Elsbeth would dare wear it. The fabric was so fine that any touch would feel as if it were on bare skin.

A shiver ran down her spine. That was what she was afraid of, that the Lord would touch her.

Closing her eyes, Nadia tried to still the fear in her heart. She had come to her Hansel and Gretel moment. With a slow exhale, Nadia reached for the dress. She'd put it on. She'd put it on and pray that the Lord wouldn't finally ravish her.

She had managed to arrange her hair, though it was a loose mess of curls. Her hands had shaken so much when she'd pinned it up with clips of diamond stars that she couldn't get the sections to hold properly. But it was the best she could do without someone to help her.

In all the months she'd spent here with just the Lord for company, this was the most alone she'd felt. She hadn't minded the lack of people. She had welcomed it. There was no one to abuse her or make fun of her. No one to order her around or criticize her. But now, there was every chance she was being silly and there was no one to calm her down.

She'd managed all those years to escape with nothing more than an occasional grope, but the attempts and near-misses had left their mark. And a tiny, little voice, not the kind one, kept whispering that she had just wrapped herself up as a gift to be opened.

Nadia leaned her arms against the dressing table and buried her face in her hands. A gentle brush against her shoulder launched her from her seat with a startled yelp. She turned, gasping. But no one was there.

A nervous giggle bubbled up. Nadia drew in great, shuddering breaths. Then the line between laughter and tears quickly thinned.

Nadia put her hands on her hips and breathed deeply through her nose, willing the tears building in her eyes to stay put. She would not let the Lord find her red-faced and salt-stained.

The deep breaths finally slowed her racing heart. With one last exhale, Nadia turned to face her reflection. She could scarcely believe the exotic looking creature gazing back was herself. Her panic had flushed her face, now full and round. The fabric suggested at the curves she'd gained. Even her hair had a luster; its mess of curls a star-studded elegance. Her hands were no longer red and cracked but smooth.

She looked like an Arabian princess. Minus the veil. Though women didn't wear the veil for their husbands.

Whatever the Lord's intentions tonight, she did need to thank him for the transformation. And if that were with her body—

Nadia smoothed her skirts, her hands rippling the golden scales, and gathered her courage.

If that were with her body, he'd earned the right. And she thought he'd be kind. Or at least more gentle than all those who'd tried before.

She turned from the mirror. Crossing the room, she lowered herself to sit on the chaise and await the Lord's arrival.

Even though she was expecting it, the knock on the door caused her heart to leap, slamming it against her ribs. She managed to cross the room and turn the knob with fumbling hands.

The Lord's gaze traveled over her. "Stunning," he proclaimed. He dipped a bow and gestured with his hand. "After you."

Nadia closed the door behind her, and steeled herself to take the Lord's arm. But it wasn't offered. Disappointment or relief churned in her chest. Or maybe a combination of the two. She couldn't pick them apart to tell. "I'm guessing we aren't eating in the main dining room."

"No," the Lord replied. "Though your dress is a clue."

Her brow wrinkled. "I couldn't begin to imagine."

His smile widened at her words. "Tonight is all about bringing the imagination to life."

They headed down the stairs and followed the twisting passageways to a room placed at the far end. The Lord turned the handle, stepped to the side, and pushed the door open. Nadia's jaw dropped. She knew they were still inside the castle but the room was very much from somewhere else.

Nadia crossed the threshold and turned in wonder. The walls were covered in fabric panels seamed with embroidered ribbons. Multi-colored glass lanterns hung from a ceiling painted with geometric designs. In a corner, a fountain splashed merrily, sending sweet echoes throughout the room. A swirling mosaic of branches and stars covered the floor. Instead of chairs, a bank of cushions had been placed around a circular brass table.

"I couldn't give you the sea, and I didn't think you wanted sand, but tonight I can give you dinner at the Kasbah."

The Lord gestured for Nadia to take a seat on the cushions. Reining in her surprise, she folded her legs and took a seat on the floor, smoothing her dress around her.

"Now traditionally," the Lord continued. "There'd be a slave or servant or wife—" He tossed Nadia an amused look. "—to serve us." His cheek ticked with a smile. "And since I'm currently short on servants—" He stopped again to hold back some mirth. "I shall be performing those duties."

He dipped a low bow and turned toward a buffet table where an array of platters and strange utensils had been set out. The aroma of honey and cinnamon and savory meat drifted from the offerings.

The Lord picked up a brass bowl and flung a towel over his arm before hoisting an ewer and turning back around. "In Arabia, we eat with our hands, so they must first be washed."

He placed the bowl in front of Nadia and instructed her to hold out her hands. The water that trickled over them was warm and scented with rose oil. The Lord handed her the towel. After she had dried her hands, he returned the basin to the buffet where he washed his own. Next, he brought her a glass of wine the color of crushed raspberries. This was soon followed by two bowls of soup. He lowered himself down next to her on the cushions.

"Bismillah," he said, raising the bowl of soup in toast.

"Which means?"

"In the name of God."

Nadia bit back a smile. "So you're thanking yourself for this meal?"

The Lord's eyes twinkled. "I could, since I did provide it. But, no. It is the customary call for Allah to bless the food."

"So you're thanking Allah for the food?"

"The Supreme Being? I do." His smile wavered. "There are always gifts if you choose look for them." His lips pressed together. "And I hope I have been blessed in my confinement."

With a small nod, he brought the bowl to his lips. Nadia hesitated. It was strange, now that she could use a spoon with ease, to be encouraged, expected even, to drink directly from the bowl.

She raised it to her lips. Thick brown liquid hit her tongue, bursting with flavor. Lentils and chickpeas and onions in a broth so savory it made her want to gulp it down. Instead, she forced herself to set it down and pick up her wine. It was the best that the Lord had yet served. Neither sweet nor acid, it was truly refreshing and went down as easily as water.

It's all part of—

Nadia silenced the voice. The wine was delicious and she was going to drink as much of it as she wanted. She would *not* listen to the voice's whispers tonight.

For the next course, the Lord brought over a pastry dusted with pounded sugar and sprinkled with cinnamon in a pattern of sand dunes and a palm tree.

"Dessert already?" she asked, puzzled.

With a smile, the Lord took the knife from his belt. "It may look like that, but it will surprise you." He cut the pastry down the middle, cracking the palm tree in half. Using the knife, he pushed the two halves apart. Steam curled from the crumbly filling. "Chicken, almonds, and egg."

He pulled a section from the outer edge and dropped it in his mouth. Nadia carefully did the same, trying to get a piece that was somewhat cool and wouldn't burn her fingers or tongue.

Her eyes fell closed at the taste. Heaven. A perfect combination of sweet and spicy, crunchy and savory.

The Lord was watching her with an amused expression on his face when her lids opened. If he was trying to seduce her with food, it was working. "How does anyone want to eat anything else after this?" she asked.

"And yet," he replied. "There are three more courses."

The bastilla, as the Lord told her it was called, was followed by a refreshing salad of cold, sauteed eggplant mixed with minced and marinated carrots that they scooped up with bread. Next came a dish the Lord called "ambrosia," lamb that had been cooked in cinnamon and other spices before being covered in honey, almonds, and tiny flat, white seeds. A moan escaped her lips when the meat landed on her tongue.

"I keep thinking the dishes can't get any better and, yet, they do," she said.

"I'm glad you're enjoying it."

"It's been a magical evening," she told him.

He toyed with his glass. "If things were different, I would have added music and truly immersed you in the experience."

"What would have needed to be different?" Nadia asked.

The Lord gave her a tight smile and drank from his wine. Nadia played with the folds of her napkin. "Does it have something to do with your banishment?" she asked.

His eyes met hers over the rim of his glass, and then he set it down. He toyed with the glass while he formed his response. "I have as many people here as I need. Do you?"

Nadia's gaze fell to the table. "Sometimes I think it would be nice to have someone to help me. Not that you don't," she hastened to add. "But the ballgowns are tempting and..." She trailed off and turned her head, hoping to hide the blush she could feel rising on her cheeks. She had been thinking ladies maid, but her words could certainly be construed as an invitation for him to help her dress. Or undress.

"And I do miss the chatter of the kitchen though, at first, it was peaceful." She raised her head and squared her chin. "But if you can face it, so can I."

"Who says—" He broke off with a grimace. "Were things different, I would have filled the room with the gentle but hypnotic sounds of lute and drum and voices that warble like birds." His head bowed. "But I do not have the power to change that."

His voice was so full of regret that her heart went out to him. "I'd like to hear about where you're from. If you wish to talk about it."

A smile tugged at the corners of his mouth and a faraway look entered the Lord's eyes. "It wasn't that different from this. Not this room," he said, and waved his hand dismissively. "But the castle and the mountain. Though, of course, I had an endless amount of space and not just the garden and the park." He closed his eyes as though savoring the memory. "Tall snowcapped mountains that plunged to the sea. Wide, flower-filled valleys and meadows." His throat moved with a swallow. "Though, of course, I had the freedom to travel anywhere, so I did." His eyes opened, and he gave Nadia a sad look. "I deserved my punishment, for some things deserve to be punished. There *are* things you can never finish paying for."

The weight of his burden became something she could feel against her own flesh. "Does forgiveness not enter into the equation?" she asked. At what point could he find some ease?

He looked away. "The ones I wronged are no longer here to beg forgiveness from." The muscles in his jaw stood out as he gritted his teeth. When he looked back, his eyes held a fire that frightened her. "If I could bring her here, would you wish to forgive your mother? Or the groom who tried to rape you when you were barely more than a child?" Her eyes flew wide. "How about the town—" He spat the words. "—that gave you up so easily? Would you forgive them?"

Nadia whimpered as something clawed at her heart. Could she? Forgive them? When everything they'd done to her had made her want to die? "I don't know," she whispered with lungs that were loath to give her breath.

"I've made them pay," the Lord said. "I, who have done as they have, made sure they learned that there is a price to be paid when you poison and destroy." Anger shook his body.

Her jaw trembled. "Have you hurt my mother?" she asked, both ashamed to hope that the woman who had given birth to her may have been made to feel a measure of the pain she'd dished out and afraid that her mother was dead.

The Lord looked away. "No. Though she feels some guilt at your loss."

Nadia exhaled with a relief that surprised her. And then her brow knit in puzzlement. "How do you know this?"

He reached for his wine and drank before replying. "I have my ways of watching the world." A wry smile crossed his lips. "How else would I know when I'd need to send out Uro?"

The man sitting across from her was fierce and terrible. And the only champion she had ever known. He scared her and yet...

How do you condemn someone who comes to your rescue?

They'd brought it upon themselves, he'd told her. And he had not accepted her as a sacrifice.

"Why did Uro bring me back?" she asked, hoping for a real answer this time.

The Lord caught her gaze and held it. "He could tell you were not like the rest. That you held no blame." His mouth twitched as if he wrestled with it, eventually twisting into a smile. "But enough seriousness. You haven't yet tried the pastries for dessert."

He rose and brought them over, a plate of flaky crusts filled with ground almonds and pistachios, covered in honey and rose water. Next, he brought a brass tray with two small, clear glasses, more the size one would give a child, and tipped from on high a tall, clear teapot covered in scrolling gold paint. The tea seemed to fall from the heavens into the glasses. The aroma of mint and honey hit her before she was even offered the tray.

Nadia took hers, and the Lord set the tray back on the buffet. He gathered his own glass and then lounged on his cushion, drawing up one leg before raising his glass in toast. "To a sweet end to the evening, princess."

Her hands began to shake. "I'm no princess," she said, unable to meet the Lord's eyes, afraid of what she'd find in them. Nadia placed her cup on the table so she wouldn't spill it.

"What makes a princess?" he asked.

"Being highborn," Nadia answered automatically.

He snorted. "Like all princes are gentlemen. Being highborn gives you status but it doesn't define who you are. Let me rephrase it. What should a princess be?"

Nadia considered his question. What were the things all the princesses in the stories had in common? "Kind," she said, still searching for words. Then the story of Cinderella came to mind. Her father had been a duke, but the spineless man had allowed his next wife and her children to basically enslave his daughter. Oh, in some stories Cinderella had been adored until he died and then they had tossed her from her room and forced her to sleep in the kitchen. But in the collection Nadia had read, her father had just stood by and allowed it. Aurora, Snow White—they'd lived with hatred, too.

Not unlike herself.

The Lord smiled when he saw that she had made the connection, saw the change of understanding in her eyes. "Yes, kind," he said. "And able to survive great hardship without allowing it to harden themselves. Now, don't you think that reminds you of someone?"

He fell silent, sipping his tea and nibbling on the pastries, as Nadia digested her thoughts. No matter which way she turned them, she could not reconcile what she knew about the princesses and what she knew about herself. Her hands twisted in her lap.

"I don't know what to say," she finally told him.

His glass rose in the air. "Salute. Accept it. Now drink your tea before it goes cold. And do help me with dessert. Don't make me a glutton as well."

The Lord repeated the hand washing at the end of the meal. After placing the basin on the buffet table, he turned to face Nadia. Fear shot up into her throat and refused to be swallowed down. He reached toward her. The hair on her arms stood up as the Lord's grasp closed around her fingers. Firm, strong, yet his touch was feather-light as he pulled her up.

Her lungs demanded more air, the better to prepare her to run, as she waited for his hands to move their touch to her arms, her face. Her battle to control her breathing was one he read.

"What are you afraid of?" he asked.

Heat rushed to her face. Try as she might, her mouth refused to form an answer. He hooked a finger under her chin, lifting her face to meet his gaze. Puzzlement filled his expression when she finally met it.

Casting her gaze to the floor, Nadia stammered her explanation. "T-t-the d-dress. And the instructions." Her eyes closed. "I assumed—" She swallowed and willed her tongue to push out the words, to accept her fate. "I assumed you were... are...claiming your rights."

The Lord whirled away from her. Crockery crashed to the floor, followed by the ringing clang of one of the serving dishes as it spun in circles. "I have no rights to claim. The poisonous—"

Nadia raised her eyes. The Lord faced the wall, gripping the edge of the now empty buffet with such fierceness that his hands were white. "I meant tonight as a gift to you." His voice choked on the words. "I am sorry if my actions gave you the impression that I meant something else."

Turning her gaze away from him, Nadia focused on the fountain in the corner instead. She had made assumptions, had listened to the little voices that whispered fear, and had hurt the Lord. Her head bowed. "I am sorry your gift got spoiled."

He turned back to face her, reached out a hand that closed on air before it got to her. His hand fell to his side. He stayed silent, waiting until she lifted her eyes to meet his. "Hope is a fragile thing. It can only keep the darkness at bay for so long without being fed. It can come to feel like a lie we tell our-selves, so much so that we reject it and accept the darkness. You've lived without hope for so long, Nadia, that you expect the worst of intentions. That has been your truth. So I take no offense at your…interpretation of what I intended tonight to be." His jaw clenched. "Those who damaged you, however, I will not let off so easily."

Nadia took a step toward him. "Haven't they paid enough?"

A resigned smile crossed the Lord's face. "No. But I see that you are determined to forgive them." He chuckled. "And you didn't think yourself a princess."

Her gaze fell. "I don't feel much like one."

"In time, Nadia. In time."

The Lord escorted her back to her room, his hands clasped behind his back the whole way, as if to reinforce his assertion that he wouldn't touch her. He paused at her door.

"I told you earlier that hope is fragile. But it is also power-ful, for it is at the root of all change."

Nadia shifted uncomfortably. "What do you hope for, my Lord?"

He smiled, but his eyes were filled with sadness. "That I somehow make a difference."

seventeen

It took Nadia a long time to fall asleep. She had gotten the impression that when the Lord spoke about "hope" that he had also meant her. She was fragile. She was powerful. Somewhere in her pondering, she fell asleep and dreamt no dreams.

She dressed the next morning in a fog and wandered down to the kitchen, still lost in her thoughts. What was her hope?

That people were not as cruel as she found them. Though the Lord certainly found them that way. Why else did he have his job, send Uro out?

Nadia picked up her cup and let the richness of the tea slide down her throat, warm her belly, and spread out, giving strength to every bit of her. She sighed. And became aware that the base of each hair on her arms was tightening. Nadia stared at the forming goosebumps and then lifted her gaze.

The cup fell from her fingers, spilling its liquid across the flagstones. Her heart crashed against her ribs as the cup hit the floor. Shards tinkled as they bounced, but her eyes stayed fixed on the vapor that gathered and swirled in front of the stove.

Nadia took a step back. She'd never feared the fairy fort, even though the rest of the village did. *The dead are buried there,* they whispered. *Giants from other times.* If you got too close, the apparitions would steal you away. Take you back and slowly feast on your soul. You'd be a living corpse, flayed open, yet alive; watching as the spirits plucked the choice bits from your body and ate them in front of you.

She had never believed the stories. Had never felt anything but peace on the fairy hill. But the apparition forming before her was as real as the fear now choking her throat.

Nadia backed up, one hand grasping at the table for support. It caught the edge of her plate, knocking it off the table. Shards of porcelain showered her feet, but Nadia kept her gaze fixed on the ghostly woman now stirring a pot on the stove.

And then the apparition looked over its shoulder and met Nadia's eyes.

Nadia screamed, though her throat wouldn't let it pass. She whirled to find two more beings ghosting about their chores. One stepped toward her, its hand outstretched.

Nadia gulped, forcing air into her frozen lungs, and bolted from the kitchen.

Everywhere she turned, Nadia encountered apparitions. She pulled her arms in tight and hurtled down the hall to the foyer. Guards now loomed on either side of the heavy doors. Her one chance of safety lay beyond the half-formed men with pikes. If she could get past them, Uro would protect her.

Nadia gathered her courage and ran. There was a flash of movement from the guards, but in an instant, she was through the door. She sprinted down the stairs. And then skidded to a stop. The courtyard was a hive of ghostly activity.

Her knees buckled. She hit the cobblestones and then scrambled backwards toward the walls of the castle. Activity in the courtyard halted. Figures turned toward her.

A scream finally ripped from Nadia's throat. She flung her arms over her head and cowered against the wall. Any moment and those icy hands would be on her. Any moment, she'd feel the pain of her flesh being torn away. Anguished sobs gurgled in her throat.

But the hands did not come.

Her eyes and nose overflowed, mixing together and drenching her face. A cold triumph rose inside her heart. Nadia fell face first onto the stones, teeth chattering, body shaking. The icy fingers were already inside her, chilling her blood, spreading coldness farther with every pulse. Nadia covered her head with her arms and prayed for oblivion.

"Nadia." She felt the Lord scoop her up. Last night, she'd feared his hands, his body, but now she burrowed into his embrace, for there was safety in his arms. She kept her eyes tightly shut and listened for the voices and their reaction to her protector.

But they didn't come. She could hear the Lord mount the steps, the great doors open and shut, the echo of his footsteps in the hall, and then the mix of soft treads on carpet, sharp on marble as he carried her to her room.

He placed her on the chaise where she burst into tears again, overcome with having finally reached safety. There was the trickle of water being poured into a basin, and then the Lord returned. He gently cupped her face and began to wash the salt and grime from it. The ache in her chest blossomed again.

How long can he protect you? the voice whispered. *You're alone most of the time. They'll get you eventually. You'll be nothing but bits of bone and gore when he finally finds you.*

Nadia's gaze fell to the knife on the Lord's belt. It would hurt, but it would be quick. "Just kill me now," she whispered. "I'm going to die anyway. I've wanted to die. They'll get me in the end, tear me to shreds. So, please," she begged. "Just kill me now. I'll know it was done in mercy, not anger."

A thunderous expression entered the Lord's eyes, of such ferocity, that she shrank back. He bowed his head and turned away. "I'll let you get some rest. You've had a shock. We'll talk about this later."

He crossed the room, placing the cloth on the wash stand, before returning to tuck her in, just as he had done when she'd made the bed disappear. Once the curtains had been drawn, he departed, closing the door softly behind him.

Her heart still beat heavy in her chest, but there was something new in it. Hope. She had finally found hope. The Lord's blade would slide between her ribs and finally end her suffering.

The sound tore through her slumber, jerking her awake and readying her muscles for flight. Her brain had registered the click of her door opening and flown into a panic. One that was now easing with the familiar pattern of the Lord's footsteps. Sitting up, she saw that he carried a luncheon tray.

"Last meal?" she asked.

The Lord scowled. "Not funny, Nadia."

"I wasn't joking."

He hooked his foot around a small table and dragged it over, setting the tray on top, before sinking down next to her on the chaise and taking her hand. With his touch, a strange sensation prickled her skin. It was like the time she'd petted their fat orange cat, pushing its hair up instead of down. The fur had crackled, nipping at her fingers. But this was a hundred times more intense, stealing away her ability to move. The blood in her heart boiled and scratched at its container.

"What is the saying about sticks and stones?" he asked her.

Nadia's brow crinkled with her confusion, but she recited the children's rhyme. "Sticks and stones may break your bones, but words will never leave you alone."

"And they don't. Evil words are poisonous. Truly poisonous. They enter your ears and filter to your heart and take up residence, influencing your actions, repeating the awful things said to you, whispering lies of their own." Her heart vibrated and twisted with a snarl, sending an urge to attack down every nerve, but the Lord's hold kept her frozen. "You are ill, Nadia, because you have been poisoned. I have never seen anyone before whose heart was so filled. Usually, people kill themselves long before they've received this much."

"I tried," Nadia confessed. "I wanted to. Oh, I wanted to. But I was afraid it wouldn't work."

"And so you rejoiced when Uro came. And rejoiced when you were chosen. And had I been more observant, I would have realized..." He trailed off. "If I hadn't seen—" His hand tightened around hers, the pressure becoming almost painful.

"A thousand years has both softened me, yet also made me callous. I have not always been kind to you. Do you know when I had the first clue that you were this ill?" Nadia shook her head. "Everyone who comes to me has some poison in their heart, but with you I didn't realize, even though I could smell it from the very first, could tell that you were no sacrifice, I didn't have a clue until you wore the simple dress to dinner.

No woman before you had been able to resist the exquisite gowns in the wardrobe. I thought you were being obstinate, and when I asked you about it, you said—"

"There was no one to help me." Her cheeks heated as she remembered what came next. "And then you offered to dress me."

A wistful smile brightened his face as the Lord raised his shoulders in a shrug. "One can always wish. Though," he quickly added. "I had no idea how that hurt you, how it called up all the other attempts to take you by force. But it did make me wonder why either my staff—"

Air whooshed, drawing deeply into Nadia's lungs. She would have jumped up and ran if the Lord's grasp hadn't kept her immobile.

"Yes, I have a staff. And you are finally seeing them today."

"They weren't—?" The words refused to budge. What if she were wrong and saying it aloud would make it real?

"Ghosts?" he finished for her. "No."

"I thought of the stories people tell about the fairy fort, spirits who eat you alive," she explained.

"Oh, Nadia," he said with a chuckle. "If that were to be your fate, you would have already met it with all the time you spent camped out on their doorstep." He shook his head, still marveling at her words. "You are truly amazing. There aren't many the fairies take under their protection."

"You did say they were real."

"And just as vicious as the stories imply. Though if you've found their favor, they can be useful. Just ask any member of Clan MacLeod."

"So the people here...?"

The Lord gave her an encouraging smile. "Remember the bed?"

He tilted his head, a gesture he often used to nudge her down some train of thought. Her eyes widened. "I made them disappear?"

His lips turned down in sympathy. "Just as you did not want the bed, you did not want the people."

"But it was days before I made the bed disappear," she argued.

"But you so wanted to be alone that, from the moment you alit here, you had already sent them away."

Her brow was beginning to ache from the frown that had etched there. "So you've been without a staff this whole time?"

His laughter rang through the room. "They have not been invisible to me. You had the power to remove the bed but not the people. Not even I have that kind of magic."

"So why did I start seeing them today?"

The Lord bit back a smile. "I did tell you that when you were healthy enough, the whole castle would know."

Embarrassment washed over her. Nadia's cheeks burned. They'd been there the whole time, watching her. Oh, my God. The cake. The bulbs. The shoes. The running screaming from the castle today.

The Lord gave her hand a gentle squeeze. "My staff would not laugh at you, but the poison in your heart would have you believe it so."

Nadia tried to pick through the pieces and put them into a picture she could understand. "So I'm ill because I've been poisoned?"

"Yes."

She had heard about the remedies for poisoning. Sometimes, it could be lanced and drained like a fresh snake or spider bite. But her wounds were years, decades old, continually topped up fresh. Some poisons had an antidote. Though if that were the case, she was sure the Lord would have already given it to her. Some just had to run their course, waiting until the worst of the damage had been done and then hope for some kind of recovery.

"Is there a cure?" Nadia asked.

"Yes." The word was an affirmation, but it rasped in his throat.

Much like the undulation in her heart. The muscle twisted and thumped as though it had been filled with a mass of roiling snakes. Nadia grimaced and pressed her free hand over it.

The Lord tilted her toward him and placed his lips on her forehead. They burned against her skin but calmed the snarling mass inside her. His forehead tipped to meet hers.

"When you're stronger, it will need to be drained or the voices will always rule your life, seek your death."

The poison growled like a caged dog, unable to lash out with anything but its voice.

"Will it hurt?" Nadia asked.

"Oh, yes," the Lord said. "The poison never willingly leaves."

The Lord insisted that Nadia eat something and then tucked her up again on the chaise. He brushed a stray lock of hair from her eyes and took his leave, promising to check on her later.

With her ear pressed into the pillow, Nadia could hear her blood swish, pushed through her veins with every heartbeat. It sounded thin and fragile compared to the steady thumps of the Lord's she'd heard while crushed against his chest. She blinked against the tears that rose with the realization. He had rescued her from a situation of her own making.

No, corrected the other voice, the kinder one. *From the fear that sought to enslave you again.*

The poison in her heart still slithered around, but more like a snake returning to its resting place.

She had never thought much about war, but it occurred to her that she was stuck in the middle of one—the poison fighting to keep her, the Lord fighting to free her. The idea made her feel both very small and insignificant and yet, at the same time, very valuable.

Nadia managed another nap. When she rose, she dressed her hair and then crossed to the bank of wardrobes to choose a new gown to wear for dinner. The one she had on had become hopelessly wrinkled.

She paused and gathered her courage in front of the one that held the most exquisite gowns. Blowing out a slow breath, she opened its door. Satin and silk and lace hung in shimmering folds. She reached out a hand, daring to touch them. Soon, she might have someone other than the Lord to lace her into them. Though they still seemed too fine for someone like her.

She shut the door and opened her usual wardrobe. The Arabian dress hung there, an orchid among the lilies. In its own way, it was far more beautiful than the untouched ballgowns. Her fingers traced the embroidery. Unlike the fancier dresses, she had actually worn it. And been served like a princess.

The memory of the previous night filled her with courage. Her hand went to a dress dyed the full green of summer, everything growing and strong. The color had sung to her, begging to be worn, but Nadia had left it alone, her ears filling with Cook's superstition every time she'd considered wearing it.

Green's all fine and dandy, but it doesn't last. It withers too quickly and turns to dust. Mother Nature like to keep it for herself and claims them that wears it, just like the leaves in the fall.

Nadia slid it off the hanger. Enough of listening to voices and fears and superstitions. Tonight, she was going to put on summer and grasp for the feeling of sun on her face. Be the growing thing made strong.

"Ready?" the Lord asked.

Nadia slid a piece of paper into her book and set it aside. She exhaled slowly and smoothed her skirts.

"They're not going to be hiding," he warned her.

"What if I've made them disappear again?" she asked.

"Then you'll just have to wish to see them." He held out his hand.

She had been so afraid of his hands only yesterday. But after the way they had calmed her, had tamed the poison that seemed to have developed a life of its own, she was willing to risk the other ways his hands made her feel. The poison in her heart snarled before slinking away to some tucked up corner.

She curled her fingers around his, trembling at the sensation. It was as if she had grasped living steel, a sword come to life yet wrapped in flesh and very much alive. He gave her hand a gentle squeeze. "They just want the best for you."

Nadia nodded and followed him out the door.

A foggy shape of a maid, her hands upturned, holding a stack of linen, stood pressed against the wall a short way down. Nadia faltered. The specter was making sure to stay well away from her. How many times had she passed people and they'd backed out of her way? Nadia remembered the brush against her shoulder and how she'd jumped in fright.

Of course, they did. They were trying not to frighten her.

And they had been exceedingly successful. She'd had no idea they were there until this morning. Nadia managed to give the girl a shy smile as she passed by. The sympathy in the specter's eyes caused prickles of a different sort inside her heart.

All along the halls, they passed people who regarded her kindly. She was so distracted, busy watching them, that she nearly bumped into the Lord when he stopped. "I thought you'd feel less on display here," he said, pushing open the door to his private dining room.

She had thought she wanted to practice, to get used to the ghostly presence of the others, but tension eased from her shoulders as she stepped in. No footmen to watch her every move.

As they had been. All along.

Nadia only just stopped herself from grabbing at the Lord with her other hand. His staff had been there the whole time, watching her clumsy attempts, a pig at the dining table. She had been afraid of what the Lord had thought of her, and yet she'd had an audience for every pathetic performance: at the table, in the kitchen, probably even her room. Had she known they were watching, she might have found the courage to drop herself over the edge.

"Thank you," she said, grateful for the privacy he offered.

The food was simple, familiar fare, so unlike last night's meal. Had it really only been twenty-four hours? The soup was spring pea, imported from somewhere for the late March weather was not yet conducive to planting. The main course was a simple lamb roast flavored with sage and thyme.

Amidst the safety and familiarity of the room, Nadia gathered her courage. A question had been gnawing away at the back of her mind for a while; unspoken, unrealized, but there.

"When I'm cured, when you've drained the poison, what then? And don't say I get my 'happily ever after.'"

The Lord wiped his mouth on his napkin. "Always in such a hurry." He took his wine and drank as she sat impatiently awaiting his answer. With exaggerated care, he set his glass down, his gaze fixed on it, a wry smile tight on his face. "Had you known you were not alone with me here, what would you have done? Had you known that your heart was filled with poison, what would you have done?" Nadia shrank back in her seat. The Lord lifted his gaze, fixing his eyes on her, serious and scolding. His voice, however, was indulgent. "You would not have survived. I keep telling you, the truth can kill you if you're not ready for it."

Not ready for it. "So things are going to get worse?" The idea filled her with dread.

The Lord gave a wavering hum. "A matter of perspective. Are you going to end up face down on the floor again the next time you see one of my staff?"

Nadia shifted uncomfortably, a burn rising on her cheeks. "No. But I didn't know they were there."

"Do you now welcome or fear their presence?"

She knew the answer should be "welcome," but years of pain, years of being taunted by everyone she had ever met made the truth something else. The Lord continued when she didn't answer.

"You know what you need to do next."

"Drain the poison," she answered. Though what would that entail? And how badly would it hurt?

"That's the thing to be focused on."

"How will I know when it's time?" Nadia asked.

"The people will be solid. You will ask me to drain it."

Nadia touched her fingertips to the table. "What if I asked you to drain it now?"

The Lord inhaled deeply, and the poison unfurled in panic. Tiny needles like kitten claws pierced her heart, digging in. The Lord pulled at his lips as he thought.

With a heavy exhale, his hand fell away. "I tell you this, not to scare you, but because you asked for the truth. Were I to attempt to drain the poison tonight, or even next week...I doubt that you would survive."

The pinpricks squeezed once more and then let go, satisfied they were safe for a while longer.

Having been given a taste of what was to come, Nadia nodded an acknowledgement and let her gaze fall to her empty plate. The Lord lifted it from the table.

"I think it's time for dessert." He set their dinner plates on the serving table and raised the last silver dome. "Ah. Cook has prepared floating island. Would you like one island or two?"

Nadia flinched with the reminder of the woman who had beaten her. She back a shudder. "One," she managed to say, while her mind skipped ahead to breakfast where there would literally and figuratively be ghosts to face.

He set a small bowl filled with vanilla crème and a poached meringue island drizzled with caramel sauce in front of her. Nadia picked up her spoon and sliced off one creamy end from the island.

"So my goal is to make the people solid?"

With his dessert in his hand, the Lord replaced the cover and returned to his seat. He offered Nadia a tight smile. "Sounds simple enough."

Nadia stuffed the first bite into her mouth. The sweet silkiness wasn't enough to dispel the unfinished sentence.

But it's not.

eighteen

Nadia stared into her open wardrobe with no real impetus to get dressed. Breakfast awaited. Downstairs. Where there'd now be a kitchen staff. Yes, they'd always been there, but she hadn't *known* that. She'd been able to eat breakfast in peace.

A gasp tore from her chest, and she beat her head against the door. *Stupid, stupid, stupid!* The magic kitchen that had so impressed her wasn't magic. It was staffed. They'd witnessed her every foible, watched as she nearly set the kitchen on fire, watched as she stood in amusement when the dishes disappeared.

Because they'd picked them up.

Her stomach grumbled its complaint at her delay. With a resigned huff, she pulled out the first thing she touched, not bothering to see what it was.

Three ghostly shapes met her. One stood at the opposite end of the table from her breakfast, chopping vegetables; another

186

at a counter, measuring out ingredients; the third stirred a pot simmering on the stove.

Shyness came over her. Nadia dipped her head as she slid onto her usual stool. The girl on the end smiled at her over her chopping. "Thank you," Nadia said. "For all the breakfasts. And...and I'm sorry about the messes I created."

No problem, the girl mouthed wordlessly.

Nadia forced her faltering smile to stay in place. She had given them form, such as it was, but not voice. Words of reprimand echoed in her ears, half-formed but still with the power to accuse, and her eyes stung with them. Hiding her discomfort behind a sudden interest in her tea, Nadia gently blew on it before raising it to her lips.

She didn't linger over her breakfast of buttered toast and thinly sliced meats, gathering up her dishes as soon as she'd placed the last bite in her mouth and placing them in the sink. With a heartfelt, "Thank you," she all but raced for the comforting solitude of the library and offered up a prayer that it would be as empty as before.

Forms smiled, bobbed, and bowed to her as the passed through the halls. At the door to the library, she paused, one hand on the knob, took a bracing breath, and pushed it open.

Dust motes swirled through the air that was crisp with the papery smell of the tomes. Silence greeted her in the library. Silence, dust, bookshelves, and...

Nothing else.

Releasing the breath she'd been holding, Nadia stepped in.

Wandering the library, Nadia searched for something to get lost in. She finally pulled a volume of local geography from its place. Local, at least, where she had come from. The castle could be anywhere. Nadia roamed the alcoves, looking for a more comfortable place to read than the study table. She had no desire to venture through the halls to her morning room.

She came across the Lord's reading nook and found it empty. Even the book of poetry had gone from its table. Nadia lowered herself into the space, half expecting lightning to strike her. The cushions cradled around her, but punishment didn't follow. Tucking her feet underneath her, she began to read. And read. And stumbled across some information her mind couldn't quite believe. There was no way it was true. She would have to ask the Lord when he met her for her lesson.

Lunch came, and still she sat. Yes, she was hiding. And hungry. "You've gone soft," she argued with her growly stomach, giving it a poke. "Insisting now on three square meals a day. You did just fine on two meager offerings not that long ago." She would have to venture back out to dress for dinner and that would be soon enough.

But the Lord didn't come. Nadia drummed her fingers on the table. He was probably in his study. Highly distracted. And moody.

But her question...

He'd sent things flying the last time he'd been in his study. And even at dinner two nights ago. But far from frightening her, his displays of anger strangely emboldened her.

Nadia slipped her feet back into her shoes. Pausing at the library door, she stopped and gathered a bracing breath. Tense as a cat, she stepped out into the hall. The book clutched against her chest acted as a shield as she passed the gray forms in the hall, returning their nods of greeting. Around corner after corner until she passed the suit of armor, long since rehung, and stopped in front of the door the Lord had come out of.

Nadia raised her hand and knocked.

"Enter."

She blew out a breath and followed his command.

The Lord stood, bent over a large basin. His hands grasped the wooden frame that held it. Surprise crossed his face when he looked up.

"Nadia."

"Pardon the intrusion," she said, her gaze darting from him to the door and back again. The Lord waved a hand over the basin, confirming her folly. She had interrupted. She really should not be here. What had she thought by coming? "I waited for you and then found...my questions wouldn't wait," she finished somewhat lamely.

He stepped from behind the bowl and gestured to a small sofa. "My apologies. Why don't you show me what was so important."

Nadia took a seat and tried to squish herself into the corner. There really wasn't much room. The Lord's thigh came to rest against hers as he sat. Its warmth and tingle added to her distraction.

"I...um...was curious if we were, or at least my country was, really this close to the sea? Before I came here," she breathed as the tingle continued down her leg.

The Lord's arm brushed against her as he took the book. Her heart began to pound in a way that was not unpleasant.

"Still looking for Linette?" he asked. His eyes flashed with mirth. Nadia responded with a tight nod, her cheeks heating.

Opening the book, he laid it on top of their two legs and traced the boundary of her country. "You were here. And—" He slid his finger along the illustration to the blue patch. "The sea is here. A distance of about thirty miles. Did you never get gulls during plowing?"

Nadia shook her head, unable to speak. Her leg burned from the path the Lord's finger had traced. It was as if it he had reached through the paper to her flesh.

An indulgent smile lit his face. "No matter. Sometimes they will venture that far inland in search of easy food." He glanced back at the illustration and sighed. His expression trembled, twisting with a pain he sought to hide from her.

Nadia mentally kicked herself. The one thing he couldn't have, the one thing he missed most of all, was the one thing she couldn't leave alone.

He closed the book with a soft *whump* and rose from his seat, going over to a set of shelves that held an assortment of boxes and strange contraptions. He picked up one of the boxes and returned to his seat.

The box had probably once been white but was now ivory with age. Nadia had seen a similar one, years ago when Elsbeth had turned thirteen. All of the servants had been lined up to watch their young mistress be showered with presents celebrating such a milestone. Lord Braemoor had presented his daughter with a similar box. Inside it had been a necklace of sapphire. Elsbeth had marveled at the gift as her father recited the ancient poem:

> *A maiden born when September leaves*
> *Are rustling in September's breeze,*
> *A sapphire on her brow should bind*
> *'Twill cure diseases of the mind.*

"The necklace now," Lord Braemoor had proclaimed. "The circlet when you're sixteen, and earrings when you're eighteen."

The Lord opened the lid and drew out a necklace of pearls like fat, white peas on a string. He took Nadia's hand and pooled them into her palm. Smooth and cold, they warmed quickly to her touch.

"The treasure of the sea." He closed Nadia's hand around them. "Do you know how pearls are formed?" She shook her head. "A grain of sand enters the oyster's shell. An ever-present danger when that's where it makes its bed. If that grain gets trapped between the animal and its shell, which is very rare, it irritates the oyster. To protect itself, the animal begins to coat the irritant with nacre, the same substance with which the oyster lines its shell. Over time, the irritant is encased and a pearl forms. They oyster will continue to add layers over its lifetime. What was once something that caused pain is transformed into something beautiful, valuable."

The Lord removed his hand from hers. "They are yours."

Her eyes widened. Nadia's gaze traveled from the pearls to the Lord's face. "I can't—"

"Yes, you can. They were once—" The Lord broke off. His throat worked as he wrestled with an emotion. His jaw still trembled, and his voice was scratchy when he continued. "They were once worn by someone who cherished them very much. I think you will do the same."

He opened Nadia's hand again, lifted them from her palm, and laid them around her neck. The long strand came nearly to her navel. Nadia slid her fingers along the pearls, marveling at their hardness and iridescence. Linette could not have wished for more. Legs to dance with, a voice to sing with, a handsome—

Nadia clamped down on the thought before it could go any further. "Thank you," she said. "I shall treasure them."

Despite her promise, Nadia found it difficult to truly love the gift. She could guess who the pearls had once belonged to, and she was not a worthy recipient of them. Besides, who would the Lord see when she wore them? Her, Nadia, or the woman from the poem? Not to mention that the bestowing of them had not been premeditated. Would the Lord come to regret his hasty decision?

Standing in front of her open wardrobe, Nadia debated what to wear for dinner. The white dress—that she had never worn for fear of inflicting food stains on it—which would camouflage the pearls? Or the midnight blue one which would highlight his gift?

Resigned, she pulled the blue from its hanger. If the Lord regretted his rashness, it would be better to have it known now.

She wrapped the strand twice around her neck to keep it from trailing into her food and put her hair up with simple silver pins. As she stared at her reflection in the mirror, Nadia wondered about the last woman to wear the pearls. What did she look like?

The poison woke and stretched. *You're the image of his lost love,* it whispered. *Piece by piece he's making you into her. How many times has he given them away? How many times has he taken them from the neck of a corpse and put them back until the next girl comes? That happily ever after you're looking for comes with the release unto death!*

It felt like the truth. And yet—

She had listened to her fear and spoiled the special dinner. Nadia pressed her hand against the pearls. Did she dare dream? Did she dare believe that the gift meant something, that the poison was wrong and the Lord saw her and not his lost beloved?

What's your name? the other voice whispered.

The piece of her heart that still felt like it belonged to her caught. She was not tempted to answer, "Nothing." But she could not give voice to the other meaning, the one the Lord liked to use. She could, however, stretch herself and trust. She would trust today. She would trust tonight.

And watch to see if the fear was right.

She waited for the Lord to call for her, but he never came. A one-night respite from the dining room was all he was going to give her, it seemed. Fearing the faint sound of a half-knock and having to face a spectral servant sent to fetch her, Nadia left on her own.

The halls were more alive than they'd been earlier. Or maybe that was because the figures had ceased stepping out of her way and simply carried on with their tasks, greeting her with a smile or nod as they passed.

Two footmen stood on duty in the dining room. The Lord rose when she entered and pushed her chair in as before. His gaze fell to the necklace. Nadia fingered it.

"I wasn't sure how she wore it." Nadia lifted a nervous smile. "But I thought this way should keep them out of the soup."

"She?" His eyebrow hooked in question.

"The one who last wore these pearls. Unless you're telling me they belonged to a man."

An amused smirk rose on his face. "No. And she wore them many ways." A faraway light entered his eyes. "Sometimes unclasped and woven into her hair." He shivered. His focus snapped back to the present. "But you may wear them any way you wish, for they are now yours. Out of the soup is always a good option."

Nadia spooned the mock turtle soup away from her as the Lord had shown. *Onto the cloth is always better than into one's lap.* The Lord's cook had an even hand with the sherry. There was just a hint of it in the air and on the tongue. Of course, sherry had been Lady Margaret and Lord Braemoor's favorite tipple, and Cook's version had always smelled more like veal stewed in wine.

As she ate, Nadia watched the footmen out of the corner of her eye, her nerves wound like a tightly coiled spring. When she finally put her spoon down, one sprang forward to remove the dish. Nadia gasped through her nose and gritted her teeth, trying to hold back a whimper. The figure froze.

The Lord wiped his mouth on his napkin and lifted her bowl away. He handed it to the footman with a murmured, "Thank you."

Nadia held back a shudder. The shadowy figures were worse than real people.

They are real people, a dual voice said inside her head with the echoing quality that comes from two voices speaking as one. *You've just made them so.* One voice sought to accuse, the other to enlighten.

The Lord topped off Nadia's wine and pushed it toward her, his expression firm and unwavering. He was not going to let her hide. She took the glass, anger blossoming inside her. She wanted to make them disappear again, just to spite him. But he wouldn't know they'd gone again unless she told him.

She drank deep, hoping the alcohol would numb her, obliviate the way the apparitions made her skin crawl, blind her to the fact that the Lord had ceased to be gentle and now seemed intent on schooling her.

Yes, too much truth was a dangerous thing. She knew what she needed to do. And hated the Lord for it.

In rebellion, Nadia stayed in bed long after the sun rose. But, as with most rebellions, practical needs soon got in the way of the cause. Her bladder was the first to break ranks, causing her to throw back the covers and rise to meet its demands. Her stomach deserted two hours later. She poked at it with a finger, but when her head began to ache and her hands began to shake, she finally dressed.

Reaching out her hand to turn the doorknob proved to be the most difficult part of the venture. Once in the hall, Nadia did her best to act as if the half-formed figures didn't bother her. At some point, they'd be solid, and she wanted to have caused as little offense as possible.

In the kitchen, she found the cook and maids at work rolling out pie crust and snipping vegetables. Under the long harvest table sat a bucket of water filled with live shells. Their fleshy lips were dotted with round, black things that gave the appearance of eyes, like those on a spider. A shiver traced its way down her spine. She sincerely hoped they were for Uro's dinner, though the salt smell rising from the bucket told her they were from the sea and thus likely meant for the Lord and, by extension, her.

The women smiled and kept at their work. Their bustle was familiar, and Nadia found she could ignore their half-form as long as she kept her eyes focused on her plate.

She put her empty dishes into the sink and murmured a sheepish "thank you" before leaving.

Continuing her protest, she retreated to her morning room instead of the library, irritated but not surprised when the Lord knocked on the door an hour later. Grudgingly, she called out, "Enter."

"Yesterday you couldn't wait, tracked me down in my study. Yet, today you play the truant." An amused smile played on the Lord's face.

Nadia feigned interest in her book. "Yesterday, I had questions. Today, I have none."

The Lord pulled a chair over and settled it next to her window seat. "Perhaps I have some of my own." He sat, effectively blocking off any escape.

"Ask away," she said, forcing her eyes to stay on the page.

He reached over and closed her book, trapping her finger inside. "You've been avoiding my staff."

"That's a question?" Nadia tried to pull her finger from the book.

"Avoidance rarely solves a problem."

Nadia swallowed. She tried to gather her courage, to be able to tell him without sounding ridiculous or, even worse, give life to the thing that scared her. Uttering nightmares aloud either made them real or you foolish.

"Nadia, tell me."

Her throat refused to open at first. Her fear boiled away until tears clouded her vision. But the Lord's patient presence wasn't going anywhere.

"I'm afraid of them," she finally whispered, staring at her knees.

"What scares you?"

"That I can't make them real," she said, and clamped down on the voices that renewed their protest from this morning. "That if I do..." She swallowed. "If I do..." Nadia closed her eyes. How could she confess she'd changed so little?

"They'll be like everyone else you've ever known?"

The pain rose, pricking at her eyelids until it overwhelmed her.

"Do you really think I'd allow them to treat you so?" he asked, as the proof of her belief dripped down her cheeks.

When she didn't answer, he sighed. "Do you know what it is to be brave?" The question pulled her attention from her panic, but she didn't move, didn't answer. "It's not *not* being afraid, for fear is useful. It warns you when there is danger. Being brave is doing something even though you *are* afraid.

"I know you fear a repetition of the past. The past is the best indicator of the future. And you, Nadia, equate people with pain, especially servants in a house. You are expecting to be abused and ridiculed because that is what has always happened. That will not happen here." He paused a moment and then chuckled. "Would the vengeful Lord who looses his dragon on tormentors really permit such behavior inside his house?" Nadia raised a timid smile and shook her head. "Then be brave."

"I don't think I can without you," she confessed, hating herself for saying it. She did not want to want him, to need him. She wasn't sure she really trusted him, and yet—

And yet...

Part of her wanted to believe the fairytale. That he *was* the prince. Not her Prince Charming, but her champion. With a fearsome dragon instead of a white steed. She wanted that fairytale more than anything else.

And it was too good to be true. Which meant it wasn't true. Which meant—

The Lord released Nadia's book and, with it, her finger. She looked up at him.

"Do you think I'm going anywhere?" he asked.

She shook her head, still unable to share the last of her fears.

But he could read it on her face. The Lord gave her a sad smile. "Well then. I will leave you until dinner. Do you want me to collect you?"

After a quick debate, she decided no. She did not want to be gripping the Lord's hand all the way down the halls. It would be enough to have his presence at dinner. "As long as you serve me," she said, imagining the footmen leaning over her. Not something she wanted even if they were solid. Then added, "Like you've always done," lest he think her presumptive, asking a god to wait on her.

But he merely smiled. "With pleasure."

nineteen

Nadia chose the same gown for dinner. She'd held the pearls up to the other six gowns she could get into on her own, but none of them had felt right. She could have left the pearls behind, but he had wanted her to wear them and so she did. In exactly the same way she had worn them the night before. She had played with them in her hair before she put it up, just to see why the previous owner may have preferred them that way, but then wrapped them around her neck in the double strand for the soup still threatened, and, in the end, she didn't want to draw attention to them. Have them noticed, yes. But only in that their absence would have made it greater.

Shaking the tension from her hands, Nadia blew out a breath. Then she turned the handle of the door and went out to face her doom.

Didn't you want to be Elsbeth? The kinder voice asked. Nadia tried to shut it out. The voice wasn't helping. Elsbeth would have glided through the halls unseeing. She, on the other hand, wanted to be unseen. Elsbeth wouldn't have cared what the staff thought of her; she could so easily have them dismissed. Nadia feared what the staff thought of her.

*Because...*prompted the voice.

Nadia clenched her hands.

*Because...*it whispered from the corner of her mind she'd shoved it into.

"Because you don't matter," she whispered to the voice. She was not going to go all reflective and show up with tearstains on her face.

At last, it fell silent.

Nadia found that if she remained focused on her goal—the dining room—that she barely noticed the people she passed in the halls and on the stairs. They had a job to do and so did she.

The Lord stood when she entered and helped her into her seat. "No white knuckles, I see," he said with a twist of his lips.

"Are you trying to torment me?" she asked.

He poured her wine. "Reward your success." The footmen in light green livery stood silently on either end of the serving table.

The Lord returned to his seat and passed Nadia the first course. Squares of bread no bigger than a snuff box had been smeared with what looked like cheese—some white, some pink—and topped with split chives and salmon roe that were meant to picture spring bulbs in flower.

"Your efforts should be blooming soon," the Lord said as she put a couple on her plate. "The daffodils are in bud, and the tulips are coming up nicely. The lilies, though, won't get their show until June."

"My pathetic efforts," Nadia said. She followed the Lord's example and picked one up with her fingers. The pink cheese proved to be a smoked salmon mixture and quite tasty.

"Your brilliant efforts," the Lord corrected. "Though Gregor was not happy at first that you'd hijacked his bulbs and his plans for them, he has since deemed your efforts 'not bad,' which is high praise from him." He offered her the tray of appetizers again which she declined with a shake of her head. "You should leave the books behind for a while and go look at them."

"I will," she said, but added it to the list of things she wanted to avoid.

The next morning, Nadia headed to the library in semi-defiance of the Lord's instructions. She had finished her latest book and was once again looking for something about the sea. The shellfish that had caused so many shivers viewed at the previous morning's breakfast had turned out to be quite delicious. Firm, yet tender and sweet, and covered in a light mustard sauce that made her drool again just thinking of it.

She wandered the section where Linette's tale was housed, coming across one entitled *The Sea King's Daughter*. A flip through the pages showed that this tale was different from Linette's. Nadia tucked it under her arm and turned to go. Then she spied the Lord's poetry book back on its familiar table.

Nadia fingered her throat. She shouldn't read the book. They were the Lord's private thoughts.

But don't you deserve to know if you're her? If he's making you into her?

Nadia's stomach turned. If he was molding her into his lost beloved, she had a right to know.

She snatched up the book and leafed through it. The ink and handwriting changed over time. As she neared the end of the book, having read only a word or two per page, she found the confirmation she'd only half-consciously sought. The hand that had scratched these lines was indeed the Lord's. Nadia scanned the poem on that page and sank to the floor with what she read.

My beloved's heart lies in a thousand pieces
Torn asunder by whispered lies.
Yet I rejoice that it is broken
For if it is broken, it can be mended.
If it had simply gone
She could not love again.

Nadia sat in stunned silence, the book open on her lap. The Lord had written these words. Recently, too, for there were only a few more pages in the book. The poem looked just like those he'd penned for her to copy to practice her handwriting. But it couldn't be about her. Could it?

Once more, she read the lines. His beloved had a broken heart. She didn't. Hers was filled with poison and still whole.

Unless draining would break it.

Her finger traced the next line. *For if it is broken, it can be mended.*

The puzzle twisted in her brain. It couldn't be about her for she had never loved anyone. And yet...yet...he'd lost his beloved a thousand years ago. Nadia's fingers crept to her neck again, reaching for the pearls that weren't there.

Had the voice been right? Had he done this time and time again, finding a new beloved with each new girl?

Not so beloved. Only desired.

And then written up, a document of his triumph.

Nadia snapped the book shut and tossed it back on the table. She wiped her hands on her skirt, trying remove the feeling that she'd been touching something nasty. Her stomach twisted with the thought of someone immortalizing their conquests in poetry.

Lies...

The war in her head started up again.

Nadia picked up the book she came for and left. The library was not a place of peace and calm today.

Disappointment settled over her like a wet cloak. She found no interest in the musician in her story and eventually laid the book down, taking to pacing the room instead. Her gaze kept drifting to the windows, dotted with moisture from the light, misting rain that had wrapped itself around the castle. With a sigh, Nadia opened the door to the wardrobe. She may as well have an actual soaking cloak to go with the phantom one.

The figures in the hall barely drew her attention, and the courtyard was blessedly empty. She gave a moment's pause to the notion of visiting Uro, but found that the thing that drew her most was the thing she had wanted least of all. Curiosity had grabbed her somewhere around her middle and drew her attention to the garden beds in which she'd labored in the fall. It managed to drown out, though not obliterate, the voice that whispered, *Foolish!*

Yes, she had certainly been that.

But, according to the Lord, her efforts were turning out to be not unpleasant. Nadia raised her hood against the mist and trod across the park's grass to the beds, her stockings soon soaked with the rain gathered and shared by the passing blades. Tall green stems rose from the earth. She recognized daffodil buds; thumb thick, their yellow blossoms visible beneath the confining green skin of the buds. Broad, cupped, hand-like leaves of tulips were also poking from the ground, as well as the fringed stems that would later hold lilies. The arrangement was disorganized but surprisingly cheerful.

And you didn't even know what you were doing, the kinder voice whispered. *You didn't know, yet you were willing to try.*

It felt like a gentle reprimand.

Nadia's gaze swept over the beds. She had been kicking herself for her efforts ever since the Lord had laughed at her about it that night.

The scene rose up in her memory. Nadia gasped as it played out in her head, this time with new understanding. The Lord had remarked on how she smelled of roses, looked at the wall—where the footmen stood!—and then laughed, saying how she must have needed it as she had spent the day in the garden. She'd thought it was because he found her efforts pathetic, but it was really because the footmen had informed him, and he'd been imagining his gardener's reaction. A grudging "not bad" that was apparently high praise, now that her efforts had come to fruition.

A tingle along the back of her neck gave her warning that she was not alone. Nadia turned, expecting to see the Lord striding toward her, but it was a ghostly figure. The gardener, she hazarded to guess from the way he was dressed.

He came alongside her and spoke, but she was unable to read the silent words on his lips. Nadia shook her head. "I'm sorry."

He gestured to the beds and then took her hand and patted it. His touch prickled, but not as much as the lump of regret that churned in her stomach. He seemed to be reassuring her it was fine.

Blinking back tears, she managed a "thank you." The man nodded his head, patted her hand again, and took his leave, touching a finger to his cap. Nadia hugged her arms around her. If he had forgiven her, then maybe she should forgive herself.

♪ ♪ ♪ ♫ ♪ ♪ ♪

There was no wine at her place setting at dinner. Instead, a cup of tea sat centered where her plate should have been. From the corner of her eye, Nadia followed the Lord as he took his seat. There had to be some hidden message in the cup. He raised his wine to his lips and watched her ponder.

Did it have something to do with the dress she'd found lying on her bed when she'd returned from her walk? No note, but its message had been implicit—*Wear this to dinner.*

The Lord set down his wine and steepled his fingers as Nadia's gaze flicked from the cup to him and back again. Neither his hands nor his face revealed a clue.

Nadia gave a soft, exasperated sigh. "I give up. Why the tea?"

"You are looking at the invention of the fabric you are wearing tonight."

Nadia fingered her dress but failed to make any connection.

"An empress sat by her favorite mulberry tree, enjoying a cup of tea with her ladies-in-waiting. A breeze ruffled the leaves, dislodging a cocoon from its anchorage. It fell into her cup. The hot tea dissolved the glue that held the worm's transformation place together. The empress noticed that the cocoon was actually a long thread and, when she lifted it from the tea, found that it was both strong and very soft, suitable for weaving." The Lord smirked. "I have now shared with you what was once China's most closely guarded secret. Once upon a time, not so very long ago, it was forbidden for the fabric to even leave the country. And it all began with a cup of tea and an accident.

"You berate yourself for your accidents, Nadia. But imagine if that highborn, high-ranking empress had cursed her misfortune and tossed her tea instead. You'd be—" The Lord reddened and bit his lips. He turned his gaze to his plate. When he'd regained a measure of control, he continued, gaze down, cheek twitching. "You'd be wearing cotton or wool instead of silk. Accidents are there to teach us things we've never dreamed of. And we learn more from our failures than we do anything else. Success is born from failure and the willingness to try again."

"So what's my happy accident?" Nadia asked.

"Landing here. You sought death but found life. You just have to want it."

Want them solid, Nadia heard. "And what do you want, my Lord?"

"You well, of course."

Well, you...of course.

Foolish, the poison hissed.

"And then what?" she asked, wading through the voices clamoring in her head.

"One step at a time," the Lord said.

Which neither answered her question nor brought her any comfort.

Nadia began the tale of the musician again. Sadko was so unlike her. Poor, true, but happy with his town and happy with his music. He had been taken to a place as foreign as this, offered everything, and had chosen to return instead.

He knew who he was, the kind voice whispered.

And who, or what, was she? No scullery maid, though she could certainly return to that if she had to. The repetition of the job had been burned into her soul. No man would have a woman for a secretary or a scribe, and most wouldn't want an educated wife, though she had no desire to be a wife or mother. In truth, she feared children, having her own children. A husband would treat her as others had, and she could handle that. But having a child or children who would turn on her...

She blinked back the tears that rose. So, if she did not live out the rest of her days in the castle, what would she want? It was time to start finally answering that question.

Nadia gathered her courage and approached one of the figures in the hall. "Is there a music room?" she asked. The ghostly shape of a footman nodded. "Would you mind showing it to me?"

The figure smiled and nodded then beckoned her to follow. He led her to a door she'd tried before but could never open.

"It doesn't work for me," she told him.

It was strange to watch the transparent hand of the footman grasp the brass handle and see the knob turn, almost of its own accord. He left it ajar.

"Thank you," she said. The man gave her a little bow and returned to his task.

She pushed the door fully open. A harpsichord sat by the window. Its dark ebony wood was inlaid with scrolling patterns of ivory. A gilded harp stood not far from it; its player's seat covered in red velvet. Simple spindle-backed chairs sat in front of music stands; lutes, violins, flutes, and recorders waiting upon the seats. A fine layer of dust covered everything.

Nadia trailed one hand along the strings of the harp. Sweet notes rose from it. She would have sat and truly tried it but feared tipping the enormous instrument toward her. The violins were too dusty to bring to her chin, and there was no way she was putting her mouth on the recorders or flutes. Lifting a lute, she blew the dust off. She plucked at the strings, but the tones they emitted were harsh. She set it back down.

There was only one instrument left. Nadia removed her handkerchief from her pocket and wiped down the keys to the harpsichord. A sheet of music still sat on its stand: "O Rosa Bella." Though she could read the title, she had no clue what to do with the dots and squiggles that were scattered across the lines on the page. She pushed one of the keys. A bright tinkling sound emanated from the plucked string. Using her index finger, Nadia pushed the keys in sequence for several notes. This was easier than the lute and safer than the harp.

Hesitating for just a moment, Nadia fanned out her fingers and tried to match them up with the keys. It was awkward, her hand resisting the strange use, but the sound from the harpsichord was not. It must be wonderful to be able to make music like Sadko with his twelve-stringed gusli in *The Sea King's Daughter*. She hummed along with notes her fingers played. Soon, with only a few missteps, she was able to pick out the tune "Though the Rose Out in the Rain."

An hour or longer she sat, at first astonished by the music she was able to make, then lost in time and space as she connected with and nearly became one with the instrument. Learning to read had been work. This was more like learning to ride, the few times her father had thrown her over the back of Nib, the horse that pulled their plow and wagon. Uncertain of each other at first, but slowly learning how to work together.

Eventually, Nadia drew her hands into her lap and sighed. Tonight at dinner, she would ask the Lord for music lessons, even though she suspected her teacher would be one of the ghostly figures, even though she wouldn't be able to speak to him, even though she'd have the strange, prickly feeling when he adjusted her hands to where they should be.

Nadia brushed the keys with her fingertips. She produced nothing by reading. She'd produced nothing since she'd come but burnt cake and hijacked bulbs.

The keys were soft and cool to her touch. If she learned music, then she'd have something to *do*.

It didn't occur to Nadia that she had totally missed the Lord that afternoon until she dressed for dinner. He'd always checked in before. She wrapped the pearls around her neck and wondered at his absence. Had he been absorbed in his work? She thought it had something to do with the basin she'd found him staring into that one time.

Nadia checked her hair and adjusted the pearls and went down to dinner. She half expected to find the dining room empty, but the Lord sat, drinking his wine, when she entered. He stood and assisted her with her chair.

"How was your day today?" he asked as he pushed it in, his breath warm on her neck.

"Very nice," she answered, distracted by the sensation. "Yours?"

"Productive. Informative."

Nadia sipped her wine and hoped it would quiet the butterflies that had strangely found a home in her stomach. She must be hungrier than she realized.

The Lord returned to his seat and watched her. As the seconds ticked by, she grew more and more uncomfortable. And hungry.

"Are you waiting for something, my Lord?" A stray thought shot through her, causing her heart to skip a beat. "Or someone?"

"No, no. I...just..." He gave her a tight smile. "Never mind. In its own time then." He held a round platter out to her. "Shaved asparagus and cheese?"

They had finished their dinner of veal cutlets in a sherry sauce and had started in on the meringue filled with berries and cream when Nadia finally gathered enough courage to ask for music lessons.

"I spent some time in the music room today," Nadia started.

"I know."

Nadia lifted her eyes from her dessert. "Y-y-you know?"

"You were quite entranced when I stopped by. Seemed best to let you be."

Had she really been so engrossed that she'd failed to notice him standing in the doorway?

"You asked me months ago what I'd like to be...and I think I'd like..." She faded off. It was too grand a dream to speak aloud. But she could ask for his help with the first step. "I'd like to learn to play. For real. I'd like music lessons."

"Even if you teacher isn't fully solid?" the Lord asked. Nadia nodded. "Have you solved the auditory problem yet?" Her eyebrows knit together in puzzlement. "Could you hear your teacher?" he amended.

Heat filled her cheeks. Nadia lowered her eyes. "No." She hadn't thought about that particular obstacle.

"Well," the Lord said kindly. "It will certainly give you motive to correct that."

They agreed that Nadia would continue to meet with the Lord for an hour in the afternoon and then spend as much of the remaining daylight hours as she wished in the music room.

She almost bolted that first lesson. Nadia arrived first and sat running her fingers along the keys. A frisson of awareness tightened the hairs on her arms. Looking up, her heart hit the floor. Standing in the doorway was a tall man with wild white hair that stood out at odd angles. His semi-transparent face was thin and severe. His eyes had a fierce, bird of prey glint to them.

Nadia gulped. Was this another of the Lord's trials by fire? Had he chosen the person he thought she'd find the most intimidating?

The man's sharp eyes took in the room. He snapped a handkerchief from his pocket and marched over to the chairs of instruments. Small clouds of dust rose as he flapped the cloth over the them. Not that his ministrations seemed to do much good.

The man sneezed and finally turned to her when she uttered the obligatory, "Bless you." He began some explanation or instruction she could neither hear nor read on his lips.

"I'm sorry," she said, interrupting him. The man scowled. "I don't know if the Lord told you about my situation. I—" But the words wouldn't come. "I—" Her head bowed. She twisted her fingers in her lap. "I...I..." Pulling in a deep breath, she tried again. "I am unable to see you properly or hear you. I understand if that is too big a challenge for you to have me as a student."

A shiver ran up her spine as the man took a seat beside her on the bench. She shivered again as he lifted her chin to meet his gaze. A smile had softened his severe countenance. He pointed at the music propped up on the harpsichord's stand.

Nadia shook her head. "No, I don't read music. I only learned to read after I came here. Words, that is." His eyes widened, and then he nodded, apparently impressed with her statement. "I don't know anything about music," she said. "Other than it's beautiful."

The man raised a finger and rose from the bench. Crossing the room, he opened a cupboard she hadn't noticed before. Its hinged door was perfectly concealed by the green and gilt scrollwork of the wall. He rummaged through and took from it a sheaf of paper and an inkpot and quill.

My name is Herr Montfort, he wrote at the top of one of the creamy sheets.

"Nice to meet you, mein Herr." Her eyes widened. Where had that greeting come from?

Shall we start at the beginning? Herr Montfort quickly sketched a diagram of the harpsichord keys. He pointed at one labeled "C" and lifted Nadia's hand, placing her thumb on the key represented in the diagram. He labeled four others and pointed from the paper to her fingers. He waved his hands, gesturing at her to play.

Nadia pressed the keys in sequence from her thumb to her pinky and back again, reining in a shiver when Herr Montfort lifted her palm so that her fingers curled. He smiled and nodded for her to continue.

And so they did. Herr Montfort worked on the way she held her hands and began to translate the keys to a piece of music that he scribbled notes on. At first, he communicated mainly through sign language, but Nadia encouraged him to talk.

"I'm supposed to be making you solid," she said. "Your appearance to me is more ghost-like."

Herr Montfort clapped a hand to his heart. He pulled a blank sheet to him and scribbled. *My dear lady, I am so sorry. Do I frighten you?*

"A little," Nadia admitted. "But it's of my own doing so I suppose I must live with it." Herr Montfort gave her a sad smile. "And please feel free to speak. Since I'm supposed to be working on that, too. How will I know if I've been successful if all you do is write? Though," she added sheepishly. "Please don't be offended if I scream. I fear it will be quite startling to hear a voice other than the Lord's after all these months."

His arm reached toward her, a movement that was arrested, and he laid it on the instrument instead. But his smile wrapped Nadia in an embrace that warmed her battered heart.

twenty

Spring warmed into early summer. Nadia could now hear Herr Montfort at her lessons, which were progressing well. His voice had, as well as those of the other servants, not come on all at once, as she'd feared, but gradually. One day, she thought she heard something as if from far away. As her ears searched for the source, she came to realize that the sound came from next to her. Herr Montfort had been giving her a demonstration on staccato. Her mouth dropped open in surprise when she perceived the noise as his instruction.

In her joy, she had placed a hand over his and announced, "I can hear you!" only to be clapped into an embrace when he shared her happiness. It had been uncomfortable for the first few moments until she realized that he truly wished her well.

As she relaxed into his embrace, the poison hissed. It was quieter these days, slyer. Whispering things so in such hushed tones that she nearly didn't notice. It didn't try to turn her against the others that inhabited the castle very often, but it always made sure she questioned the Lord's intentions, and she often thought that it spoke the truth.

Even with that, she found it more and more difficult, found herself falling for his "beguiling charms." As much as she feared his possible ulterior motives, part of her had begun to revel in the attention. He could play the handsome prince exceedingly well.

This early June morning, he'd called for her in her morning room. "Lesson outside today," he announced. "You spend too much time indoors."

Nadia slipped a bookmark between her pages and closed it. "You're one to talk, locked up in your study all day. I, at least, have windows."

"And this afternoon, we will have the sky. We are taking our luncheon al fresco and shall continue your studies out there." He waved a beckoning hand. "Come, come. Bring your book."

With a small sigh of exasperation, she followed.

The servants had laid out a picnic on a cloth spread in the shade of one of the towering maples in the park. The Lord tossed himself onto it and took up the bottle of wine, pulling the cork with practiced ease. Nadia sank down and arranged her skirts. He filled her glass and then handed it to her, swiping and munching on a handful of stuffed olives before pouring his own. The kitchen had supplied a selection of thinly sliced meats and cheese, buttered bread, vegetables, fruits, and small, iced cakes. She had helped Cook pack luncheons such as these, but had never dreamed she'd have the chance to partake in one.

The Lord wound an arm around one knee and handed Nadia an empty plate. "I'm curious, o resident expert. Does the staff hate or look forward to serving meals such as these?"

Nadia gave him a sideways glance before arranging an assortment of breads and meats on her plate. "Does it matter?"

He cracked a roguish smile. "Not in the least. Though I am wondering if they're praising or cursing me right now."

"Don't they always curse you?" she asked, assuming a coquettish smile.

The Lord threw back his head and laughed. "I suppose they do. Would you have cursed having to prepare a meal such as this?"

And there it was, her past slapped in her face. "Praise, I suppose," she said, steeling herself. "Ultimately they—the family—are less picky with picnic fare. As opposed to the soup or the birds having to be at just the right temperature."

He tossed an olive in the air and caught it with his mouth. "Do you miss it?"

The questions needled her, but she found they bothered her less asked out in the sunshine than in the confines of the library or dining room. "No," she said, releasing both her answer and her last bit of longing for her old life. While she now faced uncertainty, the familiar but abusive life she'd had at the manor house was not something she still longed for. They had saved her from the streets, but even the dogs had been treated better than her. "No," she answered again, and hardened her heart around a surprising pang of loss that welled up. She had once dreamed of a manor kitchen where she was treated with kindness, but that would never be.

"And how are the music lessons coming?" the Lord asked.

Nadia smiled. "You should know. Or was that some other figure in black lurking by the doorway as I played?"

"I always stop to listen to "Come Again, Sweet Love.'"

Her cheeks heated, much as they had when she'd read the lyrics of the song Herr Montfort had set her to the day before. They were credited to one John Dowland, though they could have come from the Lord's poetry book. "It is your castle. You may do as you wish."

The Lord cocked an eyebrow at her. "May I?"

The heat became a burn. Such teasing still somewhat frightened her, but, more concerning, had lately caused a thrill she found unsettling. Nadia averted her gaze. "You are a god, after all, and we are all in your power."

The Lord sighed. "You do so like to spoil my fun." He gathered things into a sandwich and reclined with it on the cloth. "You may read to me instead. The Sonnet from Amoretti."

Nadia wiped her fingers on a napkin and found the place in her book.

What guile is this, that those her golden tresses
She doth attire under a net of gold:
And with sly skill so cunningly them dresses
That which is gold or hair, may scarce be told?
Is it that men's frail eyes, which gaze too bold,
She may entangle in that golden snare;
And being caught may craftily enfold
Their weaker hearts, which are not yet well aware?

She lowered the book, though the poem continued. "Is love really so painful?"

The Lord took a moment in answering. "It can be, if it is false or unrequited." He cracked an eye open and looked at her. "Or withheld." He closed it again and inhaled, savoring the breeze or the memory, she couldn't tell. "But if it is true...if it is true, it is fire and wind and earth and sky. It is the scorching rays of the sun and the gentle light of the moon. It is the still quiet in the last hour before dawn. It is everything worth living for...and everything worth dying for." He swallowed. "Most people settle for just a taste of that, for generally love is surface deep and doesn't last. True love is rare, Nadia, and worth nearly any price."

He fell silent, unmoving, and so did she. Even the poison recognized the truth of his words and went still. She had always hoped that love would be protection, a caring great enough to keep someone from harm. But this, this was vast. And for the first time since she'd read those words all those months ago—*My beloved, how I yearn for your love*—she had an inkling of his loss. And to have been responsible for her death...

"And he gave me the pearls." In her surprise, she had uttered the words aloud. Whispered, but enough that the Lord cracked one eye open again.

"What was that?"

"I said, 'The folly of some girls.' Those who'd settle for less."

He shrugged and stared at the sky. "They don't have much choice, do they? Find a chap to keep them in hearth and home. Or go where their parents want them to."

"Because that works so well in Arabia," she said, her voice full of sarcasm.

"It's all about keeping the community strong. Did your Elsbeth choose love?"

Nadia grimaced. "No, nobles go for prestige—"

"Which is community," the Lord interjected.

"And I wouldn't know, for after Uro came, Lord Gilroy cancelled, and I wasn't around for what followed." Nadia paused. "So she didn't take my place?"

"Oops," the Lord said. "And no, I won't tell you who it was."

Nadia pondered a while longer. The Lord closed his eyes again, and the meadow fell silent but for birdsong and the occasional insect.

"Is that what saved them?" she asked, her thoughts coming back around to the missing princesses. "Aurora and Rapunzel and—"

"You ask too many questions," the Lord said. "If the Amoretti bothers you, find another. Find one that waxes poetic about the view."

Nadia sighed and flipped through the book. Most of them spoke about love, mainly one sided. "What is this great interest in poetry?" she asked.

"It is the best expression of the otherwise unrepresentable," he answered. "A portrait or painting *shows* you that person or place, but only poetry gives voice to the feelings that surround it. I, or the poet, could *tell* you about the person or place. But the emotion, that's left out of everything but poetry. And if you were to sit down and try to capture your feelings about something, you would naturally fall into poetry to do it."

"So poetry is emotion captured on a page?"

"Exactly."

Her face heated as she recalled other poems, ones the villagers would recite after ale had loosened their tongues. "But I've heard more...colorful rhymes that didn't seem to contain much emotion."

The Lord chuckled. "That is true, but they made you *feel* something. Poetry is all about feeling."

So the Lord wrote poetry to capture how he was feeling. Which again begged the question, *Who was his beloved with the broken heart since the one who'd worn the pearls was dead?* Nadia couldn't shake the suspicion that that someone was her.

For all the progress she seemed to be making, Nadia had a constant reminder, actually reminders, of what she hadn't accomplished. No matter how she tried, she didn't seem able to make the other occupants of the castle solid. She occasionally conversed with Nicolette, the maid who served her room, but shied away from asking her for help. The wardrobe that contained all the fine gowns that laced up the back mocked her for it, how it was all her fault that they were shut up in there, especially now that her original excuse for not wearing them had been solved.

She knew her excuses well, and, as much as she agreed that they were pathetic, she could not overcome the fear they were rooted in. They should have just been dresses, but they weren't, and even walking by the wardrobe caused so much discomfort that she would have avoided it completely if she could, much to the delight of the poison, which reveled in her distress.

One major change to her former routine that Nadia had consented to was taking breakfast in her room. It was not an acceptance that she deserved to be waited on, but an act of cowardice. Now that she was no longer alone in the kitchen, she could no longer pretend that she belonged there. She was of no use to the women and, if truth be told, feared what could come of trying to befriend them. So every morning, Nicolette brought her a tray, and every morning Nadia ate breakfast alone.

Now that the weather had warmed, she spent little time in her morning room, choosing instead to take her book and find a secluded place in the park in which to sit and read. Lunch, too, she now took elsewhere, in a small room off of the library, where she ate the meal brought to her by one of the footmen. Initially, she'd done it to save time, cutting out her trek from her room to the kitchen and back upstairs again. But once she'd discovered how blessedly peaceful the practice was—only the footman arrived and then departed—Nadia had made it an everyday ritual.

Besides, she spent the whole afternoon in the company of others. And dinner with the Lord. Though this evening, she could tell he was distracted. Troubled even. He avoided meeting her eyes and placed far more interest in his food than usual.

His avoidance strangely pained her. Had her actions with the staff finally offended him?

When she could stand it no longer, Nadia took a great gulp of wine for courage and asked. "My Lord, have I done something to cause you distress?"

His gaze flicked from her then back to his plate. "You? No."

Nadia poked at her salmon. If it wasn't her, what could it be? "They say a burden shared is halved."

His voiceless laugh was a whirlwind of air. "And when have you ever taken that advice?"

Nadia blinked and stabbed at the pink flesh of the salmon. "You're right, never. I'm sorry I intruded on your solitude."

With a groan, the Lord gritted his teeth. "I am burdened with knowledge that I don't know whether to share with you or not." The gaze he fixed her with was tired, weary. "I fear you would find it upsetting, and that it would be best if I didn't share it with you."

Nadia's breath caught in her throat. Did she want to know why he was reluctant to share it? "Is it about me?" she asked, fearing the answer.

The Lord's head bowed. "You could say that."

Nadia bit her lip. "Well. Then I guess you should tell me."

He raised his gaze to hers, the weight of his secret heavy in his eyes. "Would you truly open Pandora's box?"

What matter of evil could it be? "If I were not here, if Uro had never come, would this be something I would have learned?"

"Oh, yes," he answered. "And I fear your reaction will be the same."

She lifted her chin. "Then tell me."

His mouth disappeared in a thin line before he spoke. "Your mother is dead."

A hole opened up in the floor, ready to take her, chair and all. Or maybe it only felt that way. A part of her rejoiced that her mother was no longer there to ignore her. But mostly, she just felt loss. Loss for what had never been and now could never be. "How?"

"Childbirth."

Of course. Though it had been years since her mother had last been with child, having reached an age when such things were rare. "And the child?"

"Another son, farmed out to another family to nurse."

At least it wasn't a daughter to replace you, the poison whispered. *Though the timing is right.*

She tried to stuff the thought away, but it contained too much truth to go willingly. "Well, thank you for letting me know." She looked at the concern in the Lord's eyes and couldn't hold back the words that roiled up from her heart. "Did you fear that I'd think you caused it?"

"Frankly—yes."

"Are you really that much of an avenging angel?" Nadia asked.

He didn't answer. He didn't move. An icy chill collected in her heart and pushed out through her veins. She'd almost forgotten how deadly he was, how he had savored the idea of making her village suffer. How he'd boasted to her just months ago that he'd made them pay—the groom, her village.

And her mother.

Nadia reached for the now blurry shape of her wine glass. She missed, knocking it over and spilling the liquid across the table cloth, the stain blossoming like pooling blood.

A whine began at the back of her throat. The more she fought, the stronger it grew. Every hope she'd had as a child that her mother would take her in her arms and cuddle her, accept her; every hope that had been stuffed away, hidden away in the recesses of her heart, now screamed out their loss.

And proved too strong for her.

Her hands grasped at the air, unable to find any comfort to hold on to or way to stop the wail that had taken command of her voice and fought with her lungs for their mastery, leaving her breaths to come in great shaky gasps. Her grief became a thing of its own, taking control of her and leaving her helpless.

But not friendless.

With a scrape, the Lord's chair slid back. His arms came around her. Her heart gave one attempt at protest, to have her push aside this man who'd wanted her mother dead, but his arms offered the comfort hers never had. Nadia let herself get lost in them. The Lord didn't speak, just tucked her head under his chin and held her.

When she could sob no more, and her grief felt like an empty thing, a foolish thing, Nadia forced herself to ask. "Did you?"

"No," the Lord said, the word echoing in the ear she still had pressed against his throat.

She didn't believe his denial. "You said you'd make her pay."

"She already has."

"If not her death, then what did you do?"

The arms around her tightened, and the Lord gave a small sigh. "Haven't you had enough grief for one night?"

Nadia's stomach turned. "Tell me."

The Lord's arms loosened so that Nadia was all but sitting on her own. "Your brother George died putting out a barn fire the night you arrived."

"I see." Nadia swallowed, holding back anger and another wave of grief. George had always been her mother's favorite. And he had never let Nadia forget it.

The Lord removed his arms and rocked back on his feet to squat by Nadia's chair.

Part of her wanted to lash out at him and shower him with hatred for having harmed her family. But another unspoken but vaguely conscious part of her told her that family didn't do to each other what hers had done to her. True family cared for you, didn't harm you. That it was actions that made someone a mother or father or brother, not blood.

Nadia reached out an unseeing hand to steady herself. She flinched when the Lord's hands grasped her arms. "I thank you for dinner, but I'm not feeling well." She pushed herself up from the table. "Good night."

Only months of having walked the same route enabled Nadia to make her way back to her room unaided. She threw herself on the bed, fully dressed, and waited for a second round of grief to come and carry her away. But it never did. There was nothing but a hollow feeling in her heart and in her stomach. And, though her eyes were heavy with them, new tears didn't fall.

She lay her head on the pillow and watched the moon rise. The pillow was soft beneath her cheek, but her heart whispered to her that it was tainted, that she was being housed and fed by a murderer.

And you're thankful for him, it hissed. *So what kind of person does that make you?*

Nadia lifted her eyelids. The throw from the chaise held her legs firm. Someone, most likely Nicolette, had removed her shoes and placed it over her, but all her thrashing from her nightmares had transformed it from a cover into a noose.

In her dreams, her mother, distorted with anger and hate, had shouted at her, *Nobody wants you! Nobody loves you!* Her brother George had spat on her and called her, *Filth!* Her family had lined up and pushed her into the arms of the Lord, telling her that she was a fit prize for a murderer, for what other kind of man would have her?

And yet, in the light of day, it was his arms she remembered most. Her family's words had sickened her, yet once the Lord's arms had closed around her, she hadn't cared what he was. They'd felt so right. So longed for.

Nadia hugged her pillow closer. Last night she had mourned the family who had always mistreated her and had found comfort in the arms of the man—the person, she corrected—who'd had a hand in murdering them. George, anyway, though it was probably the loss of her son that had found her mother pregnant again after all these years.

To be replaced. With another son.

The truth that she had never really been part of the family, at least in her mother's eyes, worked its way into her heart.

She never mourned you, the dual voice whispered; one gleeful, one sad. *Was it murder or revenge?*

I'll make them pay.

Could it possibly be both?

♪♫♪♫♫♪♫♪♪♫♪♪♫♪

Nadia wrestled with the question all morning in her room. Nicolette brought in a tray with tea, a soft boiled egg, bacon, and toast with marmalade and left it for her on the bedside table. She didn't even need to rise to eat. Her hollow stomach was soon filled, but her heart was a different matter.

She curled her arms around her legs, still under the covers, her head on her knees, and contemplated the Lord's nature; the dueling voices in her head banging like a blacksmith's hammer while the poison in her heart laughed. Of one thing she was certain—the Lord had killed. Countless times. It was hard to accept the kind voice's argument that this was a war and that generals are responsible for deaths on both sides. Though its argument that murder requires malic did give her pause, enough that the other voice whispered, *But he's banished because of the death of his love.* There was a counter-argument to its statement, but she was unable to capture the thread to it through the clamor of voices banging about in her head. When the clock chimed noon, she gave in and threw back the covers. Might as well ask the Lord about it than let the voices keep up their arguing.

Nadia didn't bother to put up her hair. A band of pain had formed, wrapping around her temples. Piling her hair on her head, securing it with pins, would only add to the pressure. Instead, she caught it up with a ribbon tied in the back. Though she avoided her reflection in the mirror, she did catch one glimpse. Her eyes were red and dark circled.

The Lord waited for her at the reading table in the library. Nadia sank down onto the chair next to him and stared at the table.

"Are you a murderer?"

"I kill, yes," he said. "And though at times I enjoy taking revenge, making those who have caused so much suffering learn what it is to hurt, I do not kill for the fun of it."

Nadia thought back to the stories she'd heard at church, before her mother had tossed her out and ended her ability to regularly attend. One sermon in particular had been about angels who guarded those God had chosen and smote their enemies with flaming swords. Beside her sat a god, which was something like an angel. He didn't have a flaming sword, as far as she knew, but he did have a fire-breathing dragon whom he loosed to avenge and protect others. Would she consider angels murderers?

No. She would have considered herself blessed to have received such protection.

But she didn't consider herself blessed or even lucky. She was cursed. Her only champion—her only champions, she corrected—weren't angels. They were monsters. And she was a monster for accepting them. Her mother was right to have thrown her out. They all were.

"Please make my excuses to Herr Montfort," Nadia said, rising from the table. "I don't feel able to perform my lesson today."

She staggered away, aware of the Lord's gaze upon her back. But he let her go without another word.

twenty-one

If she'd had the energy, Nadia would have dragged herself down to the stables and begged Uro to eat her as he should have done all those months ago. Only the poison had spared her. She had poison in her heart, so Uro and the Lord had accepted her as one of their own.

She was worse than "nada." She was evil.

She was no princess to be rescued. She was being groomed to be the evil queen. That's why Aurora and the others weren't here. They'd been too good. But her...she was still here, waiting for her crown. She'd already accepted the pearls and the dragon. A crown was sure to follow. And then she'd take her place with the Lord and hunt down those who displeased her.

And so it continued all afternoon. Lying on the bed, staring at the wall, counting her sins, wishing for death.

The shadows were lengthening, though day hung on as long as possible in the early summer, pushing dusk and night to the outmost reaches, when a knock sounded on her door. She lacked the energy to even call out "Enter" to Nicolette.

Though the figure that entered and then loomed over her bed, placing a tray on the bedside table, was not Nicolette.

The Lord gave a gentle sigh and sat beside her. "I know you are mourning, but I do not think it is for the woman who threw you out or the brother who did not love you." Her heart cracked, sending out new fingers of pain. "What do you mourn, Nadia?"

Her lips trembled, but she could not speak. She flinched as he reached over and freed the ribbon that had become tangled and half-undone in her hair. Then he brushed the hair out of her face and waited.

"A mother," Nadia whispered. "I never had a mother to cherish me...and now I never will."

"The woman who bore you did not value you and, therefore, could not cherish you."

"She named me 'Nothing,'" Nadia whispered.

The Lord gave a gentle laugh. "That was certainly her intention, but she actually named you otherwise."

"Hope," she whispered automatically, having heard it so many times before.

"She intended you for nothing, but she armed you with hope."

"I have no hope."

The Lord ran his fingers through her hair. Squeezing her eyes shut, Nadia tried to ignore the comfort of the action. She wanted to wallow in her misery, not lean into the solace that his hand promised.

He'll stroke you. He'll kiss you. He'll finally have you.

A sob burbled up. The voice was right. She could feel her resolve fading. The desire to reach out and let him take her was growing. If her mother didn't want her, if the village didn't want her, why should she keep herself from the being who did?

"What else do you mourn?"

Nadia gulped back a sob. "That I am no longer a kind person who stands up to evil." She sucked in a horrified breath as her words rang in her ears.

The Lord's hand stilled. "Do you think me evil?"

A tangle of answers tied up her tongue.

He removed his hand. Words formed and then were taken away as he struggled with her accusation. "I have not always been kind, but I hope that does not make me evil. I am a judge and executioner, but I hope that does not count as evil. I am many things, but I hope that the one thing I am not is someone who revels in the misery of others for, to me, that is true evil."

Nadia let his words sink in. The poison hissed and slunk off.

No, she was not that kind of person. And neither was he.

"I am sorry," she said.

The mattress shifted as the Lord rose and crossed to the window. "You say that you have no hope, but you must hope for something."

"Death," Nadia said.

"That is your fear, fed by the poison. If I granted you death, what then? What would you want then?"

"That the pain would finally have stopped."

"Because you had ceased to be or because you were transformed?" he asked.

Nadia frowned. In all the years she'd wished for death, she'd never thought about what would happen if she got it. Though—a shiver ran down her spine—she never thought she'd cease to be. Just the pain. "Transformed, I guess."

The Lord inhaled slowly. "Eat something. Mourn tonight. Mourn for the woman and brother who never loved you. Mourn for what should have been. Then tomorrow, I want you to rise and seize the life you have now. You are not the 'nothing' tossed out into the streets. You are not the 'nothing' who subsisted on scraps and the meanest of beds and feelings. You are the 'hope' that learned to read. You are the 'hope' that has learned to play music. One day soon, I would wish you to be the 'hope' who has learned to dance. You are no longer what you were, Nadia. You have been transformed."

He turned from the window. "Good night, Nadia. I will expect you at our usual time tomorrow." With a nod of his head, he left her, closing the door softly behind him.

Nadia dried her tears and ate the dinner the Lord had brought for her: an omelet made with a soft, white cheese and chives, and a glass of young white wine. He had, again, softened her pain all by the simple application of truth and without making her feel ridiculous.

The hollowness remained; a place that should have been filled with a mother's love and, yes, the loss of that mother. But Nadia realized she mourned for what could have been. That her mother was now gone would have mattered very little if Uro hadn't come. So Nadia said her goodbyes and left her mother to the fate she had made, a different judge to face than the Lord. She wondered if he'd be as kind.

She had fewer warm thoughts for her brother George. They'd shared a bed and played as children, but once she'd been turned out, he'd treated her like a guttersnipe, always among the first to torment her. He'd probably cursed her, blamed her, when the dragon returned and continued wreaking havoc, cursed her from the grave for the circumstances that took his life. He was the evil one, according to the Lord's description. Both George and her mother.

Should one mourn the loss of evil?

Your mother and brother weren't all evil, the kind voice whispered.

No, they weren't.

Nadia slipped to her knees beside the bed. She thought she remembered the prayers for the dead. Maybe, with her efforts, God would have mercy on their souls.

She had intended to take a walk the next morning, but after she'd breakfasted and dressed and collected her book, her feet found their way to the grand ballroom with the moving ceiling. Sitting on the floor, her skirts puddling around her, arms wrapped around her knees, Nadia watched the globes swirl, humming the dance tune that Herr Montfort had set her on a few days before.

Her last thoughts before she'd drifted off to sleep last night had been about transformation. Aurora had gone from cursed to free. Cinderella from abused to loved. Gretel from lost to found. And the signs were all there that it had happened in this place.

If the stories were true, then the balls were true, perhaps taking place in this very room. Cinderella's slipper left on the steps when she rushed out, seeking the comfort of Uro when fear took over as she had done herself. Aurora getting a victory dance after battling dragons of her own making.

It was too soon for her to dance, too soon after the loss of her mother and brother. It would be too much like dancing on their graves. But she did want to learn. Fill herself with something other than fear.

Nadia hummed the tune again, set her gaze one of the globes and watched it spin. It twirled, changing places and partners as it traveled across the indoor sky. At night, it would be a star moving across the heavens.

What must it have been like to watch the stars in the Lord's world? With a start, Nadia realized that he, too, was mourning. She'd only lost "what could have been," but he'd lost everything—his love, his family, and his home. He was banished, cut off from all of it, with no hope for return. Condemned to spent the rest of his days as a virtual prisoner. And tasked with meting out punishment to those who were once like him. She couldn't imagine him being cruel. Foolish, careless—yes—as he had been at times with her. A thousand years he'd been at it. A thousand years to be reminded and mourn.

And all without hope.

No wonder it was so important to him. It was the greatest thing he was denied.

Nadia collected her book and rose. It was time to be thankful. And she'd start at the beginning where it had all started, with Uro.

"How do you do it?" she asked the Lord that afternoon. "Live here and not go mad?"

"What makes you think I haven't gone mad?" he asked, a teasing grin lighting his face.

Nadia bit back a smile. "You're usually so sane to talk to. Rarely the ravings of a lunatic."

He gave her a sidelong glance. "Only rarely?"

"Well, you do occasionally talk in riddles." Nadia bit back a giggle and then sobered. "Seriously though, I thought about what you said about hope, and then I realized, it's the one thing you're denied."

He reached out and poked her between the eyes. "So shortsighted again. I always have hope. I hope that every time someone arrives that they can be changed and—" He broke off abruptly. His eyebrows lifted. "Spoilers. Some things you're just not meant to know until it's time. As for me, I may not have the freedom I once enjoyed, but I always hope for change, that one day I may not be needed." He sighed. "But after a thousand years of watching, it is difficult. Humans do seem to forget the lessons their fathers learned." He shook his head as if to clear it. "What other conclusions did you come to in your ponderings?"

Nadia turned the book in her hands. "That I want to learn to dance. Not right away..." She swallowed heavily and raised her eyes to meet his. The Lord nodded his understanding. "But soon...if you'd like that."

His hand went out to her but then changed course and came to rest on the table.

"I would, indeed."

A little more than a week had passed when Nicolette knocked on the door just as Nadia was dressing for dinner."

"Beggin' your pardon, miss." Nicolette curtsied and cast her gaze to the floor. "But the master says I'm to help you dress, that you can't get into the gowns alone."

Nadia turned and fingered the yellow dress she'd laid on the bed. She blew out a breath and then hauled the frock back up. "Thank you, Nicolette. You can put this back for me then."

She handed over the dress, and then took a breath to steel herself. Stepping over to the middle wardrobe, she exhaled again and opened it, her hands shaking.

Nicolette gasped. "My stars, they're pretty."

Nadia swallowed. "Yes. Yes, they are."

"Which one would you like, miss?"

The sight of them still took her breath away and, for a moment, she wasn't able to find words. "I don't know. Which one do you think?"

Nicolete came to stand behind her. "The blue one? It's as pretty as a lake on a summer day. And your pearls would look so nice against the color."

Her heart gave a strange thump. It seemed she just couldn't avoid references to water and the sea.

Just like his beloved, the poison whispered.

But Nadia let Nicolette lace her into the gown anyway.

"Would you like me to help you with your hair?" Nicolette asked as she adjusted the bow on the lacings.

"No, thank you." She'd had to work hard to suppress her shivers as Nicolette had pulled and tugged on the strings against her back. Her fingers running through her hair—

Nadia closed her eyes and hauled up a smile to hide her panic. "I'm fine. You may go now."

She opened her eyes to find Nicolette bobbing a small curtsy. "Very well, miss."

Putting a hand on her hip, Nadia exhaled again, trying to control her breathing. When some of her shaking had stilled, she crossed to the full-length mirror in the corner for a better look. The gown swept across and molded to Nadia's bust and waist. It fell from her hips in a froth of fabric that swished when she walked. Not even Elsbeth had looked so fine.

Nadia sat and twisted her hair up, trying for a more artful arrangement than the simple knot she usually went with. A task that left her kicking herself that she hadn't sucked up her courage and let Nicolette do it. She wound the pearls around her neck and pinched her cheeks like Daisy had always done to add some color.

She blew out a slow breath. Tonight was different, as different as the Arabian nights dinner. Only, this time, she didn't think she was the dessert course. But still...dancing, putting herself on display...

Enough. Nadia gave her reflection a sharp nod. It was time to go out and face the music. Literally.

The music had a reprieve in the form of dinner. The Lord met her at the foot of the stairs by the dining room and offered her his arm.

"Escorting me in?" she asked. "Are we being that formal or—" Her heart thudded. "Are there others joining us?"

His eyes twinkled. "Have you made them solid since I left you this afternoon?"

"No." Shame colored her cheeks. She'd made no progress in solidifying the other inhabitants. No progress at all since she'd given them back their voices.

The Lord chuckled. "Didn't think so. No, I've planned no grand dinner this evening, in the formal dining room anyway. Tonight, I thought we'd eat in a smaller one not far from the ballroom."

They walked down the hall, up another staircase, down another hall, and entered a room two doors down and to the left of the ballroom. It was just like Henry's stories. At night, as she and the girls would be finishing up the last of the work in the kitchen, Henry would sit at the table and regale Daisy and Hazel with tales from his footman duties. Stories about the lords and ladies and how they acted and what they said. Throwing in descriptions of what they wore. Though his face turned gloomy with the telling when begged for details by the girls. Occasionally, Oliver would come in and rock a chair back on its legs so that he could cross his feet and use the table as a stool (risking a beating if Cook ever caught him) and try to outdo Henry's tales when he wasn't finding ways to torment Nadia.

Her first thought upon entering the dining room was "white." From the silk on the walls and the scrolling molding that edged it, to the porcelain chandelier that hung from a great medallion on the ceiling. White flowers arranged in great silver vases sat on white and gilt buffet tables and scented the air with the fragrance of roses and exotic lilies. A white cloth covered the table around which six low-backed chairs had been arranged. Even the china was white, with a raised basket weave pattern which, to break up the monotony, contained hand-painted pink roses and blue forget-me-nots. The most colorful thing in the room was herself for, in his usual black, the Lord looked as out of place as a crow.

Dinner sat beneath large silver domes. The Lord took his usual place to Nadia's left and removed the cover from one. Underneath it was a large pink and white thing that looked like an overgrown crayfish tail but must be from a lobster. Beside it were spears of white and green asparagus in a lemon sauce, a tart made with fresh morel mushrooms, and sugared grapes.

"Don't want you too full for dancing," he said of the more meager offerings than usually appeared at their dinner, and poured Nadia a glass of white wine.

Of all the meals that she had eaten with the Lord, this one had to be the most strange. Even more than the Arabian dinner where they'd sat on the floor and eaten with their hands. The reason for it first eluded her. As she followed her thoughts, trying nearly as many ideas as she had doors, what finally emerged was that the meal was just the prelude. It was what came next that was the focus of the evening. The idea left her somewhat tongue-tied.

"Have you hosted many balls?" Nadia asked.

The Lord paused in his meal, a tight smile forming on his face. "A few."

"Would you tell me about them?" Her eyes met the Lord's. "I've wondered..." She lowered her gaze. "You tell me they got their happily ever afters. Couldn't you tell me one of their stories?"

She dared a glance back up.

"They're not really my stories to tell." Nadia's face fell. "But I suppose I can think of something. Who would you like to hear about?"

"Cinderella?" Nadia ventured.

"There were other balls, you know," the Lord answered with a warm chuckle. "Where would you like me to begin?"

"Was she...like me?" Heat crept across her cheeks. "I mean, did Uro bring her?"

"Yes. In a lot of ways, she was like you. Mistreated. No real family to speak of." A thoughtful smile crossed the Lord's face. "She volunteered though. Her stepmother nearly didn't let her, didn't want to lose the free help, but then her daughters threw a fit, saying that they'd be at risk if Ella didn't go." His brows lifted, and he met Nadia's gaze, pinning her with his intensity. "Though once she arrived, she never tried to get Uro to eat her."

Nadia ignored the barb. Now that he'd started, she wanted details. "What about the slipper?"

"She was much more social than you. Never made anyone disappear." That one hit its mark. Her cheeks heated again as he continued. "I treated her to court life, taught her to dance." He paused, his face clouding over. "But then Uro returned with...someone new. His roaring alert frightened her and she ran from the room." He leaned in closer. "Dropped a slipper on the stair." He gave a small laugh that quickly faded away. "It was hard for her to trust me after that. Having another brought in made it seem less like a rescue." He lifted his wine and drank before he continued. "I was not the handsome prince who wanted to find a mate to the shoe, though I think she was hoping I was."

"I see," Nadia said. Her heart had suddenly grown smaller, tighter.

"She did get her happy ending though, in the end. And I think the ball gave her the strength to go through what came next."

The poison. Nadia's heart twisted. "Is that what this is about tonight?" she asked. "Preparing me for what comes next?"

The Lord took her hand. "No, Nadia. This is about all that you should have been doing and trying to make up for that. I've told you before, no one has ever come to me with so much poison. And even with a dose half of that of yours, hate has found a home. But you…you have never uttered one word against anyone. The only hate in your heart is for yourself, and others have put that there." He squeezed her hand. "You have mourned, and now it's time to dance, to start collecting some of the good things in life that should have always been there."

He gave her hand another squeeze and let it go. It felt strangely empty.

Her gaze fell to her plate. "You seem to think I'm something special."

"You are, Nadia. Much more than you seem to understand."

Butterflies had entered her stomach and were banging around as the Lord rose and held out his hand. At least it was the butterflies that were crashing into each other and not her knees.

The ballroom was dim as they entered. The globes swirled and danced, lit with a phosphorescence that made them look more like fireflies than stars. She had watched their unlit movement for hours, but now…

But now...

Nadia turned in a circle, taking it all in.

The lights swooped and swirled across the sky, the ceiling having vanished into darkness.

"The stars...where you're from, they aren't really like this, are they?" she asked.

"And the moon so close you feel like you could reach out and touch it." Longing etched lines into his face until Nadia couldn't stand it. She grasped his hand and held it.

"I'm sorry," she said to him. "The things you've lost." The people.

His fingers curled around hers with a gentle squeeze. "That's what happens when you aren't careful."

Her heart swelled. He thought her special for her lack of hate, but she marveled at his courage. To have lost so much and still hope.

"I think you know our musicians," the Lord said. "Or at least, their leader."

Nadia's attention was finally drawn to the back of the ballroom where candlesticks lit up four music stands. Herr Montfort and three other gentlemen Nadia hadn't seen before stood or sat, waiting for instruction. Herr Montfort sat at a harpsichord that had been brought in. The others held a recorder, viola, and a drum.

"He was quite glad you asked for lessons, you know," the Lord said. "I'd locked him out of the music room for...many reasons, including the fear that you might begin to hear ghostly music."

So that explained the dust.

The Lord led her to the center of the room. "What do we do?" she asked, trying to keep her hand from clasping his in a death grip.

He nodded to Herr Montfort. "We bow and curtsy." Nadia managed to make her foot move and her knees bend, and the Lord bent toward her. "And now, we dance."

She had seen dancing before, of course. Both the dances the gentry performed at events like Elsbeth's birthday, when they were held outside, and the country dances the common folk did. She'd just not actually done any of them herself. The Lord masterfully led her, providing just the right amount of pressure to draw her forward or push her back.

Then his arm wrapped around her waist, and he hoisted her into the air, resting her hip on his, their left arms intertwined. It only lasted two counts, and then she was free again and dipping a small curtsy. Her heart pounded and shivers scattered across her skin. Their hands linked again, and they proceeded down the ballroom several steps before stopping and beginning the sequence anew.

"Usually, we'd keep changing partners," the Lord said as they drew close again.

"I know," Nadia answered, breathless from the contact and the way her heart pounded.

He smiled and looked into her eyes. "But tonight, I get to keep you all for myself." Nadia forced a tremulous smile onto her face.

Around and around, he kept her at it. Turn right, turn left, promenade, down and back, hands high, hands low, around the waist—

And down I go, she said to herself every time he released her, her body dropping while her heart lingered in the air. She wondered if this was how the poison was drained, if it wasn't some magical dance meant to capture it.

He walked her through the next dance and then the next. The lifts gave way to an arm held around her waist as their right hands formed an arch under which they turned, again hip to hip, but much closer to the earth. He had to be able to feel her ribs, vibrating like a drum from the pounding mallet of her heart. She could feel his; a firm, steady beat that never seemed to race or tire. Watch it pulse in his neck, so much closer to her gaze than his eyes. And just as hard to pull her eyes away from.

The fourth dance ended with the Lord, hands on her hips, lifting her up and tossing her into the sky. She probably only went a foot in the air, but it felt like her fingers could brush the globes as they passed by. He'd told her about touching the moon. Now, she could almost reach out and touch the stars.

And then he caught her about the waist again. Her hands reached out to break her fall and slid down the Lord's chest. Her feet hit the floor, but her hands lingered. His slid up her back.

Looking up, all she could see were the stars in his eyes. The globes reflected in his yellow irises turning into dancing lights. He stared at her with an expression she'd never seen. He brought one hand up to cup her face. The other pulled her closer. Nadia closed her eyes, certain that she was going to get her first real kiss. This was what it felt like to be wanted.

He stroked her face with the back of his hand. Her arms reached for him of their own accord, draping around his neck. Her body pressed against his. Her lips raised themselves toward his.

Only his didn't come.

Nadia's eyes snapped open. The Lord's expression held both longing and loss. He traced his fingers along her jaw.

She moved her head away from his touch, blinking back the tears that rose. Something was wrong.

His free hand settled on her waist again. "I could kiss you," he said. His index finger traced a pattern on her back. "I want to, very much." He inhaled deeply, and then gently pushed her hips, creating an inch or two more space between them. "But it wouldn't be fair."

The words hit her like a slap. Nadia's arms fell to her side, and she stared, unseeing, at his chest. "Why?"

He took her hands. "Oh, Nadia. My brilliant hope. There are still truths to be told."

He continued an explanation of some sort, but all she heard was his months-old warning, *Too much truth can kill you.* Her heart certainly felt like he'd pulled her close and plunged in a blade. Like the king's grandfather, Black Edmund, had done to his uncle to steal the throne.

The Lord had stolen her heart. And then stabbed it.

Why shouldn't he? What are you to him? You're nothing compared to the others.

The music started again, and Nadia forced a smile onto her face. At least she was moving. At least she had a task to give her legs when they so desperately wanted to run. Down the hall, back to her room—Nadia stifled a sob—back to her room where one of the filmy nightgowns still hung, unused in the wardrobe.

How many others had he taken to bed? Stroked their skin, made them want him?

Oh, saints help her. She did want him. Wanted him more than she'd wanted her mother's approval and love. More than she'd wanted the villagers' acceptance. More than she'd wanted to die, though that desire was quickly overtaking the other.

He'd held them close and stroked their skin and made love to them. But he wouldn't kiss her.

The dance that had thrilled her, that had made her hope she could have a taste to what it was like to be a princess, became a dance of death. Nadia turned and twisted and changed hands with unseeing eyes, wearing a smile that never reached them, unable to look at anything but the floor; moving with the

Lord, even after the music faded away and she heard nothing but the shuffle of their feet and the slap of their hands as the dance continued, now unaccompanied. She kept her gaze from the music stands. Seeing them empty would only confirm how much things had changed.

How greatly she had failed.

When she and the Lord had dipped their final and deepest bow to each other and the dance was over, Nadia gathered her voice. "Thank you, my Lord. This was an evening I'll never forget." She curtsied again and turned from the room, walked straight and quick, and had just enough strength to keep from breaking into a run.

It was only when she was safely back into her room that she gave into the sob that had threatened for so long. Another soon followed as reality hit her, and she sank to her knees. She was laced into this stupid dress with no way of undoing it herself. No Lord's hands to unlace her, only Nicolette's that would mock her with every tug since they weren't another's.

Nadia reached behind her and grasped at the bow at the small of her back. She'd been laced from top to bottom so that the decoration fell where it would accent most and not be lost to the square outline of her shoulders.

She managed to remove the ribbon from only the three bottommost sets of loops before she surrendered and pulled the bell. Freeing herself would take all night.

And she had better things to do.

twenty-two

Nadia slapped herself a few times before Nicolette arrived. Slapping something had always seemed to focus Cook. Though, truth be told, Cook had always slapped her and not herself. Nadia continued to fiddle with the laces and worked at putting a dreamy expression on her face while she waited for the knock.

"Oh, thank heaven," she said to Nicolette when it finally came. "I knew I couldn't get myself into it but—" She turned around. "—I can't seem to get myself out of it either."

"Not to worry, milady." Nicolette stepped in and closed the door. "That's what I'm here for."

Nicolette whipped the satin ribbon from the eyelets with nimble ease. When she at last pulled the ribbon free, Nadia sighed and then gulped lungfuls of air. "Oh, bless you," she said, glad to be free of at least part of the evening, and quickly stepped out of the dress.

"Would you like me to brush out your hair?" Nicolette asked, collecting the dress from the floor. "You've danced so much your arms are shaking."

And they were. Nadia pulled at one of the pins holding up her hair. The jeweled flower snagged in her curls. If she tried to free them herself, she'd probably tear out chunks of hair. Nadia clenched her jaw and gave in to this new defeat. "Yes, thank you, Nicolette."

Her legs wobbled as she crossed the room to her dressing table chair. Nicolette closed the wardrobe door and joined her.

"You have such pretty hair," Nicolette said, picking up the hairbrush. She worked at the strands wound round the clip and pulled it free. "It's got a lovely curl to it. Not so curly as to make you look like one of those fancy dogs, but just enough to frame your face nicely."

Nadia had never noticed. She still too often saw the thin, haggard face with hair drooping from exertion when she looked in the mirror. "Thank you," she replied automatically.

Nicolette's fingers gently massaged Nadia's head as they pulled out the pins. The smooth, even strokes of the hairbrush soothed her as nothing else had done this evening.

"There you go, miss." Nicolette did one last pass and set the brush back on the table. "Have a good evening." She bobbed a curtsy.

"Thank you," Nadia called at Nicolette's retreating form. Hopefully, her evening would soon be fruitful.

Nadia waited until all signs of activity had ceased in the castle and on the grounds, waited until the moon sank lower in the sky and the Lord was sure to have gone to bed. Then she slipped a robe over her nightgown and eased open the door to her room.

The corridor was empty except for a candle in the sconces at either end. The light did not meet in the middle and cast shadows into what would have been nightmarish forms if she had been scared of such things. But a lifetime of working in semi-dark made it comforting. In fact, a little less light wouldn't be remiss.

She slipped down the hallways and staircases, her bare feet silent on the floors—wood, marble, and carpet alike. Nadia slowed her steps as she passed the dented suit of armor around the corner from the Lord's study and continued cautiously. Her heart pounded with every step. Perhaps her plan wouldn't work, her hand wouldn't be able turn the knob, but it did. She inhaled and exhaled and thought of an excuse if the Lord was within and not in bed at all, and then pushed it open.

A dying fire lay in the grate but otherwise the room was empty. And dark. Reluctantly, Nadia closed the door behind her. She should have brought a candle with her. Curling her toes in to keep them from stubbing against things hidden in the shadows, Nadia crossed to the fireplace. She ran her hand along the mantle but found nothing to light her way. *No matter.*

Turning, she stepped toward the thing that had brought her—the basin. If it was what she thought it was, the answers she sought were in there.

Nadia stifled a small cry as her little toe caught against something. She limped the remaining distance and came around the stand that held the basin. Larger than the circumference of her arms, it glinted dully of silver. Though it was hard to tell through the gloomy dark of the room, it appeared to be about six inches deep.

Opening her hand, Nadia waved it over the bowl. Dark clouds formed and gathered, growing lighter in color until they became a swirling, silver mass. Nadia swallowed. This was the window that the Lord used to look upon the world, past and present. All answers were in here. Even her most desired ones. *Why wasn't she good enough? Why wasn't it fair?*

I could kiss you. I want to very much...Oh, Nadia...there are still truths to be told.

Well, if the Lord wasn't going to be forthcoming, maybe the basin would.

Gripping the edges of the wooden frame, Nadia spoke the question on her heart. "I wish to know why it wasn't fair."

The clouds continued their undulating, their light casting an eerie glow on her face.

"I wish to know what it wasn't fair," she repeated. To the same result.

Nadia tapped a finger on the frame. Did it refuse to answer her question? Or was something else needed? Her breath caught as a possibility entered her mind. Maybe it wasn't enough to ask. She'd had to wave her hand over it to open it, as the Lord had done to close it. Maybe she had to touch it.

And trust that she wouldn't be pulled in and sent somewhere else.

As the folly of her actions became apparent, Nadia raised her hand to close it. And then heard a familiar whisper.

Or maybe it will show you your heart's desire. You want to know, don't you, Nadia? Why you weren't good enough. Why he didn't kiss you like all the others. Why he pushed you away. The answers are there. All answers are. Are you afraid of the truth?

The truth. The one thing that the Lord kept hiding from her. Nadia curled the fingers of her left hand around the frame to anchor herself and reached tentatively toward the swirling clouds with her right. Lightning crackled in the bowl, casting off images that quickly disappeared beneath the swirling clouds.

Why wasn't it fair? she thought as her finger touched one of the clouds, cold as ice but fluid as oil.

Color erupted from the spot. Nadia drew her finger back. The shapes twisted and turned, changing from one thing into the next but slowly becoming a steady picture—a study, not unlike this one, and familiar.

No, the figure in it was familiar.

Lord Braemoor sat at his desk. He wrote on a slip of paper, sanded the ink, blew on it, and folded it up. He tossed it in a basket and put a mark next to a name on a list to his left. Nadia's knees wobbled. Why was it showing her this?

The basin answered her thoughts, focusing in on the slip of paper as Lord Braemoor wrote the next one. Nadia's eyes widened. Lord Braemoor folded the slip of paper with her name on it and tossed it in the basket. The basin followed his hand to the paper where he made a mark next to not her name, but the name of Sonja, the baker's daughter. Nadia grabbed the frame as the floor shifted beneath her feet.

Lord Braemoor began again. A slip of paper, Nadia's name, a check mark.

And then, the world went black.

twenty-three

The sound of screams woke her, blood curdling cries like those of a pig to the slaughter. Only it wasn't a pig. It was her.

She'd asked the wrong question and gotten the wrong answer. She'd wanted to know why the Lord hadn't kissed her, why it wouldn't have been fair for him to do so. Instead, the basin had answered the first question she'd asked herself when she'd arrived: why hadn't the Lord counted her as a sacrifice.

Because the lottery hadn't been fair.

The Lord had told her she was no sacrifice, and now she understood, had seen the proof. She had never fully understood the depths of the village's contempt until now.

Her screams turned to wails as she finally grasped what they had done to her. Nadia pushed blindly at the floor. She needed to leave. She couldn't be found here. But her arms flailed like the legs on a newborn calf and without their success. Pressing her palms to her eyes, Nadia tried to blind herself to the scene burned upon them—the name Lord Braemoor wrote on the slip of paper, every single one, was her own.

Nadia Crofton.

That big speech had been just for show. It all had been. One big charade to rid themselves of the thing they needed least. Her.

They'd plotted and carried out her death. No—her murder. Poisoning hadn't been good enough for her. They'd needed her death, too.

The poison twisted in Nadia's heart, laughing. Laughing until it filled her ears and echoed in the room. It had her, even if they had failed to dispose of her, to send her like a pig to be roasted on a spit.

"No." Nadia moaned and shook her head, desperately trying to dislodge the words. "No."

The laughter became maniacal and so powerful it took over her voice, making the room ring with it. Nadia fought for control, tears streaming down her face as the poison laughed and laughed.

She clamped her jaw shut. Out. She needed the poison out. It had controlled her too long.

Come and get me! it shouted in a joyful singsong, a depraved child ready for a game of hide and seek.

Nadia scratched at her chest, determined to get at it. The poison laughed and laughed until she was seized by a fit of frenzy. It was too late to get it drained. If it didn't come out now—her fingers dug deeper, drawing blood as her nails scraped away strips of flesh—there'd be nothing left of her by morning. Oh, why hadn't the Lord drained the poison? Why had he waited so long?

Nadia snarled as something bound her arms, keeping her fingers from finally reaching her heart, from squeezing out the poison.

"Nadia."

The poison took up where she'd left off, viciously slashing at the insides of her heart.

"Nadia, stop."

Nadia wailed as the poison released its claws, leaving a thousand pinpricks through which she could feel her blood seeping. "Gone!" she cried, gasping for air. "I want it gone!"

"Ssh," the Lord said. "I'll take it, but not tonight."

Nadia struggled to loosen her arms. "Now! No more! They can't have any more of me."

The Lord wrapped his arms around her. "You are mine. They cannot take you. I'll drain it in the morning if you still want."

She wanted to shout, to insist that her wishes would be the same in the morning, but her voice, finally released, refused to work anymore. She collapsed into his arms. As her cheek came to rest against him, her brain noticed that he was clothed in green silk pajamas and a green and gold paisley robe. Where was the black? Then he scooped her up.

Mere hours ago she'd lamented that she hadn't ended up in the Lord's arms, and now here she was. He carried her to bed like a child, her head lolling against his chest, as one thought kept repeating in her head.

They tried to murder me!

twenty-four

The Lord sat on the bed and stroked her hair until she fell asleep. In her dreams, she was finally able to reach her heart and squeeze out the poison. It ran in rivulets of bilious green into the grass, turning it brown and burning holes in her shoes.

The Lord looked at her with eyes that had gone black. "You have no heart," he said. "How did you ever think I could love you when you have no heart?"

She awoke to find a bandage on her chest and ripped it away, certain there was a scar to prove that her dreams had been real.

Dark red scratches, only just beginning to scab, showed where she'd tried to rip out her own heart. Nadia forced her gaze to her fingertips. They looked clean and well kept. Someone had washed them.

Nadia curled her fingers to her palm and rolled onto her back, fixing her gaze at the ceiling. The poison began to pace like a caged animal.

He'd been right. The Lord had been right. Too much truth could kill you.

But now that she knew just how damaged she was, how expendable she was, and how much the poison could control her, she knew she couldn't live with it any longer.

Even if it killed her.

The Lord himself came to ready her, picked out the dress and then slipped outside while she put it on. He put up her hair with deft hands that made her heart ache. How had he gained so much practice yet he wouldn't touch her?

"Don't want it coming loose," he said. She found the energy to nod.

The poison backed into a corner and dug in, ready for a fight.

The Lord took her by the hand and led her down the stairs and out the doors. A gnawing feeling grew in her stomach. Something was missing. Something else was different. Breakfast. He'd not allowed her to have a last meal.

Through the maze they went, all the way to the center. He stopped in front of the fountain. The aroma of bitter laced with over-rip fruit blew over her. So that was what was in her heart.

"You don't have to do this yet, you know," the Lord said. "Last night nearly killed you."

"Exactly," Nadia answered, drifting on a sea of exhaustion and indifference. "It tried to kill me. It's time for it to go." She let go of the Lord's hand. "What do you need me to do?"

"Just stand there."

He left her side, taking up a place behind her. Why? Wouldn't it be easier to get at her heart from the front? Nadia closed her eyes and waited for his knife to strike.

The Lord ran his hands down her arms and interlocked their fingers. Then he crossed their arms, locking her in his embrace. His lips came close to her ear, and he whispered. Just seven little words, but the response was immediate.

Nadia fought against them long before they reached the poison. The Lord repeated them, holding her tighter as she struggled. A scream that was both her own and the poison's ripped from her throat. If she'd thought last night had been bad then, compared to this, she'd merely gotten a splinter. Again, he repeated the words, more insistent this time.

Nadia felt her heart shred. The words cut through the inside of her heart like it was seeding a melon. A melon of living kittens hanging on the curtains and refusing to go.

Hot tears dripped down her face. First, a few, and then a river. Through her screams, she could hear them splash, joining the contents of the fountain.

As the world spun and oblivion beckoned, two thoughts raised their voices.

My, God! How many people has he done this to? was soon followed by *How do any of them survive?* and then darkness swallowed her.

twenty-five

Nadia expected Cook's toe to connect with some part of her at any second. Her body ached as though Henry and Oliver had worked her over and not Cook's ladle. She just couldn't muster up the energy to care.

A thought popped into her half-conscious brain and then scampered off. There was something important about that thought. Nadia groaned and tried to follow it.

Her efforts were interrupted by a message from her face to pay attention to what it was on. She tried to tell it that it didn't matter, and then realized that the texture was off.

Grass.

Groaning again, Nadia opened her eyes. She lay partially on her side, chest to the ground, arms flung wide, cheek against the grass. The trickling sounds of water met her ear.

Wait. Not water.

Poison.

Pushing herself up, Nadia braced her palms flat on the ground to keep from toppling over. The fountain trickled merrily, giving no hint as to the danger of its contents or the price paid to get them.

She placed a hand on her heart, felt its steady beats and...

Nothing else. No whispers, no movement other than the muscle as it pumped the blood through her body. Nothing. A great, empty nothing as vast as the sky.

Nadia stifled a sob. It wasn't supposed to be like this. The poison was gone so she should feel free. Instead, she felt horrifically empty.

Her eyes finally focused, changing the garden from smears of color to the tableau she was familiar with. Except for the rose that lay about a foot from where her head had been. That was new.

Nadia snatched it up and crushed it, crying out when the thorns ripped her palm, but glad for its destruction. Whatever reason the Lord had left it for her didn't matter, for he had lied. She wasn't healed, she was...

Was...

Nadia fought for words but couldn't find any. Hollow didn't fit. Neither did empty. There was just an utter absence of feeling that left her desperate for some emotion. Even desperate wasn't a feeling, any more than lack of air or food or heat or water were feelings. Something essential had been taken from her. Or, at least, something her body thought was essential and now missed.

It wasn't supposed to be like this!

Nadia swayed and slammed her hands down to catch herself, crying out as the thorns shoved deeper into her palm. The tap of her pulse filled her hand. Raising it, Nadia stared at the ragged red streaks oozing blood. She flexed her fingers. The thorns rippled with the movement of her muscles. They were painful, but pain was something. It filled the seemingly endless void inside her.

Turning her palm down, Nadia ground it against the grass, gritting her teeth as the throb grew and tears gathered in her eyes.

Tears.

A shiver wracked her body, and Nadia lifted her hand. Her face ached from the torrent that had flowed down her cheeks and into the fountain. Her ears focused on the merry trickle splashing next to her, and she scrambled to her feet, her stomach twisting and roiling. A fountain of poisonous tears.

Nadia staggered away. She actually missed the voice. The one that would have whispered she was a failure. For she was. This was no happily ever after. This was a shell. *She* was a shell, an empty thing. There'd been nothing inside her but poison and, now that it was gone, she was nothing. Nada.

A bitter laugh rose from her throat. So much for hope. The Lord had lied to her or been mistaken. Either way, there was nothing left. Not even poison.

Nadia skidded to a stop. Something about that was important. Her feet renewed their journey as her mind began to trail the thread of possibility.

This was not a life she wanted—no feeling, a great crushing emptiness. She had a lifetime of nothing to look forward to. But now, if there was no poison...

It hadn't worked before, but now...but now...

A sob lodged in her throat. Resolve rose up and molded itself around her heart. She did not want this life. And she finally had an out.

twenty-six

Uro raised his head as Nadia entered and then lowered it to the floor. He stared expectantly over his snout at her with what she called his please-come-scratch-me puppy dog eyes. Nadia huffed a laugh, which felt odd in her heart, and did what he asked.

"I've failed, Uro," she said. His inner lid slid halfway open at her words. "All these months doing what the Lord asked were for nothing. The poison is gone, and I'm nothing."

The lid slid completely open. The pupil contracted, a fiery mass of red and orange with only a slit of black, as he focused on her. Fully armed knights had fled in terror from the angry, glinting look it held. Just the promise she needed.

Nadia pulled her hands from his snout. "There's no more poison so..." She took a deep breath and prayed for the courage to face what came next. Wasn't this what she'd wanted all those months ago? Hadn't he been her savior then? "Please eat me."

Uro snorted and scrambled up. Closing her eyes, Nadia prepared herself be enfolded in his massive jaws or burned to a crisp. A few moments of pain, easily endured after all she'd been through in the last day or so, and then there'd be peace. *I wonder what heaven's like.*

Then Uro's tail smacked into her, knocking her over, and she landed hard on her butt. Uro slunk out of the stables, grumbling.

Opening her eyes, Nadia watched him go. The ultimate failure.

I've insulted a dragon and lived to tell the tale.

Nadia curled up against the hard stone wall of the stable and laid her cheek on the floor. There was nothing for her in the castle. Nothing for her here. And she was still too afraid to throw herself over the edge. For a moment, she let herself wonder what it would be like to fall so far that one might be flying. Though with a sudden stop at the end.

The shadows lengthened, and Uro did not return. Nadia listened to the comings and goings in the courtyard, afraid that someone would find her and want something from her. She cringed when the door finally opened, admitting the last person she wanted to see.

The Lord strode over to her, one hand wrapped around the neck of a bottle of wine, two glasses clasped in the other. He peered down at her.

"Something wrong, Nadia?"

Her tongue was dry, and she had trouble making it work. "You lied to me," she croaked.

The Lord settled himself across from her and began to twist a wire that held a strange, bulbous cork to the mouth of the bottle. "What did I lie about?"

"All of it." She choked back a sob and ground her teeth, recalling the words he had whispered in her ear. "The poison's gone, and I feel *nothing*!"

The Lord tossed the wire over his shoulder and grasped the cork. "I've never lied to you." She glared at him. "I told you I'd never seen anyone with so much poison in their heart. It didn't leave much room for anything else." A sigh escaped his lips. "Frankly, I'm surprised, and relieved, that you survived." He made a strange, choking sound. "At one point, I thought we'd lost you. But you're strong." He nodded. "You'll recover. You'll begin to fill your heart with things you do want to feel. It's just going to feel strange for a while."

He wiggled the cork. It shot out of the bottle and into his expectant hand.

"What's that?" Nadia asked.

"Something every special. Your prize for surviving."

"I don't like prizes." Nadia paused as a shudder racked her frame. "They're given so you can boast and gloat and prove that you've won, or else to supposedly console you."

She paused, waiting for the voice that didn't come, but long enough that her body cried out at its last memory of a prize. How Lord Harris hated having to kiss her, being forced to acknowledge in front of everyone that he had lost.

Nadia continued, her voice wavering. "But really, all they do is remind you over and over and over again that you weren't good enough. That you played. And that you lost!"

"I see." The Lord frowned. "So to you, there is no token of comfort?"

She didn't answer. The Lord cocked his head and looked at her. "The pearls I gave you were a prize. For me, a consolation prize in that I looked at them and found comfort. They reminded me that I played. And lost." His face twitched as he sought to control some emotion. "But I'd rather have lost than—" The word caught in his throat. His lips trembled as he attempted to twist them into a smile.

Her heart burst, suddenly swelling with emotion so strong that it caused her eyes to sting. She finished the sentence in her head, "*than to never have loved at all.*"

She pushed herself up. "So what is my prize?"

"The Devil's wine," the Lord said, a twinkle returning to his eye. "A wine that's managed to capture the stars, though they do try to escape." He held out a glass to her. Nadia reached out and took it from him, their fingers brushing briefly. Again, something flared in her heart. A sleeping ember, dark on the surface but harboring a glow deep within its depths.

The Lord filled his and set the bottle aside. He raised his glass. "To new possibilities."

He drank, but Nadia couldn't bring hers to her lips. "I'm really nothing, you know. The poison's gone, and the proof is there. I feel nothing. I *am* nothing. I'm what they give you when you lose."

The Lord raised her chin and waited until she met his gaze. "If you were the consolation prize, I'd lose on purpose."

Nadia gasped, choking on a sob that rose in her throat. The ember swelled and burst into a flame that burned like the sun. It ate away the emptiness and then settled down into a warming spark.

He raised his glass again in silent toast and drank. Nadia brought hers to her lips, intending to sip, but ended up with a gulp that made her sneeze.

"Careful." A look of mock horror widened his eyes. "You do not want to know what I went through to get this."

"More difficult than the scallops?" she asked.

The Lord snorted mid-sip, nearly spraying his wine. He wiped it from his mouth. "Definitely. Scallops, I can get anywhere. Along the coast, that is. This I had to get from some Benedictine monks."

Her brows rose. "That is some feat. You're nothing like their God."

His mouth thinned in a smirk. "Not intentionally."

Nadia sipped. The wine was like sparkling spring sunshine bottled. Though she could see how the Lord thought of stars. The bubbles dancing in the glass were like miniatures of the globes on the ballroom ceiling. The wine warmed her insides, adding to the ember in her heart—a spark in the emptiness—and it gave her a fragile hope.

"So what comes next?" she asked the Lord after they'd sat in silence, drinking until their glasses were nearly empty.

He picked up the bottle and refilled her glass. "You still have some healing to do." His eyes flicked to hers, their depths filled with fear and pain. "You sought the truth too soon and it nearly killed—" He choked, the word catching in his throat. "...killed you. What *were* you doing in my study?" His eyes closed, and he held up a hand. "I know what you did, but why?"

Nadia whimpered and would have scrambled up and dashed away but for the wine in her hand and fear that the Lord would grab her by the ankle to stop her. "I wanted to see why I wasn't good enough," she said. The bowl had misinterpreted her. Maybe the Lord wouldn't see through to her foolish longings.

"But it wasn't *you*," he said. "It was them. You were no sacrifice, not just because the lottery was a sham, but because the definition of sacrifice is to give up something you value. Did they value you, Nadia?"

"No," she whispered.

"So when I told you that you were no sacrifice, I meant it just that way. I had no idea—" He broke off, drained the rest of his wine, and filled it again. "I had no idea that you'd take it that *you* were not worthy." The Lord stared at the flagstones and turned the glass in his hands. "I've been here a thousand years but sometimes I think—I know—I've not really changed. I'm careless with my actions and my words. I cause great harm." One side of his mouth came up in a half-smirk. "And I'm not talking about the burning of fields. Or the ones Uro—" He looked down again and took a gulp, unable to continue.

"I met Uro with great joy, you know," Nadia said, awed that the Lord would let her see how much he suffered. "I sought death for so long and then it came." She smiled and closed her eyes. Drawing in a deep breath, she let the remembered emotion wash over her. "It came, and I was chosen. I was so excited to finally meet Death." She opened her eyes. "I would have died happy, you know."

The Lord ran his thumb along the bowl of the glass cradled in his hands, still unable to look at her. "And I messed that up for you, snatched your peace away. Brought you here. Drove you to such desperation that you tried to rip out your own heart. If William hadn't heard you and alerted me—" A shudder wracked his body. "And the poison had to go. The truth had made it too powerful. And you nearly died!" The horror of the memory passed over his face. "You convulsed in my arms and your heart stopped. It stopped beating, and you stopped breathing. And I thought you'd gone." She was shocked to see tears in his eyes. "I thought you'd gone."

The Lord coughed and surreptitiously wiped his eyes. "And then, just when I'd lost all hope, you took a breath." He raised his head, his eyes filled with remorse and pleading. "And all that was my fault."

He was begging for forgiveness, but she couldn't let him hold all the blame. "No, it's not. If I had listened to you, if I had had hope instead of fear, I wouldn't have looked. I should have been stronger."

"I think we both underestimated just how powerful that much poison was," the Lord said.

Nadia turned her gaze to the floor. "So now what?"

"Now, unless you can walk, I'm going to carry you to bed. You nearly...you've been through a lot in the last twenty-four hours. Your heart needs the rest."

"No, I mean what comes next? The poison's gone."

A disbelieving laugh shook his body. "One step at a time. And would you trust me on that this time? Please?"

"One more question," she said.

"Just one?"

"Why did you leave me there? By the fountain?"

The Lord looked away. "I thought I might be the last person you'd want to see when you awakened."

And hadn't he been? Nadia looked at her palm. The thorns were still embedded in her flesh.

The Lord pulled her hand toward him. "And I see I wasn't wrong." He bent her fingers back, opening her palm wider. "Would you like me to remove them?"

She nodded. The Lord pulled his knife from his belt and gently scraped its tip against the thorns. It stung, but not as much as if she had tried to do it herself.

"There. All finished." He stroked her fingers with his thumb. "I'll send Nicolette up with some salve. Don't want it to get infected." He turned her hand over and stared at it. For a moment, she thought he would raise it to his lips. But then, with a gentle squeeze, he released her. "Can you stand?"

"How do you think I got here?" she retorted, determined to not end up in his arms again.

"True. But you've had some wine, and you did...you're still recovering. There could be some delayed reaction."

Nadia pressed herself up with her good hand, mildly irritated when the Lord took her other arm to steady her. "See. I'm fine. You can take the glasses."

"I'll send someone else out to get them," he said. "You could still collapse. I'm keeping my hands free and walking you to your room."

Nadia shook her arm free of his grasp. "You are impossible, you know," she said.

The Lord grinned. "Always."

♪♪♪♪♫♪♪♪♪

Nadia ordered him out as soon as they got there, all but slamming the door in his face. She turned and staggered to her dressing table, sinking down onto the chair. Her bruised eyes spoke of her lack of sleep and the trauma of the last night and day.

She reached up and pulled the pins from her hair, feeling the Lord's touch as he'd put them in with each one she pulled out, her heart aching but silent.

It still felt empty, like the vast hollowness of Lord Braemoor's tithe kegs before the autumn collection. No, that wasn't quite right. There was something still there, off in the recesses. Maybe end-of-winter empty, then.

Had not the scabs on her chest been so tender, Nadia would have poked at her heart, wanting to wake whatever was there, fearful and yet hopeful at the same time.

She half-heartedly tried to brush out her hair, but her arms began to go as limp as three-days-dead pheasants hung for ripening. She set the brush down and attempted to lift her dress off instead. A knock sounded on the door before she had much success.

"Enter."

It was Nicolette with a bandage kit.

265

"Oh, let me help you with that, miss. You look as done for as a newborn kitten!"

"Thank you, Nicolette," Nadia said, sinking back down onto her chair. "I do believe you are right."

She managed to stand so that Nicolette could pull the dress over her head, flinching when the girl gasped at the sight of Nadia's chest.

"He told me about your hand," Nicolette said. "But that will want dressing, too."

She had just assumed that Nicolette had been the one to bandage it the night before, but now she realized it must have been another. And there was only one other person she could think of to have done it.

"The poison and I had a wrestling match," Nadia told her. "It nearly won."

Nicolette sorted through the kit she'd brought with her. "I can see that." She gave Nadia a gentle smile. "Well, you don't need to worry about that anymore."

It was then that Nadia realized she could see Nicolette properly. For the first time, she wasn't dealing with a ghost. "You're right," Nadia said, choking on her emotion. "It's finally let me go."

Nicolette finished her bandaging on Nadia's chest and took a look at her hand. "It did seem to take a piece of you with it, though." She dipped into a pot and smeared some salve on the cuts.

"Tried to take all of me," Nadia said, admitting for the first time how close she'd come.

Nicolette gave her a tight smile and began to wind a bandage around Nadia's hand. "It likes to do that." She snipped the end and tied it off. "There you go."

"Have you been here for others?" Nadia asked.

Nicolette put her things back into the kit. "One or two." Nadia got the feeling she wasn't supposed to talk about it.

"Well, thank you." Nadia rose slowly, testing her legs. They wobbled, threatening to go like her arms.

Nicolette quickly put an arm around her. "I'll just help you to bed. Don't want to have to bandage your nose."

"Thank you again," Nadia said. "And I'm sorry if I've been difficult."

"Oh, not you, miss. You've been ever so kind." Nicolette flipped the covers back and helped her slip in. "I'll check on you later," she said, folding them back up and tucking them around her. "But I suspect you need the rest. Best thing for you." Nicolette gave her a sad smile instead of the usual curtsy and left Nadia alone.

♪ ♪ ♪ ♫ ♪ ♪ ♪

Nadia's stomach growled her awake, complaining that it had had nothing to fill it but wine, long since spent. Everything about her ached, every muscle, every nerve, but especially her hand. The scratches on her chest were now beginning to itch as well, just to add even more discomfort.

She rolled over. Nicolette had already come and gone. Breakfast sat on the bedside table, a pot of tea and a plate covered by a silver dome wrapped in its own tea cozy to keep the heat in.

Nadia scooted up and placed a pillow behind her back. The tea was strong and soothing. She lifted the lid and found an omelet with crumbly white cheese and chives and shoveled it in like she was a farm hand late for chores.

She faltered as she put the last crumbs in her mouth. She'd rushed through her meal, and now what? Everything had changed.

She'd thought the loss of the poison would have freed her, that the world would be filled with possibilities. But instead, she felt...bereft. All the work she'd done to move forward had been for naught. She did not feel like the girl who'd learn to read or play music.

Or to have danced.

There was a catch in her heart as she thought of that evening. Not that many hours ago, but now a lifetime. She'd hoped—

A jumble of thoughts twisted and pushed, causing an ache behind her eyes. Nadia let the half-formed ideas slip away.

Her bladder wanted relief. Nadia threw back the covers and slipped from the bed, testing her legs. They buckled, sending her to the floor. Swallowing down her humiliation, she crawled to the cloze stool.

Nicolette found her sitting next to the bed, unable to get back in unassisted, when she came in later.

"Milady! Why did you not ring the bell?" Nicolette exclaimed. She helped Nadia back up.

"I was hoping to make it back in on my own. My legs worked just fine yesterday," she explained.

"Your body's adjusting to the difference. It's a shock to the system. They make it back—" Nicolette abruptly broke off.

"I understand if you can't talk about it," Nadia said.

Nicolette gave her a tight smile. "Did you ever see men back from the battlefield?" Nadia shook her head. "There's a blessing. Well, their bodies do what they have to for survival, but once it's over...it's like the body uses itself up, a fire stoked with paper or dry grass to get it blazing and then—"

Nadia nodded. "It's done, and it gives out."

"That poison kept you, I'm beggin' your pardon, weak. It's gone and you've been through a trauma—" She eyed Nadia's hand. "—or two. Let it settle, let the embers build. You'll be back on your feet in no time...if you let yourself rest." She tucked the covers around Nadia. "Anything I can get you?"

Nadia sighed. She had no desire to read, but it would be better than staring around the room or out the window. "My book, I suppose."

Though she'd spent months sitting around reading, being forced to do it in bed was something entirely different. More than once she was tempted to throw her book across the room, despite the many adventures of King Arthur's court.

The Lord left her alone through the afternoon, but as dinner approached, the knock that she had thought was Nicolette turned out to be him and a series of footmen bearing things that transformed the small table in her room into a near replica of the one in the Lord's private dining room.

Nadia clutched the covers to her chest even after the string of footmen took their leave of her, each with a bow.

"Do you think it appropriate to be dining in a lady's chambers?" she asked when they were alone.

"Sick room," the Lord corrected. He opened one of her wardrobes and pulled out a dressing gown. She kept her arms firmly across her chest, her fists holding the covers to her chin. "I've seen it all before," he said. "Well, not *all*." He snapped the robe open. "Who do you think bandaged you up two nights ago?"

Two nights. Was it really only two nights? It felt like a lifetime ago. "Not Nicolette?"

He stared at her with a shocked expression. "Did you really want the staff to know?"

"No." Nadia sighed. "But she bandaged it up again last night."

The Lord hummed in acknowledgement. "Poor thing. I'd only warned her about your hand. I'd thought you must have been right about your legs. Yet, here you are—jelly." He shook the robe. "Come on, some movement is necessary for healing. Especially if that movement is toward food."

Nadia threw back the covers and scooted to the edge of the bed. The Lord slipped the robe onto one arm and then the other. His eyes rested briefly on the bandage on her chest before he folded the robe over and tied it closed. He caught her elbow with his hand, creating a shelf for her to lean on, and steadied her as she slid off the bed. Her legs wobbled but held. Slowly, they crossed the room, the Lord more walking stick than assistant, for which she was grateful.

Dinner was an omelet filled with strawberry jam and covered with pounded sugar. Crumpets had been smeared with an herbed butter and topped with thinly sliced ham. For dessert, there were slices of a hard, caramel-colored cheese and sugared grapes.

The Lord poured her a glass of white wine. "How many days until I'm up?" Nadia asked, leaving her glass untouched, afraid of the buzz the wine would create when her skin was already buzzing.

"Yesterday morning, I would have said three days. Yesterday evening, none at all. I am done making predictions," he said.

The salty-sweet smell of the omelet drifted up, but Nadia played with her fork instead. "And then what?"

He swallowed his bite and washed it down with a sip of wine. "You are singularly focused on the future," the Lord said with a sigh. "You carry on as you have been, as if the poison had never left."

Her eyes narrowed. "Why?"

"Are you the same person you were when you arrived here?"

Nadia cringed as she thought of how fearful she'd been and desperate to die. "No."

"You are not yet the person you need to be to move—" The word caught in his throat. "—on to the next thing...you need to do." The Lord gave Nadia a smile, but it kept slipping from his face. "The fairytales you're so fond of gloss over this point. You've won a battle, but you're not yet strong enough...to take its reward." He managed to hold his smile in place, but his eyes held a sadness.

They all leave him, Nadia suddenly realized. *That's why they're not here. He saves them, heals them, and then they leave.* Which would mean, at some point, she would leave, too.

A strange ache blossomed in her heart that had nothing to do with the emptiness left by the loss of the poison. She picked up her fork properly and finally cut into her omelet. *That would mean they all found their happily ever after somewhere else.*

Her heart clenched. Crying out, Nadia pressed a hand to the bandage on her chest. The Lord was out of his chair in an instant. "What's wrong?"

"Achy, itchy." Nadia grimaced, leaving out the real reason.

He gave a relieved sigh and patted her hand. "That just means it's healing."

Nadia lifted a fake smile of her own. "Of course," she said. But it was more likely that her heart was breaking.

The Lord didn't stay once they had finished eating. He didn't want to tire her out, he said, and helped her back to bed, summoned the footmen who'd been waiting just outside to clear away the things. He snuffed out the lights, leaving just one burning—probably so it would be easier to check on her—and wished her a, "Good night."

The candle flickered, playing hide and seek with the drafts in her room. Nadia laid awake, waiting for the moon to rise, and thought about what came next in the fairytales.

They get their prince and live happily ever after.

But they didn't get the Lord. He'd warned her that he wasn't their handsome prince. And she hadn't cared. Until now. Until he'd saved her, not once, but twice. Three times if you counted her being sacrificed to Uro and her wish for death. She had feared he'd been making her into a replacement of his beloved. But now, she feared he wasn't. And that, to her surprise, frightened her even more.

But why? What had changed?

The words he'd whispered in her ear that had cut out the poison, she'd been so certain they had been lies. And yet... what if they weren't? What if they were true?

If you were the consolation prize, I'd lose on purpose.

He thought her a prize.

Nadia rolled over and stared at the moon as it rose. Its gentle face looked down and smiled at her. Maybe fate was finally smiling on her, too.

She snuggled down into her pillow and prayed. Prayed for the strength to finally embrace who she was and become hope.

twenty-seven

When Nadia tested her legs in the morning, they held. She had Nicolette help her into a dress the color of the sky and consented to Nicolette's offer to put her hair up. There were other activities she had in mind for her energy reserves.

After eating breakfast alone, Nadia slowly made her way down to the library. She could always curl up in the Lord's chair if she tired.

Nadia sat down at the table and consulted the Lord's map. She sought a different book today, one that could give her a clue as to who he was. If the fantastic was real, if all the fairy stories were true, then they all began somewhere. Including the Lord's story. It occurred to her that he might keep it hidden, as he had hidden his name. It might be the one book that wasn't in the library.

She noted the area and marked it in her memory before pushing out of her chair. The trek to the section seemed to take forever. Nadia had to pause several times, one hand against a bookcase for support, as she gasped for breath and willed her legs to stand.

Her energy had faded by the time she reached the shelf, leaving none for a thorough search. She pulled down two volumes that were close at hand, ones that might be good for a general overview—*Legends of Cornwall* and *Encounters with the Fae*. She'd look again when she was more recovered.

The trek back was even more arduous. Fearing she'd end up on the floor, Nadia changed course, setting her sights on the Lord's reading nook. It was closer than the large reading table.

His book of poetry was not in its frequent spot. Which was probably for the best. She hadn't the energy to work at that mystery today.

Encounters with the Fae proved to be a collection of fairy, or faerie, stories. These were not tales of princesses rescued, but encounters with creatures seldom seen in the human world. Creatures that were hidden away, separated by a veil that they, and occasionally humans, could pass through in certain places and at certain times of the year. One story told how the stars would leave their sky dance and journey to Earth as the summer began to wane and the harvest was nigh, flying to Earth in hoards to dance upon it and warm themselves before the season crept back toward the cold dark of winter, like their sky.

Slowly, the morning light crept across the floor of the library. When the shadows bent in the other direction, Nadia pulled the bell by the chair and asked the responding footman for tea and sandwiches. She managed to limp back to the reading table by the time her luncheon arrived. Nadia continued to read, nibbling at the cucumber and salmon sandwiches.

The book said that most of the creatures lived close to the human world. The veil, it seemed, was as much for human protection as for the privacy of the fairy folk. These stories were more like the ones told in her village, the ones that kept people from the fort on which she'd found protection.

The Lord found her, hours later, still reading. He picked up the books. "Research project?" he asked, reading the titles.

Heat bloomed on her cheeks, and Nadia swiped them back out of his hands. "I've decided since I've entered the world of the impossible that I should get better acquainted with it. So yes, I guess you could say I'm doing research. Though I doubt—" She stared at the name on the spine. "—we're actually someplace called Corn...wall." Nadia frowned. A wall of corn? She shook her head to clear away the buzz of puzzlement.

The Lord laughed. "No, not Cornwall."

Nadia stacked her two books and rested her hands on them. "If I ask some questions, will I get straight answers?"

His eyes twinkled. "Probably not."

A sigh left her. She wasn't up for pretending today. "Very well." Once again, he was keeping secrets from her. Why wouldn't he just tell her what came next? Did he fear what she'd do if she knew?

Nadia pushed up from the table, unable to rein in her irritation at the Lord and his puzzles, desperate to return to the peace of her room. She tottered, coming dangerously close to falling, and grabbed for the edge. The Lord sprang from his seat and took her arms.

"Definitely not ready for any answers," he said.

Nadia pulled an arm free and smacked his chest. "I'm going back to my room." Her plan to march off was foiled when her right leg gave out. A moment later, she was in his arms.

"Put me down."

He simply looked at her with an amused expression, as if she were a kitten, hair fluffed up to make it look monstrous, spitting at a ball of yarn on the floor. "You're not walking back."

Nadia crossed her arms. "Well then, at least give me my books."

"I like my nose where it is, thank you very much," he said. "I'll send someone back for them."

Realizing she'd be on show the whole way back, Nadia deflated. "Please." Her eyes stung. "Put me down."

The Lord met her gaze. His arms tightened around her ever so slightly. "I don't trust your heart," he said. "It wasn't ready. I'm not going to risk the walk being too much for it." Her heart thumped once in agreement.

"I thought the danger was gone once the poison was gone," Nadia said.

"The danger from its whisperings is gone, but it tried to shred your heart as it left." He swallowed hard. "It usually clings and tries to remain, that's why it's removal is so painful. But you had so much..."

She could read the fear in his eyes. Was her pride really worth her life? A life so newly won?

"Very well," she said, giving in.

He adjusted her weight in his arms and strode off through the library.

It was not the first time she'd been in his arms, but it was the first time she'd had the ability to observe how it felt. With no distress to distract her, she noticed how the contact made her shiver, and not unpleasantly. Though, as she looked at the Lord's jaw and neck from this vantage point, her heart did feel funny.

"So, you don't think I'm out of danger yet?" Nadia asked, recalling stories of the ill and how they rallied.

Right before they died.

Her heart gave a frightened thump.

"I'm sure you are. The worst is probably behind you. Let's just not take any chances. Any unnecessary chances."

"Well," she argued. "You did tell me I was supposed to just carry on. That's all I've been doing."

His head tipped, a gesture he usually combined with an eye roll but not visible from her current vantage point. "I also told you that you needed time to heal. Let's focus on that first, shall we? You have plenty of time to continue."

Plenty of time. That was good news, at least.

The Lord settled her on the chaise in her room. A footman he had spoken to on their way up handed Nadia her books and bowed out again.

"Dinner in here again, I think," the Lord said.

"So much for my reputation," Nadia replied, her eyes full of mischief. "They'll be thinking you're wanting to make use of all those nightgowns you placed in my wardrobe."

His cheeks reddened. "When Uro first brought you back, you weren't quite what I expected."

"Obviously." She hummed a tune in her head to keep it from pulling up his first words to her, fearing her face would surely burst into flame. "You were obviously expecting a different kind of woman."

"Oh, you were different all right," he said. "I certainly had no idea what I was getting when I got you."

"Why didn't you?" Nadia asked, puzzled that he knew so much but not that.

The Lord finished tucking the throw around her. He fixed his gaze on the chaise, avoiding her face. "I try not to look too closely. Once I've determined things need to happen...well, let's just say, I don't like looking too closely at the hearts of men. If they already believe that they're owed the world at no price, they often try to cheat having to pay that price when it comes due." He fiddled with the throw, checking again that it was tucked properly.

"I knew they'd chosen you." His gaze flicked to hers. "Though not how. And you looked so happy to be there, on the hill. I thought...I thought you'd heard the stories about the dark dragon master who grants every wish. I thought you'd be one of those women who'd want to please me so that I'd want to please you, too."

He looked ashamed. "A thousand years is a long time to be alone. And I was usually not alone before I was banished, before—" His voice caught. He swallowed. "I thought that Uro had brought you back here to comfort me. I hated that I was so weak and that so were you." His eyes met hers, pleading their apology. "I misjudged you from the very start." He dropped to his knees.

"When did you know?" she asked.

"That you weren't some slut after riches or power?"

"Do they really do that?" Nadia asked.

"They intend to." A smirk crept across his face. "But they learn the error of their ways."

Hadn't she wanted something from him? Hadn't she hoped he'd give her what she desired—her death. "So not that different from me."

"In some ways, no. They have poison in their hearts, too. Usually acquired the same way but with a different outcome. They seek the things they think will keep them from gaining more of it." He grasped her good hand and stared at it. "You are unlike anyone who's ever passed through here. And I wished I'd seen it from the start."

Her heart contracted, but not from the kind words he'd spoken. They had passed through, the others. They hadn't stayed.

And she was determined to find out why.

Nicolette came to help her tidy before dinner. She had Nicolette put her hair up with the pearl hair pins. Nadia wrapped the strand of pearls around her neck, wanting to remind the Lord that he had given them to her. All the better to help her on her fishing expedition.

She sat reading on the chaise when the Lord arrived with the footmen and dinner. She felt better after having rested all afternoon but still used the Lord's arm as a crutch to travel to the dinner table. Mostly so she could hold it. And it didn't hurt to have him think her weak. Or, at least, not at her best.

The cook had fixed a shoulder of lamb, broiled and herbed new potatoes, and a cool, refreshing cucumber salad. There were fresh strawberry tartlets with heavy cream for dessert.

The Lord poured her a glass of raspberry wine. His eyes drifted to the pearls around her neck. Nadia fingered them.

"Will you tell me about her?"

His hand froze, leaving the wine decanter hovering above the table for a moment, before he slowly lowered the bottle.

"I know my gift was of great value to you," Nadia continued. "So I'd like to know a little more about her. About why you think I'm worthy of such a gift."

The Lord returned to his chair. He sank down onto it and pulled his wine to him but didn't drink, just twisted the glass between his fingers. A ghost of a smile crossed his face.

"Vivienne was a water spirit." His face twitched with almost laughter. "She was so beautiful but so shy that men—" The Lord glanced up at her. "—humans—that caught sight of her drowned, wading in after her as she fled from them. I'd heard tales of this enchantress and, wanting to meet a kindred spirit, sought her out." He looked at Nadia again. "She wasn't what I expected." A look of sadness crossed his face. "It had seemed so easy, to have succeeded where so many others had failed. I loved her and the watery world she introduced me to. But I was a god. The whole world was mine." He closed his eyes and slowly inhaled.

"I guess you could say I was neglectful of both her and the way others felt about me." He glanced at Nadia again. "Others grew jealous and whispered to her, pouring lies and doubt into her heart." Nadia's hand strayed to her bandage. "She came to me with her fears, but I paid them no mind. The world was my oyster with all the pearls to pluck. Why should I listen to her fears?"

This was why she hadn't heard the story with the poison in her heart. Even empty, she could feel its twisting echoes wanting to claim her.

"My father told me what had happened. Came with his rage and thunder to make me pay. Vivienne had become distraught at my neglect, convinced, as others had told her, that she'd simply been a challenge. A notch on my bedpost, if you will. In her watery home, the poisonous words twisted in her heart, not unlike what happened to you in my study. But imagine that in the sea with the water responding and adding itself to every movement." He covered his mouth with his fist, blinking back tears.

Nadia waited.

After a time, the Lord drank some wine and then, as she sat quietly, continued; each word heavy, reflecting the burden of his guilt. "The resulting storm, when she tore herself apart, wiped out a village under my father's protection. I'd been an 'arrogant fool' who could not be trusted, so he cast me out. Cast me out and gave me charge to keep others from doing as I had done."

"But they weren't your words that tore her apart," Nadia said.

"No, but I did nothing to counter them. My actions made them seem as if they were true. And..." He paused, tapping a finger against the clear base of his wine glass. "I don't think I've changed all that much. I was responsible for her death and... sometimes I wonder if Father hadn't cast me out, if I wouldn't have done it all again."

He bowed his head, as if he were waiting for her to add her affirmation to his claim, for hadn't he been careless with her, as well?

"I don't think that's true," she said. "You've saved me time and time again. You have not always been kind, but then I've not always been brave." She toyed with the napkin in her lap. "Your Vivienne sounds a lot like me. If she'd been brave enough to trust you, the poison may not have found a home." Tears gathered in Nadia's eyes. "If I'd trusted you, I wouldn't have gone looking for answers that you had told me I was not ready to hear. The poison was there, but I am the one who gave it power."

Nadia swallowed. "In that moment, I had no care for you or anyone else who would have found me. And I would have only destroyed myself. Vivienne must bear part of the responsibility for what happened for, as one of the sea, she must have known the kind of storm she'd raise. Those deaths are on her. And the ones who poisoned her against you."

The Lord lifted a sad smile. "And what is the one thing that is always spoken of about the gods?"

She knew it too well. "That they are not always fair."

"The fault may not be totally mine, but I am responsible. I did not cherish her and opened the door for the lies to take hold." Power gathered, crackling around him. The Lord's head came high. At that moment, there was no mistaking the god he was. "Actions have consequences, and it's best not to forget that."

Nadia bowed her head. "And what about justice? You are judge and executioner. At what point is a debt paid?"

"Some debts can never be paid."

"You have saved me over and over again." Nadia lifted her chin though she could not raise her eyes to his. "At what point would I stop being in your debt?"

"But—"

"But you've hurt me?" She finally met his eyes. "That debt was erased when you sat me down at your table and—" Nadia choked back her humiliation and her tears. "—*taught* me. You sat me in a place of honor and overlooked my utter baseness. Put a fork in my hand without rebuking me."

He looked away. "I was only doing what others should have."

"Exactly! For a thousand years, you have been doing what others should have. You haven't just paid for your crimes, you've paid for Vivienne's and everyone who poured poison into her ears.

"For a thousand years, your actions have had consequences. How many people have you saved? How many people have left you?" The Lord shifted uncomfortably. "I don't see any of them around to thank you, to remind you of how good your actions can be.

"I am not brave. I listen far too often to fear. My actions have had consequences that *you* have forgiven." She drew herself up as he had. "Your father may never forgive you, but I think it's high time you forgive yourself."

The Lord sat in stunned silence. Like a pricked balloon, her courage deflated.

"So. Thank you for answering my question." Nadia looked down and touched the pearls at her throat. "And thank you again for the pearls. I will endeavor to be worthy of them."

The Lord steepled his fingers and pressed them against his mouth. "You never cease to amaze me," he said through them.

"Is that a compliment?" she asked nervously, all too aware that she'd been arguing with, nearly shouting at a god. Her heart sunk with a sick realization. Oh, my! She'd all but insulted his father.

He burst out laughing. "Yes. Yes, it is." He picked up his wine. "To you, Nadia. And to Uro. He certainly knew what he was doing when he brought you back."

Shyly, Nadia raised her glass, embarrassed at the compliment. "To Uro," she echoed, and gently knocked her glass against his.

The meal proved delicious and the conversation turned to things less serious. She had gotten one burning question answered, but it had raised more. She'd sought to compare herself to the Lord's beloved and wasn't sure she liked what she had found.

twenty-eight

With a last desperate effort, Nadia jerked upright, the scream still harsh in her throat. Darkness filled her room, the shadows offering a quiet comfort. Nadia tugged at the bedsheets, freeing herself from their confines. They had twisted around her, trapping her, in much the way the Lord's arms had done when he drained the poison. Still gasping for breath, Nadia lay back and willed her frantic heart to slow.

The dream had been too real. Even now, in the moonlit dark, it felt like she could slip back beneath the waves.

Nadia clenched her hand. But what was this? She sat up again. Opening her palm, Nadia peered at it in the moonlight, only to suck in a breath when she spied the bandage from her chest.

Tears pricked her eyes. The story the Lord had told her about Vivienne had chewed away in the back of her mind as she'd drifted off to sleep. And then took new form. It was her, not Vivienne, whom the men pursued, a kelp forest instead of a fairy fort that she retreated to. It was her, not Vivienne, whom the Lord pursued. And won. Wrapping his arms around her, he whispered words of love in her ear until she neither knew nor cared where one of them left off and the other began.

Until he left.

The next one needs me, he cried as he rode away on Uro.

You were only one of many, voices echoed in her ear. *Did you really think you could hold the Lord's attention?*

In her dream, she had sought to escape to the safety of the forest, but Uro burnt it down. *Did you really think you could stay?* Uro asked her.

The voices shouted at her, each one saying something new, tearing apart her dreams in an ever-growing cacophony. In the chaos, she became Vivienne and Vivienne became her. They knew what they needed to do. They needed to rip out the poison.

But as they reached for their heart, the part that was her, Nadia, hesitated. The poison was no longer there. The Lord had drained it. And she knew that if Vivienne wasn't stopped, the storm would be raised and the village wiped out. They would die. And the Lord would pay for it for eternity.

With a desperate effort, she attempted to split herself in two, wrestling with the energy that was merging them, all the while trying to keep Vivienne from ripping out their heart. She had nearly succeeded when Vivienne transformed into a monstrous fury with eyes of lightning.

You just want him for yourself! Vivienne had screamed and, as Nadia froze in shock, ripped at their heart.

Blinking, Nadia let the dream slip away. She glanced down and stared at the bandage in her hand. How much of it had been real? Nadia ran her fingers over the scratches on her chest and slipped from bed to light a candle and check.

A study in the mirror revealed no new damage. Sinking down onto the chair, Nadia buried her face in her hands. The pearls shimmered in the candlelight, a lumpy, white snake on her dressing table.

In the dark, at that late hour, and with Vivienne's words till ringing in her ears, she began to wonder if the pearls were cursed.

Or if it was something else altogether.

With the light of the day, her dream seemed to be just that, a dream. But not entirely. Dreams were said to be messages from God. What could hers be? She didn't like the most obvious one. Still, just to be safe, she ought to ask the Lord a bit more about the pearls.

Her legs had regained most of their strength, supporting her weight as she moved about. Her heart, however, had fear camped out in it. And it showed on her face when they met.

"What is wrong?" he asked, concern etching his face.

Nadia wasn't sure which question to ask first. The pearls, she decided. That way one answer wouldn't be tainted by the other. "Has...have..." Nadia wavered, trying to figure out how best to ask the question. "Am I the first person to wear the pearls since Vivienne?"

He frowned. "And you want to know, why?"

Hesitating, Nadia ruffled the pages of the book in her hand. "Is there any chance...they could be cursed?"

"You've worn them for months and they were just fine." His eyes widened. The puzzlement vanished and a knowing look crossed his face. "My story gave you nightmares."

She nodded her confirmation. "It was like she was there, angry with me."

"Angry with you for what?"

With a jolt, recognition buzzed along her nerves. "Forgiving you," she whispered. And lied. If she couldn't admit it to herself, how could she confess it to him. But Vivienne's accusation rang again and again in her ears. Nadia shook her head, trying to dislodge it.

"At first, it was me—" *You were kissing.* She shook her head again. "—in the water—" *Leaving.* Nadia clenched her hands, desperate to keep them from straying to her ears. "—raising the st—"

The Lord's hands curled around hers. Nadia cried out. This was not what she wanted. She wanted a place to belong. This, as she'd seen last night, felt last night, could only destroy it all. Had his rejection of her in the ballroom taught her nothing?

Nadia choked back the emotion constricting her voice. "Raising the storm, destroying it all. Because you could never be forgiven," she said, weaving in her lie, hiding her heart. "They all leave you, so how could you be forgiven?"

But the falsehood ate at her. She risked hurting him, having him think the nightmare was a result of his guilt. "Why do they all leave you? Why don't they stay?" Nadia raised her head, certain that that fear, and not her longing, now rested in her eyes. "Do they not forgive you?"

He leaned toward her and placed his lips on her forehead. "Always so worried about me," he murmured. "Even in your dreams." He gave her hands a gentle squeeze. "I was not their happily ever after. And you need to let this go. I think Vivienne reminds you of yourself. You both love the sea. You both had the poison tell you to destroy yourselves."

"And you saved me."

"I got there in time...I was not able to do that for Vivienne." He squeezed her hands again. "Maybe your dream was a message for me. You have forgiven me, Nadia, but my debt is not paid."

She longed to slip her hand from his and caress his face, smooth away the pain she saw there. "Will you ever believe your debt paid?"

He released her. "It's not for me to believe or disbelieve."

If only he still held her hands. It was harder to keep them from his face when they were empty. "I'd set you free if I could," she said.

"Free to roam the earth and cause pain again?"

Which was exactly what he'd done last night in her dream, but Nadia shook her head. "Do you believe you've learned nothing in a thousand years?"

He didn't answer.

She reached out and touched his face. "If you were truly that selfish, would you have done everything that you've done for me?"

His fingers folded around hers, and he lowered her hand. The light faded from his eyes. His voice took on a deadness. "I was just doing my job."

Nadia slipped her hand from his. "I'd still do it," she said. "Your debt would end with me."

She got up from the table and turned her back on him. *I'd do it,* she whispered in her heart as she left him there. *I'd give up everything to set you free.*

♪♩♪♪♫♩♪♩♪♪♩♪

Nadia rested her arms on the sill and stared out the window of her morning room. She'd made a bargain today in the library. Whether the Lord's father would accept it remained to be seen. She rarely prayed. Despite the general concern of the church for everyone's souls, she had seldom been given leave to attend services. The Sabbath as a day of rest did not apply to her. To be fair, few of Lord Braemoor's servants rested on the

Sabbath, but they did get an afternoon a week off. All of them, except her.

As a result, she loved the peace of the sanctuary the rare times she found herself there. It had fulfilled the promise of its name. Nadia closed her eyes and inhaled, drawing up the memory of incense and beeswax, a muffled hush, patches of multicolored light cast by the stained glass windows.

The priest would surely think that she had landed in hell. Or, at least, was being held captive by a demon. She did not have the experience or the knowledge to reconcile the church's teachings with her situation, but she did not think the Lord evil. Lord Braemoor would be more deserving of that label. He had lied to everyone, and he had murdered her, for surely they thought of her as dead, as he had intended her to be. God had not chosen her as the sacrifice, for Lord Braemoor had stolen that choice from God.

But was the God of her church the Lord's father? She only knew that the world and what was in it was bigger than what she'd been taught within those four walls.

Still, if God heard prayers—and she believed he did, for hadn't she been rescued? Then perhaps he would hear this one.

"Dear Heavenly Father, thank you for sending Uro and the Lord to save me. I pray now that you will help me find a way to save him. He's been paying for his mistakes for a thousand years. I would ask that you consider his debt paid."

She hesitated. What was a thousand years to someone eternal? "And if you deem it unpaid, I would ask you to show me what can be done to help him. He is no longer neglectful, Father. And he suffers. Did you not say, 'Come to me all of you who are weary and carry heavy burdens?' I would ease his burden, and I ask you to show me how...Amen."

Nadia put her chin on her hands and continued to gaze out the window. As much as she longed to ease the Lord's burden, there was still some massive secret he was keeping from her. Of that, she was sure. And it frightened her as none of the others had.

♪♩♪♪♪♫♪♪♩♪♪

Despite her prayer, Nadia wondered if the Lord would show for dinner. She had crossed some line today in the library. He was, apparently, allowed to touch her, but she was not allowed to touch him. All those other women had caressed him, but he'd gone dead at her touch, shut himself off from her.

He was truly Vivienne's.

But he wanted to kiss you, the kind voice whispered.

She brushed the thought aside. It had been surprising when the voice continued to speak to her. Unlike the poison, this one was easier to ignore.

He's Vivienne's, she told herself again. And Vivienne could have him. She only wanted the safety this place offered. In Westfold, she had been the chicken at the bottom of the pecking order, subject to abuse from every other member of the flock so they could prove they weren't her. But here, no one scrambled to be better than anyone else. Either because it wasn't allowed or because they actually cared for each other. Somewhere else, she might not be so lucky. How could her happily ever after be anywhere but here?

And she had overstepped. Maybe he wouldn't let her stay if he thought she was like all the others.

♪♩♪♪♪♫♪♪♩♪♪

The Lord was not at dinner when she entered. Nadia sat and poured herself some wine. Perhaps she had scared him away. Perhaps she would now eat her meals alone.

And then he walked through the door. "Forgive my tardiness," he said as he entered, looking harried.

"Is the lord of the manor ever truly late?" Nadia asked. "Aren't all clocks set by him so the perfect time for anything is when he appears?"

"Still—" He took his seat. "One would never keep a lady waiting."

Would a lady have done what she had in the library? "I must apologize for having been so forward this afternoon," she said. "I fear my actions were unwanted." Nadia raised a smile. "But I stand by my words. You have no debt to me."

The Lord simply set his napkin in his lap without looking at her or even acknowledging that she had spoken. "Are you well enough to continue your music lessons?" he asked. He pulled the decanter toward him and filled their glasses, still avoiding her gaze.

Nadia's breath hitched, a sourness filling her stomach with his silent rebuke. "Yes."

"Herr Montfort would like to make up some of the time you've missed the last few days. I told him he could take my time in the afternoons so you could have one long, uninterrupted lesson." He paused for a moment and then slowly looked up. His face was guarded.

He was avoiding her. Or punishing her.

"Of course," Nadia replied. "After all, I don't know how many more lessons I'll get—" *Now that there's not much reason for me to be here,* had been on her tongue, but the words froze. Quickly, she changed it to, "Before he realizes I've gone as far as I can. My fingers just aren't all that flexible. They're more used to working together to scrub."

"They learned how to hold and use a pen."

"Yes," Nadia said. "But that's another exercise where they work together. They don't like having to work independently of one another on the keyboard." It killed her to admit it. Tangled up in her unease lay the dream that had led her to ask for music lessons. If she were to become something, why not a musician?

"They learned to work together to scrub from practice," the Lord said. "I'm sure they could learn to work independently the same way."

But his words were of little comfort. Despite the loss of the poison, her worry for the future sapped her ability to hope. "You're probably right," she told him. "I spent all that time practicing to improve my reading and that's coming along nicely." Nadia steeled herself. "I hardly need you at all now. I guess it's Herr Montfort's turn to see what he can do with me." She lifted a sweet smile that was really a mask. She had committed an error in the library and this was how she was paying for it. She'd just have to make him believe that it didn't bother her in the least.

For the next two weeks, she only saw the Lord at dinner. She would smile and pretend everything was fine. Answer his questions.

And try to get answers from others. At her music lesson, she asked Herr Montfort how long he had been in the castle.

"Many years, milady." He gave her a kind, grandfatherly look.

"How did you end up here?" There had to be some pattern she could tease out.

But his smile faded. "This is not a place to ask such questions, Fraulein."

"I'm sorry. I've just lived with such uncertainty," Nadia explained.

Herr Montfort patted her arm. "He has good reasons for doing what he does." He frowned, debating some internal question. "Do you remember the dust that lay here the first time we met?" Nadia nodded. "He had kept this room from me. When it was given back, I appreciated the instruments and—" He smiled kindly. "—the student. So, indulge an old man. Let me teach."

It was a kind way to tell her to stop with the questions. Nadia obliged him and worked on her lessons, missing the dark figure that no longer hovered outside the doorway when she played.

She tried again with Nicolette and got the same response, but with a, "Just let me serve you." She didn't know the other servants as well and lacked the courage to ask. What if they found her impertinent?

As the days dripped by, she began to feel shut out of the castle. In many ways, as friendless as when she'd been alone. More so, for the Lord had been there to lift her spirits. If he noticed her growing melancholy, he didn't comment on it.

After yet another night of stilted dinner conversation, Nadia couldn't take it any longer and excused herself early. Back in her room, she pulled the pins from her hair. As she placed them back in the box, her fingers brushed the pearls. She'd not worn them since her nightmare. And it wasn't like they were actually hers. They were Vivienne's. Just like the Lord was still hers.

It was time to return them. Leaving her hair hanging free on her shoulders, Nadia picked up the pearls. She'd just slip them back into the box. The Lord needn't know.

The corridors were empty. Her heart began to beat frantically as she neared his study, as though it remembered what had happened the last time she was there.

"I'm not touching anything this time," she told it.

She didn't knock. Grasping the handle, Nadia pushed. The door opened easily under her hand.

But the room wasn't empty. She'd been so busy arguing with herself she hadn't noticed the light from under the door.

"Nadia."

"My Lord." She gulped.

He closed the book in his hands.

"I...uh..." Nadia wrapped her fingers through the strand and held it out. "I wanted to return these."

A hurt look crossed his face. "Why?"

Nadia turned her gaze to the floor. "I don't feel that they belong to me. They were Vivienne's and, by rights, should belong to you."

He crossed to the fire and leaned an arm against the mantle, turning his back to her. Her arm wavered in the air.

"They were a gift," he said.

"To you," she argued.

"And I gave them to you."

Nadia let her arm drop. "Why?"

He met her gaze over his shoulder. "Because I miss the sea." He gave her a sad smile. "Because you have never been. Because I wanted to make the stories real for you."

"Too real," Nadia said.

He turned from the fireplace. "I should not have told you that story."

"And kept yourself hidden away?" she asked. He didn't answer. "At the manor, I knew everyone too well. I always got to see the worst. But here?" Nadia searched for the words. "Everything is hidden. There are secrets everywhere." She held out the pearls again. "I can't take them. If they are going to make you hide away, I don't want them."

His jaw ticked, and he looked away. "You don't want to see who I am."

Her hand dropped again. "I've a pretty good idea who you are. You are death and salvation. You are vindictive and kind. You are fury and sorrow. You are the kind of person who would take the lowest of the low and make her a princess time and time again.

"And you're afraid. You are afraid that what you've done can never be forgiven but, even more, never should be." Nadia lifted the pearls. "So take them. If you need to be reminded of all the wrong you've done, then you need these more than I do."

The Lord closed the distance between them. He clasped his hands around her fist and raised it to her chest. "I should have let them go long ago." He squeezed her hand. "You deserve them, perhaps more than Vivienne and definitely more than me for, though you think it not true, you are brave." He leaned closer and whispered. "How many people are willing to stand up to a god?"

With that, he released her. The pearls trickled down along her chest. "Good night, Nadia. I will see you tomorrow."

Nadia turned in a fog of confusion. What had just happened?

"I'm locking my door from now on," he called after her. "You just can't seem to stay out of trouble."

Nadia stared at the strand of pearls resting beside her on her pillow, shimmering in the moonlight. She ran a finger over them, a bumpy, silky path inches from her nose.

He thought her brave.

Well, you did face a dragon with a smile on your face.

"I thought I was facing death." Nadia closed her eyes. "I thought I was finally facing death."

The kind voice laughed, a tinkling sound like a brook. *And how many people go happy to their deaths? Death is their greatest fear. They hide and hope to cheat him. But not you.*

"I would now," she whispered.

For now, you have a reason to stay.

Tears gathered in her eyes. She didn't want the wanting of it. It hurt too much.

It?

"Him!" she said, lashing out at the voice, tossing the word like a knife. "I don't want him!" But, God help her, she did.

Nadia clutched the pearls in her hand. She had feared becoming Vivienne's replacement. Had rebelled at the idea. Now, she wanted nothing more.

You sought to be a better Elsbeth. Why couldn't you be a better Vivienne?

"Because he'll just shut me out again. He doesn't really want me."

Are you so sure about that?

twenty-nine

Once she'd broken her morning fast, her intention had been to work in her morning room, but Nadia found herself walking along the corridor and then pushing open the door to the starlit ballroom instead. The globes danced across the ceiling, much as she and the Lord had danced not that long ago. The night she'd tried to rip her heart out. After it had broken. After he'd told her he wanted to kiss her and then didn't.

Something forgotten buzzed in her brain. Nadia reached out to capture it.

There are still truths to be told.

He'd said something else, but she'd lost it. Lost it when her heart had broken. Just the first of many wounds it had suffered that night. And the next morning.

Nadia sat on the floor and watched the celestial dance. It amazed her that she had survived the hours that had come after that one magical, nightmare ball. She nearly hadn't, she reminded herself. The Lord had thought she'd died, feared she had died, for a while.

She hugged her knees close, still trying to work out what he'd meant that night. What about his kiss wouldn't have been fair? That the poison could have twisted his words and deeds until she believed he'd taken advantage of her? That she didn't know the truth about his banishment, about Vivienne?

Nadia considered that last question more carefully.

He'd been here a thousand years, with no hope to leave.

Maybe that was what was not fair. To fall in love with him, to choose to love him, would mean to join him.

Maybe that's why they never stayed. Finally free of the poison, they came to see this place as a prison, not a sanctuary. An angry huff escaped her lips. The Lord's father had ripped his son from the world, made him judge and executioner of those who behaved as his son once had, had him heal those who'd been poisoned like Vivienne, and made sure no one would stay. No wonder the Lord sought comfort where he could.

No wonder he wouldn't touch her. He'd pursued Vivienne, and look what that had gotten him. And he didn't think he'd changed very much.

Stupid! Stupid! Nadia screwed her eyes shut. He didn't trust himself and she'd gone and caressed him. What else was he to do but shut himself away.

Nadia laid her chin on her knees. Heaven help her. She loved him even more than she'd thought.

A shockwave coursed through her, nearly sending her to the floor as the words registered in her brain. She loved him. *Oh, Lord—oh, God!* She loved him.

Hurling herself to her feet, Nadia paced the floor, chewing on her nails in her distraction. She wasn't supposed to love him. And yet, how could she not?

She stumbled over to a wall, unseeing, and rested her hands on it. Her heart beat joyfully against her ribs, but Nadia couldn't shake the fear that played at the edges of her soul. At least the poison was no longer there to add its voice.

He'd wanted to kiss her. But hadn't. The poison was gone, and he hadn't. She knew about Vivienne, and still he hadn't. He'd pushed her away. So she wouldn't stay?

But she wanted to stay...

Even if he takes the next one to bed?

A splintering crack ran down her heart. Nadia pressed a hand to her chest.

Could you bear it, if he takes the next one to bed?

Maybe that's why they never stay. They can't stand to watch him do it all over again.

I was not their happily ever after.

"No," Nadia whispered. "But you were mine."

Nadia stopped by the library that afternoon to exchange her book before her lesson with Herr Montfort. She meant it to be a quick trip, just to find additional stories about the piskies. She hadn't meant to look in the Lord's reading nook.

But she did.

His book of poetry was back. He'd probably thought it safe since they no longer met for lessons here and she had her morning room. But, as ever, it drew her like a moth to the flame. And usually with the same results.

She flipped slower this time, reading snatches of what were definitely poems the Lord had written about Vivienne, watched his handwriting change over time. But as she got to the newer ones, the ones written in a hand she'd recognize anywhere, the poems changed. It was true that Vivienne's heart had been torn apart by lies, but Vivienne's heart could never be mended. Nadia's breath caught. But *hers* could. Though she had never loved.

Nadia shook her head to dislodge the whisperings the kind voice started before they fully took shape. Sitting on the floor, she leafed through the book, reading the heart of the Lord. Her hands dropped to her lap when she read the last entry:

She has suffered, so she understands suffering.
She has cried, so she recognizes pain.
She looks at me and I don't have to explain.
She just sees me as I am.
She just sees me as I am.

The ink was fresh. Grains of sand still stuck to the page.

Nadia gathered all the reasons the poem couldn't be about her. One, he was constantly having to explain himself to her. Two...two...

She fought to come up with a second reason, but all she could picture was standing in his study last night, yelling at him that she knew who he was.

You just can't stay out of trouble.

Nadia laid the book back on the table and scrambled up. Apparently, the Lord had a pretty good idea who she was, too.

The dark shadow that had loitered in the hall outside the music room returned. Nadia took that as a sign that she'd been forgiven. It also strangely emboldened her, though she'd have to tread carefully.

That night, she dressed for dinner with a care to catching the Lord's eye. She had Nicolette lace her into a gown of aquamarine and put her hair up with the pearl-studded pins. Nadia wrapped Vivienne's pearls around her throat for the first time since the nightmare.

"You look stunning, milady," Nicolette told her.

Nadia smoothed her hands over her skirts and reviewed her reflection in the full-length mirror. "You don't think it's too much? Does it look like I'm trying?"

Nicolette's eyes twinkled. "Do you want to be trying?"

A blush burned its way up to her ears, heating her face long before it appeared in the mirror. "No, I—" Nadia's gaze fell. Her face became like flame.

"You can just tell him you finally feel like you can wear the gowns." Nicolette moved to the wardrobe and shut the door. "Heaven knows it took you long enough." She turned back around, a saucy smile on her face. "If you get his attention, too...just count it as gravy."

Nadia turned from the mirror. "Why don't they stay, Nicolette? The others?"

The question brought an abrupt change in Nicolette. The smile vanished. Her expression became guarded. "I wouldn't worry about that, milady. Just enjoy yourself while—" Nicolette sucked in a breath. "While the summer sun is shining." She bobbed a curtsy. "Have a good evening, miss. Ring when you need me."

Nadia sank down onto the dressing table chair. Why did that question frighten everyone so?

The Lord's gaze lingered on Nadia as she entered the dining room. She was nearly to her chair before he jumped to his feet and pulled it out for her. "I see you decided to use Nicolette again," he said.

Nadia took her seat, avoiding his eyes. "I did. I figured it was time to truly start putting her to use."

He pushed her in. "She will appreciate that more than you know." Nadia shook out her napkin, all too aware that his gaze was still fixed on her as the returned to his seat. "You're wearing the pearls, as well."

Nadia fingered them. "Yes. Since you wouldn't take them back, I decided I should wear them. Try to make them mine." Heat ran to her face at her slip, and she rushed to cover it up. "Try to remember that you gave them to me because we share something you love." Nadia slowly raised her eyes. "If I never get a chance to see the sea, between the stories and the pearls, it will be like I've been. Just like you took me to Arabia." She managed a small smile.

"I hope you will see the sea someday." His lips curved into a smile that didn't reach his eyes, and then he picked up his fork. He poked at the trout on his plate but didn't eat.

He hoped she'd leave.

"I wish there was some way for you to see it, too," Nadia said.

"I have my scrying bowl. Just as it showed you your heart's desire, it would show me mine." A pained expression crossed his face. He poured some wine. "Though without the sound of the waves and the salty tang of the air." He forced a smile onto his face as he handed her the glass and met her eyes.

Nadia took it from him. "You did the ceiling. Why not a room or a lake with waves?"

The golden stream of wine trickling into his glass came to a halt. He set the decanter down, his glass only half-full. He gave Nadia a tight shake of his head and then picked up his fork and started in on his dinner, his gaze firmly fixed on his plate.

She'd done it again, crossed some line. Nadia looked down at her food. It was only a fillet, but she felt as if the glassy eyes of an entire fish were staring at her. She was completely useless. What did she think she was playing at?

The answer floored her. The poison was gone. It was time to go. The Lord was preparing her for her departure.

A pain nearly as great as that of the poison leaving scraped the inside of her heart. Nadia clutched at the arm of her chair. The Lord glanced up, concern written on the furrow between his eyes.

"I'm not feeling well," she said. "I think I'll go back to my room."

He was at her side in an instant. One hand went around her wrist, taking her pulse, the other brushed her face. "You're so pale."

Fire trailed across her skin. Unable to stop herself, she leaned into his hand, wanting to melt into him, wanting the fire to burn away her pain.

"Your pulse is thready."

Because my heart is broken, she wanted to shout. "Please," she whispered. She couldn't do this anymore—any dinners, any pretending everything was fine.

"What do you want? Water?"

Nadia blinked back the sting in her eyes. She needed to be back in her room where she could fall apart properly.

With a jerk of his head, the Lord motioned for the footmen to leave. When they were alone, he repeated his question. "What do you want, Nadia?"

The hand around her wrist tightened, anchoring her to the chair, as if he knew she wanted to run.

What did she want most of all?

She wanted him, but he was not hers to have. She could make herself live without the Lord.

Even when the next one comes?

The kind voice knew her heart's desire, both of them, twisted up into one large knot of longing.

"I want to stay." She raised her eyes to his. "They always leave, but I want to stay." A tender smile crossed his face. "Please," she said. "Let me stay."

"Oh, Nadia." The Lord took her hand in both of his. His thumbs brushed against its back. "You worry too much. What is true for every person who passes through here?"

Nadia shifted her weight away from him. "Their poison gets drained."

He chuckled. "Yes, that's true. But what do they get?" She longed to pull her hand from his and be done with it. "Think, Nadia. What do they get?"

She stared at him, but her mind wouldn't go where he asked. Her brain buzzed, and her hand tingled.

"Aurora, Rapunzel, Snow. Do I need to go on?"

Her brow furrowed. She'd know what they had in common, once upon a time.

Once upon a time...

That was the beginning.

And how did it all end? the kind voice asked.

"Happily ever after," Nadia whispered.

"Exactly!" the Lord said. "They all found their happily ever after. That's what you should be focused on." His gaze fell to his grasp. "If I let it go, are you going to bolt?"

Nadia shook her head. The Lord gave her hand a squeeze and released it. "So what does your happily ever after look like?"

Nadia clutched her hand to her chest. If felt empty, yet tingly. "Um." She fought for focus. "I'm here."

"Why?"

She prayed the flush she could feel creeping across her face wasn't visible. "It's my home. It's my home now." Her lungs shuddered as she drew her next breath. "I haven't really had a home in so long." Nadia squeezed her hand to stop her trembling.

The Lord leaned in and placed a kiss on the top of her head. "No, you haven't," he murmured. "I can see why the idea of leaving would upset you. What else, what else does it look like?"

"Um..." Nadia fought to find the answer, but her brain refused to land on anything solid. Her thoughts kept getting lost in a swirling fog of sketchy images.

"No matter." He leaned back from her, straightening. "So that will be your next task. Figure out what that looks like. But not tonight." He handed Nadia her wine. "Tonight, you need only eat your dinner."

The Lord knocked on her morning room door, surprising her with his appearance. He had a blanket over his arm and a basket in his grip. Nadia tucked a scrap of paper between the pages of her book. "I see you have a picnic planned."

"I spend too much time in my study and you spend too much time in here. The roses are in bloom." Nadia flinched. "Or we can venture out into the park." He hoisted the basket. "You pick the spot."

A fine sunny day, with the Lord by her side? "Well, if you insist."

She chose a spot on the vast lawn of the park, not too far from the shade of a willow tree. The Lord spread out the blanket, avoiding the butterflies that fluttered from flower to flower around them.

"Let's see what we have." The Lord dropped down. Hiking up one knee, he began to hand her the contents of the basket. "One bottle of wine—Riesling. Two glasses." He passed them to Nadia. "Sandwiches—chicken salad, I think." He placed them on the blanket and then pulled the lid off a small serving dish. "Ah, gurkensalat—cucumber salad." He set that down next to the basket. "Grapes. And plates."

Nadia accepted hers with a murmured, "Thank you," and ran her finger over the pattern of blue and rose accented with curling, gold scrolls. "Your picnics are always so fancy."

"If one is to dine al fresco, it should truly be at ease." He worked the cork from the bottle and poured her a glass. "What should we toast to?" he asked, filling his.

Her nose crinkled as she thought. "Fine summer days?"

"Of course." The Lord brought his glass to hers. "Fine summer days."

Nadia took a sip. A bright, sweetness greeted her tongue. "So this is my happily ever after?"

"Do you want it to be?"

Lifting her face to the sun, Nadia savored the warmth on her cheeks. "Today it is."

"There you go then." He clinked his glass against hers again. "One happily ever after."

"Do I get only one?" Fear gathered in her chest. Maybe they were like wishes.

The Lord laughed. "The term 'ever after' does imply a continuance. You could consider this yours for today." He took a sip of his wine. "What would it look like tomorrow?" He placed a few of the finger sandwiches on her plate and then dug two forks out of the basket as she considered.

Nadia gathered her knees to her chest and looped her free arm around them. "I don't know. Something simple."

The Lord put the container with the cucumber salad between them and placed a napkin at Nadia's feet. "If you would permit me to be so bold, how about something you failed at earlier? The cake?" Nadia colored and focused her gaze on her knees. "I know you burnt the last one, but this time you could have a teacher. Would you like to learn?" He turned a sandwich over in his fingers like a worry stone. "I'd understand if you'd prefer to stay away from the kitchen, but it was something you desired once."

Her cheeks heated. Nadia prayed the Lord would think it was just the sun. She picked up one of the sandwich squares and nibbled at it. The creamy salad with its savory spices and tender chicken brought a moan of pleasure to her lips.

"Darla is quite the cook," the Lord said, agreeing with her assessment. "It pained her to watch you try so hard and fail. She and Elsie and Meg got quite used to having you every morning and afternoon, always trying to help them. Won't you let them help you?"

Nadia speared several slices of cucumber, breathing in the aroma of sour cream and vinegar that wafted up from the bowl, before shaking them off her fork and onto her plate. She leaned her chin against her knees and ignored the small hairs batting against her face in the gentle breeze. *I'm not always brave,* she had told him. Could she go back and face her failure? Face the people who'd watched her stumble around like an idiot all those months? People whom she hadn't even wanted to exist?

I thought you wanted to stay, the kind voice said.

If this was to be her home, shouldn't she make it her home? The Lord would say that if she was brave enough to stand up to him, then she could face anything.

Nadia blew out a slow breath. "Very well." She lifted her face to meet his. A warmth spread through her chest, cancelling out her doubt. "Tell...Darla? Does she go by Cook or Darla?" She couldn't imagine a cook being called anything but "Cook."

"I call her 'Cook.' She finds 'Darla' too impertinent coming from me." His eyes held a merry glint. "But everyone else calls her 'Darla.'"

"Tell Darla, I'd be glad to have her show me how to bake," Nadia said. Hope and desire began to spread in her chest.

The Lord grinned broadly. "I'll look forward to sampling your efforts."

thirty

Nadia had anticipated eating her breakfast in the kitchen, but Nicolette arrived with the tray before she'd finished dressing. She drank her coffee and ate the toast with cheese and then took the tray down with her.

As Nadia carried it through the corridors, it occurred to her how much of her old self was gone. She hadn't carried anything heavier than a book in months. Her hands were now smooth and supple. And her place was no longer in the kitchens. There were a thousand other little things, but they added up to a completely different person. The idea brought a furrow to her brow.

Nadia pushed the door open to the kitchen. Three women looked up from their work.

"Oh, here miss. Let me get that for you." The girl with gray eyes and nutmeg colored hair braided up in a bun took it from her.

"Thank you…" Nadia trailed off, having no idea what to call her.

"Elsie," the girl said, filling in the blank. "I'm Elsie. This here is Meg." The blond girl shelling peas gave her a nod. "And Darla is our cook."

Darla wiped her hands on a towel. "Go put that in the sink, Elsie, and take over this for me." Elsie gave her a nod of acknowledgement. "Well," Darla said, stepping away from the stove. "I dare say you know your away around a kitchen, but I take it you haven't done much actual cooking."

Heat blossomed on Nadia's cheeks. "No ma'am."

Darla chuckled. "No matter. We'll soon get that fixed. Eh, girls?"

Meg and Elsie smiled and murmured their agreement.

"Broke my heart to see you so upset over your cake attempt. But I'll get you fixed right." Darla motioned Nadia over to a place on the large harvest table. "Bowl," Darla said, and handed her one, the woman's large, muscular arms rippling with every movement. "Whisk. That's the secret to a light cake. No mixing it with a spoon."

"Whisk," Nadia echoed, and set it next to the bowl.

"I don't have receipts written down. When you've done it as much as I have, it's all up here." Darla tapped her finger to her temple. "But I'll talk you through it." She handed Nadia a measuring cup. "One cup flour. One cup sugar. One and one-half teaspoons leavening. Whisk that together. Gently!" she added as the flour tried to jump out of the bowl.

Nadia smiled and did smaller movements.

"It's all in the wrist. Just like scrubbing but with more turning." Darla watched her. "That looks good. Now—" She handed Nadia another bowl and a spoon. "—we mix the wet ingredients. They mix better if you do them separate and then combine. One cup butter. I've packed it in with a spoon to get any air pockets out. Just run a knife around it and tap."

Nadia did as she was told. The creamy, yellow fat fell with a splat into the bowl.

"Two eggs. Beat those together. One half-cup milk." Darla slowly poured it in as Nadia stirred. "Next time you can do this part on your own." She watched the stream. "Okay, now switch to the whisk. And now—" Darla turned an pulled a small brown bottle from the shelf. "One teaspoon of the best spice there is—vanilla." A secret smile glowed on the woman's large face.

"Ooh! Can I just smell it?" Meg asked.

"Please!" Elsie added.

Darla laughed. "Oh, all right." She gave Nadia a nudge with her elbow. "It's an aphrodisiac," she whispered to Nadia as the girls left their tasks and came around the table.

Darla pulled the stopper from the bottle. A sweet, creamy, lightly floral scent rose from it and caressed Nadia's nose. She closed her eyes and breathed in again just as Darla whisked the bottle to her other side and held it out to the other two girls.

"Oh," Meg sighed. "Isn't it amazing?"

"A couple of dabs behind the ears and you'll have every man running after you," Elsie added.

Darla moved the bottle away from them. "This is not a perfume. I catch any of you messing with this bottle and you'll be on laundry duty instead."

"Yes 'em," Meg and Elsie said in unison, hanging their heads.

"Anyway, one teaspoon of this." Darla measured it out and poured it herself. "Here's the best part." She filled a cup with milk and stirred the spoon in it. "We don't let any of this go to waste. Taste it."

Nadia brought the cup to her lips and nearly swooned. And she'd thought chocolate magical! Meg and Elsie looked at her longingly.

"Here." Nadia offered them the cup. "I don't need more than a sip."

The girls began to bolt in Nadia's direction, but one glance from Darla slowed them down.

"Thank you," Meg said. She took the cup from Nadia.

"Thank you," Elsie echoed.

"Now whisk the dry into the wet," Darla said. She handed Nadia another cup to use as a scoop. "Just break up any lumps with the back of a spoon."

Once the batter was mixed, Darla handed Nadia a cake pan. "Grease it with lard—butter burns too easily—and then put a spoonful of flour in. Bang it around until the pan is covered."

Nadia did as instructed. Darla then had her pour the batter in and use her finger to scrape the edges of the bowl. "Don't want any of that to go to waste." Darla had Nadia hand the dirty dishes to Meg to be washed and then motioned her over to the oven.

"The true secret to baking is the heat. Anyone can mix up batter. But a good cook knows the right heat and how to control it."

Darla opened the oven door and stuck her hand in. "Feel that?" Nadia stuck hers in as well. "Hot, but not too hot. You can linger, but you don't want to for more than a moment or two. That's the right temperature. We need to keep the fire consistent at this temperature. Too much hotter and the cake will burn. If the temperature drops, it will rise funny and be dry. Stick it in."

Nadia slid the pan in.

"Now we have time for one cup of tea. We don't want to open the door to check it until we think it's done, and we don't want to get distracted." Darla took down two cups and poured water from the kettle into a teapot. "I developed this method to help me time it." She smiled widely at Nadia and tossed three scoops of tea into the pot.

It was strange, sitting and drinking tea with Darla while the other girls worked. "They'll get some of the cake," Darla said in response to Nadia's glances at them.

To fill the time, Nadia asked Darla about her favorite dishes. It seemed a safer topic than inquiring about the woman's past.

"I cooked for a duchess, you know," Darla said, leaning close and whispering. She sat back. "You would think cooking for a god would be more difficult, but no. Pickiest person I ever came across, that duchess. I learned to be real creative. I like decorating things."

"Those picture sandwiches you did were lovely," Nadia said. "And delicious."

Darla gave a hearty laugh. "That's an old one I pulled out of my hat. The Lord doesn't do fancy too often, but that's one I managed to squeak by."

When their tea had been drunk and Darla deemed the cake ready, she had Nadia open the door. A delicious, sweet smell wafted out when Nadia peered in. The cake was perfectly golden and held when Darla instructed her to touch it with a finger.

Nadia pulled the cake out with padded mittens and set it on the table. "Time to wash up our cups, and then it will be ready to take out of the pan to finish cooling. Don't want it to stick," Darla warned her.

Once the cups were washed, she had Nadia run a knife around the edge of the pan, and then tip the cake out onto a wire rack to finish cooling. When it was ready, Darla sliced the cake into two discs, beat up some cream with sugar and vanilla (and proved why her arms were so muscular), spread a layer of strawberry jam on the bottom layer, added the whipped cream, put the top back on, dusted the cake with pounded sugar, and made another pot of tea.

Meg and Elsie came over to join them. "Ring for Bertram," Darla told them. "We'll send a slice and some tea in to his lordship."

Even though it was not a smoking mess and Darla had helped her, Nadia was still nervous to try it.

"The cook should always get the first bite," Darla said, and gave Nadia some insight as to Darla's bulk.

Come to think of it, Cook had been on the hefty side, too. Must be the result of tasting everything.

Nadia's hand trembled as she cut her fork into the cake and then lifted it to her mouth, three sets of eyes watching nervously. "Delicious," she decreed from behind her hand.

Darla nudged her. "Couldn't be anything but. Just let me know if you'd like to learn anything else." Meg and Elsie nodded their enthusiasm for that idea, their mouths being full. "Now what was that receipt?"

Nadia rattled it off. If the Lord's intension had been to make her feel at home, it had certainly worked.

This is what a kitchen should be like, she thought as she ate the cake she'd baked and drank tea with three people genuinely glad for her presence. She didn't even mind that her face hurt from smiling when she finally begged her departure, for Herr Montfort was waiting.

He had a surprise for her as well.

"I've asked Fritz to join us," he told Nadia. A lanky young man with red hair and the scruffy beard of youth nodded from the corner where he tuned the strings of a lute. She couldn't remember if he had played at the ball or not.

She gave him a tremulous, "Hello."

"You've been doing well on your own, but a true musician can play with others. It's tricky," Herr Montfort warned her. "You must listen to your partner and adjust your playing to match theirs, otherwise it's all gobbledygook." He opened "When the Nightingale Sings" on the stand above the keyboard as Fritz's dischordic twanging settled into a melodic running of scales.

Nadia shook out the nerves that were trying to freeze the muscles in her arms and blew out a slow breath. Not half an hour ago, she'd been pleased with the Lord's maneuvering. Now she would have placed him on Father Christmas's naughty list. Not that she truly believed in the old man, but anything was possible.

Two weeks later, Herr Montfort had Nadia give her first concert. Fritz on his lute, Abner on recorder, and Rafe on drum. They sat at the head of a white room with gold silk panels. Rows of white gilded chairs marched back toward the door. Herr Montfort was expecting sixty people. She hadn't even realized that sixty people lived in the castle, but there had to be more. There'd been at least forty at Westpark, not that she'd stopped to count, and the manor was tiny compared to the Lord's castle. Though vast and relatively empty, there had to be a hundred or more living here.

Nadia warmed up her fingers and waited as people began to file into the room. The crowd stood as the Lord entered and walked down the aisle like a dark ghost, taking their seats again with a rumble of feet and creaking of chairs.

Herr Montfort gave no introduction, just raised his hands in the air, flicked his baton, and they were off.

They received polite applause at the end of every song. When Nadia and the others stood at the end to take their bow, the Lord rose, clapping, the rest of the audience following behind him.

Nadia took hands with Fritz, Abner, Rafe, and Herr Montfort, her heart thrumming in tempo with the applause. The air shook with the force of it. The Lord gave Nadia a smile full of pride but with a hint of mischief as his hands beat out their praise.

Heat crept across her cheeks. Nadia dipped her head as she curtsied yet again. What else would the Lord orchestrate to prove how much she'd changed?

thirty-one

"Would you mind working as a servant again?" the Lord asked Nadia at dinner a few days later.

Her face went cold. It had finally come, the time to return. He'd found a place for her as a servant. *Just be brave.* She set her fork down before it fell from her grip. "If that's what you think I should do," Nadia said, afraid to lift her eyes.

"Once a year, I hold a fête for the servants. Though they are here to learn to serve, they still deserve a party, don't you think?"

Relief filled her heart. "Very generous," she said, smiling. Lord Braemoor had never done anything for them. They'd had to make do with the leftovers from events like Elsbeth's birthday or Christmas.

"Since I am giving them a day off, I think it's fitting that I serve them. And since you are no longer a servant, and they are serving you, I wondered if you would be interested in helping me?" He gave Nadia an encouraging smile.

"I guess it wouldn't be fair," she said. "One person waiting on a hundred. Where, since I could do it in my sleep, I could be counted as two. Or three." Her eyes sparked with glee.

"Good," the Lord said with a nod. "All settled then."

When Nadia looked out her window the morning of the fête, maids and footmen could be seen hauling chairs and baskets of supplies in the direction of the park. Kegs of beer and cider rolled by, rumbling on the cobblestones before they hit the gravel of the path.

Nadia put on her loden-green dress and tied up her hair without Nicolette's help. She'd excused her after Nicolette had brought up the breakfast tray, sending her out to help with the final preparations instead.

Making her way through the courtyard, she passed a servant carrying a goose. The creature, sensing its danger for being used in one of the blindfold games, squawked loudly and beat its wings, throwing feathers into the air.

The park was a hive of festivity. A large marquee had been set up to house the tables of food that were basically self-serve. Another covered the kegs where she and the Lord would be working. Colorful ribbons fluttered in the air, tied on the crossbeams of the quiots and coconut shies booths. Beneath them stood tiers of cakes that Darla had decorated up "all fancy." Both were to be offered as prizes at the games. A checkered queek mat had been spread out and sat ready and waiting for the wagers to be made and stones to be tossed.

"Are they actually going to be gambling?" she asked the Lord as she entered the tent.

He laughed. "Yes, with the only currency they have here— time. They're betting how much time the loser has to take over from the winner's chores."

He looked strange with his white shirtsleeves rolled up to the elbow and an apron covering him from his collar to his knees. He handed Nadia one.

"This is a first," she said, taking it from him. "No one ever cared about keeping my clothes clean before."

"You were the one doing your laundry before," he said to her. "And today is about giving them time off."

She tied it around her. "Beer or cider?"

"Beer for the gentlemen, cider for the ladies," the Lord said. He twirled a mug in his hand. "So I'm beer, and you're cider."

In many ways, it was like a repeat of Elsbeth's birthday. Nadia pulled drinks while other people enjoyed the games, though this time she actually got lunch. The Lord manned both stations while Nadia ducked into the food tent and brought back sandwiches which they sat and ate during a lull.

She was even pulled from her chore and herded away. Late in the evening, when the moths had come out to bump against the glass of the lanterns, several members of the staff came in, untied their aprons, and put them on, insisting that Nadia and the Lord join the dance.

Once again, she found herself standing hip-to-hip with him, their hands clasped. This time under a starlit sky that did not move. Right turn, left turn, hands high, hands low, around the waist—

The Lord hoisted her into the air, balanced her against his hip, and turned. She stared into his eyes even after she slid down, nearly missing the curtsy she was supposed to do.

And then he handed her off to one of the footmen she thought was called Adolf. For a moment, she stood there, confused. The Lord bit his lips as he turned to join hands with Darla. Nadia realized how lucky she had been to have had him to herself for a whole ball. But then Adolf put his arm around her, and her attention was pulled back to her partner and keeping his rambunctious feet from stepping on hers.

♪♪♪♫♪♪♪♪

When she awoke the next day, her arms ached from the work, but she relished the feeling. She'd done something productive. Today, she'd go back to her lessons.

Nicolette came in a short while later but without the breakfast tray. "Beggin' your pardon, miss," she said. "But the Lord would like you to join him in your morning room to break the fast."

Nicolette pulled the forget-me-not blue dress out of the wardrobe. It had become Nadia's favorite for it was like the color of the August sky. It wouldn't be long before the days began to get chilly. She found it hard to believe that she'd been here almost a year. Nicolette kept her eyes downcast while she helped Nadia dress.

"Anything else, milady?" Nicolette asked.

"No, thank you."

Nicolette took a step toward Nadia before she arrested the movement and clamped her arms to her sides. Was she not feeling well? Nicolette's face bore a pained expression as she curtsied and then departed.

A breakfast of eggs, toast, sausage, and fruit had been laid out on the table in Nadia's morning room. The Lord poured her a cup of coffee and added cream.

"What's the occasion?" Nadia asked as she sat, taking the cup from him.

"A thank you for all your hard work yesterday," he said. There was a serious cast to his eyes that his smile didn't quite hide. She chalked it up to his having stayed up late, helping to take down the tents and seeing everything safely back to the castle before the evening's dew could settle on them.

"It was nice to feel useful again," she told him.

The Lord simply smiled and handed her a plate.

"Shall we take a walk?" the Lord asked as Nadia finished her last cup of coffee.

"Of course," she replied, though she was puzzled by the change in their routine.

He slipped her hand around his arm and escorted her down the stairs and out the heavy main doors. The last bit of the night's crispness was giving way to the summer sun. The workmen in the courtyard gave her a nod as they passed. Their smiles held a hint of sadness.

Gravel crunched under their feet as Nadia and the Lord made their way into the formal gardens. He stopped and took her hands in his.

The Lord bowed his head and swallowed deeply. "For months now, you've asked where they are, the other princesses, and I told you they got their happily ever after." His hands tightened around hers. "It is time for yours, Nadia. You have grown. You have healed. And now the time has come to choose."

Her heart skipped a beat, and then another. The Lord's hands trembled in her grasp. "You have a choice to make." He paused and inhaled slowly. "You can return. Or you can go on."

The world shifted beneath her feet. "But I don't want to go," she insisted.

The Lord's next breath rattled as he inhaled. "You need... to choose," he said, each word heavy, as if he had to force them out. "Do you wish...to return...or go—" His voice wavered. "—go on?"

Nadia's heart hammered. Her head slowly moved from side to side, trying to reject the Lord's words. She didn't want to leave, had feared having to do it. But this! How could she return? What sort of life awaited her at Westpark? She bit her trembling lips. "Go on to where?"

"To the reward that awaits you after death."

Her knees nearly buckled. "I'm to die?"

The Lord looked up. Tears filled his eyes. "No," he said with a small shake of his head. "You'd cross into the next existence whole."

Tears gathered and dripped down her cheeks. Nadia let them fall. Her hands tightened around his. "I don't want to go," she whispered.

The pain in the Lord's eyes shifted. First to determination, then they filled with a cautious hope. He leaned over and whispered in her ear. His gaze locked onto hers as he straightened and gave her the, *Think!* look that was so familiar from the library.

Nadia opened and closed her mouth, stunned mute. Why? Why had he just offered her the one thing he kept hidden? Why had he told her his name?

Her hands became like a worry stone beneath his. She looked down, fire trailing across her skin at his touch, and then raised her head.

His smile faltered. His eyes began to lose the hope they had held. She couldn't do this. She couldn't leave him.

His eyes clouded over again. "What do you choose, Nadia?"

She wanted to pull her hands from his, to caress away the painful mask he now wore.

"Do you choose to return or go on?"

Nadia looked down, ran her thumbs across the back of his hands. His name. She now knew his name. Something he kept hidden, as some names were from everyone but—

Her eyes widened as the realization crashed into her. Her gaze flew up to meet his. She saw a flicker of hope return. He gave her a ragged smile and squeezed her hands again.

"What do you choose?"

She clenched the Lord's hands in a death grip and jumped into the unknown.

"I choose to stay."

thirty-two

Thunder crashed. Winds whipped around them in a sudden storm. Lightning cracked the air. The Lord pulled Nadia into the protection of his arms.

"Hello, Father," he said over her shoulder as the winds died down.

Nadia turned. Standing before them was a giant of a man. His long white hair and beard were wild with an unseen wind. Robes of gray, more smoke than form, wrapped around his dusky armor. His hands rested on the hilt of a flaming sword, its tip buried in the ground before them. Living mercury, swirling like storm clouds, filled the space where his eyes should have been.

"Still breaking the rules," his voice thundered.

"No, I offered her a choice, and she chose to stay." Nadia backed farther into the Lord's embrace. "Oh, where are my manners? Nadia, my father, Odin. Father, this is Nadia."

Bolts of lightning crackled in Odin's eyes. "I know who she is. The rules are very specific. You are here to judge and to cure. You don't get to keep any of them."

"You said nothing of the sort," the Lord argued. "You told me that, when they were ready, I had to offer them a choice, to go on or go back."

"Exactly."

"I gave her the choice, and she chose to stay."

"Not one of the choices."

The Lord laughed lightly. "It may not have been one of your choices, but it's always been hers. If you'd been paying more attention, you would have seen that."

"I choose to stay," Nadia said, keeping her eyes averted from the burning intensity of Odin's gaze. The Lord pulled her closer. "For months, I've feared leaving. I can't leave." Her chin trembled, but she lifted it. "This is my home. I choose to stay."

"What are you going to do when the next one comes through?"

"Probably help," the Lord said. "Nadia is very empathetic."

Odin turned his focus to Nadia, pinning her. "My son is very weak. Easily distracted. He can't be trusted."

"So you would have him believe. But that does not describe the person I've spent the last ten months with. I know why you imprisoned him here. I know what he's done, and I know how it pains him. He has learned from his mistakes. He doesn't need to stay."

Fire erupted from Odin's sword, encircling Nadia and the Lord within a wall of flame. "Oh, yes he does. He owes a debt that can never be paid."

"My choice stands," Nadia said. "This is my home." The Lord's hand grasped hers. Nadia squeezed it, drawing strength from it. "I choose to stay. I will not be parted from this place or from him."

The flames crackled around them, but she felt no heat other than the warmth of the Lord's embrace.

"You would doom her?" Odin asked his son. "You would have her spend eternity here with you?"

The Lord looked into Nadia's eyes. "If she'd have me."

Her heart swelled until she thought it would break. "Forever."

The flames around them shot into the sky and then crashed back down to earth and disappeared.

"Take her arm," Odin commanded.

The Lord turned his hand over and gripped the underside of her arm by the elbow. Hers naturally fell and grasped his. Their inner arms lay together, pulse points pounding against the tender flesh of the other. Odin pulled his sword from the ground and brought its tip to their linked arms. A rope of lightning wound itself around their arms, binding them together.

The Lord's face filled with awe as he looked at her. "I am hers and she is mine," he said, staring into her eyes. "From this day forth 'til the end of time."

Her heart broke, unable to contain the emotion bursting inside it. Tears streamed down her face. "I am his and he is mine," she repeated. "From this day forth 'til the end of time."

"Eternity is a long time," Odin said, and tucked his sword into his belt, where it flamed unsheathed. "Enjoy your banishment."

"Oh, I intend to," the Lord said, a smile curling his face, still staring into her eyes.

There was a whoosh of wind that bent the grass and blew Nadia's hair around her face as Odin traveled back up into the sky.

"Not quite what I expected to happen," Nadia said. She bent her head. "I didn't think you wanted me to stay."

"I didn't think I'd get to keep you. I didn't want to break your heart, having to send you away." The Lord smiled. "But you clever, clever girl. Figuring out my clue. Realizing what I wanted."

"It was what I wanted, too. I wasn't going to go that easily."

The Lord sobered. "And now you can't." He took her hands and stared at them. "Any regrets?"

"Just one," Nadia said.

He paled. "What's that?"

"Well..." Nadia removed her hands from his and ran them up his chest. She locked her arms around his neck. "Where I come from, a marriage is sealed with a kiss. And I haven't gotten one yet."

"Ah." The Lord's eyes twinkled. His hands settled on her hips. "I guess it wouldn't be fair. To leave you without one, that is."

Her heart pounded against her ribs. The Lord's hands were like fire, encircling her, melting her until she flowed into him. She closed her eyes as his lips came down on hers.

It had all been worth it. Every kick, every taunt, every hungry night. She'd do them all again if this was the reward. His lips moved against her, drawing out her soul. Her fingers ran up into his hair, pulling him closer, offering up all of herself. The Lord scooped her up in his arms.

"Now what?" Nadia asked, fighting to catch her breath.

"I'm going to carry you across the threshold and introduce you to some of those nightgowns that have made you blush. Most places, a marriage isn't valid until—"

She cut him off with a kiss, hearing only the echo of the words he'd spoken to drive out the poison, now knowing it was no lie.

You are loved. You are truly loved.

about the author

Catherine "C.S." Hale has been writing fantasy since she could hold a pencil. When not holed up in a comfortable corner writing all her books out by longhand, she can be found somewhere by the sea enjoying tea and pastries. Visit Catherine at CSHALEBOOKS.COM and on Facebook at AUTHORCSHALE.

www.ingramcontent.com/pod-product-compliance
Lightning Source LLC
Chambersburg PA
CBHW061629190726
48289CB00006B/1532